The Brooklyn Stories

A Rousing Collection From New York's Most Colorful Borough

ANDREW BERNSTEIN

Published by
Hybrid Global Publishing
301 E 57th Street
4th Floor
New York, NY 10022

Manufactured in the United States of America.

Bernstein, Andrew
The Brooklyn Stories: A Rousing Collection From New York's Most Colorful Borough
 ISBN: 978-1-951943-89-9
 eBook: 978-1-951943-90-5

Cover design by: Joe Potter
Interior design by: Suba Murugan
Cover illustration by: Bosch Fawstin

www.andrewbernstein.net
TheBoschFawstinStore.blogspot.com

To Penelope Joy,
The love of my life.

Contents

The Clock Strikes

News of Julian LePort's terminal illness thrilled me with pleasure. The lecherous bastard was barely sixty—but the cancer would finish him before the end of the summer. Justice, I thought grimly, was often not pretty. I briefly considered a mini-celebration to commemorate the event, but it was more than two years since our irrevocable split and much of the simmering rage had dissipated.

It was the beginning of the summer term at Brooklyn University, and the May breeze wafted rain-laden, scented air across the tree-lined quad. The cool temperature veiled the humidity and temporarily obscured from view the steamy months inevitably to follow.

I sat in my office in the Philosophy Department in Covington Hall when Barbara Stenmark entered without knocking to tell me the "heartbreaking" news regarding her celebrated colleague in the English program.

"Julian is dying." She spoke without preamble, her dark brown eyes puffy around the edges.

My head jerked up from my lecture notes. "Good," I said firmly, holding no desire to dissemble.

"Jack," she said softly, more sympathy than reproof in her tone. "It was a long time ago."

"Not so long that I either forget or forgive."

She stared into my implacable gaze, shook her head, and quietly withdrew.

I had only a few peaceful minutes alone with my notes, then came a soft tapping at my door.

"Jack!" a familiar male voice called.

"Come in," I said, unable to resist a smile, even though I knew the plea that would follow.

Ted Werner had been Dean of Humanities for as long as I'd been at Brooklyn. He was a genial guy with flaxen hair and a wind-blown look even when the air was still. He dressed nattily in pin-striped blue suits and colorful ties and the only thing warmer than the city's summer weather was his smile. His own background was in literature and he had long striven, within school guidelines, to free up my time and Julian's for the work we had all deemed so important.

He'd been in my office many times over the years but, always harried, had never sat down. This time, he made an exception. Though lean and fit from daily workouts, he sat slowly, heavily down.

"You heard?" he asked, coming directly to the point.

I nodded.

His eyes looked as they would if the news concerned a close family member, which, in a way, for him, it did. There was a long silence. He finally broke it. "I just spoke to my sister."

"Yeah? What does she think?" Deborah Werner, whom I had met several times, was an accomplished oncologist who consulted at Memorial Thorpe Kennedy Cancer Center, a top New York hospital for cancer treatment.

"Those symptoms? Probably not long."

There seemed nothing else to say. I could not match his sense of loss and was too brutally honest to try.

"Any chance of re-considering?" he asked, trying to manufacture a grain of hope in his voice.

I took a moment before answering."Professor Werner," I said, choosing my words carefully. "Not even for you. No."

He nodded his understanding. "I know it was shattering," he said for possibly the hundredth time in the past two years.

"And final," I stressed, utterly sick of the whole affair and ready to fill my life with work. I turned quickly from him and shoved my nose back into my notes. I barely heard the sound of the door closing softly behind him.

It was less than a week later. I sat at the computer in my walk-in apartment on East 16th Street near Avenue W. The stacks of books overflowing my wraparound bookshelves represented my complete library and explained the bareness of my office at work. Papers covered with scribbled notes littered my desk and necessary reference texts were piled on the floor at my feet, near to hand. The superabundance of writer's materials over brimmed my tiny apartment, making it—despite a mere few sticks of battered furniture and a toy-sized TV rarely switched on—a congested fire hazard through which I navigated happily, a man in his element.

My book on "Aristotelian Thought and Human Civilization" took form. But it was a massive undertaking, tracking the rise, the loss, and the re-discovery of Aristotle's writings—and their profoundly positive impact on the development of advanced culture. I had been poring over the screen for hours, when a sharp tapping—although somehow deferential—was heard at my unlocked door, as if the visitor had stood there indecisively but then willed himself to overcome all trepidation and proceed to fulfill his purpose.

"Come in!" I snapped.

I was focused on the role of Aristotle's writings in promoting the medieval renaissance—but I knew who it was before I heard the voice or saw the face. My subconscious immediately registered the confident rat-a-tat clicking of high heels on the hallway tiles and the barely perceptible fragrance of fresh cut flowers, wafting subtly from an unforgettable perfume. I willed my stare to focus exclusively on the computer screen for several moments as I fought to control my breathing. Then I looked up into the face of Victoria Scaffidi.

It had changed little since I'd last seen her over two years ago. She had the same reddish-brown hair curving gracefully to her shoulders; the same green eyes gazing forthrightly forward—exhibiting now the pacific serenity of the sea at calm, with only a hint of the tempest that could mount suddenly under the wrong atmospheric conditions. My unslackening avoidance of her at school had, after all this time, become habitual. But now, I no longer feared looking at everything I had lost, every facet that had been seized from me on a day so maleficent it had left me crumpled on the underside of despair: the exposed skin of her neck, cheeks, and wrists— the fair complexion so bursting with animal vitality that her white skin seemed almost red from its network of glowing capillaries; the hips, thighs, and breasts of her full figure— spreading now in her mid-forties—but stretching the clinging fabric of her sky blue cotton dress in a manner calculated to torment one who could never again have her but who could never be reconciled to his loss.

"Hello, Jack," she said, the musical quality of her voice that had dazzled students for fifteen years once again tinkling in the narrow confines of my apartment. Her gaze was level and I looked up from my chair and met it squarely.

"We had dinner," she said gently, as if in answer to a question that had never been asked. "At a French restaurant near his apartment on Third Avenue. I asked him, actually—part of my research on Dostoyevsky. I knew right away. I fought it for months, but I knew right away. I tried to tell you...but you didn't...want to hear it." She drew herself up to her full height in an unconscious way she had of facing painful truths. "I didn't betray your trust for something casual."

The diamond on the ring finger of her left hand was not the one I had placed there—and the gold band that bracketed it attested to her claim. They'd been married quietly barely a month after our breakup and she had moved into his famous duplex on the Upper East Side. He had been a superstar for a full three decades, since he had burst on the scene just two years out of graduate school with a brilliant critical examination contrasting the writing styles of Tolstoy and Dostoyevsky. Since then, he had demonstrated his virtuosity by writing incisively on Milton, Goethe, and Hugo, showcasing his fluency in four languages—and in the universal language of art. He lectured all over the world, was a visiting professor at Columbia, taught as many classes at Princeton as he did at Brooklyn, and transformed his residence into the most sophisticated literary salon that New York's intelligentsia had witnessed in many decades.

But he had never married, preferring, in his flamboyant style, to conduct front page affairs with sundry socialites, Broadway actresses, and network news analysts. The marriage of the world-renowned intellectual to the beautiful Brooklyn University professor, although a small, private affair, had attracted significant press attention, including a cover story in *The City Magazine* entitled: New York's most intelligent couple? On the morning of the wedding, I took a northbound local to the outlying station of Breakneck Ridge and spent the day hiking alone the tangled green labyrinth of trails clustered in the remote hills along the river.

She stood before me now, making no pretense at being defended. Her hands were empty at her sides, her arms slack, with only a leather bag slung over her right shoulder. Her posture was straight, both her shoulders thrown back, and her open face looked ready to receive any blow, including the vilest insults a man could hurl at a woman, in order to complete her mission. She took a step forward, as if by approaching nearer she could reach out more effectively to me.

"He's the most complete, self-sufficient, monolithically self-absorbed man I've ever known," she said woodenly, as if anticipating my response but dutifully stating what had to be said. "He's more like a work of art than a human being— no inner contradictions, flawlessly consistent, even in his failings."

Now I knew what was coming. I sat like a statue, a hardened slab of marble beyond a capacity to feel, and awaited the inevitable plea. She hesitated, and I could read in the eyes I knew so well the reluctance to beg; the pride of stiff-backed spines and of driven, accomplished souls—both hers and her husband's—that bristled against assuming the kneeling posture of a mendicant. But she set her jaw and almost palpably pushed away all crippling doubt.

"You know what he wants. You above all. You were the one he worked with, had so much in common with, depended on..." Her voice trailed off, slipping down the treacherous slope toward the black abyss of despair. "Jack." Her voice was husky, desperate. "He has but months to live, not a second to waste." When she received nothing from me but a face immobile as a stone, her voice finally broke. "He feels that he has wasted his life!"

I let the reverberations of her cry ring off the walls of my studio until it seemed like the echoes of despair could be heard all the way to the Upper East Side. After moments of silence, she wheeled and headed for the door. At the entrance to the hallway, she stopped and turned back. Her thick, tousled hair was as wild as after a bout of lovemaking and her eyes colored with incipient redness. But her voice was low, controlled.

"Loathe me for the rest of your life. But don't take your hateful revenge on a dying man whose only crime was to love the same woman you did."

I had turned back to the computer screen and was re-reading my last paragraph before the click was heard of the outside door pulled shut. I felt an inner satisfied calm, a closure regarding a painful and unfulfilled part of my life. But it was peculiar to observe the pens rattling on the desk from my hands resting quietly on the keyboard.

It was Friday before the Memorial Day weekend and the campus dozed lazily in the afternoon sun, as if conserving energy for the panting marathon to come. I had no class that day, but had spent the morning ensconced at the library and the early afternoon in my office collating research notes. I was just contemplating lunch when I heard a slow, heavy shuffling of feet in the hallway accompanied by a low murmur of voices. I pushed aside my papers and waited. There came a sharp peremptory knock at the door, which opened immediately without invitation.

Julian LePort looked like he would not last the summer. He'd been heavy for the three years we had worked together, with a paunchy red face and thinning white hair. But his brilliant eyes, so dark they could be mistaken for black, had flared over every direction of the compass with a personality as large as his intellect. He involuntarily monopolized every conversation, spouting trenchant observations interlaced with terms from four languages and an inexhaustible supply of dead-on spontaneous witticisms—not from a neurotic need to dominate, but from an irrepressible creative energy that no living power could quell.

But cancer was not living. And I, more than anyone, knew that the magnum opus of his career was incomplete. He shambled in painfully, leaning on the arm of a pale skinny young man, and for an instant a stab of pain slashed my viscera at the sight of greatness reduced to the verge of collapse. But I smiled at the presence of the young man—presumably a graduate student—who in pre-Victoria days would have undoubtedly been female.

He sat uninvited in my visitor's chair and waved his assistant out with a gesture imperiously dismissive but somehow indescribably gracious, like a cultured, clement monarch politely bored by the ceaseless veneration of commoners. He faced me with the look of a man incurably ill but, simultaneously, irrevocably unabashed. He stared at me, his pasty cheeks now gaunt, his brown suede sports jacket already two sizes too big, but his dark eyes glaring as if some tameless beast had been galvanized by an injection of genius. He took his time. I held his gaze but felt myself once again, inexorably, drawn toward his massive orbit. I gripped the edge of my desk and held on.

"Jack, Jack," he said, looking at me in his earnest way that made any conversationalist feel he stood at the center of the great man's universe. "How did we lose everything we once had?" There was no denying the genuineness of his tone. I leaned across the desk toward him.

"Perhaps your theft of my fiancée had a dampening effect on our relationship. You think?"

"Of course," he said, with only the slightest twinge of sarcasm in his voice. "Victoria is a wallet to be stolen from you by any thief. She makes no more choices than a purloined wrist watch."

I knew better than to remonstrate with him. I held my fire, sensing an ultimate victory so sweet it might assuage two years of still undischarged gall.

His next words came with no trace of arrogance or a gloating sneer, only with the quiet certitude of conviction.

"Maybe you should just acknowledge that the better man won." His look was that of a man staring at the simple severity of a scientific law.

The unqualified effrontery, never unexpected from him, but stated with such guileless innocence, was experienced like a blindside left to the jaw. It stunned me. Throw him out, some stern inner voice iterated. Before it's too late, throw the supercilious bastard out. But I didn't. I just sat and stared, attracted by the audacity of this prelude to a pitch for help— and by the rare sight of undiluted self-confidence that animated it.

"You think I'm going to help you?" I said, my voice sounding hoarse even to me.

His smile had once been described by a *Sunday New York Times* writer as "that rare occasion on which a sublime miscreant swung ajar the gate to his radiant soul." It opened briefly as, even now, his devitalized smile flooded my cramped work space.

"Not me," he said pleasantly, with the calm knowledge of one who clutched a fistful of high cards. "Yourself."

I pushed back my chair from the desk and scowled.

He laughed. "Going to write on Aristotle all your life?" he mocked. "Like I wrote on Dostoyevsky and Goethe?"

His needle drilled close to home, as he knew it would.

"Aristotle was..." I began, but he cut me off.

"I know, I know. Just as Dostoyevsky was."

He looked at me, marshalling himself—and for several agonizing moments we stared, as if the meaning of two men's lives could hang suspended on a glance like so many cotton pajamas on a clothesline.

"How old are you now—forty-one?" he didn't wait for an answer. "Jack Witkin," he jeered. "Came out of the NYU Philosophy Department nine years ago—a budding megastar from a world class program with a blinding intellect and a style so brilliant that its like had not been witnessed in philosophy since the prime of William James a century before. Great things were expected, and he turned down Ivy League schools to stay in his native Brooklyn—right on the cusp of New York City's intellectual culture. And he has delivered—articles and books analyzing several of philosophy's perennial issues."

He paused, his preface complete, his punch line looming at the back of his throat, ready to be spat forward at the hard but brittle wall of the face opposing him.

"But he nursed a secret dream, didn't he? One he shared with few—because it seemed grandiose, exalted, unattainable. But he found a kindred soul—older, advanced, aspiring—and, together, they spent years planning, researching, outlining. But never actually producing. Never even starting the real work, always delaying its inception, feeling at some visceral level that procrastination was justified, because the older you get, the wiser—right? The more life experience you accumulate, the better prepared for the life's work—do it at sixty-five, at seventy even, because we're not ballplayers, we don't burn out at forty, we get more qualified as we age—yes?"

He slammed his huge fist on my desk and made no effort to dam the spurt of liquid around his eyes.

"But life has other plans, Jack!" he roared. "Whatever unholy power rules this world of crawling pathogens—it has other ideas," he whispered. "And it comes for you on its schedule, not yours, this dark wall of oblivion—not to be reasoned with or deterred or cheated—only a blind force devoid of intent or conscious will that rolls inexorably forward and tramples every poor little doll's house we erect in its path."

I looked at the crumbling mass sitting before me and fought to maintain a hard edge. But it was slipping away.

"And the great novel never gets written," he concluded tonelessly, ladling each word carefully, as though spooned from a measuring cup nearing its dregs. "We dissipate our brief span explicating the creations of others—like servile handmaidens truckling before the queen—but never ourselves dare approach such rarefied heights." He looked at me as one who shared a love deeper than Victoria. "Art, Jack," he said reverently, his husky voice barely audible. "What else justifies our pustulant existences?" When I did not respond, he finished the thought himself. "Luther was wrong. Art and art alone justifies mankind."

It was impossible to forget the years we had worked together, creating independently, critiquing each other's work—ripping it with savage glee—but improving, publishing effectual short stories in artsy literary magazines, planning, encouraging, outlining plots for the grand-scale novels surely to come. And this dream we had shared—so integral

to each it was impossible now to remember who had origi-
nally conceived it—to show the death of the Greek spirit we
both revered, by telling the story of a brilliant Athenian philosopher at the time when Justinian I closed all the pagan
schools of philosophy—a conflict not merely of men or even
of civilizations but of visions, Greek versus Christian, pagan
versus monotheist, rationalist versus irrationalist—and of the
last men of reason clinging desperately to the fading light in
the final moments before the plunge into the sunless abyss.
"Like Lawrence and Lee, Jack," he had boomed exultantly in
a time period seemingly eons ago. "An *Inherit the Wind* for our
century...and...perhaps...for many centuries."

And, after our break, Julian seeking to complete the vast
undertaking alone, but not self-sufficient in this case—needing greater knowledge of Greek and of philosophy, especially
classical thought, with a specific emphasis on the naturalistic
spirit of the Aristotelian school.

Needing me.

Needing the aid of a man whose heart he had ripped from
between its ribs and callously flung aside as if some valueless
scrap of drifting flotsam. The victim for whom the depth of
his passion measured the depth of the betrayer's guilt.

Even now I felt the pull. A secret dream, had he called it?
Or one slowly becoming a guilty one? Were all men faithless
to their heart, I wondered. Did they permit the diminishing of
their grand plans, one droplet at a time, inexorably worn down
by the trifling cavils of a daily grind, like sweeping peaks
leveled by millennia of remorseless erosion? Was there ever
a time I had wanted to be anything but a novelist? I reflected
back on the life of the young man I had been, examining it,
knowing the answer to the question, cringing at the realization but drawn irresistibly to it, like an acrophobic standing

at elevation and unable to avert his vision from the precipice he dreads.

Taking a breath, I stared impersonally at the truth. That youth more than two decades ago had studied English in college, befitting a man whose primary love was literature. But he'd wanted to write serious books, not trendy mind candy instantly forgettable, and had migrated to philosophy in graduate school, investigating the timeless issues of men's lives, preparing his intellectual foundations. He would support himself as a professor—but fiction would be his career.

And then came a job—and maturation of student loans—and scholarly requirements, first for tenure and then for promotion—and the incessant never-ending agony, like root canal projected over the course of a lifetime, of grading plebian papers hurriedly scrawled by lumpen illiterates. He had known from the first that Victoria would be unique and irreplaceable, and had made ample room in his life for her. And that had left tidbits of time—stolen hours working with Julian, like a torrid affair conducted furtively, consigned perpetually to the shadows and to the rare conscious moments between midnight and bed. And then: cataclysm.

Could he read my thoughts in my eyes or on my face? He stared at me calmly, as if probing for the right moment.

"You tried, didn't you, after our split?" he said. "Tried to write a different novel on your own terms. But you gave it up—why? Because it didn't measure up to your standards, did it?" He waited, knowing no answer was forthcoming, but needing none. "Because this is the book your heart is set on—your mind, your subconscious, your soul. You think I don't know you? Think your former lover doesn't understand you? This is your first born, Jack, your virginal birth, your seminal child. In the absence of this, you found no line."

Had the bastard emphasized the word "former?" I looked at him, but I saw Victoria—the English professor who lectured superbly on the 19th century novel, and who loved literature; the passionate fiancee who had supported in every possible form—both intellectual and emotional—her lover's aspirations. I saw her and I felt the ensuing void, the dark spaces of an unfillable emptiness, and immediately detected the old fevered anger that had risen—like steam from a grating—for interminable months, leaving my face flushed and abnormally warm. Could I reach the elusive dream without his collaboration? I didn't know—nor, at the fatal moment, did I care. Involuntarily, I leaned forward in my chair, in preparation for a kill—the inexorable outcome of a hunt enduring for two bitter years—momentarily heedless whether it was a man to die or a dream...or whose.

"'He that troubleth his own house shall inherit the wind,'" I reminded him bitterly. "Get your decaying carcass out of my office." My tone was flat and, suddenly, I felt exhausted.

He nodded once at the finality of it—and, without further plea or backward glance, pulled himself to his feet and strode purposefully, temporarily without evident pain, from my office and my life. Minutes later, having lost all appetite, and feeling as though I were the dying man, I followed him painfully out to the parking lot and home to my bed.

The summer with its lightened teaching load stretched before me, offering the prospect of expedited progress on critical writing projects. But now, in mid-June, despite the rays of golden sunshine burnishing the leaves a virile, lustrous green, I was stymied, drained of creative impetus when I should have been supremely energized. My dilatory behavior took a dozen forms: I became convinced I needed a less cluttered work space, and began to stack books and file papers. I dawdled over dinner at the restaurants I favored on Emmons Avenue. It struck me that between writing, teaching, and lecturing I worked too hard; that I needed time to recreate; that I yearned for more beach time, which I proceeded to take in abundance. And all the while, my manuscript on Aristotle sat on my desk forlornly, staring at me with mooning eyes like a forsaken, woebegone lover.

Through it all, despite my tan and relaxed insouciance, some nebulous force ate at my viscera, a mere nibble actually, like an overfed mouse unwilling to utterly refuse a last juicy morsel. My gut tried to tell me something my brain did not want to hear—and instead of angrily wresting away my focus, I observed the inner struggle impersonally, as if it did not concern me but was merely a clinical study of somebody else's conflicted aspirations.

Ted Werner called early on a Saturday morning in late June. Summer had set in, and even at seven a.m. the haze hovered over the streets and caught in your throat like a floating wave of choking cotton.

"What do you want?" I rasped into the phone, cranky from lack of sleep and the sheen of sweat bathing me in a matter of seconds upon emerging from my air-conditioned bedroom.

"Jack," he said. "Sorry to bother you so early—but could you meet me at school by eight o'clock?...Yes, I know it's Saturday...It is definitely important...OK, I'll owe you one...Right, thank you."

Without breakfast and with merely a cup of ice coffee to sustain me, I drove to campus through steaming streets whose asphalt seemed poised on the verge of melting into a black vapor exhaled from the lungs of Hell. Deborah Werner sat in her brother's office and smiled politely.

"Sorry about the inconvenience," she said. "But Ted's been bugging me for weeks. This is definitely the best time."

She was a tall, painfully thin brunette, who had little time for relationships or food— indeed, seemed not to need them— because she drew all sustenance from her work. In brief jolts of conversation, torn from her life over the course of a decade, she had indicated to me that she characteristically worked twelve hour days six days a week, relaxing on Sundays in her Park Avenue apartment with the classical music she revered. Her bony hand, when she shook mine, surprised me with its tightness of grip—and its promise of much greater strength if called upon to use it. I turned to her brother.

"What do you want out of me? It's always good to see Deborah, but an oncologist—now?" I shook my head, unwilling to hide either my exasperation or my suspicions. "Dammit, I told you 'no.'"

He smiled his charming, diplomatic smile that had helped defuse so many departmental squabbles.

"I won't say 'methinks thou doth protest too much.' I simply request the pleasure of your company for less than two hours."

"I'm not going to see Julian."

"No, you're not."

I nodded. After all the occasions on which he had solicitously helped guard my writing time, I could not refuse. "OK, two hours. Let's go."

The white marble walls of Thorpe Kennedy Cancer Center rose imposingly from the banks of the East River like a citadel designed to ward off deadly foes. The patients sprawled across its plump white beds within were warriors fallen in battle, many to imminently succumb to their wounds. The doctors making the rounds of the corridors were allied with the center's researchers as vigilant defenders manning the walls, committed unremittingly to repel the invaders. Deborah Werner, an independent mercenary, invariably came to the preservers' support.

She led us through the hospital wards, standing solemnly by several bedsides, talking quietly with her patients. Her brother and I stood respectfully in the background, saying nothing, grimly watching her work.

One of her patients was an elderly man, who, under his thin white sheet, was skinnier than his doctor. He had no hair and the skin of his cheeks was a ghastly shade of off-white, as if he had been sucked dry of blood by an omnivorous vampire. He was unconscious and his breathing came in irregular tortuous gasps. It seemed impossible that this poor octogenarian could live more than a few days. While Deborah huddled with another doctor regarding the advisability of a respirator, I glanced surreptitiously at the chart she had placed momentarily at the foot of the bed. Then I looked again. I stared at it, unable to remove my eyes from one arresting line. His date of birth was two years after mine.

I stopped, rooted for the moment in place like a decaying growth of vegetation. Had Ted seen this? I sensed him behind me, but felt paralyzed, my neck stiffened into an immovable posture. I couldn't take my eyes off the tragic patient—and, suddenly, waves of panic shot through my chest like a cold breath from some victim's premature tomb. I gripped the bed stand in a vain effort to ward off the shaking and stared at the never-to-reach forty, cadaverous clump of flesh before me. This poor unfortunate tomorrow, Julian in a few weeks, myself—when? In how many years? Like a precocious child calculating the seconds in a day, in a month, in a year, my brain raced. How many seconds left in my life? Could I hear the tick of my wrist watch counting off each beat of time—there's one more second gone. I didn't hear it, heard nothing but the doctors' muffled voices, but felt rather the remorseless march of wasted years as time slipped past like wave rivulets hissing back down a deserted beach to the eternal sea. In some form, these things would always be here...but in no form, would we...

Ted had wanted me to feel sorry for Julian. I didn't. But some other force gripped my throat, squeezing the breath out of me as juice from a de-pulped orange. I had to escape. I turned and fled, walking briskly, almost running from the room and down the corridor to the stairs, not waiting for an elevator, brushing aside Ted's urgent cries behind me, bounding down the steps and through an exit into the gasping streets beyond. I crossed the broad expanse of York Avenue and stood on the parapet overlooking the river and gazed intently downward at the brackish water below.

I stared at the water spread across my field of vision, stared at a blank expanse that could not register because other images—unbidden but inescapable—trampled through my consciousness, grinding into the dust beneath focal awareness all contrasting considerations. They were images of graves, empty now but soon to be filled—overlapping, indistinguishable one from another, but beckoning their impending residents like malignant realtors hawking domiciles of perpetual duration. I saw the fresh dirt and yawning holes and tried to imagine what the stone would look like when set in place—mine or Julian's, was there a difference at this point? What would it say? "Julian LePort...Jack Witkin...Outstanding Scholar...Dedicated Teacher..." But what would it not say? Above all, what would it not say?

I hung my head over the railing and wept, my bitter tears slithering off my cheeks into the dank pool below, the dirty lifeless water a fitting final resting place for the tears of a man who had permitted wrath and spite to dominate his existence— and who had belittled that of immeasurable value to the tragic status of embryonic hope perennially condemned to abortion.

It was raining. I stood in it, exposed, across Third Avenue from the famous duplex which I had sedulously avoided for two years. The rain hammered against the abandoned pavement, a straight slanting downpour on a windless, breathless night. The cars swept past like boats, tiny enclosed cubicles throwing aside dark spouting geysers in their wake. The water from the stopped-up drain slopped over the curb, soaking my feet. I was drenched over every square inch of my body, my dripping clothes attached like a second skin, chilling me despite the tropical night. And still, I could not move.

I looked across the thoroughfare of upscale shops and tony restaurants at the lighted windows high up the concrete edifice looming above me. It dwarfed me, as the detestable miscreant it sheltered dwarfed me. I gazed upward, unable to stop thinking of the endless parade of attractive graduate students and literary hangers-on who had always formed his devoted coterie of admirers—following him, learning from him, and catering to his out-sized sexual appetites. For all of his disciplined work habits, he had lived the personal life of a rock star. While I had loved, and would ever love but one woman. I grit my teeth until my jaw ached but it didn't help. It was trivial pain compared to what lay ahead. Was it necessary to pass through the suburbs of Hell to get what you really wanted? What was life, a Crusade in which the Holy Grail was attainable only to those willing to suffer the whips, chains, and burning stakes of flesh-scourging torture? I looked up into the rain that mocked me with its silence and its splatterings across my mawkish, slobbering face. There were no answers up there—only the night, the sky, and the driving rain. Any answers were in a man's soul. We knew them already, had known them for a long time. We only lacked the fortitude to face them.

I started across the avenue.

Victoria answered the door. She wore a sleeveless green top and white cotton slacks. She was barefoot. I had to look at her, but kept my gaze focused on her eyes. She was surprised, it was evident in her expression, but pleasantly so. She started to smile in greeting, but one look at my face stopped her. She waved me in and I stood in the spacious living room I so-well remembered. The lights were off, and the main illumination was cast by the bright arc shining from the door of Julian's study down the hall. But even in the dim light, I could see the same plush white carpeting and matching sectional sofa with its plump, luxurious cushions. He had a corner apartment on the 30th floor and, on clear days, through its broad windows the river glowed in the distance, as on equivalent nights the metropolis was a sweeping expanse of pillared towers, composed not of steel and concrete but of shimmering luminosity. Plants hung everywhere, suspended from the ceiling like green wraithlike candelabra, and stood in deep pots on the floor, their fresh earth giving off the rich fragrance of country vegetation in the heart of the city. Victoria's tawny cat, sleeker but no more of a feline animal than its owner, stalked through the plants like a jungle creature. Active, teeming life flourished in this den of looming death.

I walked down the hall and entered Julian's study. His wife came in behind me. She positioned herself across the room, its distance and its furniture between us. Julian lay in repose on an antiseptic hospital bed surrounded by overflowing bookshelves and reference texts piled high on the floor. He was propped on a half-dozen white pillows, his laptop open on his stomach, his brow furrowed in concentration. He looked up when I entered. Somehow, he did not seem surprised.

"The Seeker cometh," he said solemnly, his characteristic boom of greeting pathetically reduced now to a throaty whisper. "Finally, he nears the Promised Land."

"Shut the hell up," I said, able to admire but in no mood for his undying bravado. Before he could respond, I pointed to his wife. "You, out," I commanded. It was bad enough to be in the same building with her, profoundly intolerable to be in the same room. They both understood. Victoria looked at me for one moment, her eyes and slightly upturned mouth seeming to thank me. Then she left. I shut the door behind her. I sat down in the one chair next to his bed, and for one moment sensed only her fragrance. Violently, I slammed shut a mental door on that awareness and looked at Julian, who watched me the way a predatory beast must eye its herbivorous prey.

"Let's get this thing done," I said. "Before you go belly up."

He smiled wanly. "With such command of the language," he murmured. "You are obviously a born writer."

I ignored him and pored over my extensive notes. Most were more than two years old, but a half-dozen important pages were from the last three days. As I re-read them now, the overall impact of the past few days' work was that the material did not seem new; rather, it was as if I had never cast it aside; and I realized then in a single moment of clarity that my subconscious had never let it go, and would never—and what that meant.

"Sophia is not right," I said of the heroine after completing my review. "I've thought about this for a long time. Her character is the key to the climax. Her fate needs to be radically altered."

He had waited patiently. "You've thought about this for a long time?" he asked, smiling archly.

"Yes," I said softly, unwilling to deny it. I looked directly at him—at the pallid lump of wasted flesh, the hairless head, and the giant eyes that only death could extinguish—and nodded. There was something else, not about but represented by him, that was equally not to be denied—but it did not need to be put into words.

I looked away. The notes splayed on my lap were not necessary to remind me that we had assigned ourselves a hell of an undertaking. The panoramic story necessarily held a vast array of characters—pagan Greeks, Christians, Germanic barbarians, and a sprinkling of Jews—each of whom had to be a distinctively-etched individual. The main character, Polemarchus, the last great mind to be taught by the intellectual heirs of the Lyceum, was deeply in love with an educated Christian woman of profound personal integrity, who was wholeheartedly committed to the religious belief that her lover perceived as his gravest threat. The plot was a tangled, sweeping complexity that pit the supporters of Greek thought within the disintegrating Roman Empire secondarily against the menacing barbarians without but, primarily, against the menacing Christians within. The theme of the tragic attempt to save advanced intellectual culture from the forces of dogma and brute force—and the doomed effort to stave off the Dark Ages—had to be subtly interwoven with the story's events, not slammed against the reader's skull like a cosh. And the entirety required a deep understanding of the history of ancient philosophy, whose main principles permeated the story's people and events—but whose meaning had to be shown in action, not merely expostulated by pontificating characters.

"What about Sophia?" he croaked and it jerked my attention back to him.

The skin of his face was drawn taut across his temples and his eyes squinted slightly. The rasp of his voice was a product of a chronic struggle that would cease only with his imminent death. Suddenly, I knew the heartbreaking truth.

"You've refused all pain medication, haven't you?"

"They fog the brain, Jack. I have work to do."

I looked at his hands on the computer, the sheafs of notepaper on either side of him, and the stacks of books on the floor. I said nothing but felt my long-simmering resentment slowly give way to something else.

"Here's what about Sophia," I said. "Is it possible to project an educated individual of great strength of character who repudiates reason for faith when the evidence is presented, in action, all around her? Especially, when the main source of that evidence is the man she loves? It makes no sense."

"But it's a crushing defeat for the men of reason if they lose everything—and shows that the men of faith who dominate the next four centuries can and will appreciate neither the achievements of Greek culture nor their leading representatives."

"I understand that," I answered. "But our theme does not preclude the best of Christianity throwing off faith and dogma for reason and civilization. We gain something by Sophia's final conversion."

He did not answer—but I saw the question in his eyes.

"Here it is," I said, looking briefly at my notes. "She stands by him against both her family and the emperor, and dies with him—her husband now—in unbreachable commitment to the glories of Greek civilization. Their mutual deaths symbolize the end of the Classical period—but their understanding and devotion cannot die—so that the smuggling of their infant son to Persia, where the Greek spirit still lives, presages all the rebirth to come five and six centuries in the future."

He shook his great, unbowed head.

"No," he said. "Show the final cataclysmic doom in all its crushing horror. Don't candy coat it. Civilization is irrevocably lost. Five centuries, for a human life span, might as well be five eons. There's no hope for those poor bastards—any more than for us. Don't pretend that there is. All you can do is face the portentous void like a man."

I paused and let his words hang in the mini-void between us.

"You're a tough guy, Julian," I said finally. "You want the hard truth about the void? Here it is. You'll enter it in a few weeks. Me—not for years. You'll be nothing but random sticks in the ground by the time this book is finished. What I said— that's how it's going to be."

He stared into my inexorable eyes and knew it was too late to beat the rap. His death sentence had been invoked by forces that permitted no commutation. I would go on to write more books. This was the last one he'd put his name on. It was my way or the highway—to oblivion.

"Alright," he said bitterly. "I have no choice, do I?"

"None whatever," I said emphatically. "And you stick to the chapters on Christianity and the shutting down of the Western mind. I'm writing the chapters on Sophia. You got it?"

We spent hours together, outlining the great undertaking chapter-by-chapter; planning, plotting, working out in detail the events of each section; until, finally, despite the chronic pain, Julian's eyes closed from exhaustion and his chin sank to his chest. Quietly, I gathered my notes and replaced them in my briefcase. I rose to leave. As I opened the door of his study, Julian's eyes flickered open and he spoke from the clarity of awareness one gains in the twilit realm of half-sleep, when the drawbridge accessing the subconscious lowers and one can more readily cross the moat and enter inside the walls of its glowing domain.

"We're all on the clock, Jack. It's an egg timer in the vast scheme. Soon the void will swallow you too."

His eyes closed and he was asleep. Nodding curtly at Victoria holding vigil alone in the darkened living room, I let myself out.

The funeral took place on a sun-splashed afternoon in late September, a date that though technically autumn spoke more of the golden promise of summer than most of July's and August's days of such soupy humidity that air had to be drank, not breathed. Julian was buried at an upscale cemetery out on Long Island and, alone, I drove there to pay my final respects.

I stood at the back of a teeming crowd of luminaries from a cross section of fields composing the full range of human endeavor—artists, writers, actresses, professors, athletes, and politicians—all of whom had been touched, at one time or another, by Julian's intellect or outsized ego.

I had ventured into his apartment a half-dozen times after my first visit—and consulted him numerous times by telephone. Mostly, we had each holed up in our own private writing spaces and proceeded to pound out content. The first draft of my chapters was nearly done. Understandably, Julian had not progressed as far in his. Although I spoke to Victoria as rarely as possible, I had heard through the university grapevine of her husband's final moments—of his feverish attempt to complete a first draft; of his continuous refusal of sedatives and brain deadening painkillers; of his dauntless, gallant battle against pain and his tortuously slow progress; and of his ultimate failure as, frail as a bookmark, he lapsed into a final coma and expired, bent in bed, over his laptop. His loyal wife had shelved every one of her own projects to assist his desperate, dying effort.

I watched his casket lowered slowly into the ground. Though mine may have been the only dry eyes in proximity, I found myself hoping that, in the moments before his end, he had realized that his gradually feebler efforts were not a failure. He had made a noble beginning and I would complete his chapters myself.

Slowly, I walked past the buried casket and approached his wife's side. She sat by the grave in a lawn chair, receiving the condolences of a long line of well wishers. She had removed her sunglasses despite the glare and made no effort to dry her cheeks. She wore no make-up, her eyes were red, and the soft fullness of her body sagged in its black sheath under the groaning weight of her loss. But her chin tilted up as she looked straight into the eye of every mourner, and she gripped firmly the hand of each. I held her hand in both of mine.

"I'm glad you had what you had," I said simply.

She inclined her head, and I stepped aside to make room for a hundred others.

Over the next six months, I completed the novel's first draft. There was still massive editing to do, but, for the first time, I was within sight of land. To commemorate the milestone, I printed out a copy of the manuscript and personally delivered it to the one living person to whom it meant the most.

Victoria sat on Julian's white sofa transposed now to her new apartment in Brooklyn Heights. Though she had inherited money, she chose to relinquish the duplex and live more frugally in a tiny studio several blocks from the river. On this Saturday morning in early April, she wore a long-sleeved, ankle length green dress with faint floral patterns and high-heeled white sandals. Her reddish hair swung around her shoulders like an elegant wrap, and I observed a few silky strands curve past her cheek and come to rest delicately on her breast. In both hands she clutched the six hundred page manuscript I had placed there. For a long time, she stared at its title page, which proclaimed: *Civilization Lost* by Julian LePort and Jack Witkin. Slowly, she turned the page and started reading. I sat in the matching upholstered chair across from her and waited.

For more than an hour, she sat oblivious to my presence and read carefully, seemingly caught up in the grand sweep of the novel's action. When she finally stopped reading, she refused to lay the heavy manuscript aside but kept it lying on her lap. She looked up at me silently.

"It still needs a great deal of editing," I said.

She nodded and I could see a faint misty quality in her eyes.

"Julian will like this, Jack. I know he will," she said, both hands resting on the pages. "He'll be so proud of it."

I did not answer, but was convinced she was right.

She sat looking at the manuscript in her hands, and there was an extended silence between us—no longer awkward but one of two souls that shared a close bond regarding ideals of supreme importance to each. Finally, she looked up.

"Thank you, Jack," she said, her voice final, signifying gratitude, acceptance, and closure regarding a host of painful issues.

"I did it for my soul, Vickie," I said, permitting myself to pronounce her pet name for the first time in three years. "Not for Julian...not even for you..."

She knew the creative forces that churned in the depths of me. So many times she had observed my eyes, my tone, my creased brow or pursed lips—and had known. And she knew now. Immediately, she threw back her head and laughed in exactly the way I remembered, the rich vitality of her life force ringing through the small room so palpably that you would not be surprised if it glided to a gentle landing athwart you and playfully squeezed your arm; laughing in appreciation, in respect, and in overwhelming relief.

"Jack," she said, smiling. "Nobody who knows you could mistake your motivation." She paused. "And I'm glad for you."

I got up and stretched my legs. "I know how tough an editor you are. So go through it carefully. The editing process will take months. Let me know if you have any recommended changes."

She put aside the manuscript and rose. "I will. As you know, Julian is quite persnickety regarding matters of detail. He is determined that it be outstanding in every capacity."

Her passion—and the tense that she employed—drew me in and obscured momentarily a fact that registered only when I shook my head and strode to look out of her window. Outside the wind whipped papers down the avenues and in the distance the river cut the cityscape like a blue artery carrying shipping to vital organs. When she was not in my immediate visual field it hit me that Julian would not like it or be proud or be determined to improve it or perform any other action. His resting place was final. The only thing about him incomplete—although the most important—depended on me. If I had let it go—or did so even now—his entire potential legacy crumbled. But if I held true, and carried to fruition, the path of my own remaining years shined in a way to rival religious experience. I laughed bitterly at myself. He had known that. He had said as much in my office just months before he died. I nodded my acceptance at the implacable reality: The better man wins again.

I turned back to her. She was beautiful and brilliant and passionately alive and still years from her fiftieth birthday— but I knew with an unassailable certainty regarding which it was difficult to trace a source that there would never again be a man in her life. The strength of her love would never die—and so it had to kill all chance to love again. She would live serenely with Julian in the mausoleum of her emotional life, endlessly tidying its precious artifacts until they shined a burnished gold, and any man wooing her must content himself with being perpetually subordinate to a memory.

Mausoleums were cold places and, on cue, I shivered. Briefly, I contemplated taking her in my arms one final time— but to what end? I had what I needed, and, after thanking her, left her apartment and took the stairs rather than the elevator to the street.

It was miles to my apartment and I had work to do. But I wanted to walk. I felt light, buoyed by a creative energy that could carry me effortlessly down a path seemingly highlighted to the horizon. I walked purposefully, not hurriedly, and, hours later, when I reached my apartment, I rested. But not for long.

By the end of August, the editing process was almost complete. I had elected to teach no courses during the summer— and lived more frugally on my diminished salary. I finally took a much needed day off from the project with only the two climactic chapters remaining. I drove to the beach. After

a long swim and an outdoor shower in yellow sunbeams dancing with motes, I ate a leisurely dinner at a beachfront restaurant on the boardwalk. Evening shadows settled in, harbingers
of late summer's cooler nights, and I retired to the pens and
notebooks I kept stashed habitually now in my car. My head
hummed these days with ideas for short stories—and I already
knew the next novel I would write. I proceeded now, kissed
by the sea breezes of evening, to begin its outline. It was well
after dark by the time I returned home.

My manuscript on Aristotle sat next to my computer and,
it seemed to me, cast a yearning glance in my direction. I
grabbed it and shoved it in a drawer. "In about ten years,"
I said to it soothingly. Aristotle was timeless. My life span
was not. Julian was right, and my forty-third birthday had
just passed. The clock's remorseless tick could never slow
and soon the void would swallow me too. But first I would
accomplish what was monumentally important. Unlike some,
no part of my life was a mausoleum and I would love again.
Indeed, I already did.

Thicker Than Water

The end of Frank Torino's career as a gangster was widely covered in the New York tabloids. Police reports analyzed it for weeks—and even months later, his scowling mug could still be occasionally spotted on the front pages.

Although the NYPD homicide boys investigated my involvement fully—and never hid their suspicions—the full story behind the downfall of Frank "Frankie Tornado" Torino never made the papers.

It started with the death of the capo's eight-year old son, Paul, in a tragic accident on Bay 17th Street in Bath Beach. The kid, playing stickball in the alley of his friend's house, lunged heedlessly into the street chasing a line drive and ran headlong into a spotless new Buick Skylark driven carefully by one Chris Caravello. The impact splattered Paul Torino's blood and brains onto the hood of the white car, as well as into the gutter.

I had known Chris Caravello since he'd joined the faculty of Lafayette High School on Benson Avenue as an English teacher 10 years previously. When Chris realized who the kid's father was, he knew his life expectancy was now measured in months, not decades. He called shortly after the accident—

31

and the news hit me like a jackhammer. After we hung up, I sat with my head in my hands for a long time. He came to see me that evening.

"Tim," he said. "I got to make out my will."

"Your dad's a lawyer," I pointed out helpfully.

He ignored me, sitting in a leather chair in the living room of my apartment on Bay Ridge Avenue, his eyes already bloodshot and face lined as from sleeplessness, although the accident had occurred barely 10 hours earlier. It was obvious that no feeble attempt at humor could lighten his mood. Or mine.

"Frank Torino won't care that I was under the speed limit," he whispered, holding his head in both hands. "Or that the kid leaped right in front of the car and didn't give me an inch to brake."

It was raining outside and although the temperature of the August night might have marginally diminished, the clammy air seemed to somehow insinuate its way into your throat and constrict your breath.

"No," I admitted gently, trying not to think of the child I had never met. "He won't. You got out and called for an ambulance immediately. You screamed for help from anybody who knew first aid. You did everything you could. But Frankie Tornado won't care."

"What am I going to do?" he moaned. For a second, I thought he would bite his nails.

Though 20 years older than his 33, and raised—like him—in Bensonhurst—I didn't know the answer. We sat together in the hot darkness of a Saturday night in mid-summer, fans whistling sodden air across our damp faces. The only other sound came from cars snaking through the wet streets under my open windows.

He finally broke the silence.

"You grew up with thugs like that. How much time you think I got?"

"He can't take you out immediately—too obvious. He's got to let the accident blow over. When he takes you down, it has to be long after Paul's death. Six months to a year is my guess."

"What'll he do to me?" he asked, his white face clearly visible in the darkened room.

"You'll disappear, Chris," I said quietly.

The catch in his throat as he struggled to stay calm was discernible. "And Theresa—and Christine?"

"Nothing'll happen to them," I said firmly. "The Mafia's not the drug cartel. They don't whack wives and children."

"Just husbands and fathers," he said. He didn't sound relieved.

On a muggy weeknight two days later, I got home before ten after putting my advanced judo class through a grueling workout, practicing variations of ashi-waza. There were four messages on my machine, three from Chris. He got right to the point when I called. "Theresa wants me out of Brooklyn."

"For a long time, Chris," I said, choosing my words carefully. "Five or ten years, maybe then it'll be safe to come home again."

There was an interminable silence on the other end. Then he broke it.

"But she can't come. Her practice won't permit it."

It was raining again. Through the open windows I could hear the yielding drops splash their guts out on the remorseless concrete streets. Theresa Matarazza's practice in internal medicine thrived on 4th Avenue. She couldn't abandon it. My friend would leave alone. I rubbed my hand across the stubble of my jaw and tried for sensitivity.

"It's hell, Chris. But it beats floating off Sandy Hook with the Holland Tunnel where your skull used to be."

On the other end, he groaned. Perhaps it hadn't come out as sensitive as intended.

"Tim…" he started in a pleading tone, and I knew what was coming. When he left the thought unfinished, I completed it for him.

"I know. I'm 'the Enforcer,'" I said tonelessly. "The Dean's office has a discipline problem they come to me—veteran gym teacher, ex-Marine, judo black belt. 'Tim Viggiano,' they say, 'never has to raise his voice'—"

"—And ranks as expert with how many types of hand-guns?" he interrupted.

Now the silence was on my end. How could I tell him? The beatings I'd absorbed as a kid—the blood gushing from a nose broken one time too many—the worse ones I'd seen dished out in the alley back of Fiorito's on the Docks—the poor bastards being dragged off on a skiff out of Gravesend Bay to spend eternity in the cold deep. And later, the senseless carnage of a real shooting war as my unit blew the intestines out of the shattered forces of a conscripted desert army more terrified of the indigenous dictator than of us. "Never again," I'd vowed to nobody important—only myself.

I could hear him breathing on the other end, his own life hanging desperately in the balance. I hadn't had a drink in twenty years. Now I cursed myself for stopping.

Chris," I reminded him gently. "High school kids can be daunted. Frank Torino's henchmen are stone killers."

He couldn't take it.

"I'll give you my whole salary—my life savings—anything, take it!" It tore out of him, a defiant cry of a cornered animal girding to fight for its life.

I knew it made no sense to the lawyer's son who had vacationed at Saint Moritz, gone to Poly Prep—not public schools—and who'd studied English Lit at Columbia University. But despite my training and expertise—perhaps because of them—I loathed violence. The last time I'd cried was submerged deep in banks of filed, forgotten memories—but something welled now behind my eyes and I let it come. He knew that my wife had died years before he'd met me, and that I had a child no longer in my life. But perhaps I had never shown him how much he had come to mean to me. I spoke now as if he were not my friend but my son.

"Superior defense skills generally enable you to avoid conflict." Though he couldn't see it, I shook my head. "But not in this case."

He didn't want to hear it. It was obvious from the sharp intake of his breath that he didn't want to face the full array of facts.

"My life is here," he said, as if that elemental truth, like an irrefutable theorem, outweighed all other considerations.

But Tim Viggiano did not have what it took to be a bodyguard.

"Your death will be here, too," I said sadly.

Three days later, he was gone. Theresa and I, in tandem, were effective; Frank Torino's thugs even more so. For two weeks, things were quiet. Labor Day weekend approached and the start of a new school year loomed. I didn't speak to Chris but his wife did, as he stayed first with her aunt in Buffalo, planning his next move. But events took it out of his hands.

Theresa called me the Thursday before Labor Day. She dealt daily with life-and-death issues. She was not one to panic.

"Tim," she said, the struggle to retain control of her voice clearly audible over the wires. "Marian saw some hard-looking goons outside her house on 60th Street."

Marian Palumbo, I knew, ran a day care center out of her home for the children of working parents. Four-year-old Christine Caravello had been a regular there for several years.

"They won't touch her," I said immediately.

"Are you sure?" the distraught mother fired back. "What if they grab her to make sure Chris comes back?"

I hadn't thought of that. "Have you spoken to the cops?" I asked, fighting for time to think.

"Of course," she replied. "But what can they do? No crime's been committed—not even any threats. They can watch the house for a week, maybe two. But they don't have the manpower to do it indefinitely. What then?"

I looked out the window. The rain had finally stopped, but without blessing, for the pitiless August sun now deep-fried the Brooklyn streets to a sultry crisp. I had thought I knew them. Afterall, my father had been an underboss in the Calabrese crime family before being whacked during interminable gangland warfare. My brother was doing "big numbers" in the joint for multiple killings; he'd probably rot there until he, too, was a corpse—and my kid sister had kept the family tradition alive by marrying a mobster. And then, there was one other that was too painful to even think about.

"Did you tell Chris?" I asked.

"No. But I have to."

At home alone, I nodded but said nothing.

"Will you help him?" she whispered.

I couldn't look out the window any more. The Bensonhurst streets brought home the ugly truth too vividly. How many honest people had they robbed, beaten, even murdered? How much blood of how many good men was splattered all the way to their elbows? I bowed my head helplessly before the unsummoned memories. I saw my big brother, Dom, and his buddy, Frank Torino, beat poor Tony Valentino almost to death for insulting our sister. Though smaller than both, I'd pulled them off and fought for his life, taking a beating myself, while Nicola cursed me for interfering. I'd had nothing to do with them for decades, and maybe knew them no more. Perhaps Theresa was right. In my mind, I saw the little girl, all floppy brown hair and pink ribbons, seized as a means of luring her innocent father to his demise. The old rage, suppressed for so long, started to rise. For the first time in decades, I didn't take deep breaths to try to calm myself.

I almost said "yes." I felt myself on the verge of croaking out the word. But an image crept before my eyes, slowly, inexorably, of a face I had not seen for years, had tried desperately to avoid in both deed and memory; succeeding in the one, but agonizing over the other. Theresa did not know, nor her husband. How could they? I had played my hand secretly, keeping my shameful family history buried irrevocably in the past. But the past refused to stay buried.

"Tim?" she asked, sounding concerned about me after my long silence.

"I can't. Don't ask why," I said, hoping this was the final word. "I just can't." I was surprised myself at how hoarse my voice sounded.

Nobody who knew them ever claimed that thugs were smart. It was not merely the prisons filled with wiseguys that attested to the point; it was the graveyards moldering with corpses of endless gorillas gunned down before their thirtieth birthdays. They couldn't leave it alone. They had to make sure.

The very next night they slithered from their sewers and came for me. I walked out of the diner on 86th Street after dinner and two heavyset characters in black dress jackets and slacks emerged from the parking lot shadows and walked slowly toward me. I knew who they were immediately and stopped.

"Viggiano," the taller of the two, wearing a navy polo shirt under his jacket, said. "Let's go."

I almost laughed at their stupidity. "Like I would go anywhere with you."

I'll give them this—they weren't long-winded conversationalists. In a trice, the shorter goon had something hard pressed into my left ribcage. His head motioned to the black Buick left idling just around the corner of the restaurant. I paused and when I spoke it was in words pronounced slowly and distinctly.

"You got no cause to whack me, therefore, no authority to do it. And even you cretins aren't stupid enough to do it on a street full of witnesses. So kiss off."

The short guy took no offence. He was too accustomed to obedience to hold any trace of self-doubt.

"The boss," he said easily. "Don't want you messing in this case." Subtly, he increased the pressure of the metallic object on my ribs. "Just walk away—and leave it be. *Capiche?*"

I looked at them, from one to another, at the pale, unconscionable eyes that considered murder nothing more than business—akin to running a bakery—at the swaggering gait, and at the aura of baleful menace that exuded from them as palpably as the taut neck muscles bulling over the edge of their collars. I looked at them but I saw Christine Caravello,

saw her in rosy red jumper and dress shoes, smiling in anticipation of her mommy's caress but fated instead to be accosted
by the steely glare and grip of remorseless gangsters—and
saw the small joyous face slowly darken with unanswerable
questions and inexpressible fear.

Savagely, I pushed down the full gamut of what I felt and
looked with undiluted earnestness into their apelike mugs. I
knew my mind was made up—and the consequences that for
me, personally, might accrue.

"OK, sure," I lied with total conviction. "I learned a long
time ago to mind my own business. Tell the boss this ain't
my affair."

"Guess your college education paid off, didn't it?" the
bigger thug said, grinning mirthlessly. But before his partner
pulled away the gun, his hand gave a lingering brutal squeeze
to my shoulder. "Just be sure you don't change your mind."
They both gave me the benefit of their hardest stare—and
then they were gone.

The only person I called when I returned home was Theresa Matarazza.

Chris returned in time for the start of the school year. But
instead of spending Sunday and the Labor Day holiday preparing for his classes—at which he was expert—he spent them
with me. For several years, he had studied judo with me two
nights a week at Castelli's Academy on 86th Street, and cur-
rently approached the rank of brown belt. Now we acceler-
ated—and expanded—the pace of his self-defense training.

We spent most of Sunday in a private room at Castelli's.
We damn near wore the mats out as I trained him in one
advanced throwing technique after another. I still guessed
they'd try to surprise and seize him, then hustle him off to the

docks where they could dispatch him privately and dispose of the corpse. Gunplay in the open of Bensonhurst's heavily inhabited streets had gone out of fashion long ago.

But on Monday, his real training began. It was illegal to own, but not difficult to procure, a handgun in New York City. I was on good terms with the captain of the local precinct. They'd known me and my service record since I'd started teaching at Lafayette. Long ago, I'd obtained a license for a .45 automatic, which I still owned. What they didn't know was the small arsenal of nine millimeters I had illicitly accumulated over the past decade. I kept them oiled and cleaned, in good working order. It may have been a paranoid legacy of my past—but I'd known too many thugs not to fear a break-in even on the busy avenue on which I lived.

On Monday morning, after an early breakfast, we took the long drive up to Beacon, New York, in the Hudson Highlands. We climbed the trail up to the desolate "Devil's Ladder" peak of South Beacon Mountain, our backpacks full of two things: water and ammunition. To avoid any random hikers, we went way off-trail. There, in a clearing in deep woods, I set up anything I could find as targets: sticks, branches, empty water bottles, varying the range but always keeping it within the limit of twenty-one feet. Chris had only minimal experience with handguns, having shot at out-of-state firing ranges a number of times as a college kid, so he had developed few bad habits that had to be broken. We began with the compact Sig Sauer P228 and graduated to the full-size Glock17. Even though it was likely that speed would be of the essence in foiling any sudden attack on him, I still started with two-handed "crouch" shooting to establish the fundamentals of proper self-defense shooting. We would graduate only later to the quicker one-handed "point" shooting.

Chris had a steady grip and good eye—and he was highly motivated. I stressed that though speed was important, accuracy was even more so. He was smart enough to realize that calmness was both imperative and extraordinarily difficult to achieve—and I taught him to carefully squeeze off his shots, not to jerk his hands or fire hurriedly. Hours later, by the time we reached the bottom of the hill it was almost dark, and we were hungry and exhausted—but we had established at least the basics of proper self-defense shooting. We ate dinner outdoors at a riverside restaurant in Cold Spring, as the trains roared by on their adjacent track, rattling the silverware and glasses on our table.

"What kind of family life does a gangster have?" Chris asked over his burger and brew. "How do you whack innocent people, then come home to your loving wife and children?"

I gazed down the train track at the rear lights of the departing northbound. How easy it would be to grab a train and roll across the continent, disembarking only at the point where the setting sun kissed the lip of the western sea. Flight could solve a lot of problems. Why didn't we do it?

"What if you and I appealed to his wife and explained?" he asked earnestly. "Could she influence her husband to back off?"

His question jerked me from my pleasant reverie. "You'll get no mercy from Mrs. Torino," I said bitterly. "She won't rest until your existence has been expunged from the face of this earth."

In the decade that he'd known me, he'd never heard that tone of voice. He stared for a moment, then returned to his meal.

But a minute later, he asked softly: "You knew Frank Torino, didn't you?"

I swore. "I don't want to talk about it."

We ate the rest of our meal in silence.

Chris wanted a gun, but he wasn't ready, and despite the gangsters scoping out his family, the danger to his life was not yet imminent. He needed more training.

He got it. I lost track of how many weekend days we spent in the secluded hills, including during snowstorms just before Christmas, blazing away at immobile targets with fingers red and stiff from cold. By Thanksgiving, he was deadly accurate at close range even as a one-handed, right-handed point shooter. I gave him a Glock17 and continued his training with his left hand. By late-January, he could shoot effectively with his off hand, as well, so I gave him another 17. They were heavy, but he wore a thick woolen overcoat with deep pockets. He took to carrying books and papers in a backpack rather than a briefcase, and kept both hands in his coat pockets, ostensibly to keep them warm.

We didn't stop—and long before Spring, he was a formidable enemy, especially for careless killers expecting an easy mark.

The NYPD reports of the final showdown were not entirely accurate, but they pieced together much of it. The rest wasn't hard to figure.

It was a raw night in late March with gusting winds and slanting rain—the kind of night on which Genghis Khan was conceived. Chris made an unscheduled stop in an all-night convenience store on Benson Avenue. He varied his patterns now, took looping shopping sprees across Brooklyn's polyglot neighborhoods, and rarely indulged the same store or the same hour. Quickly, he ducked back to his car.

But not quick enough. They were on him from the deep shadows, pinning his arms to his ribs, hustling him to the black Buick left idling in the lot behind the store. For several seconds, they were exposed to the full view of the avenue. But, unfortunately, on a howling night of wind-swept rain, few passers-by were on the street.

Chris relaxed in their grip, just as I had taught him during hours of practice, putting them at ease. Then he wrapped his right heel around the ankle of the thug on his right, not seeking to throw his adversary but only to knock him off balance. It worked. The killer stumbled slightly, just enough for the victim to free his right arm.

Chris reached immediately into the deep pocket of his overcoat, wrapped his fist around the Glock semi-auto, and shot the recovering gangster twice in the chest. The slugs tore two perfectly circular holes in the pocket of his coat, and drove Nicholas "Nicky Rods" Randazzo to the wet asphalt, where his blood mingled with the rain and trickled in a thin red stream toward oblivion.

The other thug was not paralyzed with shock. Nicky Rods' body had not yet hit the pavement when he had his .44 Magnum clear of its shoulder holster and beginning its downward arc. Chris never cleared the Glock from his pocket. Rather, he twisted to his left, lined up his target, and fired from the hip. The semi-auto roared, spitting a taut stream of lead into the front line of Thomas "Tommy Meat" Castellano, splitting his 300 pound frame open at the seams and splashing blood and intestines onto his killer's face.

Chris didn't wait. He peeled off Nicky Rods' blood-sodden raincoat, exchanged it for his own, shoved his two 17s into the pockets and the stiff's 9 millimeter into the waistband of his jeans. He grabbed Nicky's black fedora and jammed it on his skull, then hopped behind the wheel of the thugs' Buick. He called me on his cell phone.

"Tim," he said, his voice as husky and breathless as if he'd run 10,000 meters. "I'm going in."

"Don't do it!" I roared. At this point, I wasn't sure what had transpired, but it didn't take a genius to figure it out. Either way, it didn't matter—I recognized suicide when I saw it.

"I'm gonna ace these bastards," he said in a voice that was unrecognizable.

"Chris!" I screamed. "If they came for you, you got a legal case against Frank Torino. Don't do it!"

"They'll never give up," he responded bitterly. "I'm gonna finish it now." Then his cell phone clicked off.

"Son of a bitch," I swore bitterly. Then I swung into action.

Chris drove at the speed limit to Frank Torino's residence on Bay 28th Street. He didn't wait outside the gated compound—but gunned the heavy Detroit iron up to forty and rammed through the high white wrought iron gate, bringing the car to rest just feet from the Torino's yellow brick stoop.

The front door of the house opened immediately and one of the Calabrese soldiers stepped out. Chris got out of the driver's side, head bent, showing the mobster only the top of his hat.

"Nicky, you crazy?" the thug screamed above the wind. "What the f—k you doing?"

Chris answered with a fusillade of lead that pinned the mortally stricken gangster momentarily to the Torino's door, before it swung slowly inward on its hinges, allowing the corpse to topple backward and sprawl spread-eagled across the foyer. Chris raced up the stairs, plunged across the threshold, and hurdled the body. He clutched a semi-auto in each paw.

A second thug, galvanized by the gunfire, banged through the kitchen door, directly in Chris's path. He swung a .45 in his right fist, but in the darkened room thought he saw

Nicky Rods barrel through the front door. When he realized his error, he opened his mouth to scream, and Chris slammed a fistful of slugs into the aperture, blowing off the rear of his skull and decorating the Torino's living room walls in a new gangster décor of gore and splattered brains.

But Frank Torino Junior didn't mistake his target. He fired a hunting rifle from the top of the stairs, pumping one shell into Chris's left shoulder, splintering it to fragments, and spinning Chris to the deck. His second shot arced high, shattering the glass of the front foyer window, and he never fired a third. With a left hand now numb and useless, Chris dropped the spent Glock from his right and transferred the fully-loaded weapon from his left. The stream of fire spewing from the living room floor tore open the left half of the young thug's chest and rammed him backward against the hallway wall, off of which he toppled slowly forward, skidding half-way down the stairs before coming to a halt, both arms outstretched in front of him.

Frankie Tornado, alone with his wife and nephew in the rec room, on Chris's left as he faced the kitchen and the stairs, stepped into the hall, nine millimeter blazing. Chris, recognizing his prime tormentor immediately, fired from the floor—and for several seconds the darkened interior of the Torino ground floor took on the appearance of London during the Battle of Britain, the night sky glinting with shrill, darting flashes of death.

Then came the silence following the all-clear.

I heard the first wailing moans of police sirens at a great distance as I raced around the corner from my parked car and reached the crumpled front gate of the Torino residence. I had several minutes before the place would crawl with cops. I went up the stairs at a bound and stopped momentarily before the unhinged front door. I was shaking with fear. I knew what I would find in here—everything. No amount of deep breaths would help. I willed myself over the threshold, praying that he wasn't here.

The interior of the Torino home was a shattered charnel house. The Normandy beach carnage hardly seemed worse. Even in the dark, I made out the bodies strewn across the floor. On the finger of one, I recognized a gold wedding band, and knelt down. He lay in a pool of blood from which he would never rise. I stared silently for a moment. Then, wearing plastic gloves and boots, I reached for the Glock still clutched in his fingers. My practiced grip told me that bullets remained in the magazine.

"Tim," a weak feminine voice said, and I looked up.

Nicola Torino squatted not ten feet away, her hands cupping the head of the husband she would never speak to again. I didn't know, but she did, that the facedown stiff on the stairs was her son. She had lost her entire family in eight months; two-thirds of it in eight seconds. In the dark, I sensed her eyes were dry, but her voice was barely audible.

"Why'd he do it?" she said, her words more the moan of a wounded animal than a human question.

I fought against the accumulated rage of forty years—a cold fury engendered by the bullying violence wrought by this cadre of preening weasels too gutless to face life without a ceaseless succession of bloodied victims—the latest of whom had been my friend. Apparently, some things remained constant.

"Maybe because you and your family tried to murder him," I said in a voice so filled with bitterness that it must have struck her like the bullets that had wasted her husband.

"He killed my son!" she screamed, rising, clutching her husband's nine millimeter with both hands.

The sirens were closing in. But given whose house it was—and the extended gunplay—the cops would proceed with caution. I still had more than a minute.

"You and your scumbag family would have killed him anyway," I said of the poor eight-year-old nephew I had never known.

She raised the semi-auto into firing position, pointing it with both hands at my face.

"You think I don't know he couldn't have done this without you?" she said in a low voice so filled with lethal menace that it scared me more than the gun.

The sirens sounded just around the corner. The cops would be on the grounds outside the house within seconds. But there was still time enough to settle the debt of a lifetime.

"He was innocent," I said to Nicola Viggiano Torino. "Unlike you and your rat bastard family."

Her hands trembled as she pointed the gun at the head of the older brother who had irrevocably renounced his family thirty-five years ago.

"Blood is thicker than water, Tim," she said. "Maybe you'll learn that now."

As if on cue, a silent male figure stepped into the doorway behind her. I stared at my worst nightmare come to fruition, at the mirror image of what I had looked like a quarter century in the past. But there was something absent in his eyes that had once shined in mine. I stared, in devastated heartbreak, at a face I had not seen for an interminable ten years, stared into the venomous eyes of a gangster, of a "made" man that stared back at me.

"Hello, Dad," said the grim voice of Alexander Viggiano.

His mother's death had been a turning point. Even before she had succumbed to breast cancer, the signs had been there—the uncontrollable rage, the failing grades, the bullying violence—but when that gentle influence had been irrevocably terminated, there had ensued a rapid deterioration. First the expulsion from Catholic school, then the incessant discipline problems in public school, and then the fatal climactic night on which his frantic father had finally lost all control and, in an unforgivable fury, beaten him into an unrecognizable bloody mass—in exact replication of every hideous vice he had perpetually foresworn. It was the final breach. Three days later, the boy disappeared. Three days after that, it became clear that he had gone to live with his aunt—with the harridan wife of Frank Torino.

Alex. The name would not come. I tried to mouth the sound "Alex," pushed into it all that was left of my wavering will, but my vocal cords had been suddenly jerked tight like piano strings tautened into rigid immobility, incapable of registering even the faintest note. I was mute.

Only my eyes moved in a paralyzed body perhaps—in seconds—to be rendered motionless for the duration. Nicola's finger tightened on the trigger. At his side, Alex Viggiano—or was it Torino now—clutched a .45 automatic in his left hand. I cared nothing what Nicola did—but I would be shot dead by my own son. The debilitating nausea that surged upward from my viscera left me so weakened that Chris's gun in my hand felt like a two ton deadweight and I could not lift it.

The cops were on the grounds. Dimly, I heard them outside the crumpled gate. With exceeding caution, they would approach the splintered door.

"Blood is thicker than water," my numbed lips repeated, as if in a trance. "Olive oil is thicker than water, too. Is it thicker than justice?"

He was already dead. He had died on the day he left the only hope of salvation and aligned himself with those who plundered and brutalized the innocent. He might not have pulled the trigger of the gun that had murdered Chris Caravello, but his armed stance now alongside of Lady Macbeth left no doubt of his loyalties.

I saw his gun rise and Nicola's finger pull the trigger in the exact instant I lurched to the right, away from the door and toward the interior of the house. All immobility fled in a rush as I felt the bullets from their roaring guns whistle inches to my left. Chris's gun was up, bucking once, twice, three times, and four as I fired unerringly into the darkness, at the muzzle flashes, even though on the move. In the horrific moments of a lethal gun fight, with acrid cordite smoking in my nostrils, amidst the ear-splitting crescendo of death-dealing weapons fired at close quarters and the screams of mortally stricken animals, a gut level epiphany swept through me—one I had always sensed, but which could rise to conscious articulation not now but only in the imminent future.

I turned and fired several warning shots out the front door, high, into the trees. I stooped and placed Chris's gun back in his hand and re-wrapped his inert fingers around it. I took one last look at the rictus of agony frozen on the face of a dedicated teacher, a loving husband, and a genuine father. I had, indeed, lost my son today. Chris was family. Theresa and Christine were family. Innocent men and women were family. Murderers were my family's enemies.

Quickly, but purposefully and unhurriedly, I headed for the back door. I didn't remove my gloves and boots until I was well clear of the Torino property.

Nothing To Do

"There's nothing to do in this town," Vic Toland complained. "It's dead. I can't see why your parents moved here."

His friend, Sarah Goldberg, sat next to him in the shade of the back porch of her family's house. Despite the early hour, the heat of the summer morning already raised beads of sweat on their foreheads and promised an afternoon like the inside of one of the steel mills fifty miles to the east.

"You know why," she responded without conviction. "Daddy was made chief of airport security. Planes don't land in the city. It makes sense for him to be out here in the sticks."

Sarah was curled in supple ease on the lounge next to the screen door. She was slender, with honey blonde hair that reflected the sun's rays and swung gracefully when she bobbed her head. Her smile was warm, her conversation vivacious, and her commitment to minimal motion indomitable.

He nodded wearily, wondering already, although it was mid-June, what they would do to while away the hot days of summer's long months.

Before he could ask, a noise at the door caused them to turn around. Sarah's younger brother stood on the threshold. Both of the fifteen-year-olds brightened momentarily.

"Hey, Superstar," Vic said. "What's up?"

"Hey," Billy said, coming through the door.

Though people always observed the ubiquitous baseball clutched in his right fist, it was not what they noticed first. For Billy "The Kid" Goldberg, although only twelve, had long arms attached to his slender frame and a pair of hands the size of baskets. The ball, which he could throw with the accuracy of a dart and the velocity of a bazooka shot, was dwarfed by his long fingers. There was not a Little League coach in the state who did not think he was heading for The Show.

"Hey, little brother," Sarah asked, although she had to look up to speak to him. "What's on for today?"

"We'll see." He drained the cup of orange juice in his left hand and pitched it unerringly in the trash. "Want to come?"

"It's hot," she said.

As Billy ambled around the corner of his parents' block, onto Joliet Avenue, Joe Hasselhoff, the butcher, stood in front of his shop, speaking to a customer.

"Billy 'The Kid' Goldberg!" he boomed above the traffic noise on the street. "In ten years, gonna pitch the White Sox to the World Series?"

"The Yankees," Billy said, crinkling his nose in distaste at mention of the inferior team.

"The Yankees," the butcher repeated, laughing good-naturedly. "Whatever you want, Champ."

Billy sauntered down the street, firing the ball off brick walls and cement steps, grabbing the caroms one-handed, as if he wore a glove. He thought briefly of his years in Brooklyn, growing up, dominating older kids in spirited games of stickball, tense physical and verbal competitions waged in streets and schoolyards. He tried to remember a time he had lost. He shrugged.   People smiled spontaneously, almost involuntarily, when they saw him, and sang out, "Billy Goldberg, the pre-teen 'K' machine!" He always smiled in reply—but his mind was elsewhere, far from this hazy Illinois town, in New York, where he pitched inning nine of game seven, gunning for his third win of the Series.

As the small business district petered out three blocks past Main Street, Billy ducked down Tecumseh Street, heading for the edge of town, toward the forest that began just beyond the Western Bank and the row of homes following it. The other kids in the seventh grade believed these woods stretched all the way to the Mississippi River and that, in the past, several boys had gotten lost and disappeared in them. When they spoke like that, Billy remained silent; for in the past twelve months, since living here, he had explored them, slogging through deep drifts on February Saturdays. He knew they extended more than ten miles due west but ended in a flat expanse of endless fields, cut only by a major east-west interstate.

As he passed the last home and ducked into the line of trees, he heard a child's voice cry out: "Billy Goldberg!"

"Hey, Amber," he said to the smallish seven-year-old girl who called him. "What's wrong?"

The child tugged at her long strands of brown hair in distress, and for several seconds she couldn't choke out any words. Billy got on his knees in front of her, and, without words, used the end of his tee-shirt to wipe her tears.

"A mean dog chased my kitty up a tree," she said. "And he won't go away."

"Where's Brad?" he asked of her teen-aged brother.

"He went swimming with his retarded friends. Told me to stay home, watch TV, and stay out of trouble."

"He left you home alone?"

She nodded.

"Did you call the Fire Department?"

"I don't know the number," she said, lowering her eyes to the ground.

Billy thought for a moment.

"Amber, have you got a club or a big stick?"

"I can get one of Brad's baseball bats."

"Perfect."

When she returned with the bat, he asked: "Where's the dog?"

"Follow me."

He followed her behind the house, where she stopped. At the end of the yard, where the tree line began, a huge black and brown dog, with a head like a cinder block, crouched in the grass. His fur was matted and his coat dull, but his sides and haunches revealed the powerful structure of a fighting dog.

"He looks like a Rottweiler," Billy said. "But I've never seen him before."

"He's a stray. He lives in the woods and eats people."

"He may live in the woods. But he probably eats wood-chucks and chipmunks."

"What are we going to do?" she asked.

As if to answer her, the big dog got up, and, growling, slowly advanced on them. Taking careful aim, not want-ing to split the dog's skull, Billy jerked his right arm high and whipped it forward, firing the baseball like a bee-bee. It struck the Rottweiler square on his rump, ricocheting high as, momentarily, the beast staggered. With the animal's cry

of pain filling the air, Billy switched the bat to his right hand
and charged. Swinging for the fences, roaring at the top of his
lungs, he looked like a Berserker warrior lunging out of Viking
lore. Taking a careful look, the Rottweiler decided to try other
fare; turning quickly, he limped into the woods.

Amber came up behind him. "What about Boomer?"

"Where is he?"

"In the tree, silly. I told you. Now, go get him."

Billy looked up at the huge oak at the far end of the yard.
On the lowest branch, at least thirty feet off the ground,
crouched the feline equivalent of a Weight Watcher's dropout.
His flanks spilled over both sides of the branch.

"How big is Boom-Boom?" Billy asked suspiciously.

"Boomer. He's big."

"And of course, we don't have a ladder, do we, Amber?"

She shook her head demurely. "No."

Billy started up the tree. The bark was rough and notched,
giving ample traction, enabling him to get solid grips with
both his arms and legs. Step-by-step, he made his way up the
oak. By the time he reached the lowest branch, his arms were
scraped and sweat dripped in his eyes.

"Here, Boom-Boom."

The huge cat backed away.

"He only answers to 'Boomer,'" Amber called from the
ground.

"Thanks for your help."

He started out on the branch, swinging arm over arm.
When he got to the mid-point, he stretched out his left arm,
reaching for the cat. The terrified animal raked Billy's arms
with his claws, carving red streaks of blood.

"He doesn't like strangers," Amber called helpfully.

Billy grabbed the cat by the nape of his neck and swung

him quickly over his left arm, onto the part of the branch nearest the trunk. The cat darted to the trunk, looked down its length, and back at Billy. He crouched and refused to move.

Billy hung on by his left hand and wiped his right arm repeatedly across his face. When he pulled it away, red streaks of blood covered his cheeks and forehead. Rolling his eyes way back in his head, he opened his mouth and snarled. Then he bellowed a cry that could be heard to the shores of Lake Michigan.

"Eat the cat!"

He advanced. The animal took one look and bolted down the tree, digging in his claws to slow his descent. When he reached the ground, he didn't stop, but waddled past Amber and parked his girth on the mat by the rear door.

"Kitty! Kitty!" the young girl clapped her hands, gazing after him.

Billy started down the tree. When he reached the ground, he retrieved his baseball and stepped through the tree line. He was in the forest.

It was cooler here. The thick foliage kept the full rays of the sun from reaching the soil, but enough filtered through to support a vast amount of ground vegetation. Billy breathed deeply as he walked, drawing in air laden with the scent of voluptuous life. Here insects buzzed and leaves rustled as chipmunks scurried from his path. A blur of bluish white flashed above him and a bird landed gracefully on a low-hanging branch. There was, he knew, a fresh-water stream just a mile-and-a-half in. He headed directly for it.

After drinking, he sat on the bank a moment and rested. He knew that the activity planned for today was strenuous, perhaps dangerous. The huge bowl of cereal he had devoured for breakfast would sustain him for hours. But if he were trapped inside for hours without water, he could be in trouble. He drank until his insides felt they would burst. Rising, he checked the sun's position through the trees, then headed on a hundred-and-twenty degree angle to his left. The cliffs were several miles to the north. He would be there shortly after noon.

Forty minutes later, when the cliffs above a parched creek bed towered over him, Billy stood in the open, with the late-morning sun beating down on him. Knowing the depths he would soon encounter, he savored, for a moment, its scorching caress of his cheek. Sensing danger, he waited. He took a dozen deep breaths. Then he shoved the baseball deep into the loose pockets of his shorts. He started to climb.

Pressing his face against the dirt, he dug for traction with ten fingers and two corrugated climbing boots. Loose earth and rocks slipped away beneath him, and he could feel sand clinging to his cheeks and grating under his nails. His lungs and legs strained with effort and sweat dripped off his hair. At last, only feet from the top, he stopped and looked into the mouth of his destination.

Cave exploring was called spelunking, he knew. Not that his father had ever used that term on their exploration of cliffs and caves in the wildest regions of the Negev. Chaim Goldberg, a former Israeli commando and special agent assigned to counterterrorism, was not fluent in English; nor was he a man given to many words in any language. But he was a man who went after what he wanted—and when he left his native land to marry Mary Rebecca Walsh, a criminologist assigned to the FBI's New York office, he did so without regret. He merely took his daughter and young son to explore the desert regions he loved so deeply. If it bothered him that one shared his passion and one did not, he never showed it. He grabbed each with equal ferocity on his arrival home in the evening. Billy hadn't told him yet of this cave he had spotted from the creek bed on an icy March morning. Tonight, he thought, he would tell all.

He crawled to the mouth of the cave and reached into his other pocket for a pencil flash. The narrow cave stretched in front of him and its low ceiling descended steadily as one went in. Billy knew better than to wait. Drawing a deep breath, he started in. It was tough sledding. He crawled because of the low roof—and a series of stalagmites staggered across the floor made his progress an obstacle course. Once a flight of startled bats scattered over his head, and, seconds later, still shaken, he cracked his head on a stalactite just above his torch's swath. He lay still on his stomach for several seconds, clutching the floor, until the spinning motion of the cave's interior subsided to the rate of a high-speed carousel. He glanced back once at the sun's dim light filtering through the cave's mouth. It seemed far away. He breathed deeply for several moments to slow his heart rate. Then he started forward.

It was on the way back, after discovering that the cave, roughly half-a-mile in, petered into a passage too small even for a child, that, returning by a different route, he found the pit. Or rather, the pit found him. He was groping forward, hurrying—precisely what his father had taught him not to do—eyes fixed on the growing brightness ahead, when his hands reached into emptiness. He dug his knees into the dirt as he pitched forward and flailed with his arms, grasping for solidity, but his momentum carried him over the edge. Falling, he twisted his body in mid-air, stretching for the wall with both hands. His flashlight was jolted from his grasp, and he heard it clatter off protruding rocks as it crashed to the bottom. It was black as tar and he could not see the wall from which he clung. He swung over an abyss, clutching the edge with his left hand, while his feet scrabbled for purchase. Finally, he swung his body in air and seized ground in his right hand. He hung. Then, slowly, agonizingly, inch-by-inch, he pulled himself up. He crawled from the pit, toward the cave's interior, and lay on his belly. His fingers clutched the base of a stalagmite, and he would not let go. He lay for a long time. Finally, on his belly, he turned and crawled with infinite caution toward the faint light in the distance. When he reached it, his mouth felt like a bone.

He sat in the cave's mouth and sucked in huge draughts of air. When he looked at the sky, he was amazed to find the sun high. It was shortly after two o'clock.

He reached the stream an hour later and took the longest sensuous drink of his life. He collapsed on the banks. In his pockets were two objects, his baseball and a protein bar. Removing them, he unwrapped the bar and ate it, chewing every morsel slowly. He took another drink. Then he lay in the sun without moving, the baseball in his right hand, letting the horror of a dank abyss melt in the summer warmth. Within an hour, his strength had returned, though whether drawn from the sustenance, the sun, or the ball he could not tell.

As he sidled to the left, out of the sunlight, into the shade, he heard three sharp cracks in succession. They sounded vaguely like gunshots and came from far-off. Hunters, Billy thought, stiffening. He loved animals—and the spectacle of well-fed humans killing them for sport made him ill. But he felt the sun seep through leaves to splash light on his face, he felt the weight of the ball in his hand, and he pushed aside ugly thoughts. There were pennants to be won, he remembered. There was the toast of the New York sporting scene to become. One day, he realized solemnly, there would be Cooperstown.

He turned toward home and started in that direction; he hurried. There was just enough time, before dinner, to reach the diamonds and take batting practice against the local high school players. Maybe, just maybe, by the time he made the American League, the designated hitter rule would be abandoned.

He'd gone less than a mile when he heard hurried steps blundering through the brush. Billy opened his mouth to call a greeting, but quickly shut it. The man he spotted wore green camouflage, hefted a large satchel in his left hand, and looked back furtively over his shoulder. In his right hand, he carried a lethal-looking nine-millimeter automatic.

Billy ducked behind a tree. The man stopped in a clearing not fifty feet away and glanced upward, checking the position of the sun. When he swung around, listening intently for sounds from his rear, Billy saw the lettering inscribed on the satchel: Western Bank, Bloomsburg, Illinois. Satisfied that all was quiet, he jerked a huge plastic bag from inside his camouflage, unfolded it, then knelt quickly and transferred the content of his satchel into the bag. He flung the empty baggage into the trees. Rising, he slung the now-full bag over his left shoulder and headed due west into the deep forest. Billy let him go, then started quietly after him.

The man made so much noise in his haste that Billy easily tracked him. But several miles in, the fugitive quickly whirled, catching Billy in the open a hundred feet behind. He fired a burst, but shot from the hip, and the bullets whistled harmlessly to Billy's left as he dived for a stand of trees. Billy crawled quickly to his right, heart pounding, as the gunman charged the tree he had just abandoned. He could still hear the roar of the nine-millimeter reverberate in his head, and the palms of both hands were wet. And yet, having used guns all his life, he knew them; they did not scare him; not like the near fall into the pit had, and his breathing was free.

Peering quickly around the tree furthest to the right, he saw the gunman twenty feet away, stealthily approaching the stand. He didn't wait. Drawing one deep breath, he stepped lightly from behind the tree and fired. This time, he did not worry about splitting his opponent's skull. The gunman whirled at the sound, just in time to see a twelve-ounce, official American League hardball come whirling at his head. The crack of the ball on his forehead was heard clearly above the terrified chirping of the birds. The thug went down as if Billy were the one with a gun. The nine-millimeter fell from his grasp and he lay without moving.

"That'll teach you to crowd the plate," Billy said.

He darted quickly to retrieve first his ball and then the gun. From the lump already forming on the thief's forehead, Billy knew he was on the disabled list for a while. Still, he should truss the creep. But how? He had neither rope nor knife.

Billy heard his father's advice in emergencies: Don't panic. His dad repeatedly told him the words heard when a child in Israel, words heard by millions around the globe, the calm terms of a man speaking from space, from the depth of catastrophe: "Houston, we've had a problem." Billy had been weaned on such words and on the kind of men who could utter them. He took a series of deep breaths to slow his racing heart. Then he looked around.

Thick vines grew on several trees. But he had nothing with which to cut them. Silently he cursed himself for venturing into the forest without a knife. He knew better than that. Then he remembered that the thug, garbed in camouflage, prepared for a forest getaway, might be so armed. Going through the criminal's clothes, Billy found a sheath knife strapped to his belt, tucked under his left pant leg. Expropriating it, he quickly hacked at the vines. In several minutes, he had the thug's wrists tied behind his back and his ankles bound together. He put the automatic on safety, shoved it into the waistband of his shorts, and hefted the heavy-duty garbage bag. He started toward town.

He sweated heavily and strained under the load. He stopped frequently to rest. It seemed he had gone miles before he heard sounds of men approaching from town. He put down his load and waited. When he spotted a khaki uniform straining across a broad expanse of chest, he knew who it was. He saw a grim black face explode into a grin—and he grinned back.

"Billy 'The Kid' Goldberg!" the black man roared. "Did you leave any work for me?"

"Not much, Sheriff," Billy said modestly.

In the months since they had moved to Bloomsburg, Billy's parents had become friends with Sheriff William T. Robinson. Ten years on Chicago's police force had hardened Robinson's hide, but nothing could harden his heart. A former minor league catcher, he spent many of his days off catching the town's young phenom. "Ice that arm, 'Kid,'" he'd say after practice. "You're carrying a gold mine."

When Billy handed him the gun and the bag, and explained what he'd done, the sheriff's grin faded.

"The Yankees gain is the FBI's loss, son," he said softly. "You did your mom and dad proud."

Billy stood and watched for several seconds as the sheriff and two deputies moved into the woods. He need not look at the sky to realize there was no time for batting practice. If he went straight home, he might arrive before his mom and dad.

Forty minutes later, as Billy dragged himself across the back lawn of his parents' house, he heard a familiar voice call to him.

"Billy 'The Kid'! How's it going, champ?"

Climbing the steps, Billy saw that Frank Hackett had joined Sarah and Vic Toland on the porch. As usual with Sarah's friends and admirers, they sipped iced tea and played gin rummy. They had a small fan plugged into an outdoor socket, blowing a soft breeze across them. The shaded porch was a cool oasis after the fire and sweat of his day.

"Hey, little brother, how was your day?"

"Good, " Billy said. "How was yours?"

"Long," she said. Her friends nodded. "It must have been ninety-five."

"What'd you do, Killer?" Vic asked.

"A little of this and a little of that."

"Did you pitch?" Frank Hackett said.

"Some."

"Got to hand it to you, 'Kid,'" Vic said. "I don't know what you find to do in this town."

Billy Goldberg stood there covered in dirt, dried blood streaking his face and both arms, sweat pouring off of him. He could count his muscles by reference to every separate ache and pain. Visions of black caves, bank robbers, and Rottweilers danced before his eyes, and he couldn't wait to be alone with his dad.

"Can't imagine," Billy said and walked inside.

On the porch, Sarah and her friends continued their game of cards.

"God," Vic said, several minutes later. "It's after six and it must still be ninety degrees."

Slowly, deliberately, Frank wiped a bead of sweat off his upper lip.

"I know it," he said. "Tomorrow's gonna be the same."

The Short Light Sets

A ngela Wong was worried. Her friend was an emotional wreck. She had called just that morning to cancel their lunch date—the fourth time in six weeks that Paula had bailed on her. It was intolerable, Angela decided. She and Paula might as well be strangers for as much quality time as they spent together.

She was sitting in the Gian-Carlo Rota Reading Room of the MIT Math Department, poring over a series of journal articles. Her qualifying exam in Partial Differential Equations, Algebraic Topology, and Geometry of Manifolds was less than a month away. She had no doubt that with proper preparation she would kick serious ass. But she couldn't concentrate. Not one to waste time, she noted the place in her reading, and headed back to her graduate housing on Memorial Drive.

The quickest way to Harvard would be the Red Line to Harvard Square. Instead, opting for exercise, she went to her tiny dorm room and put on layers against the chill April wind, and unchained her racing bike from the rack in front of her building. Fitting her helmet snugly over her flowing black hair, she pushed out onto Massachusetts Avenue and pedaled steadily across town. Arriving, she took a quick circle before entering campus, passing on her way the infamous Hong Kong at Harvard Square. Images of downing Scorpion Bowls at its uproarious second floor bar and then staggering at two a.m. into a cab flashed as vivid memories of her early years in Cambridge.

At Harvard on this Saturday morning, she searched fruitlessly through the Widener Library before finding Paula at the Robbins Library of Philosophy in Emerson Hall. Her friend was barricaded behind a hardcover copy of Kemp Smith's translation of Kant's *Critique of Pure Reason* and another of H.J. Paton's *Kant's Metaphysic of Experience*, and didn't see her coming. Angela sat down across from her and said nothing.

Paula Koehler, although a petite blonde barely twenty-nine, looked past forty. Her face was drawn and her cheeks creased with deep lines, as if she had spent countless sleepless nights grappling some intractable dilemma. But her green eyes did not droop from exhaustion; they were vividly bright from an excess of coffee—and an abundance of worry.

She looked up.

"Angela! Angela, I'm so sorry." She reached across the table with a gesture of spontaneous affection and gently touched her friend's wrist. "I know I've been erratic, but I'm so swamped, I don't know what to do with myself, I don't sleep, I just work, I—" she paused for a shallow breath and then let her jumble of words come in a rush—"I have my qualifying exam in Metaphysics and Epistemology next month, it has a reading list as long as my arm, I have a German competency test a week later—and I have to translate Kant!—I have papers to write in each of my two courses this semester—and I'll soon have a stack of finals to grade for the Intro to Philosophy class I teach at Northeastern. I'm ready for a rubber suit in a padded cell!" She looked undecided whether to rise from her chair in fevered energy or dissolve into tears.

Angela burst into ringing laughter. Friends had always said that she laughed with her whole body, and now the joyous sounds reverberated from the confines of the library's walls. Paula stared in alarm as fellow students looked up from their texts.

"Angela, shh, what's so funny?" Her eyebrows lifted and her hands spread wide. "I have a nervous breakdown—and that's funny?"

The math student stopped and grasped her friend's hand. "Paula, put the books away. We're outta here."

"But I—"

"Do it!"

Paula carefully inserted a bookmark into her translation of Kant and shut the book. She looked up. "OK," she said. "But you're buying."

Paula was silent as her friend dragged her off campus and onto the "T." She said nothing on the short trip into Boston—and the furrowed ridges under her eyes only deepened, although Angela thought she detected a more erect posture as her friend rode the Red Line inbound—and, eventually, the Green E Line to the Haymarket. A short walk brought the two friends to Boston's historic North End. With the decision made for her, and her absence from work a *fait accompli*, Paula's interest waxed and she decided on northern Italian cuisine for lunch. They selected Davide on Commercial Street.

Over pan seared shrimp in orange basil sauce and veal stuffed with prosciutto and fontina cheese, the two friends chattered as they had many times since they had met two years previously in a Mathematical Logic class offered by the

Harvard Philosophy Department. Paula breathed in the fragrance of delicious food superbly prepared and Angela could see the taut lines of her shoulders relax.

When Paula felt that her intestines would disgorge all content with another bite, she put down her fork and sighed. "It's some kind of sin to waste even a nibble of this."

"Tomorrow we eat again." Angela contentedly rubbed her belly.

Paula stared across the table at the pretty Chinese girl. "Angela, I know you inherited money—but how do you do it in school? How do you get "As" in the graduate Math program—at MIT, no less—and still have so much fun?"

Angela's smile was a look, not of mirth but of genuine warmth that her friend could palpably feel. But for a moment, her look was far away.

"Gotta have fun," she murmured. "Next weekend will be fun."

"Seeing Tony?"

"Mmm."

Paula knew that Angela's boyfriend, Tony Merlucci, was a rising chef at a Mulberry Street Italian eatery.

"Here—or in New York?"

"I'll drive down next Friday after my last class. We'll have a late dinner with my mom. "Then"—her eyes closed—"we'll go to Tony's place for plenty of alone time."

Paula stared hungrily until her friend's eyes opened and held her gaze.

"When was the last time you got laid?" Angela asked quietly.

"Laid? Are you kidding? Brad dumped me over a year ago, because I had time for nothing but study." She moaned. "Angela, how do you have the time?"

Angela said nothing. She just stared thoughtfully at her friend.

"Will you answer?"

The math student took a long sip of wine and rolled the smooth liquid on her tongue.

"Will I sound like a pompous ass if I do?"

Paula shook her head. "You won't. I promise."

Angela nodded. "Alright. I don't have time. I make time."

Paula sat motionless, her face rigid. For a long time, she remained silent.

"Philosophy's the love of wisdom," she said quietly. "I just got some from a mathematician."

"Take wisdom where you find it. I got some from a skirt-chasing, rip-snorting, lecherous old man."

Paula looked puzzled. "Who?"

Angela smiled—a dreamy, girlish, faraway smile. "My dad." She sat, undecided, for a moment. Then she made up her mind. "Listen to me."

Everyone was certain The Stick was dying. A pack a day of Chesterfields for 65 years had led to a cough so violent that people imagined they saw chunks of his lungs hurled forth with his thick spittle.

"Angel," Phil Villone, one of his illegitimate sons said to me. "You're the only one The Stick listens to. Get him to a doctor."

Yeah," I snorted. "If you find a doctor with tits like Marilyn Monroe, maybe I could get him there."

Phil, at eighteen, already had the lean, lithe height of his biological father, and the peculiarly weightless way of carrying himself that, ironically, caused the son to seem more of a man than his years allowed—and the father to move like one significantly younger than the eighty-two he was known to be.

For a moment, Phil's honest face, understandably grim under the circumstances, brightened into a lop-sided grin. "Yeah, lots of guys would get sick then."

But Brooklyn of that era had no such doctors, I reminded myself, leaving the Villone apartment on Nostrand Avenue, launching my nightly foraging for supper. Despite my mom's ancestry—or perhaps because of it—I had little tolerance for Chinese food. The Stick's superlative cooking, over the course of my sixteen years, had provided a strong preference for Italian. Jimmy Chu, my mom's one friend, an old Hong Kong immigrant who owned a connoisseur's cigar shop on King's Highway, smiled, lighting up his wrinkled face, whenever he visited our apartment. "Want to go out for Peking duck, Angel?" he'd wink at me.

Everyone assumed The Stick was my dad, although no one ever said so. I asked my mom once when I was a kid, but she just dodged the question.

"The Stick? Dear God, The Stick." She waved her hand derisively, as if to dismiss the question—but I noticed her eyes, as if back-lit by the same soft glow they showed when he was in sight.

Although my last name was Wong, everyone figured I was half Italian. But for someone supposedly Eurasian, I looked suspiciously like my mom—the petite figure, the straight black hair, the delicate Oriental features. Everyone called me "Angel," except The Stick, who had his own name for me.

"Hey, Chinkie," he said for the thousandth time as I turned my key in the lock and entered his walk-in apartment on East 29th Street, around the corner from Samantha Wong's laundry on Nostrand Avenue, where my skinny mother toiled alone throughout the day with loads of dirty clothes too heavy for her. No one worked harder than her—and no one smiled less. I rarely saw her and, as long as I did well in school, rarely heard from her either.

"Hey, Stick," I smiled immediately, finding it impossible not to. His living room was clogged with plump sofas and overstuffed chairs—and I had spent countless hours of my childhood comfortably curled in them reading many of the western, detective, and espionage novels he favored. Often he had bought me "girls" books about female detectives or glamorous princesses or adventurous ranch girls and their horses—but I never read them. I preferred to read his. The well-thumbed paperbacks still overflowed the three-shelf bookcases that lined his walls, interspersed with the battered furniture.

But The Stick enjoyed poetry, as well—mostly sensual love poems. Often, I co-opted the living room easy chair in which he preferred to read, forcing him to sit on the sofa near the TV, and one day discovered a slim paperback volume of Catullus on the floor adjacent to his chair. Although hardly cut out to be an English major, I was immediately captivated by its frank, open glorification of pedal-to-the-floor living. "Come, Lesbia, let us live and love, and value not a fig what sour old men say. Suns may set and rise again. But for us, when the short light has once set, remains to be slept the sleep of one unbroken night." I never looked at The Stick in quite the same way after reading those lines.

But it was primarily the walls above the bookshelves and chairs that never failed to attract my attention. They were filled with countless snapshots of his three children. One photograph each of the two wives he had outlived was respectfully displayed on the wall nearest his eat-in kitchen. But they were akin to beloved outcasts amidst the riotous display of his children at all ages—the three "legit" kids, as he called them—and a half-dozen or so bastards and suspected bastards. Peering out from among an endless panoply of scamps with the map of Sicily stamped across their mugs was a scattered collection of shots—at all ages—of a grinning Chinese girl.

"What's for dinner?" I asked, plopping in front of his TV in the living room and calling into the kitchen.

In all the years I'd known him, I'd rarely seen his television on—and only tuned to baseball games then. But his ancient stereo blared incessantly, pouring out the rollicking sounds of swing, big band, and jazz. Now, Sinatra crooned "The Way You Look Tonight," and I wasn't sure The Stick heard me.

But he had a calmness about him—some quiet, unflustered sense—that never hurried, allowing him, in his own good time, to process multiple sources of input. He didn't respond for several long moments, and, unabashed, I was just ready to sing out again when he muttered, almost to himself:

"Damn kid eats all my meatballs." Then, with a shout: "Why don't you get some eggrolls? Get in touch with your heritage, for Christ's sake!"

I laughed. "How about some pasta and gravy with the meatballs?" I mulled my options for a second. "Preferably ziti."

He snorted in disgust. "You want a goddamn menu? While you decide, I'll run out, get you gelato for dessert. How's that?"

"No thanks," I said off-handedly, poring over the yellowed jacket of an aging Sinatra album. "Ziti and meatballs will be fine."

I could hear him above the clatter of pots in his kitchen. "Goddamn gavone," he muttered. "Got to get a second job to feed this kid."

We sat over dinner at the rickety deal table in his tiny kitchen. The air was redolent with the spicy fragrance of The Stick's homemade marinara sauce—and with the vestigial remnants of a thousand such previous meals. The walls were painted yellow, faded now, but still suffusing the room with a soft reflected glow. A quartet of multi-colored roses, purchased fresh every few days, sat in a crystal vase on the table between us.

I had slipped back into the comfort zone of countless similar dinners with him and had forgotten my specific mission. I looked up, with a mouthful of ziti, and peered at him carefully.

Even bent over his pasta, Andreas Vinatieri gave an impression of ramrod straight, tensile strength. He had a full head of white hair, clipped short at the sides and behind, but combed straight back like a rich wavy mane on top. His face was creased and lined, making him look every day and hour of his eight decades on earth—but it spoke of a limitless range of life experience to which those of an eager youth could only aspire. His eyes glittered with the inextinguishable deviltry of a boy.

But the cough, always habitual, had become pronounced. Bouts of it no longer lasted mere seconds before desisting; now they continued for long moments of seemingly endless convulsions. His children—of whom I was the youngest anybody knew of—were scared. Though most were in their thirties, even forties, and some were themselves married, none could imagine life without the man who had stood like a sentinel through every crisis of their youth.

"Stick," I said carefully, knowing his contempt for doctors. "The cough...it doesn't...you know...seem to get better...how you feeling?"

He laid his fork fastidiously on the napkin by his right side, so as not to spew gravy across the white tablecloth. His dark eyes looked full into mine with a sternness that failed to meld into intimidation only because of the sparkle that always seemed to lurk immediately behind any other emotion revealed there. "Chinkie, what did I teach you about temporizing?"

I grinned slightly. The Stick kept a dictionary by his easy chair and loved showing off his vocabulary.

"Alright." I gripped the table's edge in both hands and blurted the truth—pretty or not—as he had taught me. "You need to see a doctor."

He smiled—"morning in Palermo," Mrs. Rossini, a neighbor, once called it—and nodded. "That's better."

"You'll do it?" I didn't dare to hope.

"Not a chance."

I returned sullenly to my meal. But shortly later, as The Stick washed dishes and I dried, I saw another opportunity.

"How's the homework for tonight?" he asked, always, like my mom, solicitous regarding my education.

"Got a few calculus problems to work out—take about an hour. AP American history test tomorrow, I'm ready, studied over the weekend."

"OK, got a mission for you tonight."

I grinned, having been trusted with similar "missions" before.

"Theresa Dimming," he said. "Over on Haring Street. Her husband's a holy roller, spends most of his spare time in church, lighting candles and wailing over some saint or other. She's tired of begging for scraps of his time, thinks a little social call might give her some...you know...comfort."

"Mrs. Dimming?" I said. "She's barely fifty—isn't she?"

He shrugged. "The young babes won't leave me alone.

It ain't easy being a sex symbol. Lot of lonely people need your—ah—ministrations."

"Yeah," I commiserated. "Your life's one of humanitarian service."

He merely nodded, unfazed by irony.

"And you want me to be lookout?"

He looked at me soberly, some solemn quality contrasting with the ageless audacity of his eyes.

"You're the only one I trust, Chinkie," he said quietly.

Momentarily, I stared. "What about Phil or Nicky or Maria?"

"Great kids. But probably not prefer I maintain a busy social calendar. In fact, they think I should play goddamn shuffleboard with the fossils in Brighton Beach."

"Nah, some of those geezers are seventy. Too old for you."

He shot me an interested glance. "You'll do it?"

I was about to answer "of course," when something struck me. "No."

He turned slowly and fully to face me. He said nothing, but was plainly vexed by my obstinacy. And yet, there was in his eyes the habitual glint of approval when I stood up to him.

"What do you want?" he asked forthrightly.

I balled my hands into fists. "You know what I want," I shot back nervously, but just as unwilling as he to yield ground.

He let out a deep breath. "So your price for supporting my social life is to see a goddamn doctor?"

I nodded. "Fishman. The pulmonary guy on Kings Highway. I'll go with you."

After a second, he exploded in laughter. "Fish-man," he said contemptuously. "That's what he is—a fish-man, a butcher, a goddamn shoemaker."

"Stick," I said sternly. "That's it. You see the goddamn shoemaker—or Mr. Dimming strolls in wondering why his wife runs around in negligee and 'f--k me' heels for some octogenarian with a hard-on."

"Jeez, what a mouth on you..."

"Can't imagine where I learned it."

The wind blew across the intersection of Haring and Avenue S, and I was grateful for the jacket The Stick had made me wear. It was a battered leather jacket, three or four sizes too large for me, and I let it envelop me against the chill October night, savoring its man smell of old leather, sweat, and years of outdoor use. The temperature dropped as the wind gained force. Clouds flitted across the sky, briefly obscuring the silver sliver of moon, seeking refuge from the storm coming hard at their backs.

My watch said 9:10. We had arrived promptly at eight, and The Stick had said he'd be out no later than ten. Good Shepherd church, a block to the east, loomed like a dark bulk on a dim night, and—by the faint glow of the streetlamps— cast a giant hovering shadow on the avenue. Few cars passed and fewer pedestrians. Periodically, I walked towards Brown Street and back, knowing that if Mr. Dimming came it would be from that direction. Each time a solitary passerby emerged from the night, huddled into himself and scurrying for home, I peered intently. Mostly I waited in the shadows and thought.

It was surprising only to those who didn't know him that such a hell-raising old rogue was generally beloved in the neighborhood. But Andreas Vinatieri had emigrated from Sicily in his teens around the time of World War One. He had been a New York City police officer for 20 years, receiving several departmental commendations for outstanding law enforcement work. He had joined the Marines the day after Pearl Harbor and, although in his forties, served with distinction in bloody island battles in the Pacific. After the war, he'd taken a job with Brinks and, eventually, became chief security officer for the Durant-Tolliver Building on 54th Street, a job he still held. He swore colorfully in two different languages, and yet, women described him as a consummate gentleman—certainly, I had never known him to raise his voice or make a threatening gesture. But he was always there for neighbors with a security issue, and often people went to him before the police. He rarely disappointed. Although he provided abundantly for his children, he otherwise lived frugally, and a lifetime of unrelenting work had enabled him to save money.

Still, the deathless legend of his prowess that had given rise, decades ago, to his nickname, circulated freely. Six pall-bearers, it was said, would be necessary at his funeral—four to heft the casket and two to press down the lid.

I had my eyes riveted on the church door a block away. It opened and a man of medium build and a shock of tangled dark hair stood on its threshold speaking to someone still inside. Then he shut the door and turned in my direction. My watch said: 9:30. I took a deep breath and pushed out of the shadows, crossing Avenue S, angling toward him. I hunched into my oversized jacket like a forsaken waif. I rubbed my eyes to make them red and daubed saliva under both of them until my cheeks glistened. I limped slightly as I advanced, making sure to meet him under a streetlight half-way between Brown and Haring.

Arnold Dimming recognized me immediately. He had a full beard neatly trimmed and the pallid complexion of a Scandinavian who rarely saw the sun. His cheeks were sunk in the manner of an ascetic who ate only sparingly. His eyes,

burning with evangelical zeal, softened in momentary awareness of my distress.

"Why hello Angel," he said. "What's wrong?"

I shook my head and paused, as if too choked up to speak.

He knelt down to me in concern. "What is it, child?" he
said kindly.

"I'm...all alone...I..."

He nodded in compassionate understanding. "Your mother
must work relentlessly to support you," he said sadly. "And
your father's a whore-mongering flesh-hound who won't take
responsibility for you. You lack parental love."

I nodded forlornly—and resisted the urge to kick him in
the kneecap.

"Do you know that Jesus loves you?"

I squinted my eyes. "But he's never met me," I said in my
best village idiot imitation.

"Come with me," he said like a shepherding angel. "He'll
meet you now."

He took my hand and led me to the church. I gazed back
longingly at the street as he opened the door. The Stick owes
me a lot of pasta dinners for this one, I thought. I took a deep
breath and plunged in.

The church's interior was dimly lighted. A few late-night
worshipers knelt in the pews' cramped spaces, offering silent
devotion. Candles burned on the altar, suffusing the atmosphere with a musky fragrance. Jesus, agonizing on the
cross, loomed above all. Mr. Dimming led me to the front.
He kneeled before the statue of a saint.

"Saint Francis of Assisi, Angel," he whispered. Kneeling
by his side, I strived for an appropriately reverent expression.
"Should we hug lepers?" came to my mind, but I figured I was
better off keeping my yap zipped.

He gazed raptly at the statue but spoke softly to me.

"In prayer, this holy man heard: 'Francis! Everything you have loved and desired in the flesh it is your duty to despise and hate, if you wish to know my will.'" Mr. Dimming pondered this truth. "Like many saints, he spurned food and drink and sex. He lived in deep spiritual devotion."

I nodded respectfully.

He turned to me and lightly touched my arm.

"Angel," he said, his voice catching slightly. "Since my calling, I have lived in the same manner."

His simplicity of tone, his open expression, his guiding touch all pleaded with me to see the truth he offered. He took my silent stare as encouragement.

"I would shout this from the steeple," he smiled sheepishly. "But pride is a worse sin than carnal indulgence. I fast. I drink only water. I have renounced sex. And I am happy, knowing that I fulfill God's plan for me."

I looked around. The worshipers were straggling out, leaving a void that suddenly seemed cavernous. Involuntarily, I glanced toward the door. His grip on my arm tightened.

"You're young," he said in impassioned earnestness. "Begin now. Give yourself to abstinence."

I turned back to him. I ignored his exhortation. I could think of only one thing. "But...but...you're married."

He nodded, pleased with the question embedded in my statement. "My wife supports me fully. I haven't touched her in eight years. She appreciates the respect shown her by not being subjected to men's fleshly lusts."

"I'm sure," I said.

"You understand?" His eyes, as well as his words, mentored me. "Women are more spiritual. More worshipful of virginity."

I looked at him, at least gazed in his direction, but I saw someone else—his wife, who I knew but slightly. I saw the attractive dark-haired woman, relatively young, who was married to a husband who regarded sex as sin, who never touched her, who rejected her attempts at love, who left her chronically, hopelessly alone in an empty bed to worship nightly at an institution that appraised carnal desire as detestable abomination. I was still wearing The Stick's heavy jacket, and it was much warmer in the church than in the street, but I was growing chilled. I would be 17 in a few months, but suddenly I felt like a little girl lost in a storm who wanted her dad. I pulled my arm away. "You'll convince me as much as you did your wife."

Some visceral seething gave an edge to my tone—and I immediately regretted such provocative words.

"What do you mean?" he asked, puzzled. He noticed my eyes for an instant burn more intensely than his before I willed them to look away—and the beatific expression faded slowly from his face, replaced by the first hint of a question. "Angel," he chose his words carefully. "Where's your father tonight?"

Involuntarily, I looked at my watch. It was approaching ten. But Arnold Dimming looked at me now as if for the first time realizing who I was, and that tonight's encounter had possibly not been wrought by chance. His face went slack in a slow motion progression that would have been comical if not for the pathos.

"Angel," he repeated his exact words, this time with a sense of incipient panic. "Where's your father tonight?"

My level of urgency matched his, but, despite the crushing pain of his nascent realization, all depth of feeling went out to Theresa Dimming. "I don't know," I said offhandedly. "With a woman, perhaps?"

He didn't move. "Oh...my...God," he said. Then he rose and bolted from the church. It wasn't clear whether, in his mind, he ran from the devil or toward him.

It was after ten by the time I reached the corner of Haring and Avenue S. Arnold Dimming stood at the intersection, remonstrating with The Stick. His right hand gesticulated and occasionally poked The Stick's lean chest. The Stick kept both hands in the back pockets of his jeans, and, as I approached, answered quietly. "Love begins at home, Dimming."

The rain was just starting. It promised to come in a hard, steady downpour. Dimming looked on the verge of tears.

"You debauched my wife!" He pointed to me emerging from the night. "And dragged down your own daughter. You'll burn for this, Vinatieri."

The Stick nodded. "Fine," he said calmly. "Then take comfort in my fate." He moved closer to Dimming, as if giving paternal advice to a self-destructive son. "But take care of your wife, you fool—or lose her. It's called 'making love'— not 'debauchery.'"

He placed his arm around my shoulder and led me swiftly away. I let my head rest on his chest and didn't look back. We didn't speak until we stood in front of the door to my mother's apartment on Nostrand Avenue.

He coughed. "You got time to complete those calculus problems before bed?" he asked, fighting to get out the words.

I nodded. I stood on my tiptoes to kiss him goodnight, but stopped. "The doctor..." I said, but couldn't continue. Tears started down my cheeks.

He pulled me and held me close—and I felt better with his arms around me. "All right, Chinkie. I'll call Fishman tomorrow." Then he walked to the stairs and down into the night and the rain.

Martin Fishman resembled a well-fed penguin. He was three or four inches under six-foot, with narrow shoulders and spindly legs. He had an enormous belly whose forward protuberance was accentuated by the slight back-leaning list of his gait. He smiled vacantly, like a politician, when he spoke—and it was clear that The Stick conceived an immediate antipathy for him.

But he gave his patient a comprehensive, grueling exam of the respiratory tract.

It was several days after The Stick's rendezvous with Theresa Dimming. He had left work a few hours early and I had met him at the Kings Highway subway station after my last class. We walked the few blocks to Fishman's office. The Stick's ubiquitous cough had worsened. He leaned forward as he walked, trying to clear his lungs.

Fishman, despite his meaningless, ingratiating smile, pulled no punches. "You're two years too late."

He took The Stick alone into his private office to pore over his chest x-rays. I sat outside and tried not to bite my nails.

When The Stick emerged after fifteen minutes he looked grimmer than I'd ever seen him—but the set of his jaw convinced me that his mind was made up. I asked nothing as we walked home, and The Stick, never a big talker, was silent. I turned away as we passed Carvel, where he had bought me so much ice cream over the years. Even Jimmy Chu waving at me from the window of his store elicited no response. Before we reached my mom's apartment The Stick uttered only two lines.

"No hospitals, Chinkie. I have to see a lawyer."

I don't know how word got out. The Stick still went every day to work, but he came home in the afternoon. I rushed to his apartment immediately after school. It was always crowded, with his kids, with the neighbors—and with younger women.

It was a matter of months. Then The Stick began to look like a stick. He was so skinny that his clothes hung on him like a tent. Then he couldn't leave the house. Then he couldn't leave his bed. His children rotated as his constant companions. Most of them had careers and families—but all I had was high school. I brought my books to his apartment every day after class and often spent the night curled up on his sofa that my siblings dragged into his bedroom. I lay awake for hours listening to his tortuous struggle to breathe, my hands balled helplessly into fists. One night, in a light sleep, I dreamed I had the power to thrust my hands into the subcutaneous interior of his flesh and rip the tumor out of his lungs, holding it aloft like a bloody prize. But I could not—and, on a gray April morning, in the damp chill of a steady rain beating against his window, The Stick, already unconscious but perhaps aware of the crowd of children surrounding his bed, passed on from the hell-raising earthly existence that he had so vigorously embraced.

In accordance with The Stick's request there was no wake—only a quiet burial at Greenwood Cemetery. No clergy were invited but a horde of friends and family members showed up, standing for an hour in a stiff spring wind. As the casket was removed from the hearse, The Stick did, indeed, have six pallbearers. I, along with Phil Villone, his two youngest children, made sure the lid was not displaced from within. Maria and Nicky Vinatieri, his two oldest children, spoke at the graveside. So did several friends. I was asked to, but chose to remain silent, not from shame but its opposite—from a selfish desire not to share treasured private memories. When the ceremony ended, I walked slowly to the car. I was surprised to see at the back of the crowd Arnold and Theresa Dimming. She had a soft smile around her lips. She and her husband held hands.

For weeks after, I moped, doing my school work and nothing else. I ate little and rarely left the house. Jimmy Chu noticed and one evening invited me to dinner. "No Peking duck, Angel," he said. "The best Italian joint on Kings Highway." Over stuffed veal and mixed vegetables in olive oil and garlic, the kindly old man asked one or two questions and then listened attentively. I talked incessantly, my mouth full of food, jabbering away about my dad and I, even laughing, although tearfully, on occasion. Finally, over dessert, I wound down.

Jimmy looked at me, his dark, usually mournful eyes actually brighter now, seemingly younger. "I was friends with your dad, as well as your mom, you know."

I nodded and waited. It was clear he had something to say.

"A long time ago, The Stick asked me to tell you something, if he died first. You know how he felt about facing the unvarnished truth."

He must have noticed the look on my face. "No," he said softly. "You don't have to take another blow." He paused. "It's like this. Your mom's not much for talking, as you know. But I've known her since she first arrived in America. She went back to Hong Kong only once. She was there for a while. Six months after she returned, you were born."

I dropped my spoon. "My mom and The Stick were never..."

He shook his head—and it seemed strange to me that there was no sadness in his eyes. "Never."

The tears came immediately to my eyes. "I don't have to take another blow," I said bitterly. "No, not at all."

Jimmy Chu took his time. He waited for the first elements of the storm to pass, waited as I daubed my eyes with a cloth napkin. "Silly girl." His face was as calm as a judge. "Did he have to make love to your mother to be your father, Angel?"

The deep truth of Jimmy Chu's words was in how much I missed him—this man who was not my father but who was the only father I would ever have. Or want.

My parents' friend moved now and sat next to me at the table. His arm went around my shoulders. "There's something else, child. Something else your father wanted you to know." I looked at him.

"He said, 'Tell Angela—'"

"—He called me 'Angela?'" I interrupted.

Jimmy Chu ignored me. "Your dad said, 'Tell Angela that life is not a tragedy. She'll know what you mean.'" He reached into his wallet and pulled out a check. It was made out to Jimmy Chu for the sum of $100,000.00 and signed "Andreas Vinatieri." In the memo it said "For Angela."

Paula Koehler looked at her friend, whose eyes glittered as she completed her lengthy narrative. For a long time, the two women said nothing. Paula, who had laughed at several points during the story, sat transfixed, her eyes alert, posture taut now and alive. Angela waited. Finally Paula spoke.

"Angela, about next weekend. Does Tony have a friend?"

Making the Grade

*T*he warning signs were present long before the end.

He was tenured and a departmental star, insofar as philosophers could be a star, but there exist boundaries not to be transgressed—not even by Harry Steinway.

The women were all adults--all 30s or 40s taking evening classes after work. And he was discreet. There were no brief flings to be quickly discarded and replaced in a month's or a week's time. A relationship lasted for a year or two years, in one case longer, long after the course ended in which the woman had met him.

His books were published by academic houses, studied by the profession, reviewed in the journals. And he planned, wrote copious notes for his great work to come, the crowning culmination of his mastery of modern philosophy, his magisterial work defining Kant's achievement in synthesizing all essential philosophic advances since Descartes. He remained at Brooklyn and visited at Ithaca and New Haven, living in a loft on a re-modeled waterfront offering a view across a sweeping bay of dark glass spires by day and towers of shimmering fire in the night.

The women all loved the course, the professor, and the view.

Until one no longer did.

David Ehrenstein's life changed when Maia Pradhwa slithered from the night and swished sinuously into his class.

She arrived twenty minutes late for the first session of Philosophical Themes in Literature on a sweltering night after Labor Day. The heat had been suffocating throughout the afternoon, resembling August in Hell more than the first day of Fall semester. She swung into a chair in the room's rear and he noticed that in contrast to her short skirt and low-cut yellow top she wore neither sandals nor shoes but high-heeled black leather boots.

"Expecting snow?" he blurted.

She made a face and waved her hand dismissively at the wisecrack. The other students snickered.

When she leaned forward to see the board, he forgot about her boots.

Though pushing thirty, she lived with her family in Jackson Heights and commuted all the way to Brooklyn on the IRT because she worked in a studio on a side street off Flatbush Avenue, teaching belly dancing to young women who desired either to titillate their lovers or irritate their parents.

A few weeks later, her first essay was so superior that his initial gut reaction was that she plagiarized. Then he realized that the belly dancer had a brain, as well as a body. Writing on Sophocles, she compared Oedipus to Job and argued that it mattered nothing whether a faithful adherent was pagan or monotheist—he would be made to suffer earthly tribulations fully as dire as those who contravened the god's authority. There was, she had concluded, no possible justice in a world governed by supremely powerful beings who imposed their edicts, however capricious, at will.

"How, in Shakespeare's tragic universe, is man to gain knowledge?" he queried in early October when the class had moved on. She still sat in the room's rear but he felt her glance on him even when he turned to the board. "Reasoning paralyzes Hamlet," he said, "constraining him from decisive action—but when he acts on impulse, as in slaying Polonius, the outcome is disastrous." He paused. "On what basis, then, should he take remedial action? On what basis, can he?"

She had an answer. He saw it in her eyes, as the other students pondered. He saw also a mischievous glitter, a playful half-smile, as if soliciting, tempting him even to come to her for the response he sought. She did not raise her hand and he turned quickly away.

He paced the room as he lectured, staying in motion, gesticulating for emphasis, occasionally banging on desks, and bantering with the students.

"Hey, George," he bellowed at one kid, Michael Washington, who dozed in the back row, several seats to Maia's right. "Should Hamlet dismiss these heartaches that come from being the rightful king and just knock down a few pitchers of Carlsberg with his boys?"

Several students snorted, as Michael rubbed his eyes. "Ha, ha," one kid chortled, "George Washington." Thelma Reeves, a meticulous note-taker and "A" student who sat habitually in the front row, shook her head, a worried expression all over her thin dark face.

"You're gonna get in trouble, saying stuff like that, Dr. Ehrenstein."

"What do you mean 'gonna'?" he snapped. She was looking out for him, so he laughed easily to allay her fears. "My whole life I been in trouble."

After nineteen years, former students had spread the word that he was not your stereotypical dreary professor,

whose lectures could more productively be bottled as a cura-
tive for sleep deprivation than deployed as a stimulus to cognitive growth. His courses were characteristically packed with
young minds seeking local color with their Kant.

And color he could provide. Unlike most of his colleagues,
who hailed from all over the map and grabbed a Brooklyn
University job because they drooled for a ripe New York plum,
he was local, growing up on Avenue X in Sheepshead Bay and
attending the area's public schools. Though pushing fifty-one,
he had never owned a car and rode the Nostrand Avenue bus
to work every day—or sometimes walked or biked or jogged
the tree-lined residential streets of Bedford Avenue.

He ran every morning on Emmons Avenue, past a flo-
tilla of fishing boats surrounded by their private air force
of gulls and an overpowering fragrance of the far, deep sea.
Accosted one early morning by a young punk swinging a
roofer's hammer, he had not hesitated but had rammed his
shoulder full-bore into the thug's chest, driving him into the
gutter and spinning the hammer sideways through the salt-
filled air. The fishermen nearby called him "Dr. Doom" and
had laughed when he told them the correct title should be
"Dr. Boom." But the bad guys learned that David Ehrenstein,
though an irremediable geek, was not an easy mark. Most
could tell at a glance—his wiry, medium height and frame
exuded a runner's vitality and his upper body was lean from
light but relentless weight training.

Maia went a month without speaking in class. Nevertheless, she had a great deal to say.

"Dr. Ehren-shtein," she said one night after class, watching as the last students left the room. He observed her warily,
noticing she pronounced his name as though she'd emigrated
not from India but from Germany. "Shakespeare has an

answer to your question. It may not be to anyone's liking." Her dark eyes were earnest, focused, single-minded.

"What?" he asked, intrigued.

"Thinking paralyzes, passion blinds. We act rashly—or not at all." She stopped for a single beat leading to her conclusion. "Perhaps that is why he upholds an exquisitely tragic vision."

He stopped. She had nailed it—had taken a hardball question and whacked it over the centerfield wall; in a terse paragraph had identified the theme of the Shakespeare chapter of his current book. He stared at her wordlessly. Her eyes were intent on a serious question but hinting now at laughter, a gentle mockery directed at a student's ability to outpace the teacher—laughing, he thought, at herself, at a desire to flaunt more than her body, a desire targeted, private, and yearning to expose content reserved only for one able to appreciate it. She would, he knew, graduate in the spring, an English major, and that graduate school beckoned.

They walked the corridors of Covington Hall. They were side-by-side. He spoke animatedly—hands moving—of the labyrinthine intricacies of *King Lear*, of the complexities of applying his thesis, and more broadly, of studying philosophy by means of great literature. She listened, absorbed; he observed the absorption but only half-noted her proximity, the ever-so-slightly-too-close, shapely presence of her.

On their right, down the hall—a haunting presence of which they were each momentarily oblivious—the classroom loomed, the "dark hole of cataclysm" a colleague had described it, a room in which for years he had sedulously refused to teach. Now, with its cautionary tale most urgent, distracted by the very cause of caution's need, he failed to notice its existence.

Harry had always liked this room. The elevated view overlooking the quad, especially the green tangled leaves and fresh-tinted scent of spring's first warm days. He had taught here so many times that the secretary—a fixture, irreplaceable, the unacknowledged departmental liege— called it simply "Harry's room." And the older man had been generous to younger colleagues with his expertise, mentoring them, one especially, outlining specific techniques to bring abstract philosophy to a plane apprehensible to university undergraduates—philosophy at sea level, he called it, combining a Brooklyn growl and radiant smile. A scowling, hunkering honey bear of a man, said one of his girlfriends. For two full decades a superstar. Two decades—then catastrophe.

The great man had friends throughout the department—colleagues, chairman, the imperial secretary—many of them, eight years later still here, loyal even unto death; they held ranks—no impropriety, they said. All knew the truth, all shuddered at a prospective resolution, all could see but none would speak. But one did. The protégé could no longer abide the deception. Strenuously, he pleaded for disclosure. No more professorship, said the mentor quietly. It all goes away. What do I have left? Truth, answered the protégé. Which aspect, Harry Steinway said. Truth is multi-faceted. Will my disgraced resignation abet or undermine the students' philosophic education? Enhance or diminish the pedagogical advancement of young colleagues? The protégé bit his lips. I will not lie, he said. Not even for you.

Not even for the forwarding of knowledge? Perforated by the genius eyes of the most brilliantly active mind he was likely to encounter, the younger man made his stand. We're philosophers, he replied—lovers of wisdom. Do we gain wisdom by denying truth—or by embracing all aspects, even the bitter. He paused. No, he answered the question. Not even for that.

Slowly, the formerly young professor strolled to the exit of the classroom building, the swinging rhythm of a graceful woman's heels pattering gently in his ears. He stopped on the building's outside stairs, on his way to the bus, and stared at her. Her black hair was thick and lustrous, hanging half-way down her back, like the fluffy tail of a healthy raccoon. On a fragrant night of early October, she wore a light sweater over one of the low-cut tops that she favored. It was unbuttoned and he wrested his gaze from the dark swell of her cleavage that she emphasized by leaning slightly forward.

"Maia," he said to her carefully. "I'm a philosophy professor teaching Plato, Aristotle, Kant, and other great thinkers—and you're a student. But I'm also a 50-year-old divorced man. In fact, in fourteen years I've had one girlfriend—for six weeks. Don't push it."

She smiled warmly and her laughter, in joyous recognition of his admission, was so full of life and vitality, that he wished he could bottle it as a gift for his desiccated colleagues.

"I'm a pushy girl," she said playfully, her dark eyes flashing in the dimly lit quad. "I'm trouble." She took his arm and said, "I'll walk you to the bus stop."

He twisted his arm from her grasp and said, "You'll walk to the subway and go home."

They stood on the top stair outside Covington Hall in the soft night air of Indian summer. Gently, she took his tie in her hand and traced its length with her finger. "You're an attractive man," she whispered. "You shouldn't be alone." A whiff of her perfume brushed his nose and lips as if pushed tenderly at him by her warm words and hot breath. For several seconds, he stood transfixed, drinking in everything she was and offered. Then he remembered the full circumstances. Mildly, he took her hand and removed it from his shirt front.

"I'm writing a book," he said, with no attempt at reproof. "I work part-time for a friend who runs a cab company on Coney Island Avenue. And I have a 17-year-old daughter. I'm neither alone nor unoccupied."

She did not laugh, as so many others did, when he told her of how he supplemented his professor's salary. She smiled, not derisively but warmly, delightedly, in simple appreciation of a surprising truth. "My professor the cab driver."

"It's what eight years of graduate school prepares you for."

Her face registered, in part, a displeased pout as he walked away, leaving her alone on the top step. But she also smiled at his off-beat sense of humor. Was it just a trick of the dark night and a quick glance over his shoulder leading him to believe that she simultaneously wet her lips as she stared at his departing figure?

Sophia Ehrenstein's face conveyed unconcealed desperation.

"Dad," she said, pleading for help with her eyes as well as her voice. "What will I do?"

He gazed out at the slate gray waters of the bay visible across the sand from their bench on the Brighton Beach boardwalk—and then back into the deer-like brown eyes that, to him, ever shined like bright city lights.

"Sweetness," he said, choosing words with care. "Do you remember when Deborah Harris knocked you down in the schoolyard two days running and the teachers would do nothing because they didn't see it?"

She stared, eyes uncomprehending at first, before slowly permitting immediacy to recede and slip stealthily into the past.

"God, that must be ten years ago." She paused. "I can't believe you still remember her name."

"It was eleven," he said off-handedly. "And I remember the night you came into my life, never mind first grade." She stared silently, as his words about her life, combined with his voice—casual but not meandering, pointed, moving to some targeted culmination—commanded her interest. "A thunderstorm in mid-March," he said. "Rare, raw, unpredicted, and your mother's cries ringing in the night above the wind and the thunder's crashing boom. But the loudest, longest sound in my ears was the wail of an infant girl drawing breath for the first time. That cry has lasted seventeen years and will never recede until the day I die."

Her head was down. "Dad..." she said, and the desperation was fading from her voice.

"Do you remember what I told you about Deborah Harris?"

She looked up. "You said not to fear, because no matter the crisis I faced, I would never face it alone. Ever."

He watched the young mothers pushing their youngsters in strollers. The children were bundled against the brisk breeze that had sprung up and blew off the sea. The kids looked warm snuggled in their bright blankets.

"You think that might apply to an unwanted pregnancy?" he asked gently.

The tears started softly at first. "I'm so...ashamed..." she said, shaking her head. "Mom will kill me. She trusted me with Jason. She'll explode. You know she will."

He smiled sadly. His daughter could have been a clone of the young Claudine DePalma. She had the identical slender figure, the same thick dark hair, oval face, and soft Mediterranean features. Everything but the explosive temper—the same. And the religious legacy regarding sex.

"Sophia," he said. "My little Miss Wisdom..."

Her smile was rueful at the name he had tagged her with as a young child. "Not so wise now, huh?"

"Contraception?"

She shook her head.

"No," he said. "Not so wise."

He looked at her.

"Are you sure?"

The shake of her head was almost imperceptible. The way her black hair fell about her shoulders when she moved reminded him of her mother.

"No. It's too soon. It's just how I feel..."

He nodded.

The sun was out, shining on the bicyclists and roller-blad-ers gliding over the boardwalk's wooden beams, but clouds converged from the south and it smelled like rain. He took her hand.

"We'll get through this," he said. "You have people who wouldn't abandon you if you clubbed octogenarians with a jack handle. It will be alright."

She was silent, staring at the boardwalk's cracks beneath her feet, but the pressure of her hand in his fractionally increased and it was as if he felt her breathing through her bones and flesh—and her breathing and her hand's touch expressed gratitude without words.

They sat for awhile until gray clouds obscured the sun and the sea wind's autumnal breath chilled them through their light jackets. Hurrying figures scurried for the sidewalks, for their homes or parked cars. Rain was imminent.

"Will you tell Mom?" she whispered.

"No," he said.

He looked out at the eternal sea. Interesting, he reflected, that its breadth and august power could not dwarf the concerns of human life but somehow underscored their grandeur, this need and undying ability to face up to and face down timeless, perennially unchanged moral conflict.

He looked back at his only child.

"You will," he said in a soft voice that would yield this point only on the day that the earth's tropics were covered by glistening sheets of glacial ice.

There was utter silence on the deserted boardwalk now as she withdrew her hand from his. Well she knew the voice of her father but she knew this voice, too, the implacable voice of the professor of moral philosophy. She backed away on the bench. She stood up.

"No," she said.

His eyes bored into her, searching the lovely exterior for the skeletal backbone beneath. He said nothing, just sat and stared at her until she turned and fled down the boardwalk, racing to beat the wind's gusts and the rain, running all the way to the subway entrance. He sat alone on the bench, in the rain, and stared until his daughter's back was no longer visible to his sight.

Joseph "Daddy" Kaplan ran the Big Dude Car Service on Caton Avenue off Coney Island Avenue near the park. Daddy had inherited a last-legs pesthole from a wetbrain father and built it into a bustling dump of ten cars, eighteen drivers, and twenty-four hour service. Daddy had gone through four years of Sheepshead Bay High School with him—cutting class, flunking geometry, and, in his case, English, as well. At sixteen, hulking, he'd already weighed in at three bills, with promise of more to come—a promise solemnly kept with the help of countless gravy-dripping roast beef sandwiches at Brennan and Carr on Avenue U. In their junior year, they'd made a pact: he wrote Daddy's English papers on Shakespeare, Hawthorne, and Dostoyevsky, while the big boy made sure the football players, bikers, and assorted hard-asses advanced their financial status at the expense of other Jewish intellectuals. The arrangement had worked so well that almost forty years later they had lost count of the times that one had rushed to the other's aid during moments of duress.

At nineteen, Daddy married a forty-year old Italian broad with a house on Voorhies Avenue and a six figure bank account. Daddy had, even before Theresa's death, credited her for his firm's success.

"Her money fueled our growth," he said. "Her personality kept me in the office."

For thirty-five years and in all seasons, since his undergraduate days as an English major at Hunter, David Ehrenstein had driven week-ends for Big Dude. It was the reason he had some shiny coin sitting in the bank—and that his will, with a pretty teenage girl specified as sole beneficiary, provided unceasing solace.

That Saturday, over coffee between runs to LaGuardia, he talked about Maia. Daddy shifted his girth in the overstuffed easy chair he'd had installed behind his desk. He was silent for a long time. Though he'd barely graduated high school, and his approach, looming out of the shadows on a moonless night, scared hell out of nuns, children, and small dogs, he ceaselessly surprised people. Once he'd seen Daddy step out of his car into a driving hailstorm to help an elderly couple stranded on the BQE. As stones the size of pellets tore at his sweatshirt, he'd rolled up his sleeves and quickly changed their tire. He had done it without having the occupants leave their vehicle. When he'd returned to his own car, blood streaked both his cheeks and his sweatshirt was stained with sweat.

"So what's the problem?" he asked quietly.

"You know the problem. You're not a dope. She's my student. It's unethical. That's the problem."

"She's twenty-nine. Old enough to make up her own mind."

"I have to grade her, you hunkering dolt. A personal relationship compromises the integrity of the grading process."

The big man snorted while inhaling a donut in the same breath. Daddy was superlatively qualified at multi-tasking. "'Compromises the integrity of the grading process,'" he mimicked. "I love the way you professors talk. You may not make sense–but you sure do talk good."

He turned away, waving a hand in disgust, but not quickly enough to hide the smile on his face. No matter the situation, for thirty-five years his friend had been able to make him laugh.

"Dave," the entrepreneur said. "Seriously. And I'll speak slowly so that your big brain doesn't get confused. Give her the exact grade—*the exact grade*—that her schoolwork deserves, no more, no less. And then it's nobody's damn business what two consenting adults do in their own time."

He was still turned away, glancing at the door. The traffic noise drifted in from Caton Avenue, penetrating the closed door into the boss's inner office. Somewhere out there on Brooklyn's congested streets people hustled to and from their jobs, their families, and their romantic relationships—a few with no regard to anything but the satisfaction of their purposes. Was it easier—or harder—if one jettisoned moral principles?

Daddy broke the silence. "Remember old Doug Lankowski, owned the grocery store on Avenue X, a few blocks from school?"

"Pops!" he replied. "Yeah, sure, used to chase us out because we were too young for beer and too jaded for chocolate milk. What about him?"

"Got to know him years later when I was still driving—and not the successful tycoon you see before you today." He held his hands at arms' length and proudly took in the confines of both his inner sanctum and the outer office beyond.

"You're a mogul, without a doubt. You and Elon Musk do lunch at the Four Seasons?"

Daddy laughed, a sound distinctive to him that combined self-deprecating derision with hearty, boundless good will. "Sure," he said. "Every Thursday afternoon when Elon's in town. But anyway, Pops remembered me and threw me some business. I drove him to the airport a few times when he flew to Florida to visit his daughter."

"Heartwarming," David Ehrenstein drawled. "But is there a point to your rambling—or great entertainers simply can't resist an audience?"

It took a great deal of provocation for Daddy to take offense. "So finally, after all these years, you acknowledge that I'm a great entertainer?"

"In addition to being a tycoon."

Daddy's voice grew serious. "Pops lost his wife when he was in his forties. He died in his seventies. He worked long hours alone in the store and left several hundred thousand dollars to his only child." He paused. "It's interesting that people confess more to bartenders and cabdrivers than they do to priests. Less moral pressure, I suppose. But Pops had no romantic relationship from the day his wife passed—to the day he died. Sad, don't you think?"

The owner drained the last of his coffee from a jumbo Styrofoam container, crushed the cup in a massive paw, and pitched it unerringly into an enormous plastic trash can in the corner. He sat behind his desk, hands clasped easily back of his head, eyes staring intently at nothing, the picture of a man making casual talk with a good friend.

David Ehrenstein smiled. It was not a happy smile.

The entrepreneur and the professor, the cabdriver and the intellectual—not a likely pair. How likely was it, he thought, staring at the detailed street map of New York City on the wall, that for near on fifteen years he would have virtually no contact with women? A monk he'd been, a secular, celibate monk. He shook his head, willing himself now to remember those times, those bitter, endless years. For so long, Claudine had filled his dreams. He'd awake in the dark, knowing in some preternatural sense that dawn was yet hours away, seeing her face and her form with no need to open his eyes and no possibility to escape her presence, though he twisted on the bed as he might. And in the brief relation that he did have, he awoke to a sun-kissed morning in June with the sleepy sense that he held Claudine's slender figure in his arms, only to be jolted out of bed by the realization that although he'd made love to this woman she was neither the one he'd married nor desired.

Where had he gone on that day, more than ten years ago, that Claudine had remarried? Before dawn, he had taken the car loaned him by Daddy and driven east, relentlessly east into the rising sun, neither selecting nor considering a destination, arriving at random at the Orient Point ferry terminal before most people were yet awake, a point from which the only drive was east into the sea or west into a vast city of empty streets and fractured dreams. He took the auto ferry across the Sound to New Bedford and drove blindly, bitterly, furiously north and east and, by nightfall, found himself inexplicably in some nameless coastal town of Maine. Exhausted, he'd taken a room in a rustic, rundown motel miles off the main highway and slept with the air conditioning running full bore and the covers around his ears. The next day, Sunday, he'd wandered aimlessly dusty beaches overlooking a foaming white sea and overlooked in turn by pallid stiletto lighthouses standing as sentinels to those lost on the expansive deep. In the evening, slowly, he'd driven a meandering path home, arriving mere hours before the sun.

A call from the dispatcher and a knock on the door jolted at the fringe of his consciousness and he looked up, startled, from his reverie. Daddy sat staring at him. Had he been staring the whole time?

"A fare from Ditmars Avenue across the Verrazano to Staten Island, Dave," the dispatcher said. "Want to take it?"

He got up. "Sounds like a good tip," he said and walked to the door. The dispatcher had left it open. He shut it and turned back to his friend. Daddy pored over ledgers on his desk, a model tycoon running a thriving business. "Your goddaughter's pregnant," he said quietly and the big man's head snapped up.

"The biologist's got a biological problem?" Daddy said almost to himself but turned instantly serious.

His voice asked: "Is she okay?" His eyes asked: "Does Claudine know?"

David Ehrenstein answered the unstated question. "Not yet," he said grimly.

Over the next ten days, though Maia's written work remained timely and effective, she looked increasingly tired—even exhausted—in class. She spoke up now, clearly intrigued by the material, providing valuable insight, but her voice was drained and her face was lined with worry and lack of sleep. Her eyes, normally lively with mischief, were dull. When she missed a scheduled quiz, he grew worried. After class, he asked several of the students but none of them knew her. The next day, he looked up her email address and sent her a message. Her terse reply came that night.

"I do not sleep. My family will be my death. I take pills and still I do not sleep. Please, please, can't we talk?"

He sat staring at her memo on the computer screen. His walk-in apartment around the corner from Bedford Avenue was lined with bookcases that surrounded the small TV he rarely turned on. There was a single photograph on the wall—of Claudine and him at Jones Beach on a long past summer's day. Two-year old Sophia, in diapers and sunhat, nestled in her daddy's arms. Print-outs of chapters from his book—"Dramatists and Novelists: The Greatest Philosophers"—lay strewn across his desk. He didn't move for some time, thinking about Maia's message. He and Daddy laughed over the reason they could never walk into an animal shelter or pet store—between the two of them they would sweep the joint clean, bringing home every stray cat and dog they found. Now a nascent, similar response germinated on the periphery of focal awareness. Remorseless, he thrust it down, permitting his consciousness to access memories of only glittering eyes and a beguiling smile. Somehow, the discordant elements coalesced into a tapestry unrelievedly positive.

"Alright," he e-mailed her back. "But at school—in public. In the cafeteria."

They met the next day. The place teemed with students in the lull between afternoon and evening courses. Maia wore tight jeans, heels, and a clinging sweater—and more than one male student turned to watch her progress across the room to the center table at which he sat. But her eyes told a different story.

"My father beats the younger children," she said. "My mother is terrified. When I object, he raises his hand to me. I must escape from him."

"Anyone call the police?"

She shook her head. "My mother will never turn him in. I must be out of the house before I can do it."

"You'll be thirty in a few months," he pointed out gently. "And you have a job. Why not get your own place—even if you share it with a roommate?"

"I will." She reached out diffidently, the first timid gesture he saw from her, and lightly touched his hand. Her haunted eyes pleaded with him. This time he did not pull away. "I'm alone," she said.

"You have your mother."

"I've worked years to help her—to raise the young ones. Willingly I've given up certain things for her—and to protect the children." Her eyes rested lightly on the stubble of his chin, the expanse of his lean chest, the hair of his brown, hard forearms below his rolled up shirtsleeves. She shook her head. "But on this, she is hopeless." She paused, her eyes moving upward to his. "And I am no longer willing to give up those things."

He nodded.

"And your studies?"

She leaned across the table. Her thick hair, as if alive as she, fell off of her shoulder and across her cheek. She made no effort to brush it back.

"Do you know what I've read since high school? No—how could you. Homer, Sophocles, Shakespeare, Melville, Hemingway, Faulkner, other similar writers. You, of all people, should understand why."

His fingers drummed rapidly on the table, generating a steady drone over which she spoke easily. He was aware of neither his motion nor its ensuing noise.

"Stories are all we have," she said. "They're the most effectual means of making sense of the world. What else is the

Bible, for example, but a collection of robust, colorful, deep impact stories?" She smiled sadly. "But absurd ones. Who could make sense of bushes speaking or virgins conceiving or women transformed to salt? These are hackneyed tales wrought by amateurish writers to provide mind candy for the thoughtless. No, only a handful of imaginative geniuses enable us to make sense of the world, including religion's role in it. Keep the Bible, the Koran, the Upanishads—or dispense them solely to those who prefer magic tricks to wisdom. Give me Dante, Milton, and Dostoyevsky."

He stared at her. How, he thought, could he be so focused on the words that poured from her mind but so aware of the body poured into her clothes?

"Did you ask about my studies? Those are not to be given up." Her words, although softly spoken, carried clearly through the cafeteria's noisy dissonance. "Next fall I begin graduate school. Nothing can stop me."

Her eyes were hard now with inflexible mental toughness. He spoke to that.

"Perhaps it is time to pursue those studies outside of a domestic madhouse," he said. He paused. "Perhaps nothing can stop you there, as well."

A soft smile at the corners of her lips relaxed her face.

"You will find, Dr. Ehren-shtein," she said, choosing her words deliberately. "That nothing can stop me with anything that I want."

The noise in the room was a din as students swirled around them. He pulled his hand from her touch but, to him, it seemed to move in slow motion, as though languishing, creeping feebly through a jug of golden treacle.

He looked up as a heavyset woman with a tray of French fries brushed past them. Maia's eyes were on him when he looked back. She recaptured his hand in both of hers and stroked it. "Do you really seek to avoid my touch?" she asked openly, honestly, forthrightly. "Do you want me to leave?" Her eyes were ready for any answer he might give, for any disappointment with which he might encumber her, to bear it, to accept it, to fill slowly with tears and to then look away.

He could not will his eyes off of her, and his body, not just his hand tingled, as though from the touch of a trained masseuse. Its effect was like a kick in the solar plexus—for a moment he couldn't breathe. How long since he had experienced this? Why, for so many years, had he neglected this part of his life? Those were precious moments spilling like vintage wine from a goblet, ineluctably lost, never to be recovered or re-lived. As some viscous liquid curled upwards from his loins toward his throat, he fought back the urge to speak in the crude bodily terms that expressed so perfectly what he wanted to do to her.

"No," he said. "I don't want you to leave. Not alone anyway."

On a Thursday night of mid-Autumn, the parking lot at Marine Park was nearly deserted. He killed the lights and drove the old Buick Maia had borrowed from a friend past a few cars with steamed-up windows to the far corner nearest the baseball diamonds. The moon was up, highlighting the cars whizzing past on Avenue U—and more, reflecting off the inlet of Jamaica Bay, wan, intangible beams reminding him of long-ago encounters filled with a promise of intensity, of vitality, and of impassioned nights with a singular woman that he prayed would endure a lifetime. The air was crisp as an October apple.

Maia stared at him, silent, motionless, her expression filled with a look of pain, loneliness, and something so elemental she could communicate it even if they deployed disparate languages with no dictionary of translation.

She had the most expressive eyes he had ever seen. But what he was about to do could not be vindicated by reference to temporary madness wrought by a Siren's seductive allure. He knew far too much moral philosophy to embrace that convenient canard. His imminent action would be done with the full awareness of possible outcomes for all aspects of his life—and the one that flashed instantaneously through his mind concerned not his career but his daughter. How could he face Sophia?

Then there was no time for reflection. Maia had removed her jacket. The top buttons of her sweater were undone and she moved across the seat toward him. He knew that if this night crashed the entire edifice of Brooklyn University around his ears like a Philistine coliseum athwart Samson, it would not deter him one iota in this moment. Without a word, his arms encircled her and he pulled her face to his.

Actions have consequences, the protégé told Harry Steinway. The older man was devastated by such consequences—quietly resign for any stated reason you choose, the administration stipulated, or be terminated in public disgrace. Stubbornly he refused resignation. Brazenly he fought termination. The weapons of his arsenal were not paltry. Neither were the administration's. The results had been unrelievedly ugly—and spectacularly public.

The betrayal of one so close was not to be lightly borne. If it takes till the end of my days, I will see you paid back, he told his former understudy. Watch your back. The younger man had not flinched. It's easy to blame others for our problems, he said. More often, we should look in the mirror. Watch your back, Harry Steinway re-affirmed as he departed for the final time. Watch your

front, the younger man replied. For your own good—and for the
rest of your days—watch your front.

He picked up Sophia at nine o'clock on Saturday morning.
She waited for him in the driveway of the private home on
Avenue S. Its well manicured lawn and flower bed, he knew,
were tended meticulously by Claudine alone. Her mother and
step father were inside and Sophia did not want him going
in there. He said nothing but let her climb into the Big Dude
town car. She had on a denim jacket over a pink top, mid-calf-
length jeans, white running shoes with a pink stripe, and no
socks. Her shoulder length hair was washed, brushed, and
smelled of fresh jasmine. She clung to his neck, when they
hugged, like a young girl ready to plead with dad for a new
toy. He held her for a long time.

They drove in silence through wide avenues and teeming, bustling boulevards. She looked out the window and then
turned to him. "I know where we're going."

"You were always a smart kid. I didn't need your teachers
to tell me that."

He drove leisurely down the Prospect Expressway toward
one of Sophia's favorite places in New York City and left the
car in a lot on Fulton Street. Side-by-side they walked the
narrow, tree-lined streets of Brooklyn Heights until they
reached the promenade overlooking the river.

The hot sun shined on their backs and a stiff wind blew
off the sea in their faces as they walked slowly, silently, gazing
at the skyline. In the shadows, she shivered and clutched her
arms.

"You're cold," he said. "Take my sweatshirt," and began
tugging at the thick cotton garment he wore over a white
tee-shirt.

"No, you'll be cold." she said, a hand on his arm restraining him. "I'm young, vital, and stupid. I'll be fine."

He laughed. "Stupid, eh? I suppose that's why you applied to Hopkins, Columbia, and Cornell." He paused. "What's the word? You've been mighty cagey about those applications."

She threw back her head and laughed—a joyous sound, as of a mature, older woman, who had lived, faced down hardship, and emerged on its distant side affirming her own capabilities. He saw it there, had from earliest childhood, apprehended the exquisite potentialities and taken every active step of which he could conceive to fan and nurture them. But he knew her face, her expression, her body language too well not to recognize also the frightened 17-year-old not quite ready to snap the parental cord, spread her aquiline wings, and soar like some robust living creature of the sky.

"I was going to tell you over lunch—with a little wine, maybe, to celebrate? I got my acceptance from the Johns Hopkins biology department two days ago. I'm going there in the fall."

He said nothing, just stopped walking and took his daughter in his arms. Something surged from within, from the innermost viscera upward to his throat, some tensile, tough-minded, hard-nosed respect he would have experienced for a neighbor's kid, acknowledging the long hours of concentrated study it had taken to earn this moment and milestone—this elongated stride toward fulfillment of a childhood dream of a superlative medical school; an admiration suffused with, heightened by a reservoir of parental pride that swept through his tear ducts, spurted to his eyes, and dripped methodically, one-by-one onto the shoulder of her jacket.

Her back was to the river and over her shoulder, when his eyes re-focused, he saw the old growth forest of skyscrapers composing lower Manhattan, blotting the sun but not assailing it, completing it rather, establishing the place in nature of those who built cities—who constructed, created, and grew—and who cured disease. "Sophia Ehrenstein, M.D.," he whispered in her ear.

She laughed but her graceful figure shook in his arms and tears stained her face and she made no attempt to stop them, nor did he—and he knew that her mind and feelings had recurred to another theme. "Daddy, I'm scared," she whispered. He nodded. "I know." He took her arm and she followed, trusting, leaning against him, a girl on the cusp of womanhood, who, for a few last moments of a virile life to be consecrated to making others well, was yet reliant upon another to do so now for her.

They walked to and fro across the Brooklyn Bridge amidst the sun, the salt wind, and the cawing gulls diving to the sea. He sensed she was tired. They lunched at Grimaldi's in the shadow of the bridge on salad, roasted pepper and sausage pizza, and imported red wine. Sleepy, safe in the glow of superb cuisine, sea air, and wine, fear seemed a rude interloper summarily evicted from the soiree.

"Mom and Peter spent an hour at church before work yesterday," she said.

"Thanking the saints for your acceptance?"

She nodded.

"I thank you," he said. "And the good sense of the Hopkins' admissions people."

She smiled but said nothing and he waited.

"It's true," she said. "The worst—I'm sure now."

His look searched her face—warm, loving, supportive—but he said nothing. He waited—searching, probing, seeking the propitious moment.

"I start college in the fall," she said. "I can't speak to my mother...and I'm not prepared for this..."

"Sweetness," he said softly. "You're still a minor. Your mother has a moral right to know. There's no way around it."

"But you and I could—"

His hand waved her off. "No," he said softly.

"Can't you at least tell her? I'll head to Timbuktu for a few days and by the time—"

"No," he said again, shaking his head. "No. I'll be there with you if you want but you must speak up—and you must do it face-to-face. You're right that she will explode, she'll think you've committed a mortal sin, she'll quote Saint Paul and bawl that 'fornication equals damnation.'" He saw her body cringe in the chair and he paused. "But only at first. You'll have to weather the storm. After that, her mother's love will trump every consideration and all she'll want is what is best for her only child. She has morphed into a religious woman— and God knows I couldn't tolerate it. But she is not a Dark Age zealot. At the end of the day, you—not the Church, but you—come first. She would consign all the popes and saints to perdition sooner than harm a single cell of your body. In your heart of hearts, you know this. Stand up. Tough it out. Your family will stand by you and we will resolve this in whatever way is best for Sophia Ehrenstein. When it's over, you and your mother will be closer. I know her, even now— and this I swear."

Her head was momentarily down but her hand reached tentatively across the table, reminding him quickly of another distressed girl, and he took it.

"I sit in the shadow of the Brooklyn Bridge," he mused, as if letting her hear a private conversation running through his head. "At the near edge of greatness with an aspiring medical researcher. How's this for a story? A man dreams for decades of building a shining bridge across a deep expanse. Finally, after years of effort he convinces men it can be done. Night and day he toils to design it—this wondrous thing. But he dies, just prior to the commencement of construction, from a horrible accident relating to it. His son, a great engineer, takes over the project. But he suffers a crippling case of caisson's disease—the dreaded "bends"—from digging one of the supports for a massive tower, and is bedridden for years. The engineer's wife—brilliant, unschooled in engineering, but fluent with her husband and father-in-law—comes now to the fore. She takes over the dig, relays information and instructions to and from her crippled husband, barks out commands to hardened construction workers—does so for years, and, eventually, the shining bridge reaches fruition."

He rubbed his chin. "Hell of a story—eh?" Her eyes were focused, no question mark there, only concentrated understanding. "I sit with someone who has the capacity to cure human disease," he said. "For a full decade, I have not doubted that for a second. You think such a cause might engender grievous tribulation? You think moral lightweights make such miracles occur? Did spineless poltroons build those skyscrapers across the river—men and women cowering from austere truth?" He detected it, the spark he sought, germinating in the depths of her consciousness, progressing toward the light of day through the conduit of her eyes. "Hiding from fearful truth crushes you," he concluded. "Facing it makes you indomitable."

He felt the pressure of her hand grasping his. She would stand up—he felt certain she would. He willed himself to return her grip. But he thought ruefully: the fearful truth. The full truth included her father's unconscionable professional transgressions. He knew a reckoning would come for him as surely as for his daughter—as it had inescapably for one much grander than he—as it did inexorably, quickly or in the fullness of time, for us all.

Somehow he stumbled now through his days and his friends reported discreetly that a zest, a sparkle, a quenchless gusto had been irremediably diminished. Oh, he still ate sufficiently to nourish a private army, and the ladies—honest, attractive career women—were in no short supply. Bonhomie, after all, was relative—and when a gushing fountain of it is reduced, it might still vastly exceed the faucet flow of a neophyte. He'd had to move to a small apartment far from the harbor view he cherished, it was true, but he had money saved. Teach part-time, his friends had urged. Every philosophy department in New York City will line up for your services. He did. But even at such a prestigious program as NYU, the public scandal followed, the demotion to part-timer rankled, the protege's betrayal stung, and the desire to avenge himself proliferated...it tormented his soul.

He unearthed the boxes from storage in the basement of the home in which he had been reared, owned now by his siblings, the cartons of notes on Kant's philosophic achievement compiled over decades of research and thought. He re-read carefully. He sat in front of a computer, he brainstormed, he outlined, he scratched out errant thoughts, he re-structured. He could do this. He knew he could. Everyone familiar with his work knew he could. The material was right in his wheelhouse. But he was stymied. He sat and stared. Nothing satisfied him. He deleted and started over. Something in his soul...was different...had dried up. He looked at the computer screen—he tried to concentrate—but he saw the vengeful face of the woman who denounced him, the implacable eyes of the dean who loathed him, the condemnatory expression

of the protege who betrayed him, and others on campus resentful
of his swaggering stature.

His head went to his hands. He breathed. They were against
him. A coterie of pusillanimous miscreants envious of their superi-
ors. Entrenched in the bureaucracy, lacking stature but not power.
A diseased world held many of their kind, aching to cut him up
and cut him down. He had to respond. But a single thought chilled
him: The miscreants had killed his career, they had besmirched
his public reputation, they had poisoned his protege's soul....What
would they do to his book?

For several weeks of November, as Indian summer persisted, and the sun rode slowly across a cloudless sky, as though June's halcyon days refused to abate, David Ehrenstein and Maia made love fiercely, tenderly, and without regard to further consequence. They used Maia's friend's car, a borrowed Big Dude town car, and, in short order, his Sheepshead Bay apartment. They did not speak of the risks, of the consequences, of his abrogated professional standing. They cared—but not very much. They were skylarking children granted respite from a severe years-long regimen and they lived exclusively in the delicious moment. They laughed a great deal. They intertwined hands.

They paid no heed to who saw them. Once he spontaneously volunteered that if they were observed together by someone from school he would tell them she was his sister. Instantaneously, without a moment's jolt of surprise, as if attuned to the subtlest nuance of his soul, she ignited into laughter. "You can see the family resemblance—right?" he asked. "Without a doubt," she replied, still shaking.

They spoke of her family, of her impending move, and of the world's great literature. Often they did not speak. They sat on the couch of his tiny apartment cluttered with books, her head on his chest and her legs drawn up sideways, his arm about her shoulders. They sat or lay together in bed deep into the night, fighting sleep, acutely aware of the other's presence, unwilling to relinquish such awareness even for a few hours of blessed rest. Not slowly but also not noticed, at a gently seismic moment preceding conscious articulation, something subtly shifted in the exchanged glance of their eyes, like turning on a soft nightlight for a beloved child.

One night a week before Thanksgiving she lay in his arms in his bed and he stroked her back.

"I'll be out of the house on December 1st," she said.

He'd been drowsing at the boundary between pleasant awareness and sleep, permitting no weighty concern admission to ruffle his becalmed inland sea. Now a slight tensing of her muscles warned him one was coming; reluctantly, he nestled his toes in the sandy bottom and pushed upward through bliss's warm pool toward the harsh, illuminating light above.

"It's worse," she said quietly, as though resisting insanity's weighty push into the one hard-earned haven of her life. "The screaming, the threatening gestures." He felt the shake of her head by the rustle of her hair on his chest. "I barely go home any more. I go to the library, stay at a friend's."

He willed himself to focus on the problem.

"Would it be best to call the police now—to protect your mother?"

"I might have to."

His touch on her back became lighter, gentler. "If you need anything, Maia, I'm here for you."

"Thank you."

Her head came up. "I know. I haven't handed in the midterm yet."

"Get it to me. It's very late but I accept late work from students." He paused. "I'll have to dock it points—but at least you'll get a passing grade."

"It's so hard to concentrate now—to write, to edit, to get an essay to my standards."

A horrifying possibility occurred to him—but it had to be laid openly on the table.

"If you need the time to complete your essays, we can stop spending this time together."

"David," she responded immediately and firmly. "This— and my future—are what keep me sane."

He breathed a sigh of relief. "OK."

Her head went back onto his chest. A moment later, she raised it again and looked directly at him. Her eyes shined in the dark.

"Whatever grade I get, I get. I know you'll be fair."

Deep in his throat, he swallowed. "You'll get exactly what you deserve. Just like any other student."

But the walls have ears, it is said—and eyes; as did the friends of Harry Steinway. Leaving class one night, Maia Pradhwa took the professor's arm, lightly, gaily, innocently. He bent, as they blissfully strolled, to kiss her on the mouth. He said something quickly—her head went back and she laughed. A long-time colleague of the professor, leaving class at the hall's far end, observed the intimate scene—the touch, the look, the gentle kiss shared only by lovers—and promptly forgot. Three days later, a casual remark from the matriarchal secretary freshened his memory and he spoke, to her alone, the truth of his observation. A faint flicker at the corner of ancient eyes that had witnessed every species of academic malfeasance bespoke interest. She spoke to neither the chair nor David Ehrenstein. But at the end of a long day, after bulldozing a small mountain of never ending paperwork, her hand went to the phone and, without a moment's hesitation, called an old friend to whom she had not spoken in a long time.

Maia did not get her midterm in until finals week in early December. She submitted it with her final paper—a month-and-a-half late. His syllabus had made clear from the course's opening night that the midterm was worth forty percent of the student's final grade. After docking her essay the requisite points for lateness, he calculated assiduously her final grade. It came to "B". "B" for a student who had never received a grade lower than "A" at any level of her educational career. She had circumstances at home that prevented her from reaching the concentration levels necessary to complete all assignments. Could giving her a higher grade be justified? He shook his head. The question was driven by his feelings, by considerations extraneous to justice and professional responsibility, by an acute depth of intimacy attained with this remarkable woman. For a long time he stared at the grade sheet. Fully cognizant of all potential ramifications—sad, nervous, but with eyes wide open—he entered the grade of "B".

She took it about as well as could be expected.

"B!" she shouted in his office in Covington Hall. "When I was working and moving and talking to the cops and protecting my siblings—you gave me a 'B' because my midterm was late?"

Quietly he sat behind his desk as she vented, as years and months of domestic frustration coalesced into a single unified fury regarding her final grade. "I apply to graduate school, Dr. Ehren-shtein," she said, articulating the name slowly. "Do you think Columbia or NYU looks at a 'B' in a course closely related to my field and will know or care about my circumstances? Do you deliberately seek to wreck my future?"

When she stopped to take a breath, he carefully interceded.

"Any superlative student would be disappointed with a 'B,'" he said softly. "But I was fair—like you said. You got exactly what you deserved—like everybody else."

"Oh, am I like everybody else, Dr. Ehren—shtein?" she asked. He saw her fighting to hold back tears and when she continued her voice was lower. "You weren't making love to them—were you? You made love to me. Did you tell them that you loved them—or did you say that only to me?" His ears registered the full sweep of emotion in her tone but his vision centered on her eyes. Despite her efforts, a single small tear formed at the corner of each.

"Maia," he said, his voice gentle, as in the bedroom. "You know—you have abundant reason to know—my feelings for you. But I can't grade any student on the basis of my feelings."

"I'm not any student!" she screamed. "I'm the woman—"

"Enough!" he got up from his desk. "I know who you are. You got what you deserved. If you think you deserve a higher grade, you can go to the Academic Dean—"

"And get you fired?" she interrupted. "Don't think I won't. " She grabbed her coat and bag and turned to the door.

"It's in your power to do that, Maia," he said. "And no doubt you'd be right." He stopped. He tried not to think of an ignominious end to a superb teaching career that had spanned two decades. It was uncanny, he thought. Your actions were part of some vast eternal network—their consequences redounded to you—like a moral boomerang, they arced silently through the sylvan glade of your life, through the environs of seeming peace, and arrowed unerringly back to the bull's eye writ large on the chest of a poor simpleton who hoped he might escape them. When he spoke, he spoke sadly. "But nothing will change the fact that you earned a 'B'". The boomerang zeroed inexorably towards her chest, as well.

She opened the door, walked out, and shut it quietly behind her.

He sat in his office, head in his hands. It was seconds after Maia had departed. He gained some relief from the touch of his fingertips at his temples, stroking the skin and the knotted tension he experienced there. Just give me a minute, he thought—one minute and I will look at this mess. His office phone buzzed. It seemed louder, more demanding than he remembered. He willed his hand to reach for it.

"David, its Claudine," his ex-wife said, as though he could ever mistake her voice. The urgency of her tone brought his head up in a snap.

"What's wrong?"

She didn't waste words. "It's Sophia. She's hysterical. She's crying like I've never heard. She won't tell me what's wrong." She paused. "I know you're busy at school—I hate to ask you—but I need you here now."

He didn't tell her that very likely he would soon not be at all busy at school.

"I'm on my way."

He was wearing sneakers and relentless running had him in shape. He bunched up his jacket and carried it in his left hand. No sense waiting for the bus, he thought. He started up Flatbush Avenue at a steady trot, then, as he broke a sweat, steadily increased his pace. When he reached the house on Avenus S, he was not sure if his sweat or his breathing was heavier. Before he could ring the bell, Claudine opened the door and he stepped inside.

Claudine DePalma looked as if she had stopped aging a decade previous. Her complexion was dark and her eyes darker but it was perhaps the darkest component of all—the fires smoldering within, for his body once, more recently for the saints—that provided a quenchless vitality that seemingly kept the years at bay. She snapped orders like the corporate vice-president she was, including to her husband, who toiled under her authority at both home and the office. David Ehrenstein smiled sadly now, remembering the long months that it had been different—when he had vainly sought to comfort an inconsolable wife who had just lost her entire family in a shattering car wreck, a period during which her godfather had voluntarily functioned like a real father to three-year-old Sophia.

"Where is she?"

"In her room." As he started up the stairs, she added: "You'll tell me what's going on?"

Quickly, he turned to her: "You'll be the first to know."

He knocked at the door of his daughter's bedroom. He received no answer. "Sophia!" He knew the door was unlocked—but he would violate her privacy only in the face of life-threatening danger. "Sophia!"

"Come in," he heard faintly through the door. He stepped in and shut the door behind him.

She'd been lying face down but now swung her legs over the bed's side and sat up. On a cold Friday evening, she wore a Johns Hopkins sweatshirt and jeans but was barefoot. Her hair was disheveled and her light makeup smeared.

He wasted neither time nor words. He extended both hands, she took them, and he pulled her up.

"It's time."

She nodded but was deathly pale.

"It's not the firing squad at dawn," he said. Mechanically she pulled on a pair of shoes.

They opened the door of her room and stepped out. She closed it behind her.

"More like," he rattled on. "The fifty-year-old researcher, Dr. Sophia Ehrenstein, and her team work on a cure for cancer." They had reached the top of the stairs. "Promising, hopeful, great acclaim." They started slowly down. "But one problem." Claudine's stern figure loomed at the bottom of the stairs. "Dr. Ehrenstein realizes the line of research is a dead end. The money wasted, the time irretrievable, the hopes hollow, the impending Nobel consideration a mockery—"

She stopped descending. She looked at him. Understanding lit her eyes. "But nobody wants to hear it," she said.

He nodded. "Or even remotely face it. One person alone must will herself to step up and rub the bitter truth in the faces of men and women desperate for it to be otherwise....and her dad is no longer with her..." She stared and his smile was loaded with every watt of warmth a child can engender in a parent's life. "But he is..."

She went to the bottom of the stairs. She turned to her mother. Her mouth opened to speak. His cell phone rang. The house's air temperature seemed to precipitously drop when he recognized the phone number—the Academic Dean's office. Wearily, with a sense of finality, he plopped onto the stairs. He took the call.

"David, am I interrupting?" said a familiar voice, the Dean herself.

"Oh, no," he said to Naomi Krasner, knowing that the end of their twenty-year work relationship loomed. "Your timing is exquisite."

Claudine and Sophia both detected something in the voice each knew so well, some hint of bitter despair it so rarely manifested. They stopped. They stared at him. Claudine's eyes were mystified. Sophia's were opened wide.

"An old friend of yours called this afternoon," Naomi said impassively, her voice sounding like a judge. "Said he had information about you—explosive information." She let it sink in. "I thought you would want to know. He'll be here in thirty minutes."

He hung up. The pit of his stomach felt like it had been kicked out by the world's reigning tae kwon do champion. Interestingly, it was Claudine who reacted first.

"David," she said, her voice emitting genuine concern. "You're ill."

He nodded. "I am."

"What is it?"

His head hung. Maia, he thought. His teaching career. How is it possible that it could all be gone in a moment— utterly, irretrievably gone? Then another thought chilled him, following swiftly on the back end of the others, like wave after wave of debilitating nausea. He brought up his head and stared at his daughter. Truth was not covert. It was part of the world, out there, living its own ghastly existence, and it was not to be shoveled discreetly into the earth, like desperate men seeking to inter Mount McKinley in their backyard. Sophia, he moaned. What would the unconcealed truth do to his relationship with her?

"Something...I brought on myself..." he answered, and even he detected the exhaustion in his voice. He grabbed hold of the banister and took a deep breath. He pulled himself upright. "And something I must rectify by myself."

He started to the door. Then a thought occurred to him.

"This is something you must see." He spoke to Sophia. She stared, confused, sensing doom, knowing instinctively that decisive action would now be taken—must be taken—but uncertain of what that consisted. He reached his hand for his daughter's and she took it. "We'll be back," he said to Claudine. Seconds later they were on the street, his jacket wrapped around her shoulders.

The Big Dude town car dropped them off at campus exactly twenty-five minutes later. They walked quickly to the administrative building. Sophia had his jacket zipped to her throat. He was no more frigid in the chill air than he had been indoors. Support staff had left for the evening but a light shined in the Academic Dean's office. The professor and his daughter knocked at the door and then stepped inside. The room was filled with old friends—and with a scent of decomposition.

He had not seen Harry Steinway in eight years. He thought, is it possible that the years could leave him so utterly unaltered? He stared closely. The full head of brown hair streaked with jets of silver—the gut so prominent it jutted forward like the prow of an invincible war ship—the dark eyes, even now, in the act of fulfilling a years-long desire for retribution, emitting the familiar glow, an unrelieved warmth not to be expunged by circumstances however baleful—all of it, undeniably identical to the figure who had for two decades bestrode the campus like uncrowned royalty. Then he spoke.

"Finally, David...finally..." The gruff patience of his tone manifested a stature almost Olympian, of one willing to wait interminably for justice and then to strike quickly at a propitious moment. His hand, waving slowly in a negligent, vaguely encompassing gesture, still moved with an unfeigned hauteur worthy of a 17th century monarch. But to one who had known him so well, his voice exhibited an uncharacteristic hesitation, the slightest timorous stammer that had never before been apparent in the monolithic self-confidence of the man.   And his initial assessment was wrong, Harry's eyes were different....Was there something new there that had been added...or something old that had been subtracted?

"These are serious charges, David," Naomi Krasner said quietly. "Although wholly unsubstantiated," she concluded, staring at his accuser. She did not glance at Sophia.

Harry Steinway lifted his girth from the chair he had occupied. Slowly but purposefully he strode across the room toward David Ehrenstein. He did not glance at the Dean but spoke in a mocking tone that carried clearly across the room.

"Perhaps, David, other witnesses might be adduced—the departmental secretary, for example, a colleague or two—perhaps even the student herself might be willing to divulge the truth, especially if assured immunity against punitive action." He turned to the Dean. "My sources did some research," he said. "The student's name is Maia Pradhwa. Did I pronounce it correctly, David? I think the administration should investigate it. Or," he asked archly, "does the Dean's office no longer concern itself with such matters?"

Naomi Krasner stared at Steinway, her hard eyes inscrutable. Nobody knew how old she was. She had been Academic Dean for more than twenty years—and, her friends liked to point out, had been part of the university since Kennedy was president. She was barely five feet tall and, now, a stooped, emaciated figure, resembled a cancer patient rather than a collegiate dean. She did not say much. She did not need to. In her youth, she had defended the rights of female students molested and intimidated by faculty members. Later, she just as vociferously defended the rights of male faculty members unjustly accused of sexual harassment. Now she no longer found it necessary to defend anybody—because she ruled the academic roost with the unquestioned authority of a Third World dictator but with the unbreachable rectitude of a Supreme Court justice.

"You might," she said in a quiet, sibilant tone somehow redolent with menace. "Be called upon to back up those words."

He laughed easily, a man once more in charge of his destiny, enjoying a delectable moment long sought. He answered the Dean but he looked at and spoke to his former protégé. "Considering that you gave the poor girl a final grade of 'B', it might not be difficult to gain evidence backing up those words. What do you think?" He turned finally to the dark-haired girl by his antagonist's side. "And you must be Sophia," he said gallantly, as if noticing her presence for the first time. He shook his head paternally. "I haven't seen you since you were nine years old. Welcome to our little witch hunt. Interesting that your father chooses to bring his child here. A cry for mercy, David?"

Sophia did not look at the accuser. She stared at her father, her eyes unyielding, trustful, questioning. David Ehrenstein felt her eyes on him but gazed at Harry Steinway. He said nothing.

Steinway turned back to the Dean. "He does not speak because he fears to incriminate himself. Is the administration willing to conduct a full investigation?" He paused. "Or does it reserve such treatment only for *special* individuals?"

He glared at Naomi Krasner. She stared back impassively. It had been an open campus secret that she detested him—despised the swaggering grandee who wielded his stature, his reputation, his buoyant, illimitable charm as arousing aphrodisiac with which to inflame star struck female students. "The Brooklyn University classroom is not recruiting ground for your private harem," she had stated emphatically on the day of their final confrontation. It had become an administrative legend. For all that, she had conducted the investigation with ruthless impartiality and been prepared to dismiss the charges irrevocably in the days before the professor's protégé had finally stepped forward.

Harry Steinway threw back his grey-maned head in a distinctively circular motion, akin to a roaring lion, and laughed. He laughed joyously, full-throatedly, bitterly. Then he halted. "Call the departmental secretary. Do it now. Then call—"

"It is Friday evening," she said evenly. "At almost eight o'clock. It will wait until Monday morning."

He stared, sensing the underlying animosity. "You'll stonewall this," he said with definitive certainty. "Won't you? You'll protect the fair-haired boy who helped you bring down the academic 'miscreant' you loathed. There's no justice here, for all your pretensions, and never was, merely unbridled favoritism and prejudice elevated –"

"I like him and I despise you," she said calmly, coldly, in deliberate insult. "That much is undoubtedly true. If you think that is why you were cashiered, you are free to clutch at any delusion you find comforting. An investigation into Professor Ehrenstein's *alleged* misconduct"—she stressed it in open provocation—"will wait until Monday morning and will most definitely not be initiated on Friday evening. You can leave. *Now.* I'll call you if necessary."

It was slipping away from him, his case foundering on the icy shores of the Dean's long-standing enmity—it was apparent in his face, which twisted now into a sneer of which for many years he was not capable.

"You two frauds," he hissed. "You"—he pointed at the Dean—"you self-righteous *poseur*, you care about gratifying your personal biases, not about justice, and you"—he pointed at the professor—"all your high-minded talk about truth, what does it mean, you hypocrite who stabbed your best friend in his back and then proceeded to commit the identical transgression?" He stood in front of his former accuser.

"Truth must be faced, you said—"

"—And you grow in stature," said David Ehrenstein quietly.

"Consequences must be accepted—"

"—Or you are vastly diminished."

"Where is that noble drivel now—"

"—Nobly facing you."

"Clear your dirty conscience—"

"—Clear yours, Harry—"

"This is not about me—"

"—Yes, it is," David Ehrenstein said. "Or you wouldn't be here."

They stared at each other. What was it in Harry's eyes that was different? They were silent for a moment. Haunted, that's what had been added. Or, he wondered, was haunted a product of something that had been irremediably subtracted?

Finally, Steinway roused himself. "I'll go to the press, if necessary," he said dully. "Truth must come out." He started for the door. But he moved heavily and it seemed decades to cross the room. Finally, he had his hand on the knob.

"Truth will come out *now*. Hard truth," said Ehrenstein softly. "You might want to hear it." Steinway looked at him silently, then opened the door. "Harry..." Ehrenstein said. But the big man stepped from the office. Did he stoop, Ehrenstein thought, as he crossed the threshold. Strange, he realized. Even now, he experienced only a sense of loss.

"I'll be right back," he said to Naomi and Sophia. He stepped out into the corridor.

"So nice to see you again, Sophia," Naomi said.

Ehrenstein shut the door. "Harry!"

The big man turned back to him. "I've nothing to say to you."

"I've something to say to you. They f--ked you, didn't they?"

"'We' is the right pronoun."

"Right, we f--ked you. Boo-hoo, poor Harry Steinway is a victim."

Harry Steinway, never one for violence, turned, fists balled, and advanced.

"Idiot," Ehrenstein said. "Cleanse your soul. Take back your power—and write the f--king book on Kant. Everybody knows it will be great."

Steinway stared but said nothing. Ehrenstein turned on his former mentor and re-entered the Dean's office.

Naomi Krasner spoke. "David, you are free to state whatever you will. But if no student registers a complaint against you—*and none ever has*—the administration will take no action. You know the rules."

He nodded in acknowledgement. "Thank you. He looked at the Dean and spoke to another. "Bitter truth must be faced." He took a deep breath, and exhaled slowly. He had hoped to speak to Harry. He looked at Sophia and, momentarily, forgot all else but what his daughter must now learn. "I had an illicit affair with a student. She was still in my class–and I had to grade her." He spoke impassively, his voice drained of all emotion save an undying respect for truth. "We broke every rule the administration could dream of—and probably a few they could not. I knew it was wrong from the first moment till the last and for every moment in between—and I did it anyway. There must be no misunderstanding and there can be no excuse." He told the full, cold truth—save for the one part so utterly personal that it belonged to his conscience exclusively: He would change nothing of his moments with Maia, and, in bitter despair, he grieved his loss. His eyes did not leave Sophia's.

Sophia did not move and she did not touch him. But something in her deer's eyes glinted—a spurt of flame on a rocky scree, and he was convinced that backbone, like muscle, could be grown.

For a moment, Naomi's head was in her hands. Then she raised it. "Lovely evening, Sophia, isn't it?"

Sophia laughed relievedly, light-heartedly, and her eyes, shining, were on her father.

Naomi's eyes were on him, too. "Any more good news you would like to share?" the Dean's voice was low, husky, controlled.

"One more piece."

"Yes, I'm sure we all want to hear it."

This time he looked at the Dean. "I'm going to resign, Naomi."

The air in the room was still, warm, and felt more like July than December. She thought about it for a long time.

"I'll say this once more—and never again. What you did is grounds for dismissal. But if the student registers no complaint, the administration will take no action against you. You understand?"

He nodded. "Yes. And nothing will happen to Maia, right?"

"Nothing." She kept her glance poker-faced. "Don't you know that she is a victim?"

"Victim or not, she's got to complete her education."

"David," she leaned forward to emphasize her words. "If she comes forward, we might suggest to her that she fulfill her sexual longings with men other than her professors. Other than that, she will get no problem from us."

"Alright," he said.

She let several moments go by. Softly he heard the Friday night street noise penetrate the calm of her office.

"You've been an outstanding professor here. For twenty years the students have learned from you and loved you. In every possible way," she added archly. "Your unnecessitated resignation will be a blow to the department and to the university as a whole."

He said nothing. How could he express what the place meant to him? Decades of memories flooded his mind—of lectures given on rain swept November afternoons when it seemed to grow dark at two o'clock—of students struggling to comprehend Descartes or Hume as snow tumbled silently to earth in late January—of the wondrous sight of a mind coming online, of seeing something dawn hesitant and breathless in a student's eyes as the sunlight shined so bright on a May morning that it seemed they were not in Brooklyn but in Naples. "When you stand in front of a classroom," Harry Steinway had told him. "You are Western civilization." For all of his flaws, he had not forgotten.

She had worked in higher education far longer than he. For all the dogmatists, the incompetents, the crackpots that infested the field, it had, at its best, a unique ability to stimulate intellectual advance. Her eyes told him she understood what he would be walking away from.

"David," she began softly. "Your contributions here—"

"—I will not let it hang over my head," he answered the unstated plea with finality. "I can't live like that. I made a big mistake. This will wipe the slate clean and I can start over again—fresh and new."

She knew when to quit. The best fighters always knew.

"And you have your books," she said simply.

He shook her hand and turned to leave. Sophia was at his side. At the door the Dean's voice stopped him. "Was it worth it?"

Without turning, he heard in her voice a devilish spark of a long-past Brooklyn girlhood that could not be extinguished by the gravity of official responsibility. Her husband had died years ago. He did not let his mind pursue the thought further.

He hesitated only a second. "You bet it was."

The town car pulled to a halt in front of the well-maintained home on Avenue S. They got out and walked to the door.

"Your mother will be frantic to know what in blazes is going on," he said. He thought, for the first time in decades he might sleep ten hours that night. But it was the exhaustion following the sloughing off of a burden recently carried, rather than that of one shouldered still.

She was silent as they walked to the door. She had not spoken since they arrived at Naomi's office. Now she turned to him. "Dad, I'll tell her right now—everything." He nodded. "You want me with you?" She shook her head. "No, I'll do it myself." She paused. "I'll call you tomorrow. Maybe you can stop by tomorrow."

"I won't be busy now."

"We can hold a family powwow. And decide what's best." Her voice was calm with a conviction that could not be feigned.

He stared closely in the dark. The look in her eyes—he thought, was it possible for a girl to become a woman in a single night? The stab of remorse at the realization that his little girl wouldn't need him any longer was submerged by the joy of a sentiment far grander. He turned to go.

"Dad." He turned back. Tears were in her eyes and she shook her head. "Wow," she said. "Thank you."

It was Monday morning. Thelma Reeves sat in his office, crying, as he cleaned out his desk and bookshelves.

"You're the best professor I've had here."

She'd taken three philosophy courses with him over the past three years and earned an "A" in every one of them. He looked at the tears streaking her dark cheeks and wanted to lay a hand in reassuring comfort on her shoulder. His classes had meant something to the best students and he was glad of it. Strangely, he felt neither remorse nor pain now—only a sense of pride at important accomplishments and a nascent excitement regarding the birth of something new.

"You have my e-mail and cell phone," he said. "Don't hesitate to contact me if you have questions."

When she had left, he took a last look at the room that had been his office for fifteen years. Everything was in a rented van parked in the lot behind the building. He sat on his empty desk and stared at the blank room. Maia Pradhwa walked in. She wore a felt fedora and a light camel's hair coat that set off her black hair. She looked radiant. She looked him in the eye and spoke with a ring of truth that could not be doubted.

"There were no circumstances under which I would have gone to the administration."

"I believe you."

"There was no need to do what you did."

His eyes thanked her but he shook his head. "There was a need."

She was silent for several moments. "I'm not angry anymore, Dr. Ehren-shtein. Regardless of my grade, you're a great teacher. I hope you forgive me."

He remained sitting atop his desk. He stared at her.

"The last official act I performed as a Brooklyn University professor was to write a letter of recommendation—an exceptionally strong letter—for a student named 'Maia Pradhwa,' recounting her superlative strengths as a student and explaining the family problems—including the courageous manner in which she resolved them—under which she labored, resulting in the lateness of her midterm exam." He paused. "I think the Columbia and NYU graduate programs will be most grateful to have you—and fortunate."

She was motionless except for the instinctive lowering of her head to hide something in her eyes.

"David..." she whispered.

She came to him and pressed herself to his chest. "Are you through with me?" she moaned. "Like with the school?"

He clutched her fiercely. "Not hardly."

It was several days after New Years. David Ehrenstein, Sophia, and Daddy sat with a platter of hot dogs and fries—and enormous cups of root beer—at Nathan's on Surf Avenue. Although it was a frigid afternoon, several derelicts panhandled on the street, the con trails of their breath forming vapor streams as they accosted unwary passersby. Daddy polished off his fourth dog as Ehrenstein took the first bite of his second. Sophia nibbled the end of a French fry.

"You want more hours at Big Dude," Daddy said. "You got 'em. Just let me know. We gotta take care of these itinerant philosophers."

Sophia laughed gaily. She did more of that recently, her father noticed. He saw that same awareness in the eyes of her godfather, as well.

"Thanks. But I think I'll teach part-time in the evenings at Kingsborough—and have more time to devote to my book.

I have money saved." He turned to his daughter. "If you don't mind me squandering part of your inheritance."

This time she didn't laugh. "I'd rather you spent it on yourself."

"You have a job at Hopkins?"

She nodded. "In a lab. Part of my work study."

"You won't forget us peons in Brooklyn—will you," Daddy asked. "When you're a hot shot doctor one day?"

"Sure," she laughed. "My education and career will cause me to forget my family."

For several minutes they did not speak. The only sound in the room came from dozens of sets of choppers gnashing up dogs and fries—and from the winter wind whistling through cracks in the door.

"Mom and Peter have set money aside for my college," she said.

"Your dad will contribute," David Ehrenstein added quickly.

"Your godfather too," Daddy said. "On condition he gets free health care in his old age."

The side door to the restaurant opened. Ehrenstein followed Daddy's line of sight as he stared suspiciously at a young Indian woman entering alone. She wore a lavender, full-length down coat and a knitted white beret. She approached the table.

"Daddy, Sophia," Ehrenstein said. "May I present Maia Pradhwa. Maia—my family."

"You don't look like his Daddy," Maia said to the big man. "But you look very much like his daughter."

"Might I add," Ehrenstein said solemnly and without a hint of nervousness. "The future Mrs. Ehrenstein."

Sophia stared, open-mouthed, from her father to Maia. Maia simply stared. "What?" she stammered.

"Somebody once told me that nothing could stop you," he said. "I thought I might as well capitulate immediately and avoid a wasted struggle."

It took her several seconds to take it in—and then her head went back and she uproariously laughed.

"Has any woman ever received such a proposal?"

"Has there ever been such a woman?" he asked quietly.

Some quality of his voice arrested her. Her eyes saw him alone and momentarily all hints of mischief were gone, replaced by something older, wiser, more elemental.

"Will you accept?' he asked.

Her head went back. A single distinct droplet of water stood at the corner of each eye.

"Yes, David," she said, voice husky, as if words moved upward through or past some sudden impediment. "Of course."

Sophia's arm was around her father's shoulder as his had been so often around hers.

Daddy blew his nose into a clean white handkerchief. "Professors," he said, "do things a little wacky."

Life Struggle

It began when his mother vowed to die should he marry his girlfriend. It ended when she did. What he did in between caused consternation among the most important persons in his life.

It was uncanny that the struggle over his doctoral dissertation mirrored that over his marriage. At times, he was tempted to revert to the religious training of his youth, the stories of which warned of sinners plagued by an outraged deity with afflictions both calamitous and unceasing. It seemed too much to be coincidental. Might there not be the hand of an inscrutable agency guiding the process toward some dark terminus of punishment for his transgressions? Certainly, his mother might construe it in that way.

He had first brought Genevieve home six years earlier, after college graduation. His mother, usually seeping goodwill from the seams, had been distant—not hostile but aloof, eyeing the new female like an aging diva might a heralded arriviste.

Genevieve had gone back to Wisconsin and for years— lonely interminable years—while he had started grad school and she had completed college and gone to work, they had suffered through a long-distance relationship. But then, as he completed qualifying exams and prepared for the dissertation, she had moved to Brooklyn.

The relentless animus his mother expressed regarding his relationship with Genevieve was beyond anything anyone had ever experienced from her—narrowly exceeding that expressed toward Trish, his first girlfriend, whom, in a combustible spurt of seething rage, she had called to her face "a little backstabbing, predatory tramp" upon discovering that she and her son, however foolishly, contemplated engagement at age eighteen. Within weeks, after more than a year together, Trish had decamped his life.

"Mom," his older sister, Amelia, said to her one evening. "Teddy's got a girlfriend. He didn't mug an old lady."

Their mother turned from the dinner she prepared at the stove.

"Amelia," she said coldly. "Don't you ever side with her."

"Are there sides?" his sister asked. "We're at war?"

His mother stared silently for several moments and Amelia said that the air in the kitchen seemed suddenly charged with a tension that she had never felt there before. He was at school that evening and his father snored in his easy chair in the basement after a hard day of teaching. Amelia was alone with her. His mother's words came softly in the still air.

"I will not let that girl steal my son from me. Do you hear me, Amelia?"

It was Amelia's turn to stare. She was in her thirties, had worked conscientiously since age fourteen, and had financially helped her parents and brother repeatedly. She was an attractive woman, who had rejected several suitors her mother had pressed on her, with long black hair swinging gracefully below her shoulders and gray eyes like the winter horizon that could penetrate to a person's core. Although unfailingly cordial, she was no trembling rosebud—for years she had been the flinty-eyed executive secretary of a workaholic CEO who described her as a bedrock of calm in a corporate stress pool. Even so, confronted by eyes as implacable as she had ever seen, she felt herself involuntarily scrape her chair back from the kitchen table. Then she checked herself, close to the wall and to some truth more unyielding than that. Her voice was tense, low.

"Me you would have married to the first bum who asked—wouldn't you?" Their mother whirled at the bitter words to face yet another agony in her life. "You would have, too—if I hadn't told you to go to Hell."

"Amelia!"

"But your son, your precious son"—her voice was a moan—"him you'll sooner strangle in a death grip than permit to marry—"

"Shut up!" his mother screamed. The piercing shriek served only to goad his sister further.

"You wouldn't let loose of your 'sonny boy' if the Chief Rabbi of Jerusalem offered his only daughter in—"

His mother advanced on her now. "Shut up, you goddamn lunatic. Who do you think you're speaking—"

But his sister was up, on her feet, brushing his mother aside and sweeping from the room. She didn't look back. She had her boss put her up at a hotel in the city and neither called home nor returned for most of a week. For a few days, anyway, his mother was frantic about something else.

Do you know what it's like to have your heart ripped from your chest? To be left gasping, trying to breathe but unable because there's a dripping red hole where your heart was? Do you? Then you know how I felt. And you know that I had to do what I did.

That girl—that duplicitous witch of a girl—intruded herself into my home and into my life and baldly, boldly with the sweet smile never leaving the corners of her pretty mouth stole from me the crown jewel of my existence. Do you possess a single, stand-alone item that makes your life worth living? You do? That's what she stole from me.

Ted introduced her when he returned home from college, the University of Wisconsin don't you know. He had to go so far? To another continent it might have been and with Germans no less. Why not go to Sweden? I said. It's about as close and they have blondes too. He didn't laugh. He didn't listen either. He never listened. Willful, my sister, Sarah, said: "Rosalind, he's willful." "Willful?" I said. "I should have a mule, not a son."

I was polite to her, like a lamb I was. "Come in," I said. "Make yourself comfortable. You're leaving when?"

She smiled. Beguiling. So beguiling I felt a chill on my breast, like a shadow on a blustery day cast across an open grave. Those green eyes, luminous, looked around my living room then back at me. A cat, she was like. A big green-eyed cat preparing to occupy one's premises and expropriate one's diamonds. "Mrs. Grossman," she said, her voice as lyrical as Chopin's personal piano. "I'm so glad to be here." Her breasts, under her sweater, heaved gently as she spoke. A cat she was, a green-eyed buxom cat and I knew my Teddy was lost.

She returned to Wisconsin but she visited. I hoped he would forget her but years later she was back to stay. She rented an apartment half-a-mile away. Rarely I saw her. Rarely also I saw my son. It was on a Friday evening in winter that I could take it no longer. He was leaving again to spend the weekend at her place. He was walking out the door. Not looking back at his mother staring at him. Just leaving.

"Teddy!" I cried and felt my face turn red.

He turned to me. His face was open to hear me out, to listen to my words—but heedless, implacably closed to my wishes or requests and I knew I could become the vessel of God's incontestable truth and it would make not a sliver of difference. The realization infuriated me.

"You're a graduate student in philosophy—you'll be a doctor soon." I strove to keep my voice measured, calm, and not grab his coat front and shake him until he saw sense. "You don't have time for this stupid girl."

He just looked, taking me in, hearing it, hearing it all, maybe in some remote way even caring what he did, but as unyielding in his judgment as an onrushing storm.

"She's after you, you fool! Don't you see what she wants?"

My hands moved now as I tried to reach him and I had discarded calm. If I couldn't reach him with my words perhaps I could do it with my hands and they pleaded, eloquently, like a trial lawyer working the case of his life. His eyes, those dark eyes I had cherished since he was a little boy just looked at me pitilessly and he gave me a slight nod.

"Have a good weekend," he said.

He was gone.

There was a pain in my side—I hoped it was cancer—and I felt every minute and second of my sixty-two years. I staggered to the living room couch. I sat alone in the darkness, pulling it around me like a black cloak, and stared at the chair in which he had so often sat across from me.

"You'll be sorry," I said to the grieving face I imagined. "Just you wait."

Professor Neil D. Rachels was not pleased.

"The theme of your proposed dissertation runs counter to every moral precept held by contemporary philosophers," he said to his star student. "No thinker of consequence for greater than a century has supported ethical egoism." He paused and let his troubled gaze rest full on the student. "Ted, your arguments could be brilliantly innovative—but I don't think a single philosophy department in the country would pass such a thesis."

Neil Rachels, although not yet fifty, had been recognized as a leading ethicist for a full decade and attracted outstanding philosophy students from across the country. Just out of graduate school he had written an original book on moral theory, followed up, two years later, by a textbook that quickly became a college standard. Now affluent well beyond his peers, he nevertheless continued to carry a full teaching load, to present public lectures, and to write essays for both scholarly and popular publication.

Observing Ted Grossman, the professor was reminded of the astronauts of his youth—not one to get rattled in the face of danger. Like them, Rachels thought, he could have been a combat fighter pilot. He even looked the part—tall, lean, black-haired, except for the glasses necessary to see distances. Even then, the dark eyes burned at you with unconcealed determination. He had always liked this kid, even though they agreed on nothing except the importance of moral philosophy.

Rachels knew the students admired him. Most graduate professors deserved their reputations as mediocre teachers, Grossman had once told him—they lacked fire, focus, and clarity of presentation—they did not prepare rigorous lectures—they schmoozed with their graduate students, as if accumulated knowledge could best be conveyed in desultory conversation. But Rachels, with a lithe frame and face like a predatory hawk, controlled the classroom and the lecture, gliding like the athlete he had been, on the balls of his feet, moving incessantly, raising his voice, gesticulating, perennially aroused by the issues.

"Regardless of whether they pass it," Ted said. "This is where I stand—and they need to consider the arguments."

Rachels slapped the desk.

"I never doubted your personal integrity! Or your ability. But I will not bring forward a proposal—much less a dissertation itself—that has no chance of being accepted. It would be bad for me," the professor acknowledged. "It would be catastrophic for you."

The student smiled. It was only a slight movement at his mouth's corners but the eyes conveyed undeniable warmth. "My career, my risk, my choice. This is what I will write."

The words hung in the air for a mere moment.

"You're an obstinate son-of-a-bitch," Rachels said.

I could have choked this kid, brilliant, original—and determined to wreck his career. Respectful and quietly adamant but would listen to nothing or nobody but his own conscience. Unteachable in some ways—but then one of the rare ones who required little teaching. Once every few years, perhaps once a decade of teaching there was one who could do it his own way—and no other. Those you had to just give them space and let them go. First you had to recognize them.

"Ted," I said gently but similarly adamant. "You've studied philosophy for years. You know the arguments against egoism— against the claim that an individual should concern himself overwhelmingly, perhaps exclusively with his own interest."

He nodded, his eyes gazing steadily into mine. His calm certitude merely provoked me.

"Ethical egoism is a specter hovering, wraithlike, over the history of philosophy," I said. *"Virtually every serious thinker is appalled by it—"*

"While they live it out," he interrupted. *"In their educations, careers, love lives, and every other endeavor in which they seek personal happiness."*

I heeded him but slightly. *"Theoretically, they are appalled by it,"* I said emphatically. *"And feel compelled to refute the theory in careful, ceaseless argumentation."*

"One reason of several," he said. *"Why it needs to be rigorously presented, vigorously supported, and dispassionately examined."*

"OK," I said and threw my hands in the air. *"So you're a modern day Socrates introducing new moral theories to challenge the principles of the Athenians—or the Americans in this case."*

"At least the Americans can't execute me."

"No, they can't. But they can ensure that your doctorate is denied—and that the only further teaching you do is as a part-time hack at a third-rate school for a pittance in salary that won't pay your carfare. Sound appealing?"

His head went back and he laughed. *"That's my life now."*

"You're in your late twenties. Want it to still be your life in your late forties? Your fifties? Beyond? With your gifts? I don't think so."

"Professor Rachels," he said quietly, eschewing the first name he had long ago earned the right to use. *"If I live out such a worst case scenario, I still live out who, what, and wherefore I am."*

I stopped. He was right, of course, and what he said was inarguable.

"True to the self," I whispered. *"Egoism from the core of your soul to the last lonely inch you step off at the end of your miserly existence."*

He smiled faintly but with an utter lack of derision, as if years of jeering had inured him and he had risen somewhere above it.

"True to the self," he acknowledged, picking out the one essential point from amidst the verbiage. I had not set foot in a house of worship for many years—nor, I was certain, had he—but the look on his face, despite my glittering mockery, belonged in one.

"Fine," I said, getting down to it. "What makes you so special?"

"Me?"

"You. Anyone. The self. Egoism teaches that my self is special, more privileged than others, and I can do as I please. Right?" I didn't wait for an answer. "It's like racism—do you see that?"

"No."

"Then consider. The racist holds that members of one ethnic group are innately better than others—and should be better treated. But is there any factual basis for claiming inherent superiority for one ethnic group over another?"

"None whatever."

"The same is true of egoism. In fact, human beings are equal—none are better or more deserving than others. But the egoist denies this. He says 'I am a law unto myself, I can do as I wish, all I need do is make myself happy—and if another man gets in the way of my pursuits, so much the worse for him.' But again, there is no rational basis for such a claim of elite status—neither individually nor collectively. An egoist lives out a false theory of human nature." I paused. He did not react. "Do you agree?"

"No."

His dark eyes stared, deep, penetrating, cutting, as if his thought processes centered not in his brain but in his visual faculty—and where he gazed his thoughts teleported automatically with all intermediary need of speech expunged. "In fact, the truth is exactly reversed."

I rubbed my hands delightedly. Rarely I agreed with him but from this student—still relatively a boy—I had come to expect thoughts that came out sparkling and new, distinctively his own, utterly unlike the recycled platitudes often forthcoming from my accomplished colleagues.

"How so?" I said.

"Exactly because human beings are equal—that's how so."

"You want to explain that? You come up before a dissertation committee at this or any university, you better have some fancy arguments to support your claim."

Any and all smile was gone from his face. He was, once again, a pitiless thinking engine that had ranged formidably across several of my classes over the past half-decade.

"One," he said. "Men are the same in needs, requirements, and rights. Two: Each must achieve his goals and needs in order to survive and to flourish—he must act in his own interest, in pursuit of his own happiness. Three: Therefore, each individual must respect the right—the' inalienable right,' as Locke and Jefferson put it—of every other person to pursue his own happiness, just as he demands that they respect his. Four: The same moral principle that protects an individual from other members of society protects them from him. Five: It is the abrogation of egoism that diminishes some man relative to others. Because if he is not permitted to pursue his own happiness—if some other individual or society or the state has the legitimate authority to demand of him a sacrifice of his interest—then he is of lesser value or importance than those to whom his aspirations are subordinated. He is a pawn, a mere means to their ends, a peon to be used as fodder to their aristocratic purposes." He paused. "Is that sufficiently fancy? If not, I can dress it up—"

"No, you supercilious bastard. I get it."

"You don't think such an argument can be developed? There's much more to be said in support of ethical egoism—but that's a taste of it."

I said nothing as my mind raced over the possibilities. He had done it. The cocksure little twerp with the executioner's eyes had reversed my argument. But he knew he was in for a struggle—the set of his jaw and hands gripping the chair showed it.

"Alright, interesting. But a little fanatical, no? Afterall, the anti-egoist need not demand that an individual sacrifice himself—but merely that he take into consideration the needs of others, as well as his own. You said before that anti-egoists act egoistically in pursuit of their own happiness. Agreed. And a good job by them, I concur. But that doesn't mean that they relentlessly focus on their own needs to the exclusion of those of other human beings. In many instances, their actions exhibit goodwill, not merely naked self-interest. The tension in human life is not so simple as self-fulfillment versus self-sacrifice, as you suggest, but balancing the needs of self with the needs and requirements of others. When is it morally right to pursue our own goals—and when to accede to the legitimate requests of important others—and why? What principle explains a proper moral decision-making process? These are the questions."

The smile at the corners of his mouth was muted, inscrutable, as if he occupied a corner of the world unbeknownst to me—one fraught with conflicts which I had not lived through, despite my advantages of age and experience.

"Is there goodwill without egoism?" he said so softly he might have been speaking not to me but to someone more integral to his life.

I was caught off-guard by something deeply reflective in his eyes and his voice and held back my initial burst of savage enthusiasm.

"Is there goodwill with egoism?" I countered.

"Egoism as the only basis of a proper goodwill—no genuine kindness in the absence of respect for the self of each individual—that's the theme of my dissertation." He got up. "Thanks, Neil, for helping me clarify it."

He walked to the door.

"You crazy bastard," I said. "You're heading to doomsday."

The initial look of his eyes when he turned back to me was of a man who fed on opposition. With an act of will he tempered it, as if the vitality within was so immense the amount loosed through his eyes must be modulated to protect by-standers. He grinned ruefully.

"You have no idea."

Genevieve Volcker stared at her boyfriend and hardened herself for the task at hand. "Teddy, it must be done. You know that. Why put it off?"

He nodded but said nothing. She saw the haunted, hunted look of his eyes and knew she must tread a narrow line between sensitivity and adamance.

"You're shielding her from the full blow—aren't you?"

He got up from the kitchen table and paced to the other end of her tiny walk-in apartment. She let him go for a moment and then followed him across the threadbare gray carpet, past the fold-out sofa and, resting before it, the tiny television on its metallic stand. She took his arm. Her head came just to his shoulder and, lightly, she rested it there. Of all the persons she knew in her twenty-seven years, this was the one most certain to do what was right—so she waited.

The dairy farm on which she'd been raised in the Wisconsin hinterlands was miles from the hamlet of Crestwood and for many years Madison was happily the largest town she'd ever seen. She had moved to Brooklyn—to the throbbing, pulsing madness of New York City—for but one reason and they both knew, with no need of further discussion, what it was. She remained silent.

"You came here for this relationship," he said. "Because I asked you to. Otherwise you're alone here." He turned to face her.

He stared at her and she smiled, knowing he liked what he saw, had always liked it—the petite stature, the full figure, the sun-streaked brown hair curling just short of the shoulders, the green eyes, the ruddy complexion of generations of outdoors ancestors that no amount of time served on New York's sun-starved streets could dim.

But despite the efforts of his father and sister a chill pervaded his family's home. She visited rarely. If his mother wanted to speak on the weekend, she'd have Amelia call and get on the phone only when Ted was on the other end. Her minimal salary as a temporary secretary and the pittance he made teaching part-time barely paid her rent and tuition in Brooklyn University's Master's program in English. Her boyfriend worked incessantly on his dissertation. Her family and friends were a thousand miles away, in the same nation but a different universe.

She could tell now that he willed himself to hold her gaze.

"I've made your life hell," he said.

I fought back tears as I stared at him, reluctant to spell out who had made whose life hell.

I smiled. He had once described the look as the first hint of Wisconsin spring after a wintry siege that might presage a dawning ice age.

"Teddy," I said. "I've never known anyone dedicated to truth the way you are. It's as much a part of you as your lungs. You don't have to think about who you are any more than you think about breathing. At twenty-nine, you're already more of a philosopher than any of our professors. You think I could want someone else?"

It bathed him—the depth of understanding and appreciation a man could receive only from a woman—it showed in his eyes, in the shape of his mouth, in the lightness of his touch on my cheek. I knew him, had made love to him so deeply, so longingly that vastly more had passed between us than mere bodily fluids. I was thrown back to intimate moments together in which he had bared first his body to me and then his soul—moments conveying tales of years gone by, when an older woman sat for hours with her only son, reading to him from advanced works, his eyes narrowed, intrigued, reading ideas that she did not understand but prayed that he one day would, showing him the joys discoverable in the realm of books.

I closed my eyes as his hands, gently, moved across my face. I had mentioned truth, a good deal of which I had learned in my year in his embattled world. Sometimes it was hard as ice and cold as death. People could be trapped in a war that rained devastation upon them and yet be too cowardly to acknowledge it. War took forms unimaginable to conventional wisdom. But the fatalities were just as real. Someone's heart would be ripped out of their chest and diced into red chunks of meat. I, who knew him so well, was confident it would not be Ted's—or mine. I wrapped my arms around the waist of his tall frame as if the soft shield of my body could effectively ward off the marshaled forces that threatened him.

It was a week later and it had to be done. It was Friday evening after dinner. His sister and parents sat in the living room, together, but light years apart, a family cozy and warm in the glow of electric light and radiated heat but whose chairs and cushioned sofas could have been arrayed in a graveyard. The television was on. Amelia sat at one end of the couch, watching the evening news; his father was in the middle, his head hidden behind the formidable sheets of the daily newspapers; his mother sat at the other end, seemingly watching the news but fretting, absorbed in concerns of her own.

He sat on the other side of the room in a chair next to the television, directly across from his mother. The announcer's smooth voice filled the room, sounding as if the mellifluous harmony of his tones could balance the grim reality of his words—reporting on a civil war in some Third World country that had produced thousands of corpses and tens of thousands of starving refugees. Was this all that went on in the world? He shook his head, trying to clear it of the depressing events that formed his reason for shunning the news. Somewhere, he thought, researchers were reporting progress in their battle against cancer. Somebody was writing an important novel. Inventors were creating devices that would revolutionize men's futures the way the automobile, the airplane, and antibiotics had their pasts. Wasn't this also news?

"Mom," he said, unwilling to any longer avoid naming the obvious truth that had hung over their family's home for at least the past year. "Genevieve and I will be married."

She knew it was coming, had to have known, had agonized over it for months—and her response came immediately.

"You marry that girl," she said slowly, articulating every syllable clearly. "Your mother will be dead inside of a year."

It was Amelia who reacted. "Mom!" It was a cry ripped out of some infernal level of truth that the conscious mind could not often afford to acknowledge—but hellishly real nevertheless.

He did not hear what his sister said. He sat still, feeling like a harpooned whale might with a barbed knife piercing its guts. He had said his piece. He was not going to defend, support, or validate it. There was no choice offered to anyone. It was not an issue for debate, discussion, or disagreement. It simply was, an incontestable truth to which any reflective individual must accede.

But his mother had also said her piece. She was not about to budge and she told Amelia so. Finally, it was his father—who rarely stood up to her absolute control over the family—who interceded to settle it. He had always been there, working conscientiously, paying the bills, supporting, supplying. If neighbors had a problem with their air conditioner, his father fixed it; with their car, he repaired it; with their tax form, he completed it. He was a silent bastion of competence, of sanity—but silent, shadowy, a tenuous presence that now, yearningly, you could almost reach but that somehow eternally receded before you could quite touch. On rare occasions he could rise though and achieve a stature dealing with his family that he perennially held in handling mechanical problems.

Slowly he put down the newspaper. "Rosalind," he said quietly. "That's enough." He did not need a hard-eyed glare when he sought to make a point; he just spoke more softly. She stopped. "Teddy," he said, turning to his son. "Congratulations. Genevieve is always welcome here."

His father and sister rose and hugged him. His mother remained seated. The strength of Amelia's arms around him, and his father's, projected a jolt of warmth from his chest and shoulders to his viscera. But the sensation was incomplete and he yearned for something more. His father and sister resumed their seats and, eventually, the spirit of good cheer subsided in the small room. His mother remained motionless. Her head was turned away and her chin was down. She breathed only faintly. He waited a moment and then started for the door.

"You're selfish," she said. She spoke to the room at large, not just to him, as if the world would finally witness her expose of his true nature. Her voice could not have expressed a contempt more blighting had she affirmed "You're a Fascist." She looked dead at him. "Only you," she said. "That's all there ever was and all there ever will be. Nobody else." She paused and her breath came shakily. "Everyone should know."

Her eyes, as she stared at me, transmitted the wrath of a trusting monarch betrayed. As if her family members were vassals whose lives were governed most effectually by a benevolent despot. Obedience was the queen's rightful expectation; unquestioning service was in the subject's best interest; non-compliance was a treason the ruler never failed to personalize.

Guilt was not my misfortune. Again, a familiar emotion surged through me—as it had so many times in the past—pushing me to stride into her space and crack her across the side of her head. The thought that stopped me, as ever, was not, "She's your mother." It was a torrent of memories cascading to the surface unsummoned—and eternally undenied.

Thoughts flooded my recollection: of Mom, who didn't drive, walking blocks in a frigid, driving rainstorm so that her eight-year-old son could study at the library—she had been drenched as she held the sole umbrella over him; of Mom, fighting single-handedly the pig-headed, entrenched public school administrators who blindly believed another student's lies that her son had cheated—who dropped all else to daily crusade relentlessly in support of her child's character—who finally prevailed when the other kid admitted he'd borne false witness—and who instantaneously dropped the matter, refusing to crucify the culprit once her son's name was unequivocally cleared; of Mom, who desperately wanted her son to attend Brooklyn University, adamantly opposing her husband's financial objections to an out-of-state university: "Jerry, he wants to go to Wisconsin. We'll come up with the money." A thousand such truths existed and could be neither mitigated nor dismissed, regardless of subsequent provocation.

Nor was that all. She had friends and relatives flung across the neighborhoods who had not forgotten a thousand kindnesses across the decades. Ethel Sullivan was merely one such instance. At eighty years of age she owned a huge corner house—and nothing else. Because of the asset, the welfare bureaucrats could not help her—and the neighbors regarded her as a senile pest. "Let her sell the house, take the money, and go into a nursing home," was the consensus up and down the block. But Ethel refused to sell the only home she had ever known. She had no surviving family, no money, and no hope. In the winter, the heat and power were turned off, the pipes froze and burst, the floors and walls were covered with ice. She had no food, no chance, and no place to turn. Mom fed her every morning for three years.

"Rosalind!" Ethel shrieked in her cracked voice as she banged on the family door at the crack of dawn. I had groaned as a teenager in my warm bed as she disturbed my sleep. "Ethyl chloride," I grumbled to myself as I pulled the pillow over my head. Mom never left her out there. She got up, day after day—not without grumbling but with a bottomless reservoir of good will—to help the freezing woman nobody else would aid. Though none of the neighbors pitched in, they did not fail to notice. Mom was loved, sainted, and taken advantage of up and down the block. She heeded neither the praise nor the mistreatment. "Human life is valuable," she said to me. "Support it in every way that you can."

I had reflected on these words over the past year—gazing at Mom but thinking of a younger woman. By what criterion did she decide whose lives to support and whose to sacrifice.

The deterioration came slowly at first, subtly but inexorably, and in fewer than four months his mother rarely rose from the couch. Approaching six months and the wedding, she barely opened her mouth for food. She had always been skinny; now she looked like a famine victim and her dark hair turned inexorably gray. She sat hour after hour, in the living room, the television softly on, all blinds drawn, so it was almost dark, head down, on her chest, barely responsive.

They were on him as the day loomed—the FoM, the Friends of Mom, as Amelia dubbed them—gad flies on a racehorse. They buzzed from the compass's every quadrant, zeroed unerringly to their target, and drove home their barbed stings.

At first, they came at him through me.

"Amelia," Doctor Sussman said. "If he doesn't relent, your mother's life expectancy is measured in months."

"Why tell it to me!" I shouted, sick to heart of her perverse obstinance. "Is that why you called me in here?"

He stared at me silently, his wise old eyes that had seen all things in multiple iterations boring gently into my skull. He had been Mom's doctor for decades, since she was a teenager—and ours—and often I remembered his big hands, always dry, always warm, always gentle on my child's skin, examining me, and the glowing feeling within, the confidence, knowing that he would soon make me well. He had delivered me—and Ted—and so many others—and doggedly he fought a rearguard action against time, trying to save them all, knowing he would inevitably lose, accepting it but struggling incessantly all the same. It was impossible, in his presence, not to experience a heightened sense of competence and life-giving prowess.

"Can't you convince her?" I whispered. I had no need to add, because his eyes inferred that I had already tried, had argued till I was hoarse, till I lost weight, till I was ready to drop after a long day at work.

"It's hard," he said. "Isn't it? Being the child of a saint—and a fanatic."

I did not respond. We both knew it was hopeless. My mother's life could be saved only by her son—who held it in his hands—and I was damned if I would demand, request, or beg that he make the obligatory sacrifice.

Finally, he broke the long silence. "I'll speak to him."

He did. I was not present—and I did not inquire—but I heard the discussion in my head as clearly as if I were a permanent resident of the doctor's office.

Doctor Sussman was kind, patient, persuasive. Ted was respectful, calm, adamant. The doctor did not ask for sacrifice but merely for the sole commodity in which he dealt: time. But he was a medical man speaking to a philosopher about time—outmanned, outgunned, outfought. How much time, Ted asked, until he should take the steps proper to the actualization of his life and Genevieve's. The time would be right—when?—in some future century when his mother accepted the rectitude of his marriage—when a sane person beat sense into her head with a hockey stick or a carpenter's mallet—when she died of non-suicidal natural causes—when?

There was no answer to his questions. All Doctor Sussman could do was shake his hand, wish him and his wife joy, and declaim huskily that he would be proud to usher into the world a new generation of Grossman offspring.

But others did not so gracefully retire into the gloom.

My first cousin resided around the corner and several blocks down. He was forty, lived with his mother, but was nobody's idea of a momma's boy. Short, curly-haired, and hyperactive, he spoke rapid-fire, as though barking orders—while at the dinner table. The small, shrewd eyes probed, never leaving the face or the hands of listeners, judging reactions, body language, tone of voice. He practiced law, befriended moguls, inveigled politicians, delighted dowagers, and angled for a judgeship. His energy flow was formidable, whether dining after midnight with city council-men at Juniors or arguing contentiously at seven am board meet-ings. Barely past thirty he had acquired a reputation as a sharp operator—but was unfailingly compliant to his mother. His mother was worth half a million dollars.

Victor Madoff upheld a single attitude in dealing with others—what's your racket?—and a single person to whom it did not apply: my mother. Her life was so alien to every waking moment of his that he was confounded, clinically fascinated, bedeviled. The beguiler was beguiled. He revered her. She detested him. But she breathed not a word to her sister Sarah.

She confided zero to him. But the calculating eyes missed nothing and, on his weekly visits, quickly observed the deteriora-tion. One task at which his lawyer's acumen excelled was inves-tigation—especially when potential scandal or controversy was involved. He dug up the truth. He said nothing to his aunt. But he said plenty to his cousin.

By the time he was ten years old, Ted was suspicious of his big-time older cousin. He did not speak, he laughed at the prac-ticed bonhomie, he nodded absently, mind elsewhere. But the con-tempt in his eyes, to one who knew him, was manifest. Victor was too shrewd to miss its reality, too unwise to reflect on its causation.

I spent marathon sessions in the office, managing the slow growth of our business into first European and eventually Asian markets. The hours were maddening, the work load brutal, the financial rewards incommensurate. It was not a job, it was a medi-eval devotion. Vaguely I heard the whispers through the office: I was not executive secretary but corporate first lady, Queen Amelia the Devout. Uttered admiringly, enviously, or in tandem—did it matter? Expertise mattered. Sense of accomplishment mattered. Respite from family insanity mattered. And now, Ted was on his own.

Do you intend to kill your mother, Victor said. Or is it you just don't care. His eyes glistened with unfeigned sincerity. Are those the alternatives, Ted asked quietly. She'll die, Victor said. Soon. She will, Ted agreed. Do you know why. Do you even care to. Victor combusted in reaction. She'll die because her son is an inhuman selfish son of a bitch who gives not a rat's ass who gets hurt as long as he gets what he wants. Ted stared at him, the heat in his eyes unmistakable. But for a moment he did not speak. Finally he did. Some might argue, he said, that she's the one who's selfish. But perhaps that's just a confused conventional way to frame the issue. Maybe she'll die not because anyone's selfish but because of its opposite. Did you think of that? Victor was taken off-guard. What the hell does that mean, he snapped. Maybe she's dying, Ted said, because she demands another to sacrifice a huge chunk of life to her. He paused. Maybe she's not as unlike you as you think.

Nor were these the only ones who had their say. But the toughest to face was one who refrained to speak: Dad. The wedding was on a Saturday morning in March. This was one Saturday I did not work. The sun was high in a sky so bright it might have been polished blue china but a bitter wind blew random detritus athwart the avenues and cut through thick layers of clothing to remind hapless wayfarers that winter was yet to abate.

Dad's lips were compressed, thin white chalk lines like those he scrawled on the board at school. He supported his son. He had almost given up attempting to speak to his wife. Slowly, he walked the hallway to the Justice of the Peace. His shoulders bowed under an invisible weight. His sunken eyes looked neither left nor right. It was not clear whether he walked to a wedding or an execution.

The Justice of the Peace was a tall, balding man in judge's robe with the solemn eyes of a priest. Ted and Genevieve stood immediately before him. A few of Ted's friends were there. Genevieve's parents stood next to her, her mom clutching flowers and shedding tears, her dad stalwart, red-faced, stretching his neck, uncomfortable in jacket and tie. Dad stood just behind his son. My mother was not there.

Just before the ceremony, Ted turned around. He shook his father's hand; they stared at each other; and in the moment before they both turned irrevocably to the official—a moment in which my presence was forgotten—it was impossible for silent meaning more unspeakably heartbreaking to be transmitted between family members gathered in joyous celebration.

The Justice of the Peace commenced to speak. We turned our attention to his words.

The three committee members, arrayed around the table like judges, stared at Ted Grossman. They noticed his disheveled clothes and unshaved face, the dark lines under his eyes and the way those eyes darted nervously, distractedly across the room. This was not the way, they thought, to face a dissertation committee empowered to determine the merit of a student's proposal and his worthiness to be advanced to candidacy. Five years of graduate level work, they knew, had been necessary to reach this critical point at which a student was judged qualified—or not—to embark on the gut-jarring, brain-paralyzing, years-long odyssey to write a doctoral dissertation. One of their mentors had confided long ago that a graduate philosophy program was not a means of cognitive training but a process of natural selection—the weak were attrited by the towering, incessant obstacles in their paths— and it took not brains but tenacity to surmount them. The committee understood that it was a panel of experts hand-selected by the philosophy department to determine nothing less than the future of Ted Grossman's career. Virginia Davies and David Volkovonich knew the candidate but slightly. Neil

Rachels alone knew that less than thirty-six hours previously Ted's mother had collapsed in the bathroom and been rushed to a hospital.

Rachels, the chairman, spoke. "You have a statement?"

"I do," Ted said. "A brief one. The purpose of my dissertation is to explore the logical foundations and moral requirements of a genuinely compassionate goodwill of an individual toward his brothers and sisters, i.e., mankind in general."

Rachels couldn't help but notice the eager looks on the faces of his two colleagues. He leaned forward in anticipation of the coming bombshell. Ted rolled on without pause.

"The theme of the book is that any and all forms of human kindness are predicated, implicitly or explicitly, on the theory of ethical egoism"—Rachels heard the sharp intakes of breath around the table—"the theory stating that an individual should always strive to be the beneficiary of his own actions. My title is simply: "Egoism: The Necessary Foundation of Goodwill.""

There was silence.

"That's an indefensible thesis," Professor Volkovonich stated flatly.

I looked at my two colleagues facing Ted Grossman—accomplished ethicists both, steeped in the literature, honorable as winter is long. So steeped in the literature, in the entrenched conventional schools, that it could be the devil's own road convincing them a case could be made for the new. Despite my own book, I found my allegiances shifting toward the challenger.

"Ted," Virginia Davies said. "You've read my essays in Professor Rachels' courses. You know where I stand. Let me cut to the heart. How does one care exclusively for one's own interest and avoid exploiting others?" He started to answer but she waved him off, looking at his left hand. "You're married—am I right?" He

nodded. "A man holding such a moral code," she said, beginning on a familiar theme. "How does he not act like a heel toward women?"

Ted did not answer at first. He seemed absorbed in his own concerns, a man drowning who, no sooner his head emerges from the maelstrom than another quick blow pushes him instantaneously below. "A heel toward women?" he repeated absently. His eyes were elsewhere, seeing something—or someone—not in the room. He looked and sounded lost.

Virginia's reputation as a cruel infighter was legendary, and she smiled—but this time not like an adversary pleased at her foe's discomfiture but like a hostess, gracious, putting a valued guest at ease.

"There's no hurry to answer," she said quietly.

Virginia Davies was a walking, breathing anomaly—albeit a brilliant and impassioned one. She was in her mid-forties, with a child poised to graduate college, but looked years younger. Her red hair, seemingly unstyled, fell casually, gracefully to her shoulders, like a teenage girl's. Her numerous supporters and even more numerous detractors, upon first meeting, were inevitably surprised that so strident a feminist was so attractive a woman. She was divorced, involved in a committed, openly lesbian relationship, and announced unabashedly in elegant terms both verbal and literary that males evolved as uber-competitive creatures inherently, involuntarily impelled to seek mastery over the weak—and to subordinate females to their rapacious, predatory will. She uttered such combustible statements lightly, as simple, self-evident, irrefutable fact. She was rigidly deterministic in theory and sweepingly non-judgmental in practice—uncompromisingly assertive in wording and alluringly sweet in tone—fearless in intellectual strife and clement in treatment of vanquished foes, of whom there were many.

Her son—a tall, lean, good-natured kid—cheerfully despised his mother's intransigent views. A senior at a major university in *the nation's capital, he would soon complete both a bio-chemistry degree and four years of varsity rugby. A sympathetic journalist covering the theoretician's contentious and protean existence for a feminist publication, wrote: "There's Virginia and her dainty lover, wrapped in parkas and blankets on this chilled Fall afternoon, drinking 100 proof flavored liqueur from a flask and wildly cheering as her son delivers a brutal blow in this most aggressively masculine of sports."*

The room was quiet. Ted's head was down and he made no reply. David Volkovonich left Ted to twist in the wind and I was just going to intercede when Virginia spoke again.

"You remember 'An End to Victimhood'?" she asked conversationally, lightening the tension by speaking as though over tea in her Washington Square apartment.

He nodded.

"What does it say?" she asked gently, as though speaking to her own son.

His head came up. "You make many points in that essay. Some psychological, some moral. Your theme is that women must jettison a victim mentality—acknowledge that males have and always will prey on them—look an ugly truth in the eye, stare it down, dispel the fear—and then, by unremitting strength of character, psychology, and purpose, reach the life goals they set for themselves. They must will it to happen." He paused. "At least one of your male critics commented wryly that 'Virginia Davies' writing represents the intersection of feminism and Nietzsche's theory of an ubermensch. One wonders what will be the offspring of such a marriage.'"

She smiled gaily. "One does indeed," she said.

"His essay was titled, 'Three Cheers for the Uber-Wench.'"

Thank you, I said silently to myself. She had gotten him talking, had broken the ice, had enabled him to demonstrate his mastery of sophisticated material, and now he was ready to roll. Quickly I jumped in.

"Ted, do you care to comment on Professor Davies' understanding and assessment of egoism?"

He smiled and, briefly, his face was transformed.

"She argues that egoism is an evolutionary development—theoretical among more sophisticated males, purely visceral among the lumpen masses. One critical consequence and, presumably, part of its motivation is the exploitation of women—and the desire to engage in such."

"What do you think?" I asked. I knew the way his mind worked and had an inkling that he would take the argument in a direction unexpected.

"It's interesting," he said, warming to the task. "How fully Professor Davies embraces an utterly egoistic ethic regarding her exhortations to women. Fulfill your self, she urges in effect, complete your self, do not permit the predatory male beast to impede your progress toward self-actualization. Leaving aside the accuracy of her appraisal of males, the advice to women is a healthy, assertive, generous dose of a proper egoism."

"A 'proper egoism,'" Virginia said, mocking him. "Perhaps, in part, that's true. But women do not characteristically engage in the bitter lone wolf predation of males. Their natural tendency is to bond, to form intimate connections, to establish community. They are not driven by obsessive, instinctual, brutal self-absorption. They sacrifice for others."

"Or call on others to sacrifice for—" he blurted and quickly stopped.

She looked around. "What?" she asked. She noticed something in his eyes. "Or is the question: Whom?"

He shook his head but did not reply. "The exploitation of innocent others is a character issue. It is not hard-wired into the brain,

*genes, or body of an entire gender—literally half the human race—
or even of an individual. It is a matter of principles, of personal
values, and of choice. Empirically, there are any number of men
utterly respectful of the rights of others and women who couldn't
be trusted with a nickel, never mind something of greater value.
Anybody who's lived to be a teenager in this world has discovered
that hard truth. Character is not gender specific."*

*"Ted," David Volkovonich jumped in. "May I? I actually agree
with you on this. Professor Davies and I have had long discussions of this issue." He turned to her. "It becomes quite tiresome to
harp incessantly on the character flaws of an entire gender—as
if the critic herself morphs into the shrill, carping stereotype of
misogynistic fears."*

*She laughed delightedly. "Why, David, that's the nicest thing
you've ever said to me."*

*A grin crinkled the corners of his mouth but he refused to be
sidetracked.*

*"My main criticism of ethical egoism is somewhat different. To
be blunt, the theory is logically inconsistent. In fact, it is so riddled
with logical contradictions as to be incoherent."*

*David Volkovonich made his reputation analyzing ethical
arguments by means of mathematical logic. He was a wunder-
kind: He'd finished college by eighteen, had published a book on
advanced logic by twenty-six, and, at age thirty, had applied his
expertise to the examination of moral philosophy's most intractable
dilemmas. Several years later, he was the youngest full professor
in the history of the philosophy department.*

*On one hand, he seemed too young for his position; on the
other, he looked older than he was. He was medium height with
exaggerated front teeth and dark hair receding away from his
forehead. His wire rim glasses inevitably slipped half-way down
his nose and he peered over the top of them, squinting furiously at*

interlocutors, conjuring images of a myopic chipmunk struggling to discern pebbles from nuts. He shambled aimlessly when he walked and wore mismatching garments out of style on the day they'd been purchased—a decade previous. He would have been a comical figure among the university's irreverent undergraduates but for a single overriding factor: an unwavering self-confidence that emanated, when he spoke, from his voice and person. He commanded a room—all within earshot were listeners, not speakers.

"For example," he began and internally I groaned. I patted myself down, seeking fruitlessly for a calculator. Instead, I reached for a pad and pen. "Candidates x, y, and z," he said. "All seek the presidency of nation A, which is aligned with nation B but opposed by C. The people of C overwhelmingly support candidate z but the people of B prefer candidate y. Half of the people of A seek to placate C but half hate C and support the alliance with B. You follow?" It was clear he batted off such arguments without blinking—he had dozens of them—and it was perennially mystifying to him that others followed his reasoning only with a deal of difficulty.

"So," he continued. "To win the election is in the interest of z, C, and half the populace of A—but opposes the interests of x, y, B, and the other half of A. Similarly but conversely, winning the election advances the interests of y, B, and the second half of A—but undermines that of x, z, C, and the first half of A." He stopped, gazing at Ted, clearly pleased with himself. "You perceive the insolubility of the ensuing dilemma?" Ted stared at him, glassy-eyed, smiling ingratiatingly, hopeful that sheer goodwill might stem the torrent of unleashed variables. I dropped my pen onto the scratch paper.

"Clearly," David Volkovonich said. "The interest of z clashes irrevocably with that of x, y, millions of people in C, and probably millions more in A. Even leaving aside the permutations inherent

*in the election's varying possible outcomes, the fruition of z's pur-
poses necessitates the downfall of those held by y, x, and millions
of people in C and A." He threw up his hands and smiled benignly.
"A moral principle must be universalizable—it must be susceptible
to successful enactment by all. But it is impossible for all parties
to achieve their ends. Someone inevitably loses and makes a sacrifice. Surely, ethical egoism is an abysmal failure regarding the
universalizability criterion."*

*He paused as another thought, even more horrifying, struck
him. "Or do you believe it is morally permissible for z to impose
his will on x and y, to compel their sacrifice, and to ensure the
triumph of the strong, in which case—"*

"No," I interrupted hurriedly. "He believes no such thing."

*"Neil," he said patiently, as if addressing an unruly child. "Why
do you interrupt? Allow the young man to speak for himself."*

*Ted was gathering his thoughts. He was punch drunk under
the barrage of David's arguments, sprawling figuratively across
the ropes, gasping for air—and yet the fierce gleam of his eyes
indicated a fighter far from done.*

*"I'll go you one better," he said to David Volkovonich. "Even
in non-competitive situations, the cherished goals of individuals
are sometimes unattainable. For example, I may yearn to write a
great novel. No implacable foe toils assiduously in an attempt to
thwart my purpose—but I might fail nonetheless, simply because
I do not have the requisite talent or my will is insufficiently strong
or the copious work involved is beyond my capacity. Similarly for
many other examples—building a house or completing college or
earning a black belt in karate. Whether others strive to triumph
over me or not, the possibility of failure is built into life itself. Our
world is not Eden, where all an individual need do is wish and
his desires are instantaneously granted. A person must struggle
to reach an important goal and failure is a perennial possibility."*

"True," I said, commenting before David did. "What's your point?"

"A rational human being accepts facts," he answered. "Failure is a possibility whether a man competes with rivals to reach a goal or does not. We must accept that as part of the given. This does not mean it is wrong for each—or even any—individual to strive for success. On the contrary, it is all the more important to struggle with all one's might, because such represents the only chance to overcome obstacles, obviate failure's haunting possibility, and gain enduring happiness. That the fruition of my aim or yours might be frustrated is neither a problem for egoism nor a satisfactory reason for any individual to renounce a quest for personal values. It is simply the specter of risk, loss and, ultimately, death that is built into the very structure of life itself. In effect, it is not an ethical problem at all—but an onto-logical fact."

David's fingers drummed on the desk. "Interesting," he said. His eyes showed his mind racing over logical possibilities. I moved first.

"Ted," I said. "You know my objections." It was not a question and he nodded. "Briefly," I said. "Close human relations are in an individual's self-interest; they promote personal happiness. But can an egoist be a true friend? Can he put aside his own interest to focus on the well-being of another? To concern himself with the needs of another is altruistic. So to reach the goal of egoism—hap-piness—an individual must give up egoism and become altruistic. Call it the 'paradox of egoism.'"

He leaned forward. "Professor Davies, a few minutes ago you said you would cut to the heart. Let me do the same." He took a breath and looked around the table. "The central point of my writ-ing is to demonstrate the underlying basis of a kindly, nurturing, genuine goodwill of one individual toward others—"

"Which lies in telling each person," David Volkovonich cut in acerbically. "To care about nothing but the gratification of his own will."

"Let him finish," I snapped.

"Yes," Ted said, staring directly at David. "The best thing you can do for another person—the single most important benefit you can provide—is to encourage him/her to achieve his own values, to show him it is morally right to work hard in pursuit of happiness, to relentlessly respect his moral right to do so, and to diligently support his legal right to the same."

"And when your desires clash with the person you're encouraging—what then?" David asked.

"If everyone seeks exclusively the satisfaction of his or her own desires," Virginia added, looking quickly from David to Ted. "Does human life not devolve into an amoral free-for-all in which the strong impose their urges on the weak?"

"Do professors of a dissertation committee," I asked acidly. "Holding power over a student's future life impose their will on him by refusing to let him finish?"

Quickly they both turned to me, six guns of fury blazing in two sets of eyes.

"Enough!" It was Ted who banged the table with his fist, as if he, not I were chairman. He stood up. "One," he snapped. "Human life is not necessarily a struggle of wills seeking to impose themselves on each other. Irrational people conduct themselves in this manner. A rational individual knows that friendship, love, and respectful relations are eminently in his interest. He loves certain others," he said, staring at me. "Advancing their happiness enhances his own. Viewing others as pawns or potential victims is a result of governing your life by whim or impulse—and of abdicating reason. As such, it is first and foremost an epistemological issue, only secondarily an ethical one. Abdicating reason for the guidance of blind urges is not in any human being's long-term self-interest, represents a Siren's allure to personal destruction, militates against a proper understanding of egoism, and is emphatically not the moral code advocated in my book. Is this sufficiently clear?"

He waited for no reply.

"Two," he said. "How to teach genuine goodwill? A tough question, isn't it? This is something I've thought about for years." He paused. "There's someone in my life who embodies it—but, then, who also does not. Who has provided positive inspiration for this point...and negative..." There was something inexpressibly wistful now in his tone—some quality that had traversed the dark moors and provinces of exasperation and emerged on their far side, that had yielded all hostility and frustration, and yet, yearned for some brutally refractory truth to be other than it was. His voice's profound poignancy made one want to reach a hand to his side but its intensely personal nature precluded it.

"My answer?" he said. "We must teach our children and students and others more broadly that each one's life belongs to him/her—that he should cultivate his own values and loves—that he should pursue these indefatigably—that he has the moral and legal right to do so—that he should never, under any circumstances, betray or sacrifice that which is most dear to him—and that it is right for him to help others if and only if he voluntarily chooses to."

A quick glance around the room revealed the puzzled looks of my colleagues' faces and then my attention was riveted back on Ted. "Think about it," he said, articulating words carefully in a room as still as an August night. "Other persons can be an enormous boon to an individual's life—prospective friendship and love are just two of the more obvious benefits. But if I am morally required to sacrifice for others—to give up my own dreams for them—then what? Do they cease being a boon and commence *being a threat?" He paused. It was clear part of his soul was else-where, he was wondering, groping, holding back tears. "What if I love somebody very much, what if they hold some cherished goal that is clearly beneficial in their life, almost self-evidently good? Do I express loving good will to them by demanding they sacrifice their dream to me--or by supporting their quest for self-actualization?"*

"Ted," I broke in, a question germinating in my mind.

"Hold on," he said. "One last point." His eyes showed a ruthless focus on the ideas and the haunted quality, so evident previously, had been shunted to some backstage area of his consciousness— albeit lurking, furtively skulking, not terminally effaced.

"A question rarely gets raised—if ever," he continued. "A vital question, a life-and-death question." He took a breath. "Where is the goodwill toward the poor bastard called upon to sacrifice? Where, for example, is the kindness toward a girl who yearns for education and career but whose culture or family demands that she be exclusively a mindless, will-less drone obeying their com-mands? Where is the generosity toward a young man drafted into the military and called upon to sacrifice years, perhaps life itself for the nation—or whose family demands that he relinquish career choice to follow in his dad's profession—or whose mother..." his voice, after gaining energy and passion was losing both, as if it had raced downhill only to find on level ground that it had depleted all fuel supply..."whose mother..." he repeated and stopped.

Virginia Davies' head snapped up, ignoring her notes and colleagues, staring intently at Ted.

"Whose mother—what?" she asked. For a moment, her eyes and voice were of someone more than a conscientious professor.

Silence permeated the room and Virginia did not repeat her question but let it hang, unanswered, in the stillness. Ted pressed against the table, as if he could go no further, his lean frame slumped, spent, as though exhausted by incessant struggle on multiple fronts against implacable foes. Slowly, with both hands, he pushed himself upright.

"Nothing," he said to the mother across the table from him.

He slid his papers into a briefcase and zipped it closed. Mechanically, he placed it under his left arm. Slowly, he moved toward the door.

Standing at the exit, he turned back to us. "That's a taste of my arguments. There's more—but now you have the basic idea." His eyes, when he spoke, moved slowly from one of us to another, politely acknowledging all, and yet anxious to be elsewhere. He turned the handle, stepped across the threshold, and was gone from sight.

He eased shut the conference room door. He walked down the hall, moving rapidly now but feeling like he crawled, past the elevators and to the stairs. He was depleted and yet had to be in motion. Behind him he heard a door bang and a voice sing out: "Ted, wait! Ted!"

He turned around. Neil Rachels hurried toward him. He waved his arm in dismissal.

"Not now," he said. Rachels caught but a glimpse of reddened eyes.

He started down the stairs.

Sixteen flights down in which he encountered no one but had faces with him incessantly and voices that would not depart his skull. He wanted to run when he reached West Eighth Street but he could escape neither the scornful expressions nor the critical words. He walked rapidly to the Sixth Avenue subway. The ride he had made so many times—forty-five minutes to Kings Highway—was a blur. He remembered nothing and looked forward to nothing. It seemed he departed a fiasco and moved toward a debacle.

He came down the stairs of the elevated and walked to the hospital. Half-way there, guided by muscle memory and rote, he found himself head down, seeing naught and caring to see no more. He stopped on a corner, under a streetlight, cars whisking past in its harsh glare. He leaned on the light post for support and, slowly, raised his head. He focused his eyes, willing himself to see the bare trees, the refuse strewn garbage cans, the grimy, muddy snow.

"Head up," he said.

He was surprised by the immense weight his skull had become and at the perverse will it displayed in seeking to roll off his shoulders and bounce in the gutter. He felt certain that if either of his shoulders dipped for a moment he would irrevocably lose it. He walked down the avenue to the hospital with nothing in his awareness but the straining attention to maintain an erect posture.

As soon as he arrived it was clear that his mother's life expectancy was measured in days—perhaps hours—not years. She rested comfortably in her hospital bed and was in no pain. She smiled when he entered the room.

"My sonny boy," she said to the attending nurse.

But her color was ashen and she was so weak she could barely raise her arm. The doctors suspected some debilitating muscle disease. It hadn't helped that she had barely moved for months.

His father sat motionless in a chair and neither looked out the window nor anywhere else. He just stared, a man who only now realized that the death of his spouse of forty years was imminent. His wife's fanatic, monomaniac obsession with her son, and his own bottomless lethargy had, years since, irremediably fractured their relationship; neither Ted, nor anyone his age had ever witnessed physical affection between them—

although Amelia swore, and nobody doubted her, that once, returning home in the evening, she had discovered them holding hands on the couch. But she had been there, every day, in all of her aberrant splendor—and now she would not be.

However attenuated an emotional presence his father had been, the stolid square bulk of him was a perpetual physical presence, offsetting the birdlike, chirping nervousness of his mother. Instantaneously, Ted saw that this, too, was gone irrevocably. His father sat hunched forward, his spine bent in the manner of a gnarled tree that had withstood one winter too many. He barely smiled at his son's entrance, and, for a moment, Ted wanted to join him in a state of apparent numbness. Amelia, mentally the toughest, stood at the foot of the bed, talking softly to her mother. Her eyes were puffy but her shoulders were square. She squeezed Ted when he walked in and then resumed her conversation.

Hours went by in which the little family maintained its grim vigil. Eventually there was nothing to say. Amelia's eyes met his, eager to hear regarding the dissertation, but there would be a time for that. His mother dozed fitfully. After a while, she stirred.

"There's something I must say before the end," she said.

A dying person has no time for untruth, for there is no further time to set things right. I looked at him and sent the others away.

"Jerry," I said. "Amelia, I need time alone. Please wait in the hall." Ted got up too to leave. "You stay," I said to him. I patted the bed at my side, showing him where to sit and he did.

"They'll carry me out of this place. You know that, don't you?"

A clock ticked on the table next to the bed. It seemed inordinately loud in that confined space, and, momentarily, Ted looked at it. But I was too focused to pay it any heed.

"Don't look so tragic," I said. "Doesn't part of you want to be rid of me?"

He looked me straight in the eye. "Yes," he said without flinching—and I felt a last jolt of joy shoot through me at the harsh words my ears heard and the straight spine my eyes saw and the deep truth my heart registered.

"Mom isn't always right," I said. He did not respond, just sat there staring at me, knowing now what was coming, knowing it was long overdue, and ready to accept it as love, as homage, and as justice.

"You remember all the times I called you 'selfish,' every instance I berated you for doing the things you wanted despite Mom's disapproval? I'm surprised the word 'selfish' isn't branded across your forehead like some supernatural stain that only divine intervention could efface. You remember?"

"I'll never forget." His voice was grim.

"Never forget—right. You know why?" He smiled, the lines of his mouth faintly contemptuous, like he had at me so many times since he was a teenager, and so many times I had wanted to strangle him for it but now I only wanted to press him to me as if by physical contact I could transmit the last micro-drop of my failing strength to him, a spiritual transfusion, and send him away, a stand-up man whose rigid backbone and purified soul contained a last element of his mother's best—and then expire happily, knowing his future was brighter than his past.

"I was right," I said. "You are the most selfish creature who ever tormented a mother's soul. But maybe it's a mother's soul responsible for the torment. Perhaps it's the mothers who need to revise their principles, not the sons—who need to re-think the sanctity of motherhood, including its sacred right to govern her child's life even when he's old enough to govern it himself and wise enough to live it more fully than she ever lived hers. Maybe there's some

core element in some persons, some nugget of truth they latch onto when very young that tells them to live, to do it their way, to wrap their arms around existence and wring it of all the passion, the experience, the joy they can—and this is the only irreversible moral truth—to live—and this is what must be fanned, encouraged, loved, nurtured, and no sacrifice of it demanded or requested or ever tolerated. Maybe this is what mothers need to learn and then their children who become clergy and professors and politicians might learn it too."

I stopped. I saw something in his eyes that I had seen so often in childhood but had seen precious little of for many years and had forgotten the joyousness of the look—my joy—of the look in his eyes not of contempt or dismissive repudiation or, worst of all, resigned dutifulness, but of a burgeoning, laughing life force inextricably linked to me in approval, in gratitude, in undying appreciation of Mother's undying support. This is what I had lost, what I had shamefully thrown away and never realized the sobbing depths of my despair until I retrieved it, finally, when I had a foot planted firmly in the grave and the other on its way down.

"Your wife..." I said, saying those two words aloud for the first time. But I needed to say no more, for he nodded in understanding and placed a single finger across my lips, a light touch but one, to me, reminiscent of the clinging joyous embraces of his boyhood.

I was almost spent. The expended energy had nearly finished me. But I wasn't quite done.

"Not finished," I said. "Redundant to tell you something you've always known but you should know that your ignorant mother learned it, however belatedly. Live, Teddy, live to the fullest, do it your way and achieve, live in joy, live knowing that this is the one sacred moral truth, and if you ever have children tell them their grandmother said they should only be as good as their father—and don't ever parent them the way you were."

He smiled. "You're wrong. I'll parent them in many ways like I was. Not all—but many."

"One last thing. The dissertation, I know how hard it is. Finish it, no matter what it takes, finish it. For yourself, for yourself, for yourself...but maybe...just a little bit for me... Promise."

His smile was no longer fully gentle but the warm part of it was directed at me.

"I will finish it. Whatever it takes, I promise."

I had nothing left to say. I couldn't speak it if I did. I just lay quietly, gazing at him. There was a depth of exquisite sensitivity in my son that I had angrily denied but had always known to be there and he showed it again now. He went into the hall and got his father and sister, knowing that I wanted them back.

They stood together at the foot of the bed. My heart broke for Jerry, who I knew would never recover. But as I looked at Amelia and Ted, at the light in their eyes and the chiseled features of their faces and the upright sweep of their shoulders, I knew, whatever my dying words to my son, that shame would not be my legacy. I knew, by God, that I had done something right. And even if I wasn't fully responsible for it, I was taking part of the credit and taking it with me. It was something nobody could take from me.

By midnight he was exhausted and slept soundly through the night. Early in the morning he boarded the rush hour subway and sweated, despite the outside chill, amidst its jostling, red-faced, rush-hour crowds. He got off at West Fourth Street. He walked to the university and took the elevator to the sixteenth floor of the Humanities Building. Professor Rachels was in his office.

"Neil," he said.

"Ted," the professor said, banging his desk. "I spent two hours discussing it with them after you left. It's no use, they won't approve it. Impressed?—without a doubt. They admired your arguments, your originality, your toughmindedness under intensive scrutiny. They were even somewhat contrite about the manner in which they treated you. But ultimately they believe the thesis so misguided as to be untenable. There's no sense bringing it to defense." He paused. "But I have a suggestion."

"So do I."

"What's yours?"

"I did not wait for approval to begin writing. I continue it. I complete it. I then perfect and polish it. When it's ready, I publish it."

"With whom?"

"With Dunlop-Starrett."

Neil Rachels smiled and showed a lot of teeth. He looked more like a wolf than a hawk when he did that.

"I hoped you would say that."

We sat silently for a moment. In Ted's eyes, in my glance, and in the air between us hung recollection of the spirited battles fought over the past five years and of the truce, deeply respectful on each side, we had reached.

"I called Melanie Perkins last night," I said. The interest in his eyes was manifest. "She's the chief editor at Dunlop—worked with me on my book. She's extremely interested in your project. So interested, in fact, that you have a meeting scheduled with her at 10 am a week Friday. You can make it?"

"Try and stop me."

"I won't try—I'm afraid you might rip my lungs out." I paused. "I've come to agree with you a little bit. But mostly not. What does that matter? You have important things to say, you say them well, and the profession needs to listen. The publication of your book

will make you an accomplished ethicist—and still young. How old are you?"

"Twenty-nine."

"You'll be thirty or thirty-one by the time your book is out. Perfect—a rite of passage in every way."

I have more books to write."

"Damn right you do—you prolix bastard. You'll come to out-shine your own mentor." He grinned. "One day, the Philosophy Department, in its immense wisdom, will recognize your contribution and will accept one of those books as your doctoral thesis. You'll receive your degree then. That is, if your illustriousness deigns to still desire it."

His grin vanished. "I desire it." He paused. "I promised somebody I would complete it."

There was a slight wheeze to his voice, as if the words squeezed out past an obstruction in his windpipe. I knew some conflict roiled his family but Ted was all business and had told me precious few details. He had married his college girlfriend, his mother was ill, and the rest I had to guess. When I had told him I was there for him anytime, he thanked me but was close-mouthed regarding intimate matters. His wife and his sister, he said, were the ones he confided such issues to—so I let it be. The way he could focus, could push aside personal strife and write was tough-minded and professional as hell—and had to be respected. I feigned surprise.

"Oh? The great supporter of egoism does something for somebody else?"

He did not dismiss me nor banter nor chide me for points he had made a dozen times. He spoke simply.

"Some people in your life are special," he said to me for perhaps the hundredth time. But now, some quality to his voice, something hesitant but cutting as a winter wind, made the words sound fresh. "You do for them, you do for you. It's one."

I sat motionless, not wanting to speak too soon, to speak over those words. I let them hang in an atmosphere graced by the most intimate touch I had experienced with him.

"Yes," I said. "I understand. But perhaps it takes a long time for certain points to sink in."

"Right," Ted Grossman said with a faint touch of bitterness. "For you and certain other people."

They laid her in the grave on a cold day in March, the wind driving skittish clouds across a gray sky. His mother had kept her promise; it was less than a year since he had announced his engagement. With Genevieve on his arm, providing support, he entered the cemetery, walking slowly behind his father and Amelia. In front of the fresh earth where his mother would rest forever, her sisters nodded silently at the pretty *shiksa* they met for the first time. His Aunt Ava, his mother's youngest sister, hugged her. "I'm so sorry we had to meet like this," she said. "I had no idea." It was left to him to deliver the eulogy.

Ted got up in front of the little group of mourners. For a moment he was silent and merely stared at us. He had never before looked like he approached thirty but now, for the first time, he did. Tall and lean, his dark hair stirred slightly in the breeze. I had one second to realize that my little brother had become a man and then he began.

"Nobody ever loved their family more than Mom did. But nobody ever made a more destructive error." Our family stood in the front row, with friends and neighbors fanning out behind them. By now, the secret Mom had kept for months was freed from its prison and making its way through the assembly. Genevieve, no doubt, could feel people staring at her. But the hardy

Germanic girl from the north country ignored them. She stared at her husband.

"If Judaism had saints, Mom could be canonized." He paused. "But for saints, too, comes a reckoning." They knew now, I could see it in their eyes. Her friends and family knew what was coming— the full truth—and with a sense of justice so often displayed in moments of bitter duress, they braced to hear and accept it.

"Mom had a bright dream for her son—a man of character and accomplishment. And she had a nightmare vision, too—of her son at 30, 35, 40 years old, living at home with his mommy. Such a dutiful son the professor would be, a momma's boy, eschewing all women but one. And she never saw, until the very end, the irrevocable, irresolvable, irreconcilable clash between the two components of her dream: the man of stature she envisioned would not subsist as the nebbish she intended."

They cried now—they knew it was true—all but two of us: Genevieve, who, with no hate in her soul, knew her ordeal was over—and me, who could not have loved Mom more but who had long ago faced down and accepted the full truth about her.

"So she loved her family –and tore it apart. She worshiped her son—then ensured that he would hate her. She did reverse alchemy—she transformed a wedding into a funeral, gold into base metal, joy into tragedy. And she did so much with such kindness, devotion, and goodwill that nobody—including one who is her twisted victim—could ever stop loving her."

He couldn't go on. It was obvious in his face. You've said enough, I thought. Shut it down. But he'd always been a finisher. He was daunted by neither his dissertation committee nor his mother and his concluding words, although addressed to us, were really a final private conversation between him and Mom. A private discussion with her—and a salute across the unbridgeable chasm separating living from dead.

"She fought against life—and so wrought her own death. But in dying, she came alive. She saw that a man's loves must not be denied—so she affirmed them. As she expired, she breathed a benediction to life. Her dying word was: 'live'—and because of it, in death she achieves immortality. As she faced the end, she saluted the beginning and in that moment she performed a proper alchemy. She turned a funeral into a celebration, suffering into joy, death into life. She's gone but is as alive in Amelia and me as if she stood, proudly, by the graveside kvelling that her son will write books. Will I ever return to the cemetery? Not while I live. Why should I? It makes no sense to pretend that those living are dead. She's with me when I face my defense committee—she's with me as I write my books—she is with me now as I bury her. I could not expunge her presence if I tried and I will not try. In the end I return where I must, to the only word that has genuine meaning and so forms a proper beginning: 'Live,' my mother said. 'Live.' Who's the philosopher now?"

He stepped down. With dry eyes he gripped the shovel and handed it to Dad. Dad threw in the first shovelful of dirt. Ted threw in the second, then stepped away. Genevieve took his arm and they started for the parking lot. It was clear he did not want to speak to anybody. But moments later I caught them, standing in front of him more angry than mournful.

"You didn't kill her," I said loudly, heedless of who heard, determined that this last piece of insanity be excised from the ledger. "I don't know if you feel it or you don't. She was the best mom ever—and she was a lunatic. Her craziness killed her. Not you." I stopped. For the first time—on the day we buried my mother— tears started in my eyes and I reached to him as if he were not my little brother but my own son. "Teddy, you see that—don't you?" I took the lapels of his jacket preparatory to shaking him but he smiled—a glowing rainbow at cyclone's end, a radiant smile like

his mother's on her best days. "Amelia," he said, willing solemnity back into his eyes and the lines around his mouth. "Socrates exhorted his loved ones to celebrate his death as a renewal of his existence." He paused. "Minus belief in a transcendent world, Mom told us the same thing."

I had nothing else to say and I rested my head on his chest and he put his arms around me and I cried savagely for the first time in years, not knowing whether I cried for his loss or his gain— or for my mother's or my own or if there was even a difference. It took a long time for my tear ducts to empty. I felt Genevieve waiting patiently and people's eyes on me as they passed. But Ted and Mom were not the only philosophers in our family. I had gained wisdom too. There were many ways of killing yourself and my mother had chosen one. There were other forms. Never conceiving a dream is another. Conceiving one and betraying it is yet another. I was surprised but elated to find an absence of bitterness when I reflected on a form of living death so rarely identified: demanding the sacrifice of his dream from a person you love. For one final moment I held him in my arms as if I were not his big sister but the best of the life force that had animated a woman much more important to his life.

Paid in Full

I never liked Joey Portabello. He was too smart to be the dirtbag he was. Fat and wet and soft – and smart as hell. But then again, I'm a lawyer. Plenty of people think the same of us.

At lunchtime, Joey walked into my office on 86th Street, looking to beat a four-year standing rap on failure to pay child support.

"Tommy," he said, as if he'd known me for years. "You think you can find a smaller office than this pillbox?"

"You want a big office, try Goldman and Lieber on Bay Parkway." I lowered my voice. "And it's Mr. Ruggiero to you."

He dried his face with a starched white handkerchief. He had a large bald spot running back from his forehead that he tried to cover with a few strands of long hair. It glistened like the Brooklyn streets when it rained.

"Sure," he said easily, unoffended, and proceeded to outline his story.

"Why don't you just pay for your kids?" I asked when he was done. "You got an income."

He laughed in apparent good humor. It was a hearty sound – but the smile never quite reached his eyes. "And it's mine.

It don't belong to those little bastards. Let them get a paper route."

"That what your dad said?"

It was clear within a few minutes that Joey Portabello was not easily ruffled. He had a quiet calm that did not desert him under the fire of verbal abuse. He snored when he breathed, he had rolls of fat that extended to his eyebrows, and he had eyes like a bottomfish. But he had an unperturbed confidence, almost a dignity, and he would not crack under the pressure of cross examination. Twenty years of courtroom experience told me that.

"My father was a homicide investigator. Taught me to notice things."

It was true. His fish eyes moved slowly but they missed nothing. The NYU diploma on the wall, the picture of Maria and me on the desk, and next to it the drawing of daddy that Jennifer had done for me – those dead eyes slowly registered all of it.

Nor did they miss the look in Karen's eyes when she returned from lunch and opened the door to my office.

"Tommy," she said, before noticing Joey's bulk in the chair in front of my desk. "Mr. Ruggiero," she corrected herself, starting over smoothly, flashing the brisk professional smile of an efficient secretary. "The file on the Castellano case has come in by courier."

Karen Weisfeld was only twenty-seven, almost twenty years my junior, but had already worked for me for nine years, since the day – just two weeks after she'd graduated from Lafayette – that she'd strode into my office and announced: "Criminal cases need a tough secretary."

I had looked at her slender figure and delicate features and almost laughed – until I noticed something about the eyes. Still, I'd been dismissive.

"You want to go from dolls to dirtbags? I don't think so."

"Dolls?" She hadn't bothered to smile in contempt. "Try bats and hardballs. My father was a baseball coach. I was an only child. Want to see the bruises?"

It was her total lack of humor that had sold me. The minimum of makeup – the severe black pantsuit – the short, vaguely masculine haircut – all had added up to a serious, almost grim package.

But there was nothing grim about Karen Weisfeld. Nor masculine either.

Now, my client looked at her thoughtfully. It wasn't a leer – it was far more calculating than lecherous – but it had an undertone that I couldn't quite place, one that caused something to catch momentarily in the back of my throat. When he looked carefully from her to me to the pictures on my desk, I was late to grasp where his thoughts were going. But Joey Portabello did not make his living by being slow on the draw.

I had forgotten about him six weeks after rejecting his case. But Joey didn't forget much.

Again, it was lunchtime and Karen was out of the office when, this time, the phone on my desk rang. I cut him off as soon as I recognized the voice.

"I told you. I don't defend deadbeats. Kiss off."

"Tommy, Tommy," he laughed good-naturedly. "That's no way to treat a friend."

I said good-bye, and was about to hang up when he said softly, slowly, "Maria and Jennifer might want you to talk."

There was a long moment of silence.

"How do you know the names of—" I began, my voice suddenly hoarse, but smoothly he cut me off.

"Tommy, it's what I do. It's OK." The easy going laugh was back. Joey Portabello was obviously a friend of mankind.

"Seven-thirty," he said. "Magnotta's Clam House." Then his voice wasn't as friendly. "Alone." He hung up.

I arrived just before 7:30 and waited almost half an hour for him. As I sipped red wine, I glanced at the other customers. A working class crowd. A few guys in denim and steel-plated boots. A young couple wearing sweat suits and running shoes. As much beer sold as wine. But there were a few guys in dress shirts and ties, so I didn't stand out. It was pushing eight when he sauntered in.

He wore a belted navy raincoat over a rumpled dress shirt and jeans. His smile was genuine but muted.

"We got business to discuss, don't we?" he asked.

"You got thirty seconds to tell me why you've been prying into my family. I don't like the answer, I re-structure your cheekbones." Four years in the Army had whipped me into a physical condition that I had maintained. Eighteen previous years of growing up in Brooklyn had taught me to despise every form of bully, thug, and victimizing creep. I had built a reputation of defending only those I genuinely believed innocent. My practice was small.

He didn't laugh or smile in his usual good-natured bonhomie. He merely nodded and reached for a packet inside his trench coat. Before it hit the table in front of me, I knew the contents.

The pictures of me and Karen were good. Dancing at Benvenuto's after victory in the Montefusco case. Kissing goodnight in the front of my Celica outside her apartment on 65th Street. Registering at the Rialto as Mr. and Mrs. Gianelli. Maria would have everything she never wanted to see. Divorce was inevitable. Perhaps murder.

I looked thoughtfully at the prints.

"Maria Lodato-Ruggiero is a possessive woman," he said softly as if he empathized with my pain. "Even though charges were dropped twenty-three years ago, she still cracked her ex-boyfriend with a clock radio when she suspected him of—"

"—Yeah, she did," I interrupted. Poor bastard wasn't even guilty. .

"Didn't stop her from opening up the side of his face," he said, as if reading my thoughts.

I didn't need to talk to him anymore. I got up from the table. "You're a wealth of information."

"Good to know cops."

"Glad to see their investigations put in service of a good cause."

He beamed, flashing a genuine smile a Hollywood star might kill for.

"The Joey Portabello Retirement Fund. Proud to have you as a sponsor."

It wasn't until three days later—when I got his demand for payment in the mail—that the plan occurred to me. His schedule for $10,000 in cash by tomorrow, followed by another ten K upon receipt of the photos in two weeks was handwritten—in print, not script, unsigned, and bore no return address. It had a New York City postmark. The terse note could not be pinned on him—but still, a paper trail was evidence. With evidence, a legal case could be built.

Detective Finelli of Brooklyn Vice stared long and hard at Joey's note. He let me tell my story without interruption.

"You tell your wife *first*," he said. "She screams, she threatens to murder you, then to divorce you. You apologize on your knees. Eventually, she thinks you're a hero."

I smiled. He had it all dead on. Except the last.

"It's possible that after you prosecute Portabello for blackmail, you prosecute Maria for murder."

Jon Finelli looked like one of my grammar school priests. He was tall and thin, with a high forehead accentuated by a receding hairline. Briefly, I wondered if Father Barone was still alive. His kindness had been undeniable. His commitment to moral principle even more so. Finelli's expression was thoughtful.

"That bad?"

My silence gave him all the answer he needed.

"That bad," he said.

Maria did not threaten me with death or even with bodily harm. In fact, she didn't raise her voice. She sat quietly at the kitchen table listening, as Jennifer slept soundly in her bedroom upstairs.

"This has been going on for years," she said quietly. It wasn't a question.

"You knew?"

She brushed aside my surprise.

"Other women?"

"No," I answered honestly. There'd been only Karen—for more than two years.

She looked toward the stairs leading up to the master bedroom. Her eyes were dry, but her voice was so hushed I strained to catch the words. "Two years I've slept alone."

Though I had utterly neglected her, Maria Lodato remained the most beautiful woman I'd ever known. Her thick black hair cascaded in waves to her shoulders, its dark hue heightened now by her white robe. The pain of impending loss filled me as I looked between the robe's folds at the breasts I knew so well, the surprisingly full breasts for so petite a frame. Her bone structure was so dainty, I had once—long ago—worried about doing her bodily harm. A series of intense nights had quickly dispelled that fear. In her mid-forties now, she looked fifteen years younger.

I wanted to touch her hair and run my hand over the softness of her cheek but was too cowardly to disturb the delicate equilibrium we had reached. She sat alone with her memories as the kitchen clock ticked loudly. Finally, she looked at me, and some quality in her eyes, though soft, proved stronger than any other impulse.

"I won't throw you out," she said simply. "You're Jennifer's father. You can have the couch in the living room until you find your own place." Slowly, with sad dignity, she rose from the table and left the room.

It was only hours later, in the dead of night, that I was awakened by the uncontrollable sobs from upstairs.

It was dark on the basketball courts of Kelly Park. At one o'clock on a December morning, the wind scattered random sheets of newspaper across the hard tarmac and even the Brighton line, running through the park on its high embankment, whipped past quickly, as if its shortened string of cars sought refuge in the bright safety of the yards.

The local was due in the Avenue U station at 1:05. I knew there wouldn't be another train for thirty-five minutes.

This time, he didn't keep me waiting. The lights of his car flashed on, and he whipped around the corner from the side street to pull in behind me on Avenue S. He stepped out of his car just as the train's taillights disappeared behind the row of houses on the south side of the street. I was surprised by what he drove.

He strode toward me confidently. As he approached, I could see that this time he wasn't smiling; he looked businesslike and calm.

"A Honda Civic? A big-shot like you should drive a Lexus."

There was no raillery in his response, only the simple ring of sincerity. "I save for the future, Tommy. I don't blow my dough."

"A wise policy."

I handed him the cash—$10,000 in hundreds—while he turned over the envelope with the original photos and the negatives.

"But," I went on. "Given your long-term future, you won't need much dough."

He was too smart not to immediately grasp my meaning.

"Tommy, don't do it," he whispered. "We'll both go down."

I felt rather than saw the shadows coming at us from all sides.

"Yeah," I said.

The wind seemed even colder as they hustled a handcuffed Joey Portabello out of Kelly Park.

Inevitably, though, he extracted his pound of flesh. By the time we stood in Brooklyn Criminal Court for his sentencing, my divorce was almost final.

Maria had been generous but firm.

"I'll give you no trouble about Jennifer," she had said, her dark eyes calm, staring into mine. "I want her to see her daddy every weekend. But no adulterer is ever going to live with me." She had turned away.

Looking now at Portabello as he stood before the judge, I was impressed. What little jail time he had served seemed to agree with him. Though his weight was the same, he seemed healthier, not as soft, as if he'd been working out. He wore a suit, not prison greens -- gray, pin-striped and fitted. His hair was short.

I, on the other hand, had lost weight. After Maria had ended it, I'd had little appetite. Jennifer and I spoke every day on the phone—but seeing my ten-year old daughter only on week-ends was tough.

Mostly, I was reminded of my ex-wife wherever I turned. A slender woman with long dark hair passed me on the street—she looks like Maria, I thought. A crime story in the *New York Post* told of a victim who was forty-five—Maria's age, I remembered. A woman called regarding a case involving family members—her daughter's name was Maria.

My sister, who adored her niece, struggled to control her exasperation when I told her.

"Nobody'll ever be able to replace Maria?" Angela asked. "Then why'd you neglect her—and why in hell did you cheat on her?"

I had no answer. It seemed so pointless to say that after ten years of marriage I had taken her as much for granted as the walnut dresser in our bedroom; that I was utterly immersed, day after day, in my work, with office routine—and with Karen, my sole employee, who was as fiercely loyal to me as she was quietly competent. I had dragged her into this sordid mess, too.

She would stand by me until the end. Even Maria's reputation hadn't scared her. But I had let her go, sending her off to Goldman and Lieber—who had long coveted her—with a glittering recommendation. She was still in her twenties. She deserved a shot to learn what else was available in the world.

"I'll wait for you, Tommy," she had said on her last day. "Whatever you put yourself through, whatever hell you make yourself pay. I'll be there when you come out the other side."

Her short pixie hair-do had always contrasted with her hard eyes. But now her eyes, too, were soft, filled with all the words she wanted to say, had never said, couldn't say. Maybe now would never say. I had squeezed her shoulder, then walked her to the door.

She had turned to me on the threshold. "It was wrong," she said. "If Maria wants to beat the hell out of me, I won't defend myself." Her voice got softer but somehow more resonant. "But I would never not do it." Her head could not have been higher as she left my office.

I proceeded to work harder than ever—and though, as a consequence, I now had more clients, I still hadn't hired a new secretary.

The judge looked from on high at the convicted black-mailer. He let the hush over the room linger for a moment.

"It's a despicable occupation, Mr. Portabello, to cash in on other people's misery, even though self-induced." He paused, letting his words sink in. "I'd put you away for decades, if your sentence were left to my discretion. But since this was a first conviction—indeed, a first arrest—the maximum the law permits me to impose on you is five years at Ossining Correctional Facility."

Joey Portabello was going up the river.

The judge knew something he didn't add—and the convicted felon knew it, too. Previous victims—more than one—had now summoned the courage to step forward. All it had taken was one to show the way. The DA's office had several cases pending. Portabello's tenure as a guest of the state was likely to be protracted.

He walked past the star witness on his way to the joint. He still had a little swagger left.

"Not for long," Finelli had said to me. "Once his real time starts, the grind'll wear him like a six-year old tire."

He stopped in front of me. He looked long and hard.

"You're skinny, Tommy. You lost everything, didn't you?" He shook his head, as if sad at the foolishness of an old friend. "You didn't listen to me. I would have left you alone." He was handcuffed, but made a gesture as if to pat my arm in sorrow. "For twenty thousand bucks," he whispered. "Now you got to pay a much higher price."

The guard behind him shoved him forward and he started for the exit.

"I've lost everything," I said to his departing back, but under my breath, too softly for him to hear. "Have I?" I said. As smart as he was, he wouldn't understand.

When I reached the stairs leading to the street, the sun hit me full in the face. Automatically, I reached for my shades. But I stopped. Even though I squinted in the June glare, I let the intense light hit me flush. It was Thursday. In two days, I'd see Jennifer. Though Maria was cordial, it tore at me to see her every weekend. My grieving process would take years.

But somewhere out there—I looked from the top of the stairs south toward Bensonhurst—was a mop-top secretary with a backbone of Brooklyn steel. She'd vowed to wait for as long as it took. I was betting that she would.

The Tough Get Going

Frankie Pearson was the toughest dude I ever met. He'd beat your ass in a New York second for a look he didn't like. He had a magnificent temper, volcanic in its sudden-death explosiveness.

Once when we played ball in Marine Park, he took exception to my park butcher style of defense, hacking him brutally on his slashing drives to the rim. I had him down ten-nine in a one-on-one game to eleven, and, never having beaten him, wasn't about to let up. Frankie fired the ball to the ground, where it ricocheted like a shot off of the asphalt court, careening as high as the cyclone fence that stood behind the hoop, towering over it.

"F--king Danny!" he roared, his pale face a fiery red.

I prayed, though nobody in my family was particularly religious, that his years-long friendship with me would spare me the brutal beating he'd characteristically dish out in such a setting. I said nothing, just stood there, chest heaving. For one second, the translated words of Father O'Donnell, my former Latin teacher at St. Thomas Prep, flashed through my head: "Those who are about to die salute you." Frankie turned away, his huge hands balled into fists, not to lash out but to refrain from it, and veins stood out like wires on his neck. When his breathing returned to normal, I picked up the rock and handed it to him.

"Your ball," I said.

He proceeded to come from behind and beat me—like he had done so many times before.

We were hoops mad in those late teen-age years, living with our families and unconcerned to work more than part-time jobs. I flipped burgers for several years at a fast food dump on Nostrand Avenue, whereas Frankie, though a competent mechanic, was unable because of various run-ins to hold any job longer than a few weeks. We'd grown up six houses down from each other on Burnett Street. I'd graduated from St. Thomas Prep; Frankie had been expelled from Holy Cathedral Academy, enrolled at the local public school—Sherman—dropped out, and, at seventeen, joined the Marines. Six months later, he received a dishonorable discharge and a broken cheekbone for slugging it out with a D.I. on Parris Island. Rumor had it that the D.I. didn't look so hot either. With Frankie often at my side, nobody ever messed with me at the park.

All day, we'd play ball at the courts on the Stuart Street side of the park, adjacent to the junior high school, and at night chase skirt in Frankie's Camaro. At six-foot and a lean one-eighty, Frankie was explosive both in slicing to the hoop and in getting off the ground. No one doubted that if he could've stayed in school, he would have been all-city. But with long brown hair flopping in a Maravich look, and with features as chiseled as his chest, he didn't need a coach to achieve all-city status with the babes.

Leah McCaskey lived on 40th Street in the maze of Irish-filled row houses that clustered off of Church Avenue just a couple of blocks from the cemetery. She was dark-eyed, black-haired, pretty as a pin-up, but with a mouth like a sewer cleaner. She was five-foot-nothing and tough as yesterday's steak. She loved Frankie with a passion that crossed the line into mania. Any girl even look at Frankie when she was present, she wouldn't open her mouth but physically start towards her—and Frankie, of all people, had to restrain her. Frankie noticed her, for sure. But he noticed lots of others, too.

Once I paced Church Avenue with a bogus alibi, looking to head Leah off and detain her from her date with Frankie, while he and Deirdre DeVito got it on, parked under the trees on Brooklyn Avenue just a few blocks away. But Leah was savvy and bulls--t didn't fly with her.

"You're not telling me something, Danny," she said. She had a glare like Sonny Liston and her eyes sliced and diced me for any signs of lying. Smoothly, using all of the pacifying skills I had necessarily learned to survive years of friendship with Frankie, I explained to her that the Camaro had a busted water hose and was right then in the shop.

"I'm looking under the hood and I better see a new hose," she said. "You will," I answered confidently, knowing that the work I described had been performed the day before. The bigger problem would be the fragrance of the car's interior. Deirdre, a blonde with breasts thrusting like cushions through the tight tops she favored, wore a perfume that smelled of mangoes, if a kid from Brooklyn was any judge. Frankie, with her body in his arms and her scent in his nostrils, might not notice the aroma in the car. But Leah would. I had never known him to hit a girl. But Leah, for all her delicate beauty, was more macho than the St. Thomas football team and I couldn't predict the result if she slugged him. With all my charm and what girls described as my tall, blond beach bum good looks, I lured her into Finley's Lounge to share a few pitchers. By the time we were done, neither of us would have noticed the fragrance of Frankie's interior.

I did just fine with the girls we met at the Shamrock Inn and other clubs, but I had also done well with French, American History, and Trigonometry at a leading prep school. I soon got tired of bumming, skirt-chasing, and lying—and something happened just after Frankie's 20th birthday that threatened my long-standing friendship with him.

I met Jill Shulman at a bar across the street from Brooklyn University on a night when drinks were half-price. She didn't drink or talk much, but her eyes did plenty of each, as, all night, she stared at me from her table across the room. Finally, I extricated myself from several of the hard-drinking Catholic school girls I had met at high school dances and crossed to where she sat quietly with several of her friends. I felt a little uneasy standing alone in front of four dark-haired esthers, sipping club soda, looking like they'd just walked out of the Jewish Studies Program across the street. But I took a deep breath.

"Hi," I said. "I'm Danny Malloy." I spoke to the whole table, but my eyes focused on one. Quickly, before anyone else could respond, she got up. She didn't offer to shake my hand, but got on her tip-toes and kissed my cheek. Dimly I heard her friends giggle, but her lips were near my ear. "Jill Shulman," she said. "Let's go outside." As I took her arm, I noticed that her perfume didn't smell of mangoes.

We walked for hours, all the way down Nostrand Avenue to Sheepshead Bay, passing Dunleavy's on Quentin Road, where Frankie had once decked 300-pound Charles "Pain" McHenry for calling Leah "an obnoxious little slut." Leah, it might be noted, kicked "Pain" in the head with three inch heels as he lay sprawled on the barroom floor. Jill and I stepped in there briefly to call her parents from a pay phone and tell them she'd be home late. Something happened as we strolled together, some floodgates opened inside, and we talked as if we'd known each other since first grade. Jill had gone to Edison, a top public high school, was a twenty-one-year old senior at Brooklyn University, majoring in English, who had received nothing but "A's" in her life. She was not shy when she told me she'd never had a boyfriend—but she knew it was time.

We stood together on Emmons Avenue. She was slender and below average height. I wouldn't describe her as pretty— but her delicate features, framed by long black hair swinging gracefully beneath her shoulders, and her eyes, dark windows fully open on what seemed a bottomless soul, combined into some unique package I had never experienced. She was as feminine as a satin gown. It was after midnight on a cool evening in late April and we leaned on the railing gazing out over the bay that opened onto the wide Atlantic. I hesitated only a moment before I told her the full truth of my experiences with girls, going back to the seventh grade.

"That's going to stop now," she said firmly, and I laughed.

"Don't laugh at me," she snapped, her dark eyes slicing me like Leah's might have. "You'll be true to your girlfriend. I know you will."

I stared. "Are you my girlfriend?"

"What do you think?" she answered. Without another word, she got on her tiptoes again, wrapped her arms around my neck, and kissed me deeply, her tongue probing gently inside my mouth. When she let me go, it took me a moment to realize the event's significance.

"Your first kiss?"

Tears were in her eyes now and she came back into my arms, laying her head on my chest. It was the only answer I needed.

My face was in her hair. "Jill," I whispered.

I started to think differently after that, more like the kid who had studied hard to get through prep school. But lacking both a car and a mother fond of Jews presented me with difficulties. Nor was Jill willing to wait. After twenty-one years, it was not like anyone could blame her. I made love to her the first time in my sleeping bag on the grass in the middle of the baseball fields at Marine Park. It was a soft evening in May, with no moon but a thousand stars blinking in the night, as if the heavens shined for no other purpose than to smile a benediction on us. But she had an American Lit Final in the morning.

"Jill," I'd said as we'd walked toward the park. "I'm not going away. Maybe we should wait until after your Finals."

She threw back her head and laughed. "Danny," she said. "You're very sweet. But I'm not worried about Henry James, Dreiser, or Faulkner." She stopped and faced me, her fingers in my long hair. "I'll ace the exam. Like I always do."

We were on the grass for hours. I never remembered what time I got her home to her parents' apartment on Ocean Avenue—but it was near dawn. I don't know what she told her parents, but at twenty-one I guess she didn't have to say much. She was true to her word: After several cups of coffee and a change of clothes, she went to school and crushed her exam. She made it a point to tell me that she did not shower.

I spoke of my relationship in broad terms, leaving out the details, between games at the night center at the junior high school near the park. I sat, sipping Cokes, with Frankie and Hugh Jackson in Hugh's office just off the gym, letting the little kids use the main court for a few minutes. Hugh was the boy's gym teacher at the school, subbed sometimes in History, and ran the after school and night centers. He was a burly black man, at least half-a-foot shorter than me, but, at forty-five, still a quick athlete and hard-nosed competitor. He had helped my game enormously over the past six years, advising me in tough one-on-one contests against him. "Use your rangy-ass height, Danny," he'd tell me, as he pushed and clawed at me. "Go up strong. Drill that lefty jumper over the little man." He knew but never mentioned that he was part of the reason I'd started 24 games at forward my senior year at St. Thomas. I remembered looking several times into the stands, being as thrilled at Hugh's presence as at my parents. He'd toughened and smartened me, and if I'd ever needed advice, had always been there.

"Jill's special," I said. "But I'm going to have problems dating a Jewish girl."

Frankie snorted. "All pussy's good pussy," he said irritably. "Jew or not."

I looked at him. "Not exactly what I had in mind," I said dryly. "But at least you don't hate Jews."

Hugh laughed good-naturedly. "Frankie has a definite personal stake in shunning bigotry," he said to me.

Over the years, I'd noticed Hugh subtly working on Frankie, seeking to defuse his temper, to be like a dad to the angry kid whose merchant marine father had long ago abandoned his family; encouraging him to stay in school, to get a job, to be less quick to bust some poor bastard's head. I looked at him now with renewed respect. Pictures of Arlene, his wife of twenty-one years, and his two teen-age daughters, were all over his desk and the walls. Other than one photo of him during his four-year Army stint, they were the only ornaments in his office.

Frankie seemed agitated and put down his bottle. Coke was not his preferred beverage. "What the hell makes her better than any of the other broads?" he asked.

There was an awkward silence in the room for several moments.

"I don't think of Jill as 'a broad,'" I said quietly. "Maybe you should—"

"So what does it mean, Danny?" he asked suddenly, with a catch in his throat. "After all these years, no more partying all night? No more broads at Shamrock or Desperadoes or any of the clubs in the Ridge? What—you'll be home eating macaroons, watching George Burns re-runs with your nice Jewish girl?"

He felt betrayed. It was obvious in the seething irritability of his tone, the familiar flashing scowl of his eyes, the slight huskiness in his voice, as if something were trapped in his larynx. Something pushed its way up from inside me, like a seed sprouting into a plant, a realization I had always had but never confronted—because it was a weed, a life form not of a fragrance to be inhaled but of ungainly ugliness to be contemptuously jerked from the ground. I had never before faced how empty his life was—the non-existent father; the morbidly religious, candle-lighting mother, whose life found meaning only in church; the neighborhood, middle-class, but always with toughs in the schoolyards and the streets; no supervision, no rules, no discipline, no academic ability, no affection. Except from Leah—and the other girls. Other than that, Frankie's entire family was in this room. I knew he held a murderous rage toward the two losers who had brought him into this world—one absent, one demented—and not being able to kill them, lashed out at everyone else.

The respect, or fear perhaps, I had always felt for him started to slowly dissipate, replaced gradually by a burgeoning pity—a cruel regression.

"Frankie..." I said, unable or unwilling to put the identification into words. I was no philosopher, but I sensed that one does not dole out pity to the Frankie Pearson's of the world. He felt its toxic presence though, could see it in my eyes, hear it in my voice, smell it in the room. A guy like Frankie could smell pity the way an animal could smell fear. And will react the same way.

He got up so violently, the motion jerked his chair backwards on the tile floor. He hesitated in the room only long enough to snarl, "F--k you, Danny," then he was out of the door, the gym, and, after twenty years, seemingly my life.

I saw Frankie up and down the block, but I had only one conversation with him after that—two months later in July. It was a muggy evening on which the streets smelled like limp sweat socks discarded in a musty corner. But I didn't care a rat's ass about the weather, because I would see Jill that night. I still worked at the fast food joint—but I had sent in an application to both Kingsborough and Brooklyn University. I was confident I'd be accepted at each. After a day at work, I had just showered and was about to catch the Avenue R bus, when the phone rang.

"Danny," Leah's voice said without preamble. "Frankie's sick."

I hadn't spoken to her in months, and at first I wasn't concerned.

"What's the matter?" I asked lazily, looking at my watch.

"His stomach is really bad, got terrible pains in his right side. Had them for days."

I started to worry. "Get him to a doctor."

"He won't go!" she screamed, all of her fears bursting forth in those three words.

"Where is he?"

"In the car, on 40th Street, off of Church."

"Keep him there. I'm on my way."

I had no time for buses, subways, or begging to borrow cars. I went down the stoop in a bound and hit Burnett Street running. It was miles to Church Avenue, I didn't know how many, but it didn't matter. I ran. And I ran. And I never stopped running. I was in top shape, and my long legs ate up ground like a champion distance runner. I sprinted down Nostrand Avenue, crossed Kings Highway against the light, causing drivers to lean on their horns and swerve to miss me—raced all the way down to the Junction, still running hard, staggered across Flatbush, oblivious to the lights and the screeching cacophony of brakes, and almost collapsed making a right turn onto Ditmas Avenue. I caught myself and plodded forward. I made a left onto New York Avenue, with sweat pouring off of me like a horse; a right onto Beverly Road, with a pain in my side that might have equaled Frankie's; and a left onto Brooklyn Avenue, lurching blindly past Holy Cross Cemetery, my jaw clenched in agony, finally reaching Church. Seconds later, I stood by the side of the Camaro parked on 40th Street.

Leah was in the passenger side. Frankie lay sprawled behind the wheel, his face ashen, sweat pouring off of him.

His eyes opened to slits about as wide as mine and stared at me.

"You look like s--t," he said.

I was in no mood for banter. "Shove over, asshole, I'm taking you to the emergency room."

By this time, he was too weak to object, and Leah dragged him out of my way. As I got in, I saw the remnants of white powder on the dash and a rolled up dollar bill, and knew he'd been snorting coke to kill the pain.

"Son of a bitch," I said to the whole stinking world.

They operated immediately at Kings County, but his appendix had burst, probably days ago, and the poison had spread throughout his system. It didn't look good. Leah and I stayed by his hospital bed all night, though he was unconscious.

Around midnight, I called Jill from a bank of payphones. She'd been stood up with no idea why. She stayed calm. I explained. I ended by saying, "I hope you trust me that I wasn't with another girl."

There was silence on the line for several seconds, and when she responded, she said only one thing: "I'd trust you with my life, Danny Malloy."

The tears burst from me then, probably for the first time since I was six, and I didn't care, me, the Brooklyn kid, who ran with toughs. I just let them pour from me.

"Come, Jill. Please come."

She answered exactly what I'd told Leah: "I'm on my way."

Jill didn't say a word when she arrived. She just took my arm and we all stared at Frankie.

Hours later, it was time for a break. Leah and Jill came from different worlds, practically different universes, but the tough Irish girl—daughter of a stereotypically hard-drinking cop—noticed that Jill never took her hand off my arm or her eyes off of Frankie. Around four in the morning, she fished a hardbox of Marlboro's from her bag.

"You want to go outside for a smoke?" she asked my girlfriend.

"Sure," Jill said gratefully.

I turned to her, eyes wide. "You don't smoke."

"I'm starting."

In the end, it was hopeless, as we'd all known. Frankie had the constitution of a jungle creature. He lingered for three days, fighting for life, and then he died. He never regained consciousness.

After the wake, the funeral was at Holy Cross Cemetery, just a few blocks away. I listened to the priest mouth the usual bogus platitudes, expressed condolences to Kathleen Pearson, the holy roller mother I despised almost as much as Frankie had, and, with Jill on my arm, walked blocks to catch the Nostrand Avenue bus. It was a Saturday afternoon and it was hot.

"I got to get a car," I said.

"Who owns the Camaro now?"

I hadn't thought of it, but she was right. I bought it for $500 from Mrs. Pearson, who probably donated most of it to the Church.

In the subsequent months, when I drove to Kingsborough to begin my studies, to my job, or to take Jill to dinner, Frankie came with me. I knew he would have anyway, but somehow it seemed more fitting. I liked to believe that, now, he might have approved—the Camaro no longer part of a life filled with violence and meaningless sex. I read in my Freshman English class where Thoreau had said that "Most men lead lives of quiet desperation." I remarked to Jill that "Some men lead lives of raging desperation." "Not you," she immediately responded. She'd gotten a job teaching English at New Utrecht High School and enrolled in a Master's program at NYU.

We saw Leah whenever we could. But something had gone out of her the day Frankie died. Her dark eyes didn't burn the way they had, and once when someone rudely shoved her in a crowd on Church Avenue, she neither mouthed off nor pushed back. She ate less now, and within months had lost weight. She smiled gently on greeting us, but that was about the extent of her reaction. It was Jill, not me, who grabbed her by the shoulders and shook her one night. "Leah, you're a beautiful girl! There's a long way to go." "Thanks," Leah said. "Thanks."

I learned that you take wisdom where you find it. Hugh Jackson spoke to me several months later, as I sat in his office one evening between games at the night center. Through his open door, we could see the side basket where Frankie had once challenged, and beaten by himself, three JV players from Nazareth. Of course, when one of his opponents had complained about the rough play, Frankie had dropped the ball and started toward him: "Rough?" he'd asked. "You want to see rough?" The kid had admitted that he didn't.

"It ain't about kicking ass, Danny. I think you know that. Frankie could probably have kicked both our asses. And Leah could probably kick Jill's."

"Without a doubt," I said.

He ignored the interruption. "But who's going to school—who's holding a job—who's got a real relationship?"

"Who would go to a doctor if in excruciating pain?" I asked myself.

For several seconds nobody spoke. Then Hugh continued, softly now.

"I loved Frankie—just like I love you. You're the sons I never had. You know that, don't you, Danny?" I nodded. "But truth is truth. In the end, was Frankie a tough guy—or a wimp? Did he face it—or did he run? Answer that for yourself one day." He stopped because he couldn't go on.

Neither could I. I stared at the floor. Hugh turned and looked out the window for a long time. He was still turned from me when he finished.

"Get going, Danny. Marry that girl. She's all class. Don't let her get away. And finish school. Be a tough guy, not a wimp. Just know the difference between them."

Without waiting for a response, he got up and went out the door back into the gym where the teenagers were playing basketball.

The Intelligent War

PROLOGUE

Reggie H.A.R.D. would go on to be one of the great heavyweight champions of history. But the toughest fight he ever fought was not in the ring. It was a conflict against a peerless foe invincible in any contest, fought until only one man could stand, battled with no gloves, no rules, no holds barred, no referee, and no scribe to chronicle the brutal result. It had consequences for innocent lives far weightier than the issue of who would wear the heavyweight crown.

The crime spree was savage.

The most successful persons of Brooklyn's crime-ridden neighborhoods were assaulted, robbed, raped—always accompanied by brutal beatings from naked fists and work boots. Sometimes, victims died; other times, paralyzed for life.

Surgeons were now quadriplegics; teachers were corpses; an award-winning novelist was comatose. The crumpled bodies of patent attorneys and Harvard-educated technologists were dumped in garbage-strewn alleys. From Bedford-Stuyvesant to Brownsville, from Crown Heights to East New York, educated people lived in fear.

Everyone asked: Why? The inability to discern an answer was chilling; more so, the prospect of what the answer would be.

He would kill them. It was that simple.

The hulking figure never sagged. That, of course, was unthinkable. Even while brooding over his own culpability, he was alert, straight-spined, swaggering the ghetto's dark streets. Let them come for me, he said. It would have been a plea, if he knew how. Whatever remorseless force sought supremacy over a tameless world, let them assail me as they had someone dear now fighting for life in the hospital. I'll kill them quick, he promised. No suffering like they had inflicted on her. None. He said it aloud, as if the remorseless force heard him. As if it cared.

Chapter One: Love Betrayed

The street was redolent with menace.

Gayle Forster stood at the corner, cursing Julius' obstinance. Every thug in Brooklyn infested this quarter of the ghetto. He lived here because of, not in spite of it. "Burnishes the legend, babe," he said. If her friends knew whom she dated, there would be another murder in this neighborhood. But she had not gotten where she was by letting people stop her. At thirty-one, with whom she slept—and where—was nobody's business.

She started down the dark street. There had been incidents. She had told him. He had laughed. "My babe breathe fire. Stare the homies down." She had asked his help. "No one to know Reggie be dating a professor." She hefted in her hand her briefcase stuffed with books and lecture notes. Reggie. Reggie H.A.R.D. That stupid alias. The pro fighter's stage name. She shivered—anger or fear? Maybe she would reveal his secret to the world. The dark secret whose disclosure he dreaded.

A tall figure stepped from an alley. Then another—then a third. A wiry hand gripped her throat. Contemptuously, she slapped it off. "Cretins," she breathed. "Get your porcine paws off me." One grabbed her thick black hair. She turned to him, mouth open, jaw exposed, and the explosive punch came from the other side, splintering her teeth. She was on the ground, dazed. They stomped her. "Bitch," spat one of the assailants. "Professor Bitch. Too ed-u-cated for the homeboys. Look at you now." A commanding voice rang from the alley. "Get her in here." They carried her into the alley and dropped her to the ground. She moaned in pain. "Shut the bitch up," the leader commanded. He wore shades, though the night was dark. His belt was unbuckled and he unzipped his fly. With blows, they silenced her. They seized purse, ring, bracelet, necklace. "Strip her clothes." The leader's shirt was off. He was tall, athletic, with lithe muscles that rippled when he moved. Around his neck he wore a gold band. He removed the shades. His lean face, chiseled jaw, and high cheekbones were those of a warrior chieftan. So too were the eyes, the inexplicable green eyes, the glow-in-the-dark cat's eyes. His henchmen smashed the briefcase and broke it open. "Books," one of them hissed. For a moment, the leader's eyes widened, as if he wished to know the titles. But he nodded. They tore apart the bindings and scattered the pages to the alley's dank pavement. He dropped his unbuckled jeans. The green eyes, in his taut, ebony face, would have been striking but for their Arctic Sea-cold.

Reggie H.A.R.D. landed a left hook to his opponent's cheek that would have dropped a lion. Byron "Sleepmaker" Jones hit the deck and did not move.

"Get up, mother—cker!" Reggie bawled over the Madison Square Garden crowd. "Get up, so's I beat you again."

The ref pushed him to a neutral corner. Reggie started again toward his fallen foe; again, the ref shoved him back. By the time the ref started to count, Sleepmaker stirred. At eight, he rose to a knee. By ten, he was on his feet.

To Reggie, caution was no more part of his vocabulary than when he and Beau Dancy, as teenagers, led a street gang in Brooklyn. Sleepmaker had won 33 of 35 pro fights, 30 by KO, and was the third-ranked heavyweight contender in the world. None of that mattered; it would not have mattered at any time; certainly not now, when Gayle Forster lay in a coma, in a hospital. Too blind, he had not heeded her; too late, he saw his error; too helpless, he shed his tears.

Sleepmaker was wobbly; desperately, he clinched, trying to tie up this newcomer who hit, with either hand, like the Brighton Express. Reggie pushed him off. Just seconds left in the 5th round. There they were, the thugs who had assaulted Gayle; in his imagination they were Sleepmaker, Sleepmaker was them; he hit him with a left hook to the head, a hard right to the body, and a vicious uppercut that lifted him in the air. The ref had to push him back. Everyone, ringside, knew that, this time, Sleepmaker would not get up.

"Get up!" Reggie roared.

The ref wrapped his arms around Reggie's massive frame. "You wanna be DQ'ed, asshole?" he screamed in his ear.

Later, at the press conference, he could barely concentrate. He was alone—Sleepmaker, with a busted jaw, had been been rushed to the hospital. Questions about pulverizing big-time opponents, and potential title fights, were of little interest right now. He had to be alone.

He took the subway, not a limo, to Brooklyn. He prowled the cars and the platforms, begging for a mugger—a footpad, as the British had long ago dubbed them—to assail him; but failing; walking the dark streets then, walking alone, a terrible figure with a terrible secret, walking the city's most crime-infested streets, seeking to inflict a terrible vengeance.

He was exhausted. It was four am. He had fought a top-ranked opponent. He had thrown every ounce of psychic and physical energy into smashing him to pulp. He had trained for months. He had walked miles tonight, criss-crossing Brooklyn's most threatening streets. His heart was ripped from his chest, and he did not try to stem the tears that streaked his cheeks.

Finally, just before sunrise, he entered his apartment. He threw himself face down, fully clothed, on the couch. But he could not sleep.

He got up, staggered to the kitchen. Half a bottle of bourbon would be right. But Beau Dancy had taught him well. He warmed a glass of milk, and drank it. Pansy drink. For a moment, he smiled.

He crept down the hall to the bedroom door, perpetually locked. He tried for his usual swagger, but knew he could not attain it. No one—no one but her—was let in here. No one but her was allowed to know his shameful secret.

His bedroom overflowed with books. He slept on the living room couch. His bedroom contained only a Laz-E-Boy recliner, a floor lamp, and books. Lots and lots of books. Nor were they scattered in disorderly fashion. Reggie had meticulously built, from ceiling to floor, wall-to-wall bookcases encircling his room. The shelves were divided into fiction and non-fiction, history and philosophy, novels and drama and short stories. Within these divisions, his books were scrupulously alphabetized, some sections by title, some by author. Among the thousands, there was not a book he could not find within seconds.

He browsed the titles. The complete works of Shakespeare—he had read at sixteen; the novels of Dostoyevsky and Tolstoy—eighteen; the abstruse—he liked that word—challenging texts of Nietzsche, on which he took a full year of study—age twenty.

But he gravitated toward the mid-section of his fiction collection, as he perennially did in moments of duress, to the collected writings of Jack London and to his childhood. His hardbound copy of *The Sea Wolf* was in tatters. He had newer editions, but this one he cherished. How old was he when he first read it? Eleven. The summer his parents died. He was an orphan; he had nobody. Hating the loveless discipline of foster care, he ran away; from the schools, too. He slept in alleys; in the winter, in subway stations. He fought and scrapped for food money. He stole. Huge for his age, menacing, heavily muscled, he did favors for a local gang leader. Fearless, he turned on the gang members themselves.

He was Julius Collymore then. The odds against the orphan were astronomical. But he had a shining love— books—a source of bitter mockery from a violently alcoholic father. From thugs, too, on the street. From bullies in the schoolyards. From no-hopers in the projects. From seemingly every quadrant of the ghetto. Even his teachers were no help, intimidated by the child's size, his fists, and his prodigious intellect. In response to derision, Julius busted heads. But it was no satisfaction. Quickly, he learned to hide his shameful secret.

He hid his love in the library's back rooms and his life's dark corners. But he clung to his love.

It was not his teachers but Hornsby who introduced him to Jack London. And to Beau Dancy.

Two future gang leaders met at the library. Reggie smiled. What were the odds of that? Worthy of Martin Eden or another London hero. Julius loved tales of heroes and read voraciously—historic accounts of Alexander, Julius Caesar, George Washington, Thomas Jefferson, Frederick Douglass; and incessantly of fictional giants—he devoured *The Odyssey* at age ten—any story of driven men that could inspire the orphan to rise from the gutter.

Beau loved those stories, too. But, several years older than Julius, still at a young age, he favored brutal tales of dominance and submission, of conquerors and conquered, slave drivers and slaves, great fighters and vanquished foes. He read non-fiction on how to crush rivals; by his teens, he loved Machiavelli, von Clausewitz, Sun-Tzu. Julius admired Prometheus, Beau preferred Zeus; Julius savored Macduff, Beau favored Macbeth; Julius studied Napoleon, Beau preferred Genghis Khan; Julius read Frederick Douglass and the abolitionists, Beau preferred the slave drivers; Julius admired the Battle of Midway, Beau, the Rape of Nanking.

Did Hornsby have a first name? Funny, Reggie thought, he had never asked. He was gray and gaunt but upright, not stooped, tending his stacks like a farmer's wife her vegetable garden. He dusted daily, worked laboriously to repair cracked spines, taped together torn pages, and contributed from his own meager salary that the library might purchase new editions. He had no family that anybody knew of. Did he live in the building?

He worked tirelessly to promote reading campaigns. He had many good students. But his stars, his intellectual sons were Beau Dancy and Julius Collymore.

If anyone had greatness stamped in his DNA, it was Beau. The only thing quicker than his hands and feet was his mind. In grade school, he threw away his history text, then shocked his angry teacher with his mastery of Caesar's *Commentaries on the Gallic War.* In the fourth grade, he mastered algebra. His schoolteacher mother spent much of her salary on obscure books desired by her son.

In the park, playing guys from the local high school team, four or five years older than him, Beau scampered for 90-yard touchdown runs, his speed and moves leaving opponents grasping air, his naked power leaving them on their backs. On schoolyard courts, his prowess at the city game—basketball—became a legend. Soaring off asphalt, it seemed he could look into the hoop, and more than once his crashing slams tore the metal rim from its backboard.

Reggie never knew any one to beat him at anything, from chess to arm wrestling. To many, he was a hero; a kid who would rise from the slums to superstar status in whatever field he chose. Perhaps a ten-year career in pro football; then retire and write books. Predictions regarding the prodigy were rife.

But the wild side was always there. He expected those less gifted to kowtow; if one didn't, Beau administered a brutal beating until the fool learned better. Once, a bigger kid tried slowing him with rough play on the court; Beau neither called fouls nor issued warnings; he got off the deck and beat the kid so savagely that some of the players tried to pull him off, and others ran away. Whereas Julius hid his love of the library, Beau beat half to death anyone who mocked his.

His mother tried to restrain, to civilize, to discipline his excesses. He broke curfew, climbed out his window, was more than once picked up by the cops, but always returned to the streets—a tameless soul seeking adventure. They had bitter arguments. The final confrontation came at age thirteen. She caught him, after midnight, lowering himself by rope from his fourth-story bedroom window. She called him, commanded his return. He ignored her, hit the ground, and sauntered—did not run—into the night. She called the cops, who found and returned him home. She cried. "Bitch," he spat. "You called the cops?" He pushed her to the floor, even now he didn't hit her, but gathered the few things he wanted and joined Julius on the streets.

Julius was so big, so tough—mentally and physically—that Beau accepted him as an almost-equal. And "Julius" was an emperor's name. Beau formed a gang, with Julius as lieutenant, and accepted only the street-toughest applicants as members. Beau, for all his wildness, was street-crafty and book-brilliant; he forbade his followers, on pain of death, to fight cops. "Let chumps go the joint to prove they badass," he said. "We prove it on the street." They took down thugs, heist artists, drug dealers—and the cops left them alone.

Once he caught Julius and gang members using drugs. He burst the hash pipe against a brick wall and scattered the stuff in the wind. "You wanna die, I kill you quick!" he bellowed. "Anyone?" No one, that day, chose to die. "We drink milk, not booze. We es-chew drugs. We treat out bodies like temples. Hear?" They heard. Like their leader, they lived clean and exercised relentlessly.

Hornsby suspected how they lived. He knew better than to remonstrate. He had a powerful ally—the books. But for all the kids he pulled from the gutter, for all his intuitive insight and book-smarts, he miscalculated. He introduced Beau and Julius to Jack London. *The Sea Wolf.*

Julius, as Hornsby hoped, was fascinated by Humphrey van Weyden—by the man's rise from effeminate nerd unable to do a man's work to hero's status, willing and able—both physically and intellectually—to stand up to the brutal, brilliant Wolf Larsen. But Beau—brilliant, beautiful, glittering Beau—was fascinated by the brutal, brilliant Wolf Larsen. Larsen's overt philosophy resonated. He saw life as Larsen saw it: the squirming, frothing ferment of the yeast. Life struggling for supremacy. A world of physical force in which there was a single choice: dominance or death. Intellect was a weapon.

He barked orders which had to be instantly obeyed. He tolerated discussion only from Julius. He busted faces of those who obeyed commands slowly. And, save his lieutenant, he withdrew in suspicion from a world in which all wanted to be him.

Julius, a clean-living hunk of physicality, knowing the gang leader had saved him from drugs, stuck by him.

To the death.

Rival gang leaders, though secretly in awe of Dancy, were sufficiently enraged by his brilliant raids to band together. They laid a trap. When Dancy's boys hijacked a drug deal, twenty thugs descended on them. They shot one of his followers—clubbed another—told the rest they wanted Dancy. They could flee—or die. They fled.

All but Julius.

He feigned surrender. He backed away. A lightning grab and prodigious strength wrested the gun from the rival leader's hand; a massive arm snaked the rival's throat, the other hand clapped the gun against his temple, and Julius grinned.

"Climax fill the stage with corpses. Like *Hamlet*."

They were stunned. Dancy was not. He stepped behind Julius and his captive. "Throw down your weapons. Or he's dead."

The rival leader agreed. "Throw 'em down."

There was a reckless gleam in Beau's eye, as of a man born to lead a commando raid, to climb Everest, to—Alexander-like—conquer a world. "A deal," he said. "Throw down guns and knives. You too retarded to use them, just hurt yourself. Then," he smiled wickedly. "We do this like men. Fists and feet and bone on bone. Two against twenty. Battle of Thermopylae."

"Cyrano," Julius interjected, "fight a hundred men."

"You nancy boys man enough?" Beau said. They threw down their weapons. Beau threw them in a dumpster. Julius slung the rival's down the alley, spun him around, and crushed his jaw with a thunderous left. The leader dropped, stunned, to the pavement. Twenty thugs descended on them.

Julius backed against a wall. Grim, focused, machine-like, he processed targets—faces, throats, chests—and landed solidly against them. He took blows but delivered more—and more heavily.

Beau attacked. He needed no wall behind him, only room to move. He assailed the assailants. Fists or feet, grounded or airborne, lightning or thunder, see him or they did not—they felt him. If a Homer were there to record such Achilles-like deeds, he would have sung of Beau all over the alley, in the air, on the walls, leaping from dumpster and fire escape, perennially besieged and besieging, throwing blows and receiving them, a dozen men prostrate at his feet, and laughter on his lips.

Against the wall, his friend slugged away, a heap of senseless frames before him retarding his foes' movement.

When it was over, Julius slumped to a crouch against the wall but not to his knees. Beau, with a cracked rib, a fractured cheek, and six broken bones in his hand, staggered to his friend. To his feet, he pulled the big man. No trace of laughter remained. "You save my life."

"You saved mine."

Beau Dancy said something he had never said. "We together."

"To the death," said Julius Collymore.

Ironically, Hornsby—who brought them together—pulled them apart.

Julius counseled against new gang members. "Me and you, bro. Others can't be trusted." But Beau's eyes glittered. "Power seeks servants." He rounded up a crew, he tolerated no dissent, and he savagely beat anyone who defied him. He accepted only Julius as a partner and Hornsby as a mentor.

"Let's get these chumps to the library and develop more than they muscles." Julius said.

Beau refused. "Education not for the brothers."

Julius disagreed. "Why not?"

"They not have the brain power."

"They not lions and tigers and bears. They got human brains."

Beau snorted. "Thinking make them soft."

"It make them soft—or less obedient?"

Several raids went awry—the boys too dull to comprehend the intricacies of Dancy's plan, too slow to capture its delicate timing. "They need to think on their feet," Julius said.

"I do the thinking around here," Beau said.

Secretly, Julius dragged them to the library. He introduced them to Hornsby. Started them on beginner's books. Between his browbeating and Hornsby's gentle encouragement, they slowly advanced, then more rapidly. Ready for battle and feeling his newfound strength, one proudly quoted, "Cry 'havoc!' and let slip the dogs of war." After the raid's successful completion, Dancy beat him to a pulp. He ignored Julius and raced to the library. Nobody could catch him. Julius hailed a cab.

"Don't be educating my boys," Beau told Hornsby. "That for me and Julius."

"Your boys?" said Hornsby. "They're your sons?"

"My followers."

"Perhaps they choose to think, not follow."

"They not choose, Hornsby. That not for the lumpen masses, only the select few."

"Like you?"

People stared at the threatening scene. Beau ignored them. "Only a few recognize the truth, stare at it—look into the abyss, unmindful it look back. The rest can't struggle top of the heap. They too weak-minded."

"The truth?"

"Society a machine. A steamroller. It crush you. It crush millions. But who drive the machine, Hornsby? You part of it, but you never ask that question."

"Clearly, men like you."

"Be right. You not be educating my followers. They not the designer—not even the driver. You not be educating them—or I shut you down."

Hornsby, despite his advanced age, drew himself to his full height. "I educate any mind who dares to think."

"'Dare' a strong word, old man. Need be backed by strong deeds. You not stand against me."

"I will," said Julius Collymore.

A siren was heard in the distance. Someone had called the cops. Beau stared from one to another. "We together," he said.

"To the death," Julius said.

Beau's smile glittered like a polished sword. "Whose funeral you just arrange?" Slowly, with inalienable regality, he strode from the library. Julius breathed a sigh. Unafraid, he had faced death—but he dreaded throwing a blow at the only human being he loved.

Julius moved to a different neighborhood. He began earnest training as a professional fighter. He changed his name. Years later, he still had not seen Beau Dancy. But he could not escape the look in Beau's eyes as he uttered that final threat. It came back to him weeks later, when he heard that the library burned to the ground—and months after, when he heard that Hornsby, of a broken heart, had passed on—the glittering, threatening look in those inexplicable green eyes, the glow-in-the-dark cat's eyes.

Gayle Forster was conscious.

Reggie H.A.R.D. visited her in the hospital.

Her friends and colleagues met him at the room's door.

"You don't belong here," one said.

"Even so."

"You don't deserve her."

"That's true," Reggie whispered.

Her eyes sent them away.

He sat down by the bedside. He stared at her silently. He had so much to say. He did not know where to begin. Her eyes glared, righteous anger, the eyes of the toughest fighter he knew—"Gale Force" he called her—and he knew she'd recover.

"You get him," she said. "When I recover, bring him to me."

"What's his name?"

"I don't know."

"What's he look like?"

"I don't know."

"Distinguishing features?"

"I don't know."

"How do I find him?"

"Clean up the streets!" she shouted. "The cops can't do it. They're shackled by rules of engagement. You're not."

"Gayle, I..."

"Don't go mushy on me! This isn't the time for it." She drew a breath and her tone softened. "You remember our arguments?"

He nodded.

"What did I say? A hundred times—what did I say?"

Through his personal hell, he remembered. "Ghetto culture often conducts a war against intelligence," he quoted her.

"You remember the instances? Even a few?"

"Gangbangers," he said. "At the high schools, even the middle schools beat the hell out of the smartest kids for 'trying to be white.' A black man, they said, is gangsta."

"Right."

"That college kid—"

"—Honors student—"

"Rode the subway to Columbia. Was warned not to carry books on the street. Told the thugs to 'kiss off.'" He hung his head. "They beat him to death....The composer in the projects—"

"Enough," she said. "Were you willing to oppose it?"

He shook his head.

"Would you come out of the closet?"

He shook his head.

"Coward," she hissed. "Would you man up to the best thing about you?"

He looked at the floor. Her did not respond.

"A hundred times, what'd you say?"

He looked up. "The intelligent should war back."

She let his words hang in the air. "Who, *Reggie?*" She had never used that name. "When?"

Chapter Two: Clean the Streets

R eggie H.A.R.D. single-strapped a heavy pack and sauntered past the high school yard. He was unarmed. But
he was never unarmed. Drug sales went down in broad
daylight. Dealers and their goons had bulges under their jackets not caused by obesity. Other than that, the atmosphere
was lazy. Classes would let out soon.

Reggie walked casually around the block. He crossed the
street. He sat on a bench, schoolyard in sight. For a week, he
had watched. He knew now what to watch for. Classes let out.
Hundreds of kids milling around, smoking, laughing, flirting.
Finally, a slight kid with heavy backpack and heavier glasses
broke from the crowd. He walked alone, purposefully, from
the school; repeatedly, he looked over his shoulder. A giant
detached himself from the dealers and loiterers; flanked by a
pair of followers, slowly, he trailed the skinny kid.

"Walker!" the giant boomed in a voice that rattled glass
windows.

The runt walked faster.

"Walker!" the giant bellowed.

The skinny kid turned, saw the thug's minions gaining on
him, and ran. Easily, the goons ran him down.

"What I tell you?" the giant said in a voice carrying to the
corner. "You carries books on my street, you pays a toll. Hand
it over. Ten bucks a day."

"But, Marvin, now I walk on different streets—"

The gang leader nodded. His minions stripped off the back pack, unzipped it, and flung books to the pavement. One kicked the books, scattering them in the gutter. The giant smashed the kid's face, sending him sprawling; then grabbed the kid's lapels and hoisted him six feet in the air.

"They all my streets, Sue. You pays in money or you pays in pain. And you tells the other bookworms they pay Marvin Barnes or they smartass heads busted."

"You—chump," said a quiet voice behind them. "You Stanley Kowalski, not Marvin Barnes."

"What?" The thugs whirled.

Stella!" boomed Reggie H.A.R.D.

"What the f—k he say?" one of the goons said.

"You best step off, money," Marvin Barnes said. "Or you get more than you handle."

Reggie took off the pack. He unzipped it. He pulled out a hardbound copy of *Paradise Lost,* another of *The Divine Comedy,* a third of *War and Peace.* Gently, he placed the books on the ground. From his back pocket, he whipped a bulging wallet. He opened it; it was filled with hundreds.

"Stanley," he said, a voice of gentle lethality. "You shake down bookworms? I right here, bitch."

Three thugs were on him in a trice. But, Reggie knew, wild street brawlers. He decked Stanley Kowalski with a lightning combo as the others piled on. He shook them off and made short work of them. The giant rose unsteadily to his pins. Reggie grabbed and hoisted as the thug had the kid.

"You rape the professor?"

"Whaa?" said a dazed thug.

Reggie slammed him against a tree and added a stinging slap across both cheeks. "Two months ago—professor raped, beaten—we know you dig bookworms—you do that, Stanley?"

"No, man, I—"

"The truth, *Sue,* or I comes back, rips off you head, and bowl it down Gates Avenue."

"I swear, man. I not rape anyone..." The thug gasped for air. "I just..."

"You just a thug," said Reggie, contemptuously. "You my bitch, boy?"

The thug hesitated. Reggie's left hand clutched his windpipe and squeezed. Quiet crackling noises commenced. Desperately, the thug nodded.

"You find out who raped the professor."

"How...the f—k... I..." the thug gasped.

"Wrong answer." Reggie's left hand reached again.

"OK! I ask questions." Reggie whispered in the goon's ear; he did it a second time. "You find out, call that number."

The thug nodded.

"And do it quick. I be back."

Again the thug nodded. Reggie pushed him off and he staggered to join his minions, who had fled.

"And Stanley!" Reggie called. The thug turned back. "Best find another profession. Bookworms gettin' dangerous."

"You, come here," he said to the kid. The kid's nose bled from both nostrils and his left cheek already swelled. He had picked up the books and inserted them into his backpack. Warily, he approached his benefactor.

"What's your name?"

"Walker...S...Peabody..." he stammered.

"You the school's best student?"

Walker nodded. "Next year, I go to Harvard," he said proudly.

"Meantimes, I keeps you out of Graveyard. Write this down." He spelled out a phone number. "Thugs hassle you, call that number. I be here."

"You're helping me?"

"Knew you were bright."

Reggie took a clean handkerchief and gently wiped away the kid's blood.

"Why?"

Reggie paused. For a moment, his mind was elsewhere. Then he looked straight in the kid's eyes. "The intelligent war back."

A high rise apartment complex cut the air in a gentrified section on the edge of Brooklyn's ghetto. A slender woman with long dark hair entered her apartment on one of the top floors. Dr. Sarah Barker, emergency room surgeon, had put in a double shift. One victim, early in the day, had been a young entrepreneur who started up a brilliant software company. Robbed, beaten savagely by a lean man in shades. Told him, "You a dumbass negro, think you smart enough to run the machine. You smart enough only to pay tribute." Took his cash, credit cards, jewelry, electronics. While he lay, crumpled, in an alley, maxed out his cards. Had serious internal injuries. Surgery took hours. She was disturbed. And exhausted. All she wanted was a shower and sleep.

In an alley outside her building, a lean man, flashing stop-your-breath agility, using no ropes, scaled the wall, brick-by-brick, crevice-by-crevice. He had seen it done, in the movies, by world-class mountaineers, and had no doubt he could replicate it. When he reached the roof, he stopped and stared. Empty. He climbed the parapet, strode to the avenue side, knelt, and peered over. It was late, traffic was light, and he was dressed in black. And he was quick. He knew the apartment. He tied a rope securely around a ventilator shaft and started over the edge. He reached his goal. The window was locked. He removed a glass cutter from his belt, sliced the glass neatly, placed it silently on the floor inside, and slithered through the aperture. Although in a darkened bedroom, he put on shades. The door opened, the intruder strode swiftly toward it, and light flooded the room.

Sarah Barker saw only a flash of motion, not the punch that shattered her cheekbone. She crashed against the wall and sunk slowly to the floor. The intruder pulled her to her feet, and, in one savage motion, stripped off her clothes. With his right hand, he clutched her throat and pinned her to the wall. "Hey, Doc. Do-good motherf--ker, life-saver—that how you lie to you-self?" His hand tightened on her throat and she gagged. "You just top o' the heap. That all. You smarter than most dumbass niggers, you claw up the pile. But not smart enough, bitch." He laughed, the sound harsh, bitter in the still room.

Through her pain, the revulsion permeated; she reached for his shades, to claw out his eyes. "Take them off, I kill you, sure. Not be seeing my eyes," he hissed. She hesitated. His grip tightened round her windpipe. "Why?" she gasped. He struck her across the face and flung her naked body to the floor. She almost passed out from pain. She knew her cheekbone was broken, probably her nose. "It about power," he said. He stood over her. "Nothing else. You got it by outsmarting stupid-ass creatures dumber than you. Lie to yourself there be good in the world, you do good. You top of a writhing mass of flailing limbs, is all. Or was." He advanced on her. "Don't kill me," she pleaded. "Rape me, rob me, beat me. Don't kill me." "That better," he said. "You learning." He pulled her to her feet. "Everything," he said. "Or I be back." She gave him cash, credit cards, jewelry, laptop, everything he could stuff into his backpack. He threw her on her back on the bed and when he was done, he intended to beat her senseless.

But her eyes were closed, she breathed. She strived for serenity, to not show revulsion, sensing somehow that repugnance would bring on her a fearful beating and possibly death. The robbery wasn't about plunder, the rape wasn't about sex. He craved dominance, surrender, unquestioning obedience— her feeling was a palpable certitude: The only safety with him lay in utter submission. He was done, he breathed heavily; she lay still, controlling her rage, breathing gently. She opened her eyes.

"Bitch," he said to her yielding form. "Who top of the heap now?" Sarah Barker was silent, memorizing every detail of his face, his neck and shoulders, his physique. Eventually, the NYPD would apprehend this monster. She would be first in line to testify.

He slithered out the window and up the rope. On the roof, he took a breathtaking leap across open space to an adjacent building overlooking a dingy courtyard. He secured the rope, lowered himself to the ground, strode from the back alley to a side street beyond, and into a car manned by his followers. Silently, they drove into the night.

The Westbrook Projects looked like a war zone.

Garbage was strewn across the yard; windows of the few occupied apartments were criss-crossed with iron bars; across the street, rotted hulks of buildings had been gutted. The complex bristled with crack dens; dope dealers and petty thugs from around the 'hood gravitated there, and now ruled the landscape; stabbings and shootings were weekly events; the cops called the locale, "the Wild West-brook," and avoided it. Most honest people had long since evacuated.

But Levon Robertson stubbornly refused to move. He was an Army vet, combat-hardened, and, though aging, ramrod stiff with pride. He had grown up here and remembered when honest folks sat, talking and smoking, under the summer stars without fear of wanton violence. Through decades of manual labor, he earned a living; through years of night school, he earned a degree. He ran a small school in his building's basement for the kids who wanted an education; he owned a shotgun and two illegal pistols with which to protect them. He did not mention the pistols to the local newspaper that covered his story.

Reggie ambled into the schoolroom, in which roughly a dozen kids of varying ages pored over a selection of texts. He tried to look angelic. Robertson immediately reached for his shotgun. Perhaps angelic was not a good look for Reggie.

The big man put his empty hands in the air. "I not trouble."

Robertson knew thugs. Something in the big man's voice, and in his eyes—something true—reassured him. He pointed the gun away from Reggie's chest.

"What are you?"

"Hector, I reinforcements."

"Levon."

"You the upright hero protect you homeland from outside raiders trying to lay it waste."

"That's true," Robertson said. He put the gun away.

The two men stepped into Robertson's office.

The teacher's skin was the color of coffee light and his hair was gray. He was lean as a racedog. When he smiled, his eyes lit a room. But he had a scar running across his cheek from his left ear. Reggie noticed. A piratical grandfather.

"Just wanted to let you knows I here. Not confusing me with the riff-raff," he jerked his thumb at the street.

"Appreciate it. Thugs victimize the students constantly—robberies, beat-downs, even rape."

"That gonna stop."

Robertson nodded.

"Who the deadliest, most lethal mother—ker out there? Always one, he go down, the rest de-camp. Who that be?"

"JJ," Robertson said without hesitation.

"JJ?"

"Juwan James. That's what they call him. Not a heart in his chest—but a metallic pump. No blood, just Jack on the rocks. Chill mother—ker. He choke, stab, or nine you soon as parley. He murder at least six. That I know of. Proud, not loud, no remorse."

Reggie smiled. Then Robertson did. "I live here all my life," he explained. "Maybe you'd prefer the Queen's English—I have lived here for my entire existence."

"I know you a teacher," Reggie said. "We cool. Where I find this Bill Sikes mother—ker?"

Robertson laughed. "Bill Sikes—exactly. He runs the dealers, the pimps, the heist artists. You find him in the quad." He hesitated. "He's never alone."

"A hero like that? I shocked."

The quad was an oasis of greenery amidst the ruins. Grass still grew and shade was afforded by several trees. Blood, Reggie mused, enrich the soil. A lean ferret of a man sat on a railing under a tree. Three men stood around him, listening.

Reggie stopped fifty feet distant and looked at the buildings, those that were condemned and those that should have been. Gayle grow up in a dump like this. No father. Crackhead whore of a mother. Knew early, as girls often do, that education was her way out; fought for every milligram of it. Rule her roost now, a benevolent despot. Some students questioned the benevolence.

"You, Mr. ah, Collymore," she had said that first day, two years back, in class. "The hood, the shades. Off. "

Reggie had sat in the rear row of the English class at the university in Washington Square. At twenty-one, he had plans. Future heavyweight champion. The quickest hands anyone had seen in this division in fifty years. No one to know the heavyweight champ a bookworm. Professor Forster no beauty queen but the sister tall, athletic, with the firm ass and muscular thighs of an inveterate tennis player. And the hard eyes never smiled. She more of a fighter than me, Reggie thought. The gold graduation ring on her finger featured a big "P." Princeton, Reggie guessed. She had been lecturing on *Macbeth* in this class on Shakespeare's tragedies, focused, had not at first noticed who she took as a hood in the room's rear.

"Macbeth a power luster," Reggie said, desperate to distract her. "Ironic, he not a king, want to be—Hamlet a king, not want to be. Nobody who he want to be in Shakespeare's world."

She was mildly interested. Enough, for the moment, to overlook her dress code. "Why bother to contrast him with Hamlet?" she asked. "Isn't the glaring difference between them manifest?"

"But they similar, yo. They impulse-driven. Macbeth know he owe fealty to Duncan but the desire to rule overpower his moral scruples. Hamlet know he must execute the usurper and re-establish proper order in the kingdom but—'goodnight, sweet prince'—he a gentle soul and not want to do it. They feelings prevent them from acting on moral principle. This the human condition, Shakespeare show—chronic conflict between what a man want and what be right for him to do."

The hard eyes stared. "Good," she said. "See me after class." She turned to the board. Then she turned back. "The hood, the shades. Off." Reggie took them off.

It turn to something when he see her after class. Something that must be made right. Something too special to be allowed extinction by a dense man's cruel blindness. Reggie took a deep breath to control his heart rate. No tears now.

Prepare for battle. But another thought come involuntarily: be good to have Beau by his side. Together they clean the streets. Wonder where Beau be? Probably never see him again. Reggie learn early, life be loss. Ultimate loss come at end. Only way make it matter—in between, win every battle you can.

He approached the thugs. His outstretched hands were empty and his smile broad. "Drugs, man. Having a party, need drugs."

The ferret had a lean neck, and, when he smiled, a mouthful of gleaming teeth. His skull was shaved clean.

"What kind of drugs you need?"

"Crack, man. My daughter turn nine today. Having a party. Need crack for the little girls."

"Nigga, what the f—k you say?" one of the ferret's henchmen said. "You be giving crack to little girls?"

"Yeah, man." Reggie's smile was all goofy, mindless bonhomie. "Start 'em young."

Reggie's hands, as he sidled closer to the ferret, were again outstretched in good-natured appeal. But the hand be quicker than the eye. Like a magician or the great boxer he was born—and trained—to be, Reggie's left hand, one moment splayed wide, the next whistled across space in a shortarm blow that crashed the ferret's cheek and left him dazed. Reggie grabbed the leader as he slowly toppled, jerked his body in front, and wrapped his arm around his neck. He smiled in the face of nine-millimeters.

"Down, bitches, or I snap his neck like a twig."

They hesitated. Reggie commenced snapping. They lowered the guns.

"On the ground."

They dropped them.

"Kick 'em here."

They did. Reggie bent and scooped, clutching the ferret's neck by one hand.

He pointed a gun from one to the other. "You rape the professor?" He watched their reactions. "Whaa?" they asked, dazed—and Reggie had an answer. "You find out." Mirthlessly, he grinned. "You find out, you tell me—or I come back, and, one-by-one, bare hands, I take you apart." His eyes matched his words. "Until there be nothing but a pile of bone and a pool of red." The thugs stared. "I be here. On patrol. Don't never let me find you harassing them students. Or you gone, man, you gone."

"You five-oh?"

"I look like five-oh?"

"What about JJ?"

"He going down. Mind you not next. Now get the f—k outta here."

They fled. Reggie took JJ back of a building, out of sight of the street. JJ awoke. Reggie dangled him by the ankles. "Bill, you like to kill people? How many homies you kill?"

"Whaa, no man, I not—" Reggie smashed his skull into the concrete. He did it again. "I like this," the big man said. "You not have to tell the truth." Again, he hoisted by the ankles.

"No, man, wait. I talk."

"Talk."

"Let me up and I—"

"Talk."

"I kill a few mother—kers, but it—"

"It cold blood, in'it?" Reggie again crashed his dome into the ground. JJ's skull was bleeding. "I do this till you head be mush and brains ooze from the quad to the gutter...if you have any. Fact, maybe I do it anyway." He lifted.

"No man, I kill. I kill plenty..."

"Names," Reggie said. "Details."

JJ talked. No professor.

"That it?"

"That it."

Reggie lifted again.

"No, man, I swear! That it."

"Cool," Reggie said. "You gots a simple choice, Bill. You tells this to five-oh—or I smashes you skull like a rotten cantaloupe. Wants to think about it?"

"No, man, I—"

"What?"

"I talks..."

Reggie stood him upright. JJ couldn't walk. His lean ferret face was drenched in sweat and blood trickled onto his shoulders. Reggie clutched his long neck and dragged him for blocks. Good for gangsta and wannabe to see. Marched him up the stairs of the local precinct house. "I waits, Bill, 'round the corner. You comes out without a lawyer—" He grinned. "Maybe you steps back to the projects with me." JJ looked at the ground.

"I not 'fraid of the joint."

"Yo, Big Boy, that the spirit!" Reggie boomed. Jovially, he clapped him on the back and sent him staggering into the open doorway.

JJ turned. He was hunched with pain but the snarl on his lips was something else.

"I get out, I be looking for you."

Reggie stared into the most soulless eyes he'd ever seen.

"Maybe you Stark Wilson, not Bill Sikes—"

"Who the f—k—"

"Might learn to read, 'tard. Where you going, be plenty of time. He stone cold, man. Shane tell him, you killing days be done. Right before he kill him. You get out, not have to look for me. I hunting the streets. I find you."

He leaned forward and advanced. JJ ducked through the doors. Reggie backed away and took up post around the corner, watching the station house. He watched for a long time.

Gayle Forster said, "That emergency room doctor survived. No condition yet to talk to the cops. Don't have a description."

Reggie scowled.

She was home now, in a wheelchair, doing physical therapy. She would walk again. Soon she would resume teaching.

Reggie said nothing. He was thinking, brooding. He sat in a brown leather easy chair in her living room, feet on an ottoman, seemingly relaxed. She lay on a sofa across the room, propped on pillows, her tall frame reaching from arm rest to arm rest. Understandably, she was businesslike. All hint of romance gone. Lucky she'd even speak to him. Have to accept it, Reggie thought. The reason be clear. He nodded. But I love you, screamed in his head. It be different now. Too late—too late—he finally understood.

He had another fight lined up. After his demolition of Sleepmaker Jones, he was a hot commodity. He was in intense training.

"Heat find out what I do, they'll put me away, not the bad guys. Unlawful for me to hit someone." He didn't say "some mother—ker." He spoke English to Gayle. She didn't tolerate ghetto-ese.

"You have a more powerful weapon against them, Reggie."

On the other hand, she had started to use his fighter's name.

"Not hard to outthink them," he said. "Verbally goad them into assault. Then it's self-defense."

"Also, NYPD's not stupid. Did they hassle you and Beau when, as teenagers, you took down every bad guy in the 'hood?"

He shook his head.

"They know who the thugs are," she said. "Proving it in court is another matter. The guys you lean on are generally notorious. They might just look away."

"The war against intelligence is not abating."

"Keep slugging, champ," she said. "It will."

Chapter Three: Bare Knuckles

Reggie bought an expensive suit. A large one, fit baggily, hid his true proportions. He stooped to appear smaller. He dyed his hair gray and wore glasses. His sparring partners stared at the gray hair. A glare silenced them. He shuffled slowly when he walked. He carried a briefcase overflowing with books and papers. He wore a gold ring, expensive wristwatch, and silver cufflinks. A fat wallet bulged in his back pocket. Nightly, he walked from the subway station the most gentrified sections of the 'hood, appearing a successful lawyer on his way home. He waited.

Weeks passed. One night, a driving rainstorm blackened the sky. No moon or stars were visible. Heavy clouds obscured the streetlights. A driving gust cut through garments and skin to chill the bone. The world was wet, windy, ominously dark.

Reggie wore neither hat nor hood. He both heard and saw through peripheral vision two thugs duck out of an alley, step close, and club him with steel pipe. He rolled with the blow; most of it glanced off his shoulder, but he feigned collapse and unconsciousness; the thugs dragged him into the alley. Nobody was on the street.

They stripped off his ring, cufflinks, and watch; they ripped cash and credit cards from the wallet and flung the leather away. They kicked him in the head.

Reggie grabbed boots and jerked two to the ground. Rising quickly to his knees, he dazed the hoods with lightning jabs that landed flush to their heads. They sprawled in puddles. He sprang to his feet. He stood face-to-face-with a tall lean man wearing shades. Two other thugs stood behind him.

The minions made a move—the leader sang, "Belay!"—and instantly, they halted. The leader peered closer at the victim. He took off his shades.

"We together," said Beau Dancy.

"To the death," Reggie said.

"Whose?"

"Whoever gone wrong, Beau," said Reggie quietly.

Beau was dressed in black—windbreaker, turtleneck, jeans, leather basketball shoes. He took off the windbreaker, oblivious to the stinging rain. His shoulders and arms had grown more muscular with age and ceaseless workouts. But he remained as lean—and lethal—as a sword thrust. "Wrong depend on what you think be right."

"Gangsta be right? Beating and robbing innocent men be right?" A terrible certainty was forming in Reggie's brain—in horror, he tried to push it off—but knew he must face it. "And women," he added, his voice strong to overcome inner blocks.

Beau laughed easily, simply, chillingly. "Ain't no other way, money. Strong eat the weak, like Wolf Larsen show."

"Humphrey van Weyden grow and defeat him."

"He become strong."

"Strong because be having moral principles."

"The king be killed, long live the king, that all."

"He not victimize the innocent."

"Be no innocent."

"Educated people teach classes, treat patients, start businesses, further human life—"

"Further they power. Be gaining money, prestige, influence—"

"Like Hornsby?"

"Gain power over you."

"Nobody gain power over me—you the only one wanted it—you fail."

Beau Dancy smiled. "You kicking ass on the street. Did I?"

"Think everybody like you?"

"Everybody wanna be like me. Just not as smart. Or as tough."

"Ain't what brain power be for, Beau," Reggie pleaded. Even now, he could forgive.

"Only thing brain power be for."

"You could write books, give lectures, get a Ph.D.—"

"—Got a Ph.D., yo. Doctor of the Streets—"

"—Be teaching the brothers...the sisters...the best and the brightest, not mauling them—"

"—I be teaching them, Player, teach them every goddamn day—"

Reggie shook his head. "Be teaching them Literature, Philosophy—"

"Whose philosophy?"

Reggie stopped.

"Be teaching Philosophy every day—dumbass niggas think they smart—they not—they good only to serve one smarter than them." Beau paused. "Brainpower the means to power. That true Philosophy, Julius." He sounded almost sad. "No changing it."

"You kill Hornsby."

"Old man serve his purpose."

"You maul, rape, plunder every educated person you find."

"They be ruling the machine—I be ruling them."

"You the only machine."

"A steamroller, baby, king of the street."

Reggie drew a deep breath. "You days of warring 'gainst intelligence be done."

"Who gonna stop me?"

"You looking at him."

Beau Dancy ripped off his turtleneck.

"Bring it, bitches!"

Reggie heard nothing. Around his neck, Dancy wore a gold band. On the band was a gold graduation ring. A woman's ring Reggie had seen. *Princeton.*

Dancy saw where he looked.

"Bitch wore it, think she be smart." He smiled soullessly. "She not smart enough."

For the first time in his life, Reggie was calm. Quiet hours, after midnight, in his personal library, could not match this. A clarity, a moral certainty filled him, and every step of his future lay clear to his sight.

Beau Dancy, of hand and foot, was quicker than a mongoose; he hit, with either hand, like a striking scorpion; and was a thousand times triumphant over streetbrawling foes greater in strength and numbers. A conscience-less killer, Dancy eschewed knife, gun, or club, preferring to beat his opponents to death with bare knuckles. Enemies, of whom few survived, thought him fearless. The truth, Reggie knew— he was a desperate man, driven by terror, against which his defense was remorseless aggression.

Slowly, cockily, Dancy raised his fists; the dark, dank alley assumed the dimensions of a gladiator pit; and the young prizefighter readied for a struggle beyond any he would face in the ring. This was not, he sensed, a fight between formidable warriors; this was a death struggle between forces that had clashed since men first oozed from primordial slime—those who deployed intelligence to advance human life versus those who, with or without intelligence, sought conquest, plunder, rape, power, destruction. If this was literature, the impending battle was not a play or a novel: It was an epic.

Reggie exhaled. He raised his fists.

A few lightning jabs, Reggie took on his forearms; he threw a left hook, Dancy ducked. The big man circled, lightness itself; the smaller man crouched, on his toes, motionless. Lulling. Dancy could, from a standing crouch, explode into vicious assault, with fists or flashing feet—streaking—from left or right or straight-ahead, flashing so quick that a hardened streetfighter never saw the blow that lay him on his back.

Reggie blocked a left-right combo that stung his massive forearms but did not see the lightning kick to his groin that mangled his testicles and brought him to his knees on the damp pavement with a throatful of vomit that threatened to choke his breathing. Leaping off his left foot, Dancy unleashed a right-footed kick that smashed Reggie's cheek and drove him full-length to the pavement. Then he was on Reggie, raining kicks, with remorseless savagery, to his fallen opponent's skull.

Reggie's prodigious strength was kicked from him. He could not breathe. He lay unmoving but the world moved. He slipped toward the brink of unconsciousness, into which he had pounded so many. Gayle Forster's face appeared in his delirium; not Gayle in the hospital, but Gayle in the classroom, brilliant, commanding, masterful—and threatened. Dancy would savage her, as though stomping a beetle; the professor; he wanted the professor bruised, mauled, splintered. "No," Reggie gasped.

His left hand reached from damp cobblestones and clasped Dancy's ankle—he rose to a sitting position, taking a crashing kick to the face that splattered his nose—and threw a right cross, of twice the power that had leveled Sleepmaker, against Dancy's locked knee.

The knee socket splintered and ligaments tore with a resounding snap. Dancy dropped to the ground; though in agony, he uttered no sound. On his back, one leg useless, he unleashed a kick to Reggie's solar plexus that rocked the big man, driving from his throat the puke that had pooled there. It spattered the alley. Reggie grabbed Dancy's good ankle before the foot flashed away; reached down, grabbed Dancy's other ankle, he rose, hoisted, savagely swung, and crashed his foe's body with shattering force into the near building's brick wall. Dancy's body crumpled face first to the pavement and did not move.

Reggie turned, in a crouch, on the gang members. Blood and puke flecked his cheeks. His shattered nose was pinned to the left side of his face. His hands were balled fists. Though in a crouch, he appeared his full six-foot-five; his eyes were baleful death. "Next," he croaked.

These were their master's men, trained by their leader. Four of them, with rippling biceps and soulless eyes, they fanned out, even in the narrow alley, flanking him, spilling at him from every quadrant, a coordinated assault. Reggie knew the broken bones of his face, with another blow, the pain would drive any man into unconsciousness. His eyes told him his foes knew it, too. In an instant, they would spring to attack.

"Halt!" cried a voice from the ground, wheezing but commanding.

Reggie turned. Beau Dancy. How the f--k was he even conscious? He's Beau F--king Dancy, that's how, an inner voice said. Beau staggered to one leg. His right knee was shattered; he stood on his left, his right leg bent in the air. He slouched forward like a hunchback, ribs busted, shoulder maybe separated. Sweat poured off of him even more than rain; he belonged in traction, heavily doped on painkillers. He turned to his men.

"Get the f--k outa here."

"But, Boss—"

"—Now," Dancy hissed. He pulled a nine millimeter from the back of his jeans. He pointed it at their heads. "Or I swear to the demons that rule this world, that I will spill the brains of every goddamn one of you." They scattered.

Beau threw the handgun on the alley's reeking surface. He hopped forward on one leg. His hands were not fists but striking edges of a martial arts master. "You a bad motherf--ker," he wheezed.

Reggie stared, in horror...and in awe.

"But we together," Beau said.

"To the death," Reggie said.

"Whose?"

"Yours."

Beau kept coming. He was but three feet away.

"Beau, let's call it a day."

"To the death," Beau whispered. "Someone don't leave this alley."

He leaped off his left leg and fired in midair. Suspended in space, like the greatest male ballet dancer of history, way off the ground, his left leg whistled across distance, delivering a blow like a wave crashing on a resistless shore. Reggie whirled, taking the punishing shot on his left shoulder, which immediately went numb, knowing that if Beau landed to his face, the fight was over. He crouched, he held both clenched fists in front of his face, he drove his massive bulk at his remorseless foe. Beau swung away, hopping like a one-legged rabbit, his laughter ringing in the night. Beau twisted, hopping, seeking escape from the big man's driving shoulders, hindered by the narrow confines and slick surface. Reggie threw defense to the wind, his face was exposed, he fired, he landed, a crushing combo to Beau's shattered rib cage, as Beau landed a devastating left-hand chop to Reggie's smashed face. The big man went down like axed, punished into unconsciousness for the first time in his life.

The rain woke him. Beau lay in a heap against a brick wall of greater strength than even his blows. His green eyes were open, focused on Reggie. Somehow he had never seemed more regal. "I can't move," he said. He smiled.

"Motherf--ker, you all busted up inside," Reggie said.

"You ugly ass face all busted up, bitch," Dancy said.

Reggie crawled to Dancy's side. Gripping the ground with his right hand, he fired a crashing left to the point of Dancy's jaw. Dancy's head slumped to his right shoulder.

"Shut the f--k up."

He leaned against the wall, side-by-side with the greatest foe and the greatest friend he had ever had. He closed his eyes. He was too busted up to cry. He breathed, marshaling his strength. Finally, he tottered to his feet and leaned against the wall. He bent down, gently took the ring and gold band from around his foe's neck and thrust them in his pocket. He hoisted Dancy's inert frame over his shoulder. Gayle was at his place. He would bring her tormentor to her.

He carried Dancy up the stairs and into his apartment. Gayle sat, breathing heavily, in a chair. He locked the door.

"Who is he?" she asked.

He lay Beau's motionless body on the sofa. He gave her the gold band and Princeton ring.

"Beau Dancy."

For the first time, she looked at Reggie. Both hands spurted reflexively to her face. "O my God!" She hobbled from the chair and limped to him. "Reggie, you need a hospital. Now."

"Beau need it more than me."

"I don't care about Beau." She had her phone in her hand. "I'm calling 911."

He limped to his closet and withdrew a bat. He gave it to her. Beau moaned. He was coming to. She took the bat in both hands. She looked from Reggie to Beau and back to Reggie. "Reggie, you're badly hurt."

He beat his right fist against his heart. "In here mostly."

"You need a doctor immediately."

"No doctor can fix this."

"Beau Dancy."

"Do what you gotta do. It's not like he don't have it coming."

She swung the bat in the air, then leaned on it like a cane. "I can't."

"You'll testify?"

"Yes. You?"

He nodded. He went to the window, looking for cops and the ambulance. It would be a few minutes.

"Reggie."

He turned back.

"Julius Collymore could not be forgiven. Reggie H.A.R.D. might be."

Something in his stomach, on this night of horror, flipped onto its back. It caused an immediate effect behind his eyes.

"No tears," she said. "In a hall of justice."

He wanted to embrace her, to tell her how different it would be. But she knew—and he belonged in surgery. He stood by the window. He leaned on the wall for support. The war wasn't over. But the tide had turned. Internally, too. Reggie H.A.R.D. would come out of the closet. He smiled, even though it hurt his splintered face. The professor would like that. He stared out the window. A bank at the corner of the avenue had a clock over its front entrance. Ten-twenty-five. Seemed like three or four in the morning. He noticed more than the time.

Turning the corner in front of the bank was a young professional, dressed in a suit and dark raincoat. He must have waited in the subway station until the rain abated. He carried a zipped portfolio and a T-square. As Reggie watched, three punks turned the corner, eyeing the man in front, following closely. Two fanned out into the street, barring escape. The third sneaked up behind him.

Reggie drew a deep breath and hurried for the door.

"Reggie!"

He moved remorselessly forward.

"Where are you going?"

He looked back over his shoulder. "The intelligent war back." Then he staggered through the door.

Boundaries of Restraint

The murderous rampage at William Tecumseh Sherman High School in Brooklyn, New York, did not merely end lives—it altered them. Some survivors came through physically unscathed. Morally, no one did.

Susan Siegel, the school psychologist—Davy Friedman, the ex-Marine—and Terry McGill, the pacifistic former priest—were as different as three individuals could be. But their fates intersected at an infamous moment. Their chosen routes out of it branched off like wayfarers along divergent life paths.

It was a day in late May, on which the sun shined in a dry blue sky so filled with fleecy white shrouds that one could think he resided in Arizona, not New York. There were those at the school, who, as children, had read of such days—days on which earthquakes or landslides shattered villages, crushing thousands under tons of unyielding debris, as the sun smiled its divine benediction upon the carnage.

They entered William Sherman High School with automatic weapons and the usual excuses for mass murder—the students were bullying, the teachers unfair, the administrators had expelled them—and opened fire immediately.

They focused first on the police officers. A hail of bullets sent hurtling backward the three officers at the front desk. Serious wounds to their skulls and shoulders kept them writhing on the deck.

Students scattered and dived to the tiled floor as the acrid scent of gunpowder and the rending cries of the wounded filled the afternoon air.

The would-be killers had timed their entrance perfectly, knowing it was a passing interval between class periods. The lobby and the first floor hallways streamed with students, some exiting, some scurrying toward subsequent classes. Even for those not in visual contact, the thunderous, confined-space clatter of gun shots was unmistakable: Screams instantly slashed bystanders' ears, grating as harshly as the gunfire, and students raced in every direction, some bolting for the building's exits, others fleeing back up the stairs, and some, in white-faced terror, trying to push through or climb over the backs of others.

Smoke filled the witnesses' eyes, blood slicked the floor, and an overriding sense of pervasive fear was smelled—and welcomed—by the gun-toting intruders. The perpetrators neither grinned nor snarled—but filled internally with a slowly-spreading dark satisfaction designed to war against, but somehow augmenting, a desperate sense of terror chronically pervasive in their souls.

Upstairs, in three separate rooms of the cavernous building three distinct heads snapped up at the sound of the guns. The killers made their way slowly, remorselessly, toward the stairs, toward a specific room, and toward the targeted heads for whom they came.

The three heads, ears filled with the unambiguous sounds they had hoped never to hear in a school building, reacted in distinctively different forms.

Chapter One: The Liberal

"Susan," my assistant, Hayley Bachman, said, looking up from her desk in the Guidance Counselor's office on the 2ⁿᵈ floor. "That's gunfire."

"What?" I had been so immersed in reading the psychological profile of several troubled students that nothing else had registered. But now, I noticed Hayley's fair skin and blonde hair were paler than usual—and the antiseptic, gray-slabbed walls surrounding the steel-grilled windows had never seemed so institutional.

Then I heard a burst of gunfire that sounded as if moving nearer the bottom of the stairwell down the hall from our door. I leaped to my feet, trying to fight down the panic surging into my throat.

"We've got to find Davy," was the first thought that came to my mind and lips. "Come on."

"Davy Friedman can take care of himself!" she shrieked from behind me.

"Exactly." I bolted through the door and into the hall.

The corridors were pandemonium. A horde of terrified students fled, seemingly scurrying in three directions at once, like a herd of panicked alley cats jolted from lethargy by a back-firing truck. But bigger than cats. They came at me from every angle, sweating faces and heaving chests towering over my five-foot height. One slammed my shoulder as he rushed past, spinning me to the wall, and another rammed a knee or elbow into my solar plexus as I rebounded, driving me down and expelling the air from my diaphragm. I was disoriented, I didn't know where Hayley was—then a foot pounded me down like a crashing wave to the ocean floor.

I crawled toward the wall, where I could right myself, but a passing boot to my mouth swiveled my head and made me taste blood. Fighting unconsciousness, clawing the floor and wall with my nails, I pulled myself up. For an instant, I saw a blur of pale skin reflected in the glass of the Assistant Principal's door—and was startled by the realization that the taut face with the left cheekbone already swollen and the right eye a slit was mine. I felt an overpowering urge to puke.

I caught a brief glimpse of Terry McGill and his nephew, Paddy O'Neill, in the Assistant Principal's office. Hayley was on her knees, tangled with several students, in the middle of the hall. She started to rise. I reached to her with my left hand. To my left, I saw Davy Friedman turn the corner at the far end of the hall. He held something in his hand. Slowly, stuporously, I turned the knob of the AP's door. It opened a crack. Then the stairway door down the hall a hundred feet to my right burst open and two armed men emerged. They pushed a disheveled male figure in front of them. It was the disciplinarian—and detested English teacher—Daryl Corticelli.

"Susan!" I heard Davy scream and then the world lit up with hellish red flame and bursting explosions. I felt more than saw the impact of bullets tearing into Hayley's back and shoulders. One of the students crawled on his belly toward me. Then hot searing pain across my cheek and head, like my skull roasted over a barbecue pit, and I fell against the door—and blackness.

Had it been only a year since I had sat so proudly at the dinner celebrating my initiation—along with three classmates—into the morally prestigious Society of Humanity? It had been held at Brooklyn's famed Caraveggio's on the Bay with its salt air and sweeping vista of the Verrazano Bridge. It had taken a year-and-a-half of study, training, and meditation to reach that climactic night. Terrence McGill, a former priest who had decided he loved the people more than he loved God, had resigned from the Church to form the Society some twelve years previous, and had built it now into a thriving moral agency some several hundred souls strong. Terry, a highly trained boxer in his youth, had recognized the extreme difficulty with which a select few could transcend their inherent animalistic impulses, especially in the face of violent assault, and attain a true humanity, meeting mindless violence with impassioned reason.

Terry had presided over the training sessions at the Society's headquarters on 4th Avenue in Bay Ridge. Although in his mid-sixties, he remained a commanding figure. He'd been dressed in black shirt and slacks that contrasted with a full head of silver hair, garb which made his lean chest and thick hands seem even more powerful. Although standing an imposing six-foot-six, he looked down on us only physically. He never cursed, he never raised his voice, and the respect that emanated from him for our humanity seemed a palpable presence in the room, like a thick pillar to be leaned on when exhausted. His initial words galvanized our attention.

"Although I was born after World War II had ended—and to an Irish Catholic family in Brooklyn—I am a Holocaust survivor. So are most of you. Festering in our souls is the rage of the innocent victim unjustly battered, because this is the way in which society treats many of its helpless children. We must permit ourselves to lower the barriers encaging the beast within—and feel it in all of its snarling, hideous fury—because this is the only way to understand, empathize with, and reach out to the aggressor."

Every exercise and meditative aid that followed had been designed to attain this goal. Terry had devoted years of research to understanding the principles, methods, and techniques a person must assimilate in order to overcome innate bestial responses and achieve the highest moral levels possible to humanity—a genuine and universal repudiation of violence in all forms and contexts.

Moreover, he had lived out his own teachings. Just before I'd met him but well within the memory of numerous Society members, he had given a talk on his creed to a community group in a crime infested neighborhood on the Lower East Side of New York. After the talk, he had walked alone to the subway station. He had been beset by a gang of youthful thugs demanding his wallet. When he politely declined, they assaulted him with fists, clubs, and the butt end of an automatic pistol. Though battered mercilessly and immensely stronger than any of his tormentors, he had never thrown a blow against them. He tried to wrap them up in his massive arms, restrain them, and keep his captives between them and his body. In the end, he had been robbed of the few dollars he possessed and his wristwatch—had been savagely beaten—and had held two of his assailants long enough for the police to arrive and arrest them. He'd spent two weeks in the hospital. The thugs spent two years in Juvie.

We underwent rigorous moral and physical training every other weekend for a year. Seeking to integrate throughout our souls a full understanding of the hapless futility of violence, we studied stories told about Jesus of Nazareth. We read works by or about Tolstoy, William Penn, Gandhi, Martin Luther King. We pored over the passage in *Acts*, in which Stephen refuses to resist his stoning. You could physically feel the intake of breath in the room's utter quiet when a student read aloud: "Then he fell on his knees and cried out, 'Lord, do not hold this sin against them.'"

We practiced with a Columbia University wrestler, a past Ivy League welterweight champion, regarding the use of leverage, balance, and pressure points to wrap up, take down, and restrain even physically bigger opponents. We worked with trained clinicians, striving to access the obdurate nucleus of suppressed rage we hid within, seeking to comprehend its gestation, befriend its existence, and alchemize its turbulent nature into a pacific, empathic outreach to the aggressor's violent core.

Above all, we simulated barbarous encounters. At breathless sessions in a hushed training room, veteran pacifists role played aggressive characters we would likely meet—spouses, family members, criminal assailants. Starting from casual disputes, they adroitly and casually escalated the hostility until the apprentice quite forgot he engaged in simulation and found himself embroiled in searing altercations in which he was first verbally abused and, inevitably, physically assaulted. His assignment, over and again, was to defuse the situation: to meet rage with reason, volatility with calm, and incipient violence with upright, hands-behind-the-back moral dignity. Most often, the students failed and permitted themselves to be sucked into the maelstrom of seething, mindless conflict.

But one repeatedly succeeded. No demeaning insult, slap to the face, or blow to the head sent me sprawling over the precipice of atavism. I took the blows, stood my ground, and fought back—with logic withering and incontrovertible.

In one memorable episode, a swaggering lout bullied young Paddy O'Neill, who squirmed visibly under the onslaught. Paddy, white-faced and sixteen, had the gangly body of an anemic colt and the eyes of Bambi on a rush-hour Interstate. He murmured some inaudible response to the aggressor's verbal barbs and I interceded to tell his tormentor to pick on someone his own age. He proceeded to revile me with every imprecation man had devised for officious, busybody females and then clubbed me with a thick forearm to the skull. I did not see stars and did not see red. I saw only a walking embodiment of irony. "It's clear that you are a zealous, male-bashing feminist," I said to his gaping mug. "They claim men are violent, illiterate beasts and you're intent on proving it." It caught him off-guard and he was stupefied for several moments, enough time for me to go on the verbal offensive and talk him down from his rage. To the entire class, Terry McGill admiringly stated: "You are Miss Logic." Holding ice to my puffy cheek, he added: "Pacifism is not for the faint of heart."

But I ultimately failed to discover the hidden rage he described as skulking in most, perhaps all of us. "Even you, a healer," Terry said in response to my earnest questions alone in his office. "Even your gentle nature knows latent depths of hostility that could be drawn out under the wrong circumstances. Befriend the beast, Susan," he admonished. "It might make all the difference one day."

The irony was not lost on Davy Friedman. He looked up immediately, when I broached the subject, from his reading of *Pride and Prejudice*—looked at his girlfriend over the tops of his reading glasses with eyes full of something beyond attentiveness, affection, and respect.

"Terry's right," he said sadly, knowingly. "If assaulted, you will discover the rage he describes." He put down the book. "But why do you deny its uprightness?"

I knew that his voice's slight tremor, the haunted hunted quality of his eyes was not a trait on display to others. I alone was permitted to know at what personal cost the combat Marine had performed his acts of valorous rectitude.

At least one of Terry's students, Denise Creacy—a friend from our first encounter at these sessions—immediately recognized the truth of his words. Thirty-something, blonde, plump, and attractive, she'd been exiled to a stream of foster homes in her youth, after her father's life was extinguished of alcoholism and her mother's love of onerous responsibility. She, who had barely to work to access the rage he described, toiled more assiduously than any to master the principles he endorsed. She had a spectacularly volcanic temper, had been expelled from one school for physically striking another student, and was ceaselessly remorseful for various incendiary outbursts. She came to Terry McGill with hopeful desperation.

Alone with us one day in his office, he recounted the horrific events that had transformed his life thirteen years earlier—the murder, in an armed subway robbery, of his sister and brother-in-law. Terry had proceeded to formally adopt his nephew, three-year old Paddy O'Neill, and moved to a quieter neighborhood a few blocks from Kings Highway, right down Bedford Avenue from Sherman. Six months later, he left the Church and initiated his society of pacifists. At age three Paddy had witnessed the murder of his parents. Mercifully he had no conscious recollection of the events but mercilessly his emotional life was permeated with nameless terrors. He was a supple kid with long legs and bowed head who generally walked alone the distance between home and school. He had joined the Society just before me, although remaining quietly in the meetings' background.

The child constituted one of the twin pillars of Terry's existence. The old man had no living mother or father, no other siblings, no romantic involvements, no friends. The Society was his passion, his career, his religion. Paddy was his family. With others, he was unsparingly kind and unfailingly withdrawn. He gave of his time generously, especially to me, but a gray concrete wall topped with a grim "no trespassing" sign loomed in the immediate distance. With Paddy alone, the wall was disassembled. The old man took him to the awe inspiring rites of Saint Patrick's Cathedral, to spiritual shrines, on pilgrimage to the Holy Land, and opened his heart, his spirit, and his conscience to the child. A long-time Society member said to me, in a whisper, "Terry McGill venerates only God. He loves only Paddy O'Neill."

Often I'd see the boy at meetings and in the halls of Sherman—a willowy, athletic build but a mournful presence with white skin and haunted eyes. He and his uncle had met several times with Sherman's Assistant Principal regarding a prospective seminar on pacifism to be held at the school.

Over the months, Terry had given me hours of one-on-one time as I strove to conscientiously complete the program. The combination of my psychological expertise and the seeming utter lack of rage in my soul captivated him—and an undeniable bond grew. My ultimate failure with the exercises had me on the verge of tears. But his arm around my shoulder had eased my fears. "You're quite a woman, Susan," he'd said. "A wise man would be proud to have you for his daughter."

After a year of training had come graduation at Caraveggio's. We sipped red wine and smiled in the glow of candlelight. An altercation broke out at a dinner several tables away.

A wife screamed a vile insult attacking her husband's manhood and he belted her in response. Denise, sitting closest, was the first one there. She interposed herself between the combatants, hands behind her back, utterly non-threatening, as we'd been taught.

"She lowered herself to the gutter with that insult," Denise said calmly to the husband. "Do you insist on joining her there?"

The rest of the graduates ringed Denise, forming a defensive wall shielding the wife. We nodded our assent to her words. It registered only on the periphery of my consciousness that Terry McGill stood by our table, several feet from the altercation, watching intently.

"Don't side with that bastard!" the wife screamed at Denise, rising.

"Shut your trap, Evelyn!" the husband roared. "Do you hear me—just shut up!"

He advanced toward her. Denise wrapped her arms around his waist to restrain him as the rest of us moved to do the same. He pushed her off. The rest of us tried to pin his arms—but he was of massive girth and broke our grip. Evelyn stood behind us, hurling taunts at her husband.

"Some man you are, Jerry!" she shrieked, laughing in contempt. "Held back by a gaggle of hens."

With a bellow of rage, he broke through the defensive ring and grabbed her throat. Denise was on him but he slugged her with his left fist on the cheek and proceeded to choke his wife. "You'll kill her!" I cried. "Act like a man and talk to her!" I tried to pry his grip from Evelyn's face, which was turning the first shade of purple. Denise staggered back to him and with both hands also tried to loosen his fingers. We both failed. Desperate, as Evelyn wheezed for breath, Denise pounded the assailant's chest with both fists again and again, and then, in frantic convulsion, his cheeks and his skull. Suddenly the brawl ended. Jerry let loose his grip. Evelyn gasped for air and turned toward her husband. "You don't have to play so rough, ya big ape," she said, hands rubbing her throat. "You want an Academy Award?" We all gaped, not knowing what to make of it.

Terry McGill's sad face loomed over us. "Thank you," he said to the two combatants, who stood there calmly now, breathing heavily. Turning slowly and sorrowfully to Denise, he said quietly: "This was the final test. You failed." It will stay with me to the grave—the fragrance of the tangy air and the brilliant expanse of New York Bay serving as a backdrop to the look on Denise's face as she slowly comprehended that she was now denied entry to the society whose principles she so dearly cherished.

The convention of dwarves hammered relentlessly at the unyielding metal. They made no progress, but their pounding sent wave after pulsating wave through the hard ground. Someone—the ground or the dwarves—experienced the incessant activity as pain. Why didn't they stop? The world was red, although tinged with black. Was this Hell? But it was cold, not hot—cold and very, very hard.

It was the cold tiles on the floor of the Assistant Principal's office that revived me. That and the waves of pain crashing steadily against the interior walls of my skull, causing me to retch violently. But nothing came out. And yet, the floor under my cheek felt slippery with some liquid that was not puke.

Someone was screaming.

"Do it! Do it!" a woman's voice screamed. "Get it over with!"

I struggled to my knees. Everything spun. I put my hand down to steady myself—put it down into a small pool of fluid that my slowly focusing eyes identified as red. I grabbed at a desk and staggered to my feet.

In front of me was a whitewashed wall with two rows of slate gray metallic filing cabinets standing against them, a mere few feet from the grilled window. Between the filing cabinets with her back against the wall stood Dr. Mary Jo Montefusco, the Assistant Principal. Her slender figure was dwarfed by an enormous male frame that weighed at least 400 pounds who stood between the AP and me, his back to me. To her temple, he pressed the barrel of a jet black assault rifle.

Mary Jo's glasses lay shattered at her feet, her face was white, and a purple welt already rose under her left eye. She took air in slowly, regulating her breathing, and then let it out.

"Do it," she said more calmly now, though her eyes were closed. "What are you waiting for?"

Paddy O'Neill, with blood on his cheeks from a wound on his forehead, lay unmoving on the floor against the cabinets. He breathed shallowly. Carefully, I stepped over him, advancing toward Mary Jo.

"We came for you, bitch," spat the voice so peculiarly high-pitched for a male his size—and I knew then it was Ronnie Hirsch. He grabbed a handful of her mussed brown hair and slammed the back of her head against the wall.

"Stop it!" I screamed, but my voice only croaked like a dying woman's.

"Miss Siegel," said a slight figure, turning from the window, his chronically twisted face momentarily transformed into a look of respect—and I felt my extremities turn icy. Warren Baker, I had known before his expulsion, to be a hundred pounds of body and a thousand tons of rage. He, too, cradled an assault weapon in his arms, but did not point it at me. His morbid intelligence, enthralled by the occult and the apocalyptic, had plagued me through two tormenting years of our work together.

"Welcome to the End Days," he said softly, and, astonishingly, almost kindly.

His past, I knew, might have enraged Jesus—the father he never met, shot to death in a criminal heist, the abusive, alcoholic mother steadily drinking herself to death; the kid reared for years by his elder brother, William, a drug dealer, a convicted murderer, a bull-necked punishing brute, all the more dangerous for his education and high intelligence...nicknamed "Gash" for the extended knife wound slashed across his left cheek...the family something you could not make up, a bitter clan too nightmarish to be fictitious. I had detested this kid, even in the act of feeling sorry for him, and my gut churning from the start told me I could not help him.

The room, where I had spoken to Mary Jo so many times regarding so many students, was unrecognizable. Papers flung from her desk littered the floor. Her smashed reading lamp lay at my feet, and photos of her two sons had been splintered with bullets and shot off the wall. Terry McGill's elongated frame, dressed characteristically in black, lay stretched motionless on the floor before Mary Jo's desk. Thin rivulets of blood trickled slowly from under his body and I couldn't tell whether he breathed. Strangely, I no longer felt sick, only a numbness originating in my bowels moving remorselessly upward.

"You're gonna suffer first," Ronnie Hirsch snarled at his victim.

A male voice semi-growled in response. It was a guttural sound, venting rage and gasping for air. A lean man in a brown jacket and unknotted tie was bound and gagged in an office chair in the room's corner, partially obscured by the file cabinets. The lower part of his face was covered by someone's bloody shirt tied across his nose and mouth. But the curly brown hair and rock-stolid gray eyes were instantly recognizable. Daryl Corticelli, a colleague of Davy's in the English Department, spent many Saturdays rock-climbing with him in the Catskills—and many more free periods arguing with him in the teacher's lounge. They stashed gear in their lockers, so they could head for the mountains after school on Friday afternoons. But despite the bond, their arguments were heated affairs, because Davy, who had served four decorated years in the Marine Corps, held views extreme and unpopular among the faculty of a New York City public high school. Even as Daryl struggled for air, I saw his powerful chest muscles working against the ropes that lashed him to the chair. To his right, I noticed a heavy metal filing cabinet had been jammed against the door, barring it to outsiders.

I moved toward Mary Jo. "Ronnie," I said in calm, measured tones. "She's innocent. Let her go."

He whirled to me at the sound of my gentle voice, his fat, affable face twisted into the permanent clownish leer that he habitually wore to ensure the inexorable humor would be directed at his antics, not his form. His enormous left paw was wrapped around Mary Jo's throat, pinning her to the wall. His right clutched the weapon, now pointing downward at the floor.

"Miss Siegel," he said with concern grotesquely comical under the circumstances. "You're bleeding."

I struggled for self-control. I'd had time to consider neither the flesh wound to the forehead nor the burning score across my cheek, but I felt the slow trickle of blood on my neck. "Oh my," I said sweetly. "I can't imagine who's responsible for that."

The desperate humor brought a momentary smile to his face and bought me the second I needed to advance into his space. His massive arm buried in Mary Jo's neck prevented me from interposing my body between him and his victim. But I pushed past the horror and willed my mind to work. Words, the Society had stressed. The power of reason to defuse a murderous situation—to gaze into an aggressor's soul, to feel his own victimized agony, and to respond with authentically unfeigned empathy. "You're right," I said, nodding my head in agreement. "The world has treated you like s—t." Gently, I touched his arm just beneath the shoulder. "But Dr. Montefusco is not one of them."

I knew his soul. He had felt me groping its dark recesses, rearranging his privates. He could feel it now. It was a superiority.

"Miss Siegel..." he started uncertainly, and I didn't stop to wonder that, even as he stood in the midst of the bloody carnage he had wreaked on the innocent, he still hesitated with respect before someone who had penetrated deep into him.

"She suspended me," he said, his eyes yielding their veneer of bonhomie and releasing traces of the molten heat I knew simmered below. "She expelled me, she stayed on my ass, she never cut me any—"

"She's not the one who fed you every second of the day to shut you up—and then screamed with despair that you were a fat slob who would die like your father."

His grip on his victim loosened slightly. I sensed it. He turned slowly toward me, at the glacial pace in which he moved. I had several seconds.

"She recognized your brainpower, Ronnie," I said softly, my normally animated hands clasped, motionless, behind my back. "Despite your failing grades, she placed you in Mr. Corticelli's Honors English class. She talked to me constantly about your progress—and at her initiative. Everything she did was because she cared about your education—and about you."

I didn't know if he would kill me—or if his Baby Huey jowls would soon trickle with tears—but I was never going to know. For the crushing impact into my left shoulder from the butt of Warren Baker's rifle drove me to the floor. I was on my knees in front of Daryl's chair, a separated shoulder inflicting pain I never knew existed, and the only sound for long seconds was a wounded animal's scream that must have chilled the blood of all within earshot.

But not Warren Baker's. His was already chilled. He stood above me as I screamed, patient, waiting, remorseless, the business end of his weapon pointed at the floor but ready in an instant to be raised to my forehead. I looked at him through eyes blurring with water. I understood now—I knew what Davy meant when he spoke of the kill-lust, the red raging haze simultaneously obscuring his vision but clarifying it, the draining of all fear, the fury molded into calm intent, as, in seeming slow motion, he lined up the charging Iraqi targets in the sights of his M-16, and, no longer conscious of either his slain comrades or the blood streaming from wounds to his shoulder and side, mowed them down like so many hurtling chunks of marbled beef.

You're still alive, said a voice in my head. Employ your training. Use your brain. He's a murderer—but he's a battered, frightened child. He's the first because he's the second. You know the causal link. Gently...touch the source...

"Warren," I said, with the sympathy of an angel. "Killing the innocent will not punish those guilty of abusing you."

To my left, Paddy O'Neill groaned as he regained consciousness. His eyes were open. Hirsch and Baker glanced at him. From their looks, it was clear they did not know him.

"Montefusco and Corticelli go to the Beast today," Baker said. "They die slow. But we can be merciful to the punk. Put him out of his misery."

Baker's gun was on me. Hirsch's moved slowly to Paddy.

"Ronnie, no," I gasped.

I rose from the floor. Even this slow movement generated pain that swept me to the brink of unconsciousness. I bit through my lower lip. Only dimly, I felt blood spurt onto my jaw. I stood in front of Paddy.

"You'll have to shoot me first," I croaked.

Warren Baker swiveled on his heels and pointed his gun at my chest.

"That can be arranged." His cold eyes gazed at me venomously.

Violent death was perhaps an instant away. But the periphery of my vision registered motion. Terry McGill was alive. His head rose slowly from the pool of blood on the floor.

Ronnie Hirsch's massive paw gripped Baker's gun barrel. "No. Kill the others. But leave her alone."

With strength surprising in one so slight, Baker ripped the rifle out of Hirsch's grasp. He jabbed it between my breasts and shoved me back. A wave of pain engulfed me. The world swam and I was certain I would puke. Baker pointed his gun at the head of a prone Paddy O'Neill. The child's large eyes looked imploringly at me, not at the would-be murderer.

Terry McGill was on his knees. He stared at his nephew.

"Judgment Day comes for us all," Baker said sadly. His finger tightened on the trigger.

"Yours need not come today," Terry McGill said. Shakily, he rose to his feet. Baker and Hirsch both whirled on him. Baker's gun was now on the ex-priest. Terry's face was white from blood loss but his eyes were calm and unyielding with desperate courage. "Take me, if you must spill blood. The boy is only sixteen. Let him go."

"It's his nephew," I whispered. "He raised him like a son."

Baker took in the information.

"Your nephew. Raised him like a son—is that right?"

Terry's head nodded fractionally. I could see the pain in his eyes was not merely from the threat to Paddy's life. He had no strength for wasted motion.

It was Ronnie Hirsch who first saw the possibilities. "The nine millimeter." He pointed to the pistol in his belt.

Slowly, Baker grinned. The flesh pulled taut across his face made it look to me like a death's skull.

"We finish Montefusco and Corticelli," Hirsch said. "We give the old guy the handgun. Make the old bastard fight for the punk's life. He kills us, they live. He fails, they die." A grim smile touched his face. "Like a video game—but with live rounds."

"Ronnie," I said. "He's a pacifist. He won't fight."

Baker stared at Terry. "A pacifist," he sneered. "You broken down old f—k. You won't even fight for your own kid?"

Terry was wobbly. He bled from wounds to his side and his right shoulder and it was clear he belonged in a hospital. But, pulled up to his full height, he towered over the two killers.

He shook his head sadly, adamantly. "No, I won't fight."

"You goddamn coward," Hirsch said. "Your own goddamn kid."

He lumbered toward Terry. I knew his emotional life to move as ponderously as did his body. But his jaws worked and the redness of his face seemed fueled by their motion. "Your own goddamn kid." He got right up in Terry's face. He rammed the butt of his rifle into the pit of Terry's stomach. Terry doubled over, retching onto the floor. Somehow he stayed on his feet.

"That's all you deserve," Hirsch said.

Terry straightened in seeming slow motion. But Ronnie Hirsch moved even more slowly. Terry wrapped his arms around Hirsch and pulled him to his chest in a bear hug. Hirsch bellowed in pain, surprised by the strength that even now lurked in the old man's lean frame. Terry tried to squeeze the air from his captive's lungs—but his strength was gone and Hirsch was too big. The murderer broke free of his grip and spun away. Terry was too exhausted to follow but reached to the full extent of his long arms and ripped the pistol from Hirsch's belt. Hirsch stood gasping by the file cabinets, just a foot from Mary Jo. The muzzle of his rifle pointed at the floor.

With two hands, Terry pointed the pistol at his heart. "Drop your weapon." He spoke to Warren. "Or I send your comrade to Hell."

Warren stared, his mouth open. Then his eyes gleamed at Terry. "Yes." He panted, as if with a lover. "Send him to Hell."

Terry was wobbly. I knew he couldn't stand much longer. He had lost so much blood, I wasn't sure he could survive this day. Somehow he kept the gun steady on Hirsch's massive chest. "Drop your gun."

Baker's gun clattered to the deck—for a moment he stood unarmed. But his dark eyes glittered as malignantly as the barbed blade he pulled from a sheath at his side. He knelt over Paddy and planted his knee in the boy's chest. "I'll carve him into sausage links."

Paddy was up against the file cabinets and could retreat no further. His body seemed to shrink into the floor. His white face was ashen like a terminal cancer victim's and the blood on his cheek stood out like a red, jagged scar.

"I will f--k him up," Baker said. "Slow. He'll scream. So loud the cops out on the street'll hear him through the walls."

Baker laughed. "He'll still be screaming when he draws his last wheezing breath."

Terry was a statue. Paddy—everything he loved in this world—would momentarily be carved into raw strips of bloody flesh, suffering an agonizing death at the hands of a homicidal maniac beyond the reach of words. But every moral principle to which he had dedicated decades of unremitting effort stood implacably opposed to the only remediating action that could decisively halt the atrocity. I had to act. I knew it as clearly as I knew my own birth date. But how could I act when in the climactic moment I couldn't even breathe?

"What do you say, pacifist?" Baker sneered.

He seized Paddy's right ear in his left hand and thrust the blade against it. The child's throat opened and emitted a scream that sounded as though it possessed neither human nor bestial genesis but originated instead in demonic sufferings somewhere in the storm cellars of Hell.

Terry's body turned and with both hands he lined the pistol up on Warren Baker.

Baker let the blade sink slowly into Paddy's ear. If Terry had wanted to reason with the murderers now, he could not, because no sound could be heard above the scream's decibels and no thought could be formulated through its horror. Baker faced straight down the barrel of the handgun.

"Do it!" he bellowed. "Send me—and yourself—to Hell!"

Do it, I pleaded internally, eyes closed. Please dear God, do it.

Terry pointed the gun at Baker's head. But his hands shook. Blood streamed from his wounds and his face was more ashen than Paddy's. He swayed slightly as though in a strong breeze and suddenly his lean body seemed frail and old. He lowered the weapon.

"Murdering you is not the answer." The last ounce of bodily vitality made his voice strong with dignity. Then, slowly, he sank to the desk top and from there toppled heavily to the floor.

I opened my eyes. "Yes, it is," I said aloud, and lurched sideways. I grazed the barrel of Baker's rifle on the floor and kicked it away with my foot. I fell on him before he could rise. With both hands I grabbed his knife wrist and shook it like a dog with a rat. I sank my teeth into his face, and, oblivious to his roar of pain and my agonized shoulder, wrestled him on top of Paddy O'Neill's body. Behind me, Mary Jo leaped on Ronnie Hirsch's back and clawed at his eyes.

A voice in my head, even now, said, restrain him. Disarm him, wrap him up, and hold his skinny frame until help arrives. But I was beyond that. I would rip his face off. That's all that mattered now. My teeth sunk into his neck in the instant my knee came up into his groin with all the force my adrenaline-induced desperation could muster. With the tables turned, I almost laughed insanely. The muscles of my shoulder were aflame with agony as my right arm, extended to the limit, pushed Baker's knife away from me. Knowing he was on the verge of death, Baker jabbed repeatedly at the mad woman assailing him. But I held his wrist with both hands in a bulldog's grip, laid my hundred pounds full on his chest, and raked him with my teeth. From below the melee, Paddy's bloody hand reached for and gripped Baker's knife wrist and forced it downwards. Inexorably, we were breaking his shoulder.

"Befriend the savage within," Terry McGill had exhorted repeatedly. "It might make all the difference one day." I had failed. But here it was—on the far side of vengeful mania—exactly where Terry had predicted I would find it. My left arm, almost paralyzed now, slipped off of Baker's wrist and hung uselessly at my side. But my right knee came up repeatedly in his groin and my teeth tore at his neck like a dog.

The ponderous bulk of Ronnie Hirsch threw off Mary Jo's slender frame like so much flotsam. He raised his rifle to me. Dimly was heard a smash of glass at the window and with superhuman effort Baker tossed me off. Hirsch pulled the trigger, and, at point blank range, bullets whistled past my face just inches from both Warren Baker and myself.

Outside, a male figure in harness and helmet, clinging to a rope with his left hand, crashed a heavy climbing boot through the metallic grille and glass of the window. Instinct threw me on my face—with blood and flesh in my teeth—as Warren Baker swiveled to confront the new menace. Ronnie Hirsch, knowing the Marines had landed, turned his body and his weapon in ponderous slow motion toward the window.

The menace had swung through the window and hit the deck rolling, tumbling to his right and to the cover of the AP's metallic desk. Prone on his belly, the menace pointed a semi-automatic pistol in a two-handed grip at Warren Baker's narrow chest.

"Drop your weapon!" bawled the commanding voice of Davy Friedman.

Chapter Two: The Marine

Susan's life is in danger—that was the first thought that entered my mind. The sounds were unmistakably gunshots, and in school rampages many innocent lives were at risk. But I thought of only one.

"Mr. Friedman!" one of the students in the 12th grade Advanced Placement English class screamed. "What's that?"

"I'm going out," I said. "Barricade the door with every desk and chair in the room. Turn off the lights, get on the floor—and stay there!"

I grabbed the small gym bag I carried with me at school every day. Unfortunately, it was illegal for administrators or faculty members to be armed in a New York City public high school. Fortunately, there was no metal detector to be passed through at the front gate. I pulled the classroom door behind me as I left. I surprised myself with the gentleness of the closing motion and with the door's soft click. Those were my kids in there.

The hall was swirling chaos. Students fled in all directions at once, and the wide-eyed violence of their motion resembled an unsupervised fire drill conducted in the corridors of Bedlam. I strode toward the Guidance Counselor's office, dodging sweating bodies as though in a mine field. My eyes were riveted on the steps necessary to reach my destination. With a will of their own, my hands unzipped the navy gym bag, pulled from its depth a hard metallic object, and discarded the bag. A full magazine already reposed in the Glock-17's magazine shaft, but it was not cocked. Carefully, with my left hand, I slid back the action and jammed the first round into the chamber. In my right hand, I held the gun at my side, at the full extent of my arm, next to my thigh. My forefinger rested lightly not on the trigger but on the guard. I turned the corner at the end of the hall.

Then I saw her. She was on her knees, disheveled, face already discolored, scrabbling at the door of the Assistant Principal's office. The stairway door beyond her opened. Two armed thugs pushed a man—familiar but unidentified—into the hallway in front of them. At that distance, I couldn't make out the faces but the automatic weapons cradled in their arms stood out. She was in their line of fire.

"Susan!" I roared.

They opened fire. Bodies hurtled to the deck. I dropped to both knees. I tried to line up a target but too many students—running, crawling, clawing—clogged my line of sight. I saw Susan fall through the doorway. The murderers, blasting as they came, sprayed a metallic rain down the hallway and I felt the onrushing air, so familiar from the Persian Gulf—still haunting my screaming nightmares—whirl past my cheeks and my hair. I dropped face down to the floor. The semi-automatic was lined up in both hands, its handle already slick with sweat. They kicked open the door of the AP's office, shoved their victim in, and stooped to drag Susan's body clear of the door. I rolled to my left, desperate for a clear shot but a student raced past, his thick, studded work boots flashing through my visual field even as they plodded heavily on the hard tiled floor. The thugs crashed shut behind them the office door.

I was on my feet. Twenty years earlier, I could not have covered the distance to the Assistant Principal's office in less time. But I was too late. The door was locked and a heavy metallic filing cabinet hauled flush against it on the inside. Through the thick door, I heard a woman's voice scream.

There was a roaring sound in my ears and it was several moments before I realized that it was the pounding of my heart. Think, I willed myself fiercely. The cops would take only several minutes to arrive—but it might be too late. They would set up a perimeter and attempt hostage negotiations. But the thugs' actions showed—and my gut confirmed—they were not here to take hostages.

I had to get in there—now. Think, I said out loud, thrusting my forehead against the painted wall adjacent to the AP's door. Breathe, and think. How many thousands of hours had I spent leisurely in the library or at home, reading, thinking? How could I re-capture the calmness, the clarity of those moments?

An image caught by my eyes but unregistered in my brain flashed through my consciousness. The familiar man had been Daryl Corticelli. The ropes! The rock climbing gear we had stashed for our weekend getaways. I bolted toward the stairs and for the teachers' lounge on the floor above.

The key was in my hand before I exited the stairwell. I flung off my jacket, shoved the gun deep in the waistband of my slacks, and was in the room in a flash. Colleagues of mine were there, ducked down behind chairs and tables. They saw me, they saw the gun, they knew my past—and for the first time they perhaps agreed with me.

"Davy," a male voice pleaded. "There's a thousand kids out there. Stop those guys."

I grabbed the stuff from my locker and turned to the exit. I nodded to the plea. "Keep this door locked."

I raced up the stairs to the top floor. I was exhausted by the time I slammed through the doorway, oblivious to the clanging fire alarm immediately set off. I leaped through the exit and onto the graveled roof. It was the stress not the exertion that had my lungs gasping. Slow it down, I internally commanded. It was a life-and-death emergency but I would do Susan or anybody else naught good by tumbling into this snake pit an out-of-control lunatic.

I ran down the rooftop parallel the ledge, the familiar Bedford Avenue housetops flashing by unnoticed at my feet. I looked down—the AP's office was directly below me, three stories down. There was a crowd of bystanders on the street. Some, presumably those from inside, raced to get away from the gunshots and the screaming. Hundreds of others milled about, gesticulating at the school's windows. The first cop cars had arrived, and the embattled officers struggled to set up a perimeter. As of yet, nobody saw me.

Quickly, my shoes came off. I tied on my climbing boots snug and tight, then jammed and strapped the helmet on my head. The rooftop ventilation shaft was as sturdy as the building itself. I belayed the kernmantle ropes tightly around it, wrapped the harness snugly around my waist, and secured the descender. In a second, I scrabbled over the edge.

I had no time to walk down the wall. I lowered myself carefully by a quick series of short leaps off the wall until I was directly abreast of the AP's window. It was too bright outside for me to see into the darker room. The crowd on Bedford Avenue had noticed the male figure rappelling down the building's side. They set up a tumult that might have been heard in Bay Ridge. One of the cops roared at me through a bullhorn—and time was up. If they mistook me for an assailant, they might open fire—and I was a sitting duck. I had to crash the gate now. I pushed off the wall and swung outward, intending to smash my way through steel grate and glass. At the furthest edge of my arc, it hit me full force what I would now do.

The images pummeled my interiors, of what I had done—and would do again now—the bloody screenplay that tormented my sleep, that jerked me upright, chest bathed in sweat, at three am. I saw as in high definition clarity the blood spray in the air and soak in the dust, I heard the screams of the dying—the interminable death rattle screams of the enemy soldiers whose suicide charge achieved for them a hideous immortality, an undying presence in the haunted visions and sleepless nights of the U.S. Marine who had wrought their final chapters. A U.S. Marine who had ever loved books more than guns.

I twisted my body so that my incoming dive brought my boots not to the window but back to the wall. Inadvertently my right foot kicked the grate and rattled the glass. Below and behind me the cop's roar through the bullhorn was louder. How many guns were trained on my back in this moment?

None of that mattered. Susan was in there, trapped, probably bleeding. Then I heard gunfire from within. I pushed hard off the wall, swung out into space, and came forward, boots first, in a shattering rush that crashed ajar grate and glass, and sent me sprawling chest first onto the floor of the AP's office.

I was stunned by the force of the impact, but I knew the lay-out and rolled toward the cover of Mary Jo's desk. I lined the Glock-17 up on the smaller of the two targets, the one nearest to Susan's body.

"Drop your weapon!" I croaked in what I hoped was a voice of authority. But I omitted what would have been the most brutally honest part of the formulation—for the love of God, don't make me shoot you.

It was not the love of God but the love of Susan that had saved me.

At first it had been alright. Years had gone by after my service in the Persian Gulf. Years of relative mental health in which I had finished college, started teaching, earned a Masters degree at night, and brought my lifelong love of literature to the kids, many of whom were eager, receptive students. Over a period of years, the administration's observations and the students' rousing evaluations earned for me the Advanced Placement courses. And in those seminars developed such a glowing rapport with the material that a Literature Club formed in the school's after hours, meeting once a week, continuing the penetrating, animated discussions of our class periods deep into the evening hours.

Our bodies sat in Brooklyn classrooms in the early twenty-first century but our minds ranged over the centuries and across the cultures, studying Homer and Dante and Shakespeare and Dostoyevsky. Greek councils before the towering gates of Troy sprang to pulsating life in youthful imaginations, as did searing visions of Hell and the raucous tumult of merry England during the age of Elizabeth. Often, across the span of a decade, outside the windows a winter sun had set over the rooftops during the course of our analyses but a procession of alert faces lit the room, marching through and onward toward ivy-spangled campuses and luminous careers.

It was here that I had first gotten to know Susan—the school psychologist, several years older than I, who had been drawn by the seminar's reputation and by her love of the stories—and of the bright-eyed kids. She sat quietly, watching the students, taking visible joy in their aptitude, their accomplishments, and their ruddy, fresh-faced health. Occasionally, she spoke, late in the discussions, to insert an insight into a character too important to remain overlooked. It wasn't long before my eyes continually found her, her thick, tight-curled brown hair cascading to her shoulders, her fair complexion that couldn't tolerate the sun's harsh rays but emitted its own source of light, and her petite figure curled in a chair across the room, a forty-year old woman who retained the childlike innocence of the young girl she had long ago been.

By then the nightmares had come. I didn't mention them. Susan and I spent Saturday afternoons in the crowded corridors of the Met, but alone. My eyes were on the paintings of Vermeer, Rembrandt, and other Dutch Masters, and yet all awareness centered in my tactile modality—the brush of her arm against mine, the touch of my hand resting lightly on her neck, her body in jeans, dark sweater, and high-heeled boots inches from mine; her breathing as we stood silently in front of a masterpiece, her chest slowly filling under the sweater then releasing in rhythmic tempo.

I must have smiled at appropriate moments, made the obligatory witty remarks, and behaved the part of a suitable gentleman. Of such moments, I had no recollection. All I craved was to feel my hands under her sweater, caressing her shoulders, easing downward the straps of her bra, and burying my face and my lips in the ripe female scent of her flesh.

Within months, my nights were immeasurably sweeter and unbearably tormented. I spent my days yearning to go to bed but dreading to go to sleep. The nightmares came relentlessly and their theme was an inalterable constant. No matter the clear-sighted recognition during the day's sunlit hours that a Marine unit had been under attack by the soldiers of a dictator's army, that the conflict was a remorseless death struggle, that the lives of numerous young Americans had been saved, and that the decorations bestowed by a grateful Marine Corps had been abundantly earned, the realization ravaged the inside of my skull that I had spilled the blood and snuffed the existences of human beings total strangers to me—but, like me, sons, friends, lovers, and, perhaps, husbands and fathers—snuffed them with gun, with knife...and with the butt end of a rifle expended of ammunition and wielded with the adrenaline-fueled mania of do now or irrevocably die...

Everyone was honors and congratulations, no one hinted at the remotest shadow of blame, and the in-context morality of the actions was not to be questioned. The warrior's sanity was intact, his character unblemished, his deeds valorous. And yet, under unutterable conditions, a deed could be necessary yet blood-curdling, noble yet hideous, right but perennially unendurable. In shame and in silent agony, I had kept the internal torment locked away in the private dungeon of my conscience, a torture chamber capable of inflicting as much fiendish agony as those of the dictator whose armies we crushed.

Now, for the first time, I shared it, shared the wages of unspeakable violence ironically with one who was not merely a civilian—but a gun-banning liberal, a turn-the-other-cheek pacifist. And yet, Susan's undying faith in me was like the rock walls I scaled on holidays; moral high explosives left it unscathed. It was right, it was right, it was right, she whispered tirelessly in the night and stopped whispering it only when she used her mouth and her body to perform activities that precluded words, actions so exquisite it seemed like she attempted to wash away any and all taints of pain by a freshwater ocean of her love. Many had said and nobody in our private bedroom disagreed that the pen was mightier than the sword. Likewise, Susan's love proved mightier than the gun.

By neither raising her voice nor lowering her moral expectations, she outlasted it, she licked the wounds clean, she sucked the puss from my soul, she intimidated the vile forces arrayed against her, and she sent packing the most flagrant demons, back to the acrid rat-holes of Hades where they spawned. The nightmares might never be expunged but they'd been decimated, crushed, reduced so egregiously they could never recover. She routed them like I had routed the squad of enemy soldiers. Once again I, not the miscreants of Hell, owned the night. I slept—a more potent force than the armies of the world in my arms.

But winning a battle once is not enough. The world is too much with us, a great poet had written. It reaches its tentacles for you, it sends forth its dark minions to engage you over and again, and it does so on its own timetable irrespective of your state of preparedness. Now, in this moment, killers were loose, Susan's body lay prostrate and bleeding, and the private world of blissful peace we had overcome so much to create lay just moments from its terminal dissolution.

"Drop your weapon!" I roared again at the assailants.

The sight of Susan's crumpled body lying in a pool of blood had inflamed me. In the moment, I cared not a whit for the long-term consequences. Reprise the demons! my soul bellowed at me; it matters nothing if every night between now and my last gasping breath drips with blood-covered guilt. Release your weapons, an inner voice commanded, and step away from the woman's body—or be irrevocably effaced from the plane of worldly existence. The skinny creature with blood on his hands and his face looked at me with eyes that did not belong on this earth and I knew, with no shadow of a doubt, that my battle, once won, would now be waged again.

Chapter Three: The Pacifist

The first gunshots brought my worst fears to vivid life. Paddy heard them and looked at me, his white face instantly even paler, seemingly re-living the nightmare of his parent's death—though he'd been too young to remember—and his eyes, those haunted vessels, fey now with a sense of foreboding, of impending doom.

Mary Jo Montefusco had become a friend, an ally after our initial introduction by Susan. The Society's work was important—and she wanted to introduce it to the students. Immediately she picked up the telephone on her desk and dialed Security. The line rang and rang. No one answered. A wild rush was heard in the hallways outside the office door.

I went to the door and stepped into the hall. Students tore into and by me at full-throttled pace. They knocked me back, several feet from the doorway. It was useless to try to stem the stampede; it was like trying to halt a tidal surge by madly flapping one's arms. Grimly, I fought my way back against the current and ducked into the room. I slammed the door behind me.

Mary Jo was on the phone, speaking frantically to the NYPD. "Gunshots," she said, breathing slowly, trying to calm herself. "Undoubtedly gunshots. Yes, at Sherman—hurry!"

She hung up. The door cracked open behind us. Susan, on

her knees, her face cut and bruised, tried to crawl over the threshold. Immediately, I went to help her. Gunshots reverberated in the narrow corridors, the horrendous levels of decibels shockingly loud. The assault on my eardrums sent me sprawling instinctively to the ground. I reached my arm to its full extent to Susan, but she lay dazed in the doorway.

A heavy boot kicked open the door. Guns fired at close range and I heard Paddy scream. I crawled to him but projectiles hurtled into my flesh—I felt impact but couldn't tell where. Suddenly I could no longer move—I heard shouted voices as in an underwater nightmare—the world started to go black—and I was out.

I couldn't tell Paddy what he had to fear.

He was so frail when I adopted him and his eyes had witnessed scenes that no child should endure. He was shell-shocked. He curled in his uncle's arms, his little hands clinging to my shirt and my collar, seeming to never let go. He cried when I put him down, so I took him everywhere—to church and on visits to hospitals, to parishioners, and even to stores. Eventually he grew straight, tall, but so skinny he seemed chronically malnourished and his complexion even paler than mine or his mother's. He remembered neither of his parents' lives but had hideous, sporadic flashes of their deaths, and, other than me, was chronically alone with his terror. "Father," he said repeatedly in the darkest moments of night. "Don't leave me."

I honored his needs, left the Church but not God, and nourished Paddy on spiritual fuel. He grew up around Society meetings, in which we studied Jesus and other sources of incorporeal strength. I took him to the burial grounds of men of peace—to Dr. King's, to George Fox's, founder of the Society of Friends, and to the Gandhi memorial at Raj Ghat. Ecumenically, we visited holy sites around the globe. His body lacked muscle but his soul brimmed with incipient strength. He was passive, morbidly shy in social settings but to a father's watchful eye it was clear that a germinating force—delicate as a tulip blossom in March and as tenacious—would gradually thrust through. Over the years the slow growth process was tangible—he had internalized an aura, some power source, of the world's shrines. I fanned the flames of it with every word and weapon at my disposal. Incessantly I taught the power of peace.

But incessantly I feared the power of violence.

If he had witnessed it first-hand, so had I. The eyes of the youthful gang members on the Lower East Side. The remorseless, unpitying, wildly wanton desperation of their eyes had more vivid staying power in my subconscious than the impact of their blows. They were beyond reason—no words at such a final date could deflect the course of their actions. With fists and clubs and guns they had vented insensate fury on their victim.

For the victim, though savagely beaten, it was a triumph of sorts. He had not resorted to mindless aggression; he had absorbed his lessons, lived out his teachings, and, in the absence of violence, brought two of the thugs to justice. Paddy recognized the victory and his eyes by the victim's hospital bed glowed with pride. His father was selfish enough to take from that a joy greater than his pain.

But the fear remained bottled internally. The principle, always known in theory but driven home now in practice, hammered from the inside of a man's chest. Some creatures under certain conditions were impervious to words, reason, or a magnanimous heart. A sea of goodwill washed off their hard edges like waves off an embedded boulder on a foaming shore. What if Paddy were under assault—not the father but the father's child? What if the child faced screaming death from barbarians who had willfully placed themselves beyond the boundaries of restraint? Did the child die—or did the father kill? The borders of a pacifist's creed intersected the stanchions of a parent's heart at a forlorn crossroads on the far edge of desolation. A right answer there undoubtedly was but an endurable one there was not.

The first gunshots brought my worst fears to vivid life. Paddy heard them and looked at me, his white face instantly even paler. Did those fey eyes sense the Armageddon about to strike at the heart of everything best about us?

I sank deep into a sea of blood, drowning in it, its viscous liquidity choking my throat, seeping into my lungs. I had to breathe. I touched bottom and pushed upward, gasping for air.

It was a puddle not a sea from which I slowly raised my head. But it was blood and it was mine and I could barely move. "Kill the others but leave her alone," a peculiarly high-pitched male voice said. I struggled to bring the sounds and the scene into focus. I stared.

A skinny kid pointed an assault rifle at Paddy's head. A single glance at the kid's eyes threw me instantly back to the death struggle on the Lower East Side. The size and weight and skin color were different. The eyes were the same—the eyes of a fiend. Paddy stared at Susan, who confronted the killers. Her left shoulder scrunched into her side like a hunch-back's and her face was the color of chalk. I willed myself to my knees.

"Judgment Day comes for us all," the skinny creature said.

"Yours need not come today," I wheezed. I got to my feet

but could barely stand. I was severely wounded and might be dying. The world swam in front of me. It was all I could do to remain upright and I barely distinguished faces. But one issue was clear: Paddy would be murdered.

They were talking. What did they say? Fight, they said. Kill us. Kill the killers and save the child. I leaned on the desk. Physically my world was a shambles—but morally it was a cyclone's devastation. Kill them, demanded a stern inner voice. Desperately I clung to any element of inner strength and slammed shut an inner door. "I won't fight," I said aloud. Something moved, a bulk came at me, a heavy object crashed into my stomach. I reeled. The bulk moved away. I scrabbled for it. It broke free but something came loose in my hands, a hard metallic object, a gun.

I pointed it at the fiend and the fiend panted—cold, cold, but hot for blood. Kill, the voice broke through inside, insistent, demanding. "Kill me," the fiend said aloud. "And in killing me, be like me. Kill yourself." My finger tightened on the trigger. I saw Paddy's face, I had his life to save—but the gun wavered in my hand and I could no longer see the target. Save Paddy but kill Paddy, murder everything we stood for—had worked and bled and fought for. "No," I said, no, no, no, and could no longer stand, fell, falling downward to the desk, to the floor, to the abyss of losing everything dear but clutching to the moral principles that made it possible to hold something dear.

Was I dead? Physically dead but spiritually alive. But no, a brawl swirled above me, a physical altercation. Someone screamed. Glass shattered. A body hurtled through space. "Drop your weapons!" the body roared.

My eyes opened. What I saw was a scene ripped from the lowest environs of Dante's netherworld. A fiend ready to kill and be killed. An unyielding opponent with the commanding air of a combat veteran—with horrified eyes but an implacable jaw. Imminent death filled the air in the seconds before flying lead projectiles would. It was the pre-condition of a slaughterhouse, hideous because it was a still frame that could not last—a moment frozen in a man's conscience because it was prelude to an ineluctable rush to bloody judgment.

And behind the fiend, rose to his feet Paddy O'Neill, with a look in his eyes that I had thought never to see outside the gates of Hell. His hands grasped the fiend's throat in the moment the fiend let loose at his implacable foe—in the line of the foe's fire, right in the line of fire. Paddy, I groaned and crawled to him, a bloody smear across wooden beams, crawled across the floor as the guns crashed and the bullets whined their death moan above my head.

Chapter Four: The Final Solution

Susan Siegel had the best vantage point. Flat on the floor, to the left and just behind Warren Baker, the bitter tableau unfolded to its quick resolution directly in front of her.

Warren Baker, ready to kill every living being in the room, and die in so doing, cut loose at his major impediment, spewing a metallic hail at Davy Friedman. Davy rolled to his right and bullets splattered off the desk like a spray of steel mud globules. Paddy O'Neill, snarling in rage, oblivious to life and death and every moral principle to which he had ever testified, concerned with one act only—the final termination of Warren Baker—rose from the floor and from the dead and sank his claws into Baker's throat. Baker struggled in that death grip, and, momentarily, his finger came off the trigger. Terry McGill, running on the last fumes of strength from an internal, organic after burner, crawled across the floor, desperate to reach Paddy and cover the child's anemic frame with his own massive one and absorb every bullet discharged from the start of that fire fight to its bloody, brutal terminus. Ronnie Hirsch, ponderous to the end, stared first at the struggle of Baker with Paddy, then looked for Davy's form behind the desk, and turned to line up his sights on the target. Davy's hands, head, and shoulders appeared quickly above the desk top at the room's far end. The Glock-17 in a steady two-handed grip barked once, twice, three times, four, and the slugs ripped through the layers of fat surrounding Hirsch's vital organs and mashed his heart and lungs into a mass of heaving, bloody jell-o. Hirsch's body plummeted to the deck with the finality of a plane crash.

Paddy O'Neill was caught in a mania and wouldn't let his victim go. Baker couldn't throw him off. Davy Friedman had no clear shot. "Let loose!" he screamed. Terry McGill reached the fray on his hands and knees, and, from the floor, seized Baker's ankles and then his calves. He tugged as hard as he could. Baker started to topple but did not go down. His eyes bulged and he pointed the automatic weapon at Terry. "Let him loose!" Davy screamed. But Paddy was caught in the pent-up rage of the abuse he and his dear ones had suffered. He would not release the tormentor and his father would not cease his efforts to reach and cover him. Davy wasted no further effort on screaming. He aimed through the writhing torsos and tentacles clutching Baker's body parts and he pulled the trigger twice—bam! bam!—in quick succession. The bullets crushed Warren Baker's narrow chest and slammed him backward in Paddy O'Neill's arms. Baker's finger depressed the trigger just as the slugs tore him open and jerked him back and the assault rifle's bullets whipped over Terry McGill's head and into the desk behind which Davy Friedman again ducked. Baker's body sagged, dead, in Paddy O'Neill's arms and Paddy would not let him go. His hands remained locked around Baker's bloodied throat and he squeezed the corpse as if he could kill it a second time.

Davy Friedman rose from behind the desk. His gun moved quickly from one perpetrator to the other. Then he lowered it to his side. He stood tall amidst the carnage and amidst the carnage he had averted and he breathed. He stood as he had many years before in dress uniform and on parade rest. His eyes stared at those he had killed and despite their youth his eyes were pitiless, ready to face any judgment that might be handed down—by the administration, by the law, and by his conscience. But his face and his wrists were as white as Terry McGill's.

Susan Siegel got up. The room was a charnel house at which she could not bear to look for one second further. With one arm she struggled with the file cabinet barring the door. Slowly she inched it back and then staggered through the door and collapsed in the hall. If she died, she said later, it would be outside of that room. For long moments she lay alone on the cool tiles of the hallway floor. Her body shook as she sobbed in pain, in rage, and in prodigious deliverance.

Terry McGill lay on the floor at the feet of Paddy O'Neill and the corpse in his grip. He had not the strength to rise or to move his legs or hands a single millimeter. But his eyes were open and stared at Paddy's face. He was more exhausted than he had ever been but he refused to shut them and he stared, oblivious to the rage that only slowly dissipated in his son's eyes. Terry breathed, hovering on the brink between life and death, but devoid of hurry or anxiety, lying peacefully, staring at the animated face of his only child.

Mary Jo Montefusco groaned. Unsteadily she rose from behind Ronnie Hirsch's corpse. Gingerly she checked every moving body part. She ached across her entire body, more so than the times she had given birth, and her throat felt like it had been crushed by the strangulation of Hirsch's massive paw. She shuffled across the shattered remnants of her office to Daryl Corticelli's side. She stooped to untie his gag. The embattled English teacher sucked in deep draughts of oxygen. Susan made her way back into the room, to Daryl's side, and with one hand helped the AP unbound his wrists. She and Mary Jo looked at each other across Daryl's body and words between them were neither necessary nor forthcoming. Daryl spoke for all of them. He stared at Davy, at his friend and fellow climber with whom he had so often argued about the right to bear arms.

"Davy," he said, the intensity of his gratitude ringing in every slowly-spaced syllable. "Nice shooting, bro."

Susan and Mary Jo stared at the ex-Marine, at the gun in his right hand, and for one moment remained silent. But the Assistant Principal met his eyes and inclined her head. "The Board of Education has no medals to bestow, David. But I'll sleep with you if you want."

Susan laughed. In her relief she felt almost no pain and her voice resembled a girlish giggle. She hobbled to his side. She stared at his eyes, at the chalk color of his face and his neck under the open collar of his shirt. Her eyes told him everything he needed to know. He lay down the gun on the desk and his hands went out to her, gingerly, avoiding her left shoulder but caressing her cheeks, wiping away the gore and the tears and the grime, feeling on her face as if he could similarly wipe away her horror and her pain.

It was still in that office but for those who had perpetrated no atrocity it was not the stillness of a tomb but of life taking a breath before going on. Nobody was afterward certain how many minutes elapsed before the police and EMS personnel crept cautiously down the second floor hallway and into the demolished room.

Chapter Five: Recover

Something about the questioner made people uneasy.

He was a big man and he held out a photograph from a newspaper. He had a name. Quietly, he took meals in restaurants along Kings Highway, purchased items at hardware, drug, and convenience stores, chatted benignly, looked for the friendliest sales help, talked with animated warmth, spoke admiringly of heroes, and sought to create an atmosphere of goodwill.

He dressed benignly in polo shirts, blue jeans, and running shoes. But there was some quality about him that sent a shiver of alarm down people's spines, like ominous sounds when walking past a graveyard on a blustery night. His thick black beard wrapped around his jaw and lower face, able to conceal prominently identifiable features. Standing face-to-face, one had to squint closely to notice the jagged scar that ran down his left cheek. But behind the bonhomie shining in his blue eyes was a chill that could not be adequately masked by any smile no matter the warmth. The phrase "affable fiend" ran through the mind of an avid reader he accosted outside the library on Ocean Avenue. He spoke politely and smiled in a gentlemanly form when they conversed. It was nothing he did—rather, something she could not quite identify—that impelled her to scurry quickly away when the discussion ended.

The picture he held out was of a local hero who had saved innocent lives. The name of whom he inquired, searching for an address, was Davy Friedman.

People did not know—or claimed they didn't.

The questioner searched on.

Terry McGill hovered near death.

The doctors had extracted multiple bullets from and transfused into his inert body two quarts of blood. He lay unconscious and unmoving in the ICU, nurses swarming around his bedside. Despite the blood, his skin remained as white as the sheets on which he rested.

Paddy O'Neill had been treated for bruises and lacerations. When informed he was in shock, he told the doctor he was not nearly as shocked as had been Warren Baker. He did not smile when he said it. Quickly, he was released from the hospital. But he did not go home. McGill's doctors recognized the benefits of his son's proximity; they permitted Paddy to sit in a chair by his father's bedside, for as long as he pleased. Paddy sat there, he ate there, he slept there, he stared at his father, willing vitality into the now frail body of the only parent he had ever known.

Terry McGill, though unconscious, refused to succumb. His age, his wounds, his blood loss all worked against him. But, the doctors noted, the pacifist was the toughest fighter they had ever encountered. Slowly, his vital signs improved.

Susan had been treated for shock, a separated shoulder, and flesh wounds to the neck and head. Against medical advice she had left the hospital after three days and gone home. She did not go near the school. She spoke to nobody at the Society of Humanity and attended no meetings. She permitted no visitors but one and did not answer the telephone.

For hours she lay on the chaise lounge in her fenced-in back-yard amidst the green grass, the rose-beds, the chirping birds, and the fulsome sunshine, lay still without motion, as if all activity had been drained from her on the fateful day weeks earlier and all she could do now was re-charge. She had no appetite and willed herself to eat a meal every day. She drank fresh lemonade, squeezed from an excess of ripe lemons, and savored the sweet tangy tartness on her tongue, the piquant sensations re-kindling her awareness of being alive.

Every day, Davy Friedman was there. She smiled wanly at him but said little. They did not speak of the atrocity. For days they barely spoke at all. Although her arm was in a sling their bodies healed quickly. But their souls inched forward at a slower pace and they did not make love. They sat together in the sunshine, and, finally, he reached his hand to her and she took it.

As the shock wore off, and her physical injuries healed, all that remained was the inner pain, mostly his, and she turned, fully focused now, to him, every resource of her laden soul yearning to aid. But he was not there.

Davy Friedman would not commit suicide.

He had walked miles on this sun-blazed June morning, along the pristine white sands of Jones Beach, amidst the breeze, the salt air, and the swooping, cawing gulls. He finally stopped. But he did not kneel or crouch on the beckoning sand; a restless energy ran through him, his arms swung rhythmically at his sides, he was tired, he breathed heavily after a swift, grueling walk through clinging sand, but he could not sit.

The ocean, he thought, gazing over its limitless expanse: It would be so easy, walk out through the gentle rolling breakers, walk on the soft bottom until he could walk no further, then dive into the waves as he had so many times when a boy, knife through them as a strong swimmer, cleaving a path seaward, out into the shipping lanes, out long past sight of land, out where land-based denizens no longer threatened innocents he was sworn to defend, out until weight of dripping shoes and clothes and screaming muscles dragged him down unresistingly, down into the pristine depths until, finally, his hands and soul would be washed clean.

They would never leave him be. The Marines, the Persian Gulf, were his own mistakes. But the high school Literature teacher, the Masters degree, the teaching of wisdom and culture to countless bright-eyed youths, was right, was natural, was of his essence; with such shining students, and with Susan, he had created a glittering enclave of elevated literary art that would extend well past the curtailed years of his lifetime, extend onward in the eyes, the quickened breath, and the brilliant lives of the myriad students whose souls he had touched.

His eyes closed now, fighting back some dark, melancholy surge within. "Even there," involuntarily he spoke aloud. Even there, in his private utopia of high culture, there were intrusive creatures who would not permit them to flourish, who would claw, scrap, and gash until even Susan's life was threatened and he had no choice but to take terminal remediating action. Even there.

His eyes opened but he saw nothing of the sun's glint on eternal waves. He saw only harsher images. If not there, where? the question clattered against the walls of his skull. He rubbed his eyes, as if physical pressure could blot away the image of bullets tearing into soft and resistless human tissue. I don't know, he answered.

I don't know, he thought—and for a moment, though without Susan's presence, bereft of her inestimable strength, inexorably alone, he let the images seep, then pour through inner sluiceways; pictures, passions, drives all bundled into a single bloody vision, the rage at Susan's battered body, the kill-lust, the hellish clatter of assault weapons, the bullets whining; the Glock's fire, his, arrowed unerringly into lungs, hearts, trachea of his foes, arrowed with malice aforethought at creatures who deserved to die—no one doubted, including him—but it was easier for others to make such judgment, because the life fluids of teenage boys that spewed across the room were not on their hands or heads but on his.

The sun's rays were full on his face. They warmed his body. But would anything warm his soul?

Where was safe haven from the brutes? the query rattled in his brain. Where? The truthful answer was harshest of all...nowhere....There was nowhere they could not reach him, threaten the extirpation of those dear, and transform him again into a snarling, blood-hungry killing machine.

With the unflagging regularity of a metronome, westbound jets flew overhead, descending slowly, sunlight glinting off of metallic wings. Westbound flights from Europe's every quadrant, he realized, seeking soft touchdown at Kennedy. His eyes squinted in the sun's glare, following their smooth ease of flight. One might find safe harbor from wind and hail and howling gust, he thought bitterly—but where so from human kill lust...including one's own? He turned away.

The senselessness of it, the human bodies...teens...expunged in bloody heaps...their lives cut off with sixty or seventy years to go...what might they have done...via better choices, with guidance...write books, start companies, cure patients...he shook his head, as though his willful rejection of brutality could be made universally definitive, a lone upright man pacifying the earth.

A lone upright man pacifying the earth...the image struck him now....Would that he could rise up from his human stature, assume a giant's form, bestriding the earth like a moral colossus, sweeping away weapons from those with lethal intent, striking incapacitated but not deceased those souls afflicted with terminal malice, and rain on the world not death and destruction but their antipode...a world, perhaps, not pacified but living under the aegis of an impregnably formidable protector. His hands balled into fists, as though he could will alteration in stature as effortlessly as he could will muscular contraction.

Power to bring peace, he thought...power to strike surgically with utmost precision, to render unconsciousness without demise, and to do so perennially, incessantly against every strain of violent human-like creature. He wanted to gnash his teeth and pull hair from his head, as did the wailing Trojan women, overcome with bereavement, hopelessly wishing to restore life to the moribund, they too seeking to will the impossible.

Terry McGill—the face, not the name—crept before his inner eye, the peacemaker's towering frame bloodied, crumpled, crawling forward, vainly striving to reach the same unattainable ideal, one man acting to expunge violence, another acting to expunge lives...antipodal, it would seem...but each straining to retard the inexorable, to alter the inalterable, to gain a goal priceless but perpetually out of reach.

McGill's principles lay shattered on the blood-drenched floor of the Assistant Principal's office, as devoid of breath as the corpses that had initiated their demise...a demise finalized by another. How was the pacifist's conscience today, he wondered. As tormented as the Marine's? But at least the man of peace had principles. Did the man of death?

He stared sightlessly at the incessant waves, hearing them, but seeing, in inner vision, only the incessant casualties piling up, in Brooklyn, in the Persian Gulf, god knew where next, the blood of the young, always the young on his hands. Violence as eternal as the sea...eternal...there may be no god but there was eternally violent man...

The planes streamed by overhead, conveying an endless procession of contented pilgrims from another world. But, in his immediate world, they had no reality...no god, the words pounded at his brain, but perpetually violent man.

He stood in sunlight. It blazed on his face and warmed his torso. It was as real as spilt blood, as real as violent death, as real as undying conflict. He thought of Susan and of his bright-eyed students. They were real, too. Think, he willed himself. If you could stand before murderous brutes, you could stand before inner demons.

What happens, he thought, if men of protective violence step away from the innocent? Nothing good, he knew. But what happens to the men of protective violence when they perform their safeguarding task with lethal expertise? What happened to Shane? Inevitably estranged from the peaceful family he loved by the act of protective violence that saved them. He shook his head. Somebody, he realized, in some form, always the victim of perpetration.

What was the alternative? Leave the innocent to their own resources and watch helplessly some of them murdered—or intercede, warn stringently, aim weapons unerringly, pray the violent lay down their arms, but, when prayer goes unanswered, reciprocate with withering fire that left their bodies in crumpled, blood-stained heaps. Amidst inner turbulence, he stood rock steady, like a mountain crag accepting whatever blow dealt it by wind, rain, and storm. Only two alternatives, he saw, both unacceptable.

The sea was always there. Violence, likewise, was enduring. He could retire from gunfighting, as Shane had desired, it would change nothing, murderous violence was enduring. But, in his life, so was Susan. So were his kids. Similarly, the great works of literature. Homer, Dante, Shakespeare, Milton, Goethe, Hugo, Dostoyevsky....A brilliantly cunning hero, homeward bound, strives with men, monsters, and goddesses to return to his wife and the son he's never met—a beautiful guide through a scintillating Hell of vivid imagery and just requital—a nobleman and his aggressive wife murder the king and initiate moral descent into blood-letting power lust and crippling madness—a towering prince of defiance pits his will against the Creator Himself—an eager mind's thirst for knowledge infallible, tormented but redeemable—saints of magnanimity rise to stature, although in defeat, contending with hostile social forces implacably set on oppression—murder perpetrated by four brothers, each guilty in differing forms, each in desperate need of a higher power to rescue his soul screaming from the edge of the Pit. If man was eternally violent, so was he eternally creative.

The sun was still high in the sky—but it was time to get back. Susan would be reaching out to him. He turned away from the waves. He took the first step through hot sands to the parking lot and his car. He was surprised that the thought recurred in his awareness, that it had the sharp-edge feel of a prickly concern. He wondered: How was the pacifist's conscience today?

Susan Siegel was on a mission.

She had not yet been back to work but that would soon come. It was mid-June, the school year wound down, there was but a week to go. She would be back tomorrow.

But other concerns gnawed at her. One was Davy. Where was he? More important, how was he? He did not answer his phone. She banged loudly, repeatedly at the door of his apartment but got no answer. It was not like him, she thought, to vanish without warning. With others he was often incommunicado, but not with her. She breathed slowly, deeply, her forehead against his door.

Davy Friedman would come through this. Some inner certitude, deep in her, told her that his internal fortitude exceeded that of any human being she had ever known. He would win his struggle, he would perennially prevail, until only Death, at advanced age, of natural causes, wrapped him in its clinging, non-negotiable embrace.

But what were they doing to him, she moaned. They turned his love, his innocence, his moral courage against him, they shoved him into untenable, unlivable positions and cared not a whit whether he could continue to live, his inner strength turned into a weapon against himself, a source now not of pride and joy but of unholy damnation.

Someone had to do it, she thought. Her head came off the door. But not Davy anymore. He had done enough. He had done far more than anyone else and too much for a single individual—even him. Every protective instinct she possessed--they had not been channeled into motherhood—screamed inside her; she was surprised her inner howl did not burst incessantly through her skull until the neighbors roared at her to shut it down.

Someone had to do it. To lift the unbearable burden off

of his shoulders. She turned from the door and started down the hallway. She eschewed the elevator, opting instead for the stairs. The shoulders of the petite, pacifistic liberal were back and she breathed easily. Someone indeed.

The questioner would destroy Davy Friedman.

It had taken days to make progress. He had to avoid places where people might recognize him from the past, from the drug dealing, the violence, the criminal record, the notoriety. In moments like these, of seething rage, the the old slash across his cheek throbbed in pain. He had to speak casually to strangers, make small talk, and smile blandly, when all he wanted to do was grab their lapels, shake them like helpless prey, force them on their backs, yank from its sheathe inside his jeans a wickedly barbed blade, press it to their throats, and scream, "Where is the bastard that killed my brother?"

He had finally caught a break at a coffee shop way down Kings Highway from the school. It was from a gray-haired customer with a penchant for gossip. She looked at the newspaper clipping. "That's the teacher became big news for shooting a bunch of kids."

"He's a hero," the questioner said, choking on the word. "He saved a lot of lives."

"It's all over the TV," the customer said, nodding, sipping steaming coffee from a glistening white mug. "But I hear the students hate him. He waves that gun around the classroom, scares bejeezus out of them. Should have been arrested long ago, you ask me. Those kids would be alive today if they did."

The questioner waved his hand, striving for good-natured rejection. "That sounds like bunk. Dude's a hero."

"Just telling you what people say."

He caught the eye of a waitress working the counter. "A Coke," he said. He looked around the place of white and blue tiles and silver chrome. It was spotless, like it had been scrubbed within a millimeter of its life. An image filled his mind—of his razor sharp blade shoved down Davy Friedman's throat and of his body collapsed over a stool, the floor's white and blue tiles gradually streaming red. He smiled, making no attempt to restrain the balefulness lurking at the back of his eyes. "Love to meet him." He momentarily averted his gaze. "Shake his hand."

"Was on TV," she said, "the network news reporters interviewed him in front of his building. Plenty of people here would recognize it. Summer," she said to the heavyset, overly made up waitress working the tables behind them. "What building that lunatic teacher live in?"

"What lunatic teacher?" She walked away with an armful of dirty plates.

"One that shot up Sherman and killed a bunch of kids."

"Right across the street from the elementary school," Summer said. She disappeared into the kitchen.

"There you have it," the gray-haired woman said, turning back to the questioner.

Several bills were on the counter, the stool was empty, and an untasted Coke sat next to the money. She saw only the questioner's back as he strode through the revolving door at the coffee shop's side entrance.

Terry McGill was out of the hospital.

His towering frame had lost weight, he seemed more emaciated than thin, and he stooped now when he walked, bent at the waist. More alarming to Paddy O'Neill and others who loved him, a light that had habitually shined in his eyes seemed all but extinguished, sparking occasionally like a burner struggling vainly to ignite, refusing abject surrender but lacking most vestiges of formerly robust power. He leaned on Paddy's arm when he walked.

The Society of Humanity...he had devoted more than a decade of his life to practicing and teaching peace...in addition to his son, it was his whole world...now, where were its teachings? Had more than teenaged lives expired in the bloody altercation at Sherman? Did moral principles lie in crumpled heaps on the red slickened floor as irrevocably moribund as the bodies? He could not just walk away...but he no longer possessed conviction with which to walk upright.

He returned to his two-bedroom apartment in Bay Ridge. Paddy was there, a stolidly ubiquitous presence but intuitively knowing to keep his distance, there when needed but refusing to hover, giving the old man room to breathe, to move, to reflect. Paddy now took care of the apartment and of the father, who, for years, had taken care of him. He did the food shopping, prepared the meals, washed the dishes and clothes. It appeared to those who knew him that he had put on weight, as though hospital food had agreed with him.

His movements were crisper, they noted, less diffident, as though his death struggle with Warren Baker had opened a sealed vault within and some force, long buried, now burst forth. He gave innocent persons in his compass no cause for fear but it now seemed a moral wrong to retain their familiar pity for poor shrinking Paddy O'Neill. They did not know and would be almost as shocked as he to discover that, although he retained an undying respect for his father, the man to whom he now looked as moral role model was Davy Friedman.

Paddy's fists clenched when he thought of Baker's knife to his throat—and he knew, with clear-eyed vision that, if the occasion demanded it, he would fight to the death to defend the armed teacher who had defended him.

Terry had no desire to leave his bed. He willed himself to rise, to dress, to shuffle into the living room, to stand—not sit—by the window, gazing at the Brooklyn streets he had sought to reform. He stretched gingerly, seeking to regain his full height, to straighten his spine and his shoulders. It was a burden.

One can lose battles but still win a war, he reminded himself. How does one wage a war for peace, an inner voice responded. More critically, how does one wage a crusade for an ideal when the moral principles that animate it have been ripped asunder by proponents of an adverse cause.

He leaned his forehead against the cool pane of glass. It offered little relief. He desired nothing but to close his eyes and drift into deep sleep bereft of agonizing moral conflict. He willed his eyes to remain open, staring at the harsh streets but several miles from the building in which his vision had been as definitively struck down as those who had killed it. There was something worse, he realized, than merely not knowing an answer to life-and-death questions...there was not knowing if there was an answer.

Davy Friedman—the face, not the name—crept before his inner eye, the former Marine's lean frame etched there in a hellishly unforgettable snapshot of time...gun pointed, finger squeezing, spewing flame, dispensing death. Paddy O'Neill had been rescued...his precious life saved, not through an act of peace but by one of definitive violence.

It was an agonizing truth to bear. But truth did not seek one's approval. It just was, whether it crushed one or not.

Davy Friedman was there, towering in his inner vision, armed, firing, manifesting everything he had fought against,

killing, not persuading, a centurion of violence, not a par-
agon of peace, and yet...Terry closed his eyes...the brutally
undeniable truth was that only violent intercession had been
sufficient to save Paddy's life. How was the protector, the
hero...internally, he choked on the words—but he would not
delete them from consciousness, he faced them, as he had
faced murderous gunmen...how was the conscience of the
protector today?

His head came off the glass.

He needed to know...if there was an answer, he sensed, it
was to be found there. Susan's boyfriend, it would be hard only
to meet but not to find him. He had to meet Davy Friedman.

He pressed his gnarled hands against the woodwork surrounding the glass. He leaned on them. There was a Society
of Humanity meeting in a few days, the first since the atrocity....He had to attend...Could he contact Susan, ask her to
invite....Some internal block, a boulder of jagged edge and
expansive proportion, impeded his forward path. He did not
want to push or lift or circumvent it. But he had to meet Davy
Friedman—and it blocked his way. How was the conscience
of the ex-Marine today? He had saved Susan's life. Did killing bring him peace? He had to know. He took a deep breath,
girding for the struggle.

The questioner had the building in sight.

He sat at the corner of a side street across an avenue
from the building, sat at the wheel of a battered heap he had
purchased—straight cash transaction, no questions asked—
from a shady Jersey used car dealer. The avenue poured into
a broad boulevard at the intersection. Across the boulevard,
cater-cornered to where he sat, rose the imposing red brick
edifice of a heavily-populated elementary school.

For two days, he had maintained his vigil. He had to do it intermittently. He could not risk the neighbors becoming suspicious and calling the cops. It was dangerous, he knew, to be back in his old Brooklyn haunts, a barbed sheath knife—his preferred weapon—strapped to his inner left thigh, readily accessible to his powerful right hand.

He was wanted in this town. And the deep knife gash on his left cheek, requiring painstaking effort to be cosmetically masked, largely but not entirely concealed by his thick beard, was like a swinging strobe beacon to any cop who strode through his vicinity.

But his kid brother, who, for years, he had raised—pain in the ass though he was—had been gunned down remorselessly by an armed teacher who fancied himself a tough guy, had been shot through the lungs and heart as if his life had no more meaning than a dog's. The questioner gripped the steering wheel in his hands until the veins in his wrists and forearms stood out like rigid streaks. Let us meet face-to-face, he thought, and—no matter how many guns he owns—we'll find out what kind of a tough guy he is.

The questioner was not dressed now in polo shirt and slacks, no longer seeking to deceive the unwary into believing he was a friendly hero worshipper hoping to meet his champion. He wore a studded black vest and chains over a black tee-shirt, black jeans, and heavy-duty work boots.

The familiar side streets he knew so well, the time on his hands as the solitary stakeout spooled out slowly, all brought back memories...he'd had plenty of opportunity to reflect on his childhood...although he hated it...and his eyes roved the street incessantly, searching for cops, for nosy passersby, and for the targeted teacher...but the time went by, the hours of lonely vigil dragged, and images of his poor stunted kid brother swept up from some deep internal burial sites and swamped all inner vision.

Their father a pickpocket, a break-and-enter artist, a mugger of old women, had broken into the wrong broad's home, who shot him twice in the chest, killing him instantly. He was twelve years old, their mother pregnant, Warren never knew his father, grew up hating him, left with a bitter alcoholic mother who steadily drank herself to death and mixed brief intermittent bouts of love with cursing abuse of children who were no more than a grievous burden. Scrawny little Warren had, at one point, tried to murder her with a steak knife and he had needed to pull the runt off. She had done a good enough job of killing herself.

The questioner's head jerked up. There was motion at the front door of the building. A man came out, he saw him clearly. It was seven o'clock in the evening but still full daylight, visibility was sharp. The man was medium height, lean, about the appropriate age, but he wore shades obscuring part of his face. Quickly the questioner glanced at the newspaper clipping, then back at the man's receding figure as he strolled away from the building and onto the boulevard. Was it him? He had to calculate and he had to do it now. Some gut feeling told him no, it was not Davy Friedman, and having little to go on he went with that. He stayed in the car, engine off.

The drugs had saved them, the unsummoned memories returned. It was easy money, good money, and purchased food for a starving brother that no one else cared for. But Frankie "Spooky" Ginotta, didn't think the park was big enough for rival drug dealers. Spooky had made a carload of jack over the years, should have retired to Florida, but, he knew, enjoyed the notoriety, the authority, his status as big shot, and would sooner die than relinquish it. With twin Sig Sauer P 226s strapped under his armpits he hunted the rival dealer he had warned off of his turf. At the other side of the park, he found him—clawed both fists inside his windbreaker and came out spewing hot lead.

Punk...the questioner spat out the window of his rented car...his rep scared the f--k out of college kids and local partiers, but he shot like someone's prissy sister, bullets sprayed into the night, customers screaming, ducking, running, and twenty dollar bills floating on the wind. He had always done business on the concrete softball fields, near the outfield's cyclone fence, at the gate, the steel post at his back.

He ducked behind it, bullets ricocheting off the steel like screaming pellets, and he, laughing, knowing violent death for someone had inescapably arrived, barbed sheath knife clutched in his fist, had taken a step back, metal post between Spooky and him, and fired, the blade whipping through the night and sinking to its hilt in the drug dealer's chest. Spooky gurgled once and went down like a collapsing garage. He hit the cement and lay without a twitch. But half-a-dozen eyewitnesses confirmed it was self-defense and the cops had to let him go.

He had lain low for months after that, trying to take care of the kid. Running low on funds, he had gone back in business, trying to hide it not just from the cops but from the disapproving runt whose mouth it fed. "Drug money," the eleven-year-old sap had sneered, and, losing it, he had bashed the kid in the teeth, decking him, and then stormed into the gutter, pacing the streets for hours, trying to calm himself, failing, ending at Rip's Joint in Gerritsen Beach, a mariners' dive, where an ex-con named Dibble commented on his sour look; with a roll of quarters in his right fist, he busted Dibble's jaw, who fell backward into a metal bar foot rest, which busted his skull, and earned his assailant six years in the icebox on a manslaughter conviction. Six years of reading, building on his superb Catholic school education, studying now not Paul, Augustine, and Aquinas but Thrasymachus, Machiavelli, and Nietzsche, muscular men wielding a pen like a club, who understood the earth belonged not to the meek but to the dominant.

And the kid...Warren...disgusted by all of it—neglect, alcoholism, drug dealing, lethal violence—dragged off to foster care, his foster mother a religious martyr, seeking to save him, the kid hating it, hating her, beating her saintly face to a pulp, before shoved into Juvie. There, he had gotten revenge on her, on the world...he had embraced the faith she exhorted, but the fanaticism, the sin bashing, the Hell-burning end-of-the-world death worship...released again into foster care, in Sherman's district, he had gone to school.

The questioner couldn't take it anymore. For the thousandth time he asked himself—did he really love the gruesome little punk...or did something else drive him? Damn them all, he thought, the cops, the passersby, his religious fanatic brother....It didn't matter. He was on a mission. He cared not what became of him when it was complete...but the sanctimonious son of a whore who had gunned down his kid brother would achieve a ghastly fate. He eyed the building. Eventually, he knew, the rat always left its hole.

Susan pulled up in front of Davy's building.

There were no spots available, so she-double-parked. She had not seen him in days, she had been worried, and her body yearned to be in his arms. She was a minute or two early but he knew she was coming. He would be down in a moment.

She relaxed, looking around the neighborhood in which she had grown up, the elementary school across the boulevard that she had attended, the streets she knew so well. She noted the perpetual traffic on the boulevard, the kids playing basketball in the schoolyard, a guy sitting in the driver's seat of a car parked at the corner, across the avenue, and the sun's setting rays shimmering on the towering green trees lining the side street to her left. How many times as a child had she walked down that quiet street on her way home? In all these years, she noted, nothing about the neighborhood had changed. It remained the same safe haven it had always been.

She had been surprised by Terry's request. His voice that she knew so well, and loved, like she had loved the tenderness in her father's voice whenever he had spoken to her...the voice gentle, strong, firm all at once...and now tortured...he wanted to meet Davy. She had not asked why—but she knew him, knew both of them, one as a second father figure, the other as a lover, she surmised and affirmed his request.

She did not want to see it, she had fought against it, but the memories flooded against her inner sea wall, battered it and flooded over its top, washing away all in its path. Again, she saw Paddy's bloodied form stretched on the floor, Warren Baker's knife poised to skin him like a hobbled rabbit, Terry in anguished moral conflict—his principles or his son—hesitating, she flailing futilely at the murderer, and only the resolute figure of Davy Friedman able and willing to take decisive remediating action. Violently lethal remediating action.

She closed her eyes. Terry, she knew, must be tortured by this same vision...

She heard the door to Davy's apartment building open and shut and her pulse quickened. Her eyes opened, she turned quickly, and Davy strode toward her car. Had she been mistaken to think that Davy had welcomed the request, that he had accepted not reluctantly but with a willingness that perhaps did not quite penetrate the depths of eagerness but caressed instead its outskirts?

He got into the passenger seat. For a moment, he just stared at her. Then his hands went to her shoulders, he pulled her to him, and he kissed her deeply. He let her go. She said, "I won't be able to drive if you keep doing that."

She pulled away for the drive to Bay Ridge, her man next to her in close proximity, anticipating even closer later that night, and she did not notice the car fire up at the side street corner to her left and pull onto the avenue behind her. Serenely, she merged with the traffic on the boulevard.

Chapter Six: Volte-Face

"Morality is powerless against brutes," said Terry McGill.

He stood on a riser, at the podium, facing the crowd. It was a small auditorium with glistening hardwood floor, whitewashed walls, and a brilliant chandelier hanging above. The roof, years ago, had been raised, providing a cathedral effect, and, despite the hundred-and-twenty collapsible chairs that now filled the space—ten rows with six on each side of a center aisle—the room felt spacious and airy.

Terry was gaunt but not as gaunt as, a mere week ago, he had been. He was weak but not as weak as, a few days ago, he had been. He was white but not as white as, a few hours ago, he had been. He had held the podium while speaking his first words. Now he let it go. He faced the crowd and whatever moment of truth the night might bring.

"What is man in the absence of a moral code? Nothing but an ephemeral chunk of corpulence. He swallows and gags for a few moments. He expires. He is absorbed into the abyss."

His supporters had gathered around him, moving cautiously, reaching to him gently, speaking softly. Finally, he had smiled. "I appreciate the solicitude," he had said warmly to the dozens of non-violent souls he loved. "But I am not yet ready for the scrap heap." He shook their hands and hugged their frames, letting them feel the strength that still coursed through him.

"But a creed elevates such a being," Terry said from the podium. "It makes him spiritual, not merely bestial—celestial, not just terrestrial—a man, not a brute. Scruples are the great cosmic difference maker that brings a man before God and enables him to hold his head up and say to the Divinity from the depths of his soul: 'God, you made me, and I am good.'"

Davy Friedman sat in the front row of the Society of Humanity's headquarters. He had arrived a few minutes too late to meet the speaker. But he was meeting him now. It was not just Terry's words that vibrated in the room's air, or his voice penetrating Davy's ears, it was his naked soul bared in a public room. Davy, sitting unarmed at the far right of the aisle, Susan immediately to his left, her hand clasped in his, could not avert his gaze from the speaker.

"Your scruples make you a man of peace. They lead you on the offensive against mindless aggression. So you train yourself and you train others and you reach out to any living creature of a biologically human form, and you'd grip their lapels if you could and shake them—'why don't you see it!' you'd cry. Because the endless spiral of violence is inhuman and unlivable and you'd give your life itself to be able to quell it and consider it the greatest bargain of your existence."

His eyes closed, and, for a moment, he was alone, although in a crowded room. But it was only a moment. He opened his eyes, and stared at the man sitting to Susan's right...Davy Friedman...the man of violence...the man who had saved Paddy O'Neill's life. He wanted to avert his gaze but willed himself to stare directly at Paddy's savior—and his nemesis. He never cursed. He would not now. But the temptation was undeniable.

He choked and for a moment could not continue. For several seconds the room was still. Then he went on. "But you'd be wrong," he whispered, staring at Davy. "You'd be wrong if you thought you could bring peace among men—that you could shepherd them away from the path of brutality, that you could save your loved ones by eschewing violence, or that you could successfully reach out to the perpetrator with a brimming heart of magnanimous intent."

The room was so quiet each man could hear his neighbor breathe. Susan, though caught in the public spectacle of Terry's private agony, felt Davy stiffen by her side. She knew the ex-priest's words had hit home.

For her too they hit home. A month had elapsed since the rampage at William Tecumseh Sherman High School. Twenty-two students, security officers, and administrators had been wounded. Almost one-third were still in the hospital. Miraculously, none had died.

But something had died for Susan. Davy's eyes were riveted on the speaker, his ears heard only Terry's words. She felt his body held tightly by her side and she knew that, despite the stillness of his frame, his soul writhed with Terry's in mutual torment in the face of implacable truth.

"There's a creature loose in the world," Terry said. "In multiple forms—subterranean creatures who infest the septic tanks and dank sewers of human society, rearing out of the filth as criminals, as batterers of family members, as homicidal fiends, as potential dictators, conquerors, terrorists, blood-drenched ideologues, and who target incessantly the innocent as their bloodied victims."

He paused.

"Can you talk down some of these perpetrators? You can. Can you reach all of them?" He shook his head. "Not even close. You see first-hand the look in the eye of such a creature, intent on murdering you or your loved ones, inexplicably as determined to take life as you are to save it, relentless with some dark purpose of its own, and unreachable by any appeal to logic or words or pity. Such creatures feed on violence, they appeal to violence, they can be stopped by only superior violence, and no other method deflects them—so that to live among them you become like them, you take the creature's life to prevent it taking your child's, this is the only alternative the creature permits and this is unacceptable."

Davy shifted position as Terry's words hit his core. Susan gripped his hand tighter, as though she could grip both his body and his soul, maintaining them in one place and in one vigorous piece. Her heart broke for both of them—her hand and her body's full length touched Davy but her eyes were on, and her soul was with, Terry. She noticed a growing fire in Terry's eyes and it struck her—for the first time in all the years of their relationship, he was expressing anger.

Terry breathed several times, deeply, marshaling strength, facing something it had taken decades to face, facing it as he had confronted thugs on the street and fiends in a high school, facing it unflinchingly. His voice was barely audible, as though the will to stare at repellant truth diverted energy from all life functions.

"Peace is non-negotiable but pacifism is non-viable. To protect the innocent you become like the guilty. To preserve life you extinguish life. Can you terminate violence via non-violence? Do you stop a tsunami with paper-mache walls?"

He needed to stop every few seconds, to gather himself, to publicly state the renunciation not merely of his creed but of his way of life. If a man relinquishes his code, his honor, his god, she thought, what has he left?

She tore her eyes away from him. For a moment, she must look elsewhere. Paddy sat directly across the aisle from Davy. From behind Davy's head, she saw his uplifted chin, his steady eyes, his fuller, more robust chest rising and falling steadily, his eyes pinned resolutely on his principled father, honoring him as all honest men must, feeling his father's pain, but, she felt certain, no longer his own; Paddy's eyes neither conflicted nor tormented but...unyielding.

Terry looked out over the audience, this reduced giant who had been a tower of power to hundreds of innocent men and women who authentically sought to extirpate violence from their souls, from their lives, from their society, to stop it in its footprints, to roll it back, and to promote peace. He was coming to the end...of perhaps more than his talk...and Susan could not bear to look at him.

She looked around the auditorium. It was standing room only, the unappeasable man of peace had reached hundreds, they stared solely at him—men and women, black, white, Oriental, of sundry ages, generally well-dressed in jackets, button down shirts, dresses...but a man...her eyes stopped...a white man standing in the back, dressed in studded black vest and chains, studded black fingerless gloves on his hands, a tall man, powerfully built, his deep chest rising and falling rapidly, the one person staring not at Terry but elsewhere, at her, at the man sitting by her side, with a full, thick black beard but when his head averted slightly, she saw on his left cheek, visible within the tangle of beard...a deep slash...

"There is no way to peaceably resist those intent on murdering you..." Susan looked back at the speaker. Terry's eyes were closed. Now he opened them. There was a tall, powerfully-built man striding purposefully down the center aisle.

He had metal studs and chains on his body and mayhem in his eye. Was it a vision? For one wild second, Terry was not certain. A creature spawned of Hell, embodied, as Jesus had been, but of antithetic purpose, coming to deliver definitive termination to his dream...and his life?

Terry could not take his eyes off of the advancing figure. "Peaceful men, to them," he said, voice coming as from a horrified trance, as though a deer paralyzed by sight of an advancing cheetah could speak, "represent but carte blanche to unrestrained slaughter..." The hellish creature reached his right hand for something strapped to his left thigh..."ravenous lions loosed among a flock of grazing sheep..." Was this God's judgment on him for seeking to stay the violence of the hellish human world He had created? Was he—Terry—in opposition to the world God really wanted?

Ten feet from Davy Friedman's chair, a glinting metallic blade appeared in the creature's hand. Terry stopped, trans-fixed, and Susan looked up, following his line of sight.

"Gash," she said aloud and Davy swiveled into a maelstrom of descending steel.

William Baker strode down the aisle toward the speaker.

Finally, the prey was in sight.

At first, no one noticed him. Their eyes were riveted front and center, their ears attuned to the speaker's words. The elder Baker was calm. He knew he would never escape this moment, that dozens would surround him, the cops barreling toward the building, sirens blaring, he pummeled, perhaps beaten to the floor, ground into no more than a blood-slick-ened stamp on the tiles. But it was worth it.

His right hand reached for the definitive instrument of justice.

He had heard and continued to hear the speaker's words...a whining lament for the death of pacifism. But the blade in his hand, he knew...this and the authoritative closure it brought, not puling whimpers for peace, constituted the only code by which the living world abided.

He swaggered forward, a lion among clawless herbivores, intent not on killing from hunger but on killing from lawfulness...living creatures contested...they warred...and the final arbiter of bristling dispute was force.

He was but feet from his prey. His lips set in a snarling smile and the knife began to rise. The herbivores saw him now, they observed the glinting instrument of death, and lowing wails went up from their drooling mouths. The herbivores started to rise from their chairs. But how many sheep did it take to oppose an aroused lion?

They stepped into his path. Let them come! He began a lunge toward his prey. The words of his Catholic school education flashed through his mind—the words of Jesus, of Gandhi, of Dr. King—all the paeans to non-violence, the sorrowful pleas for the meek, the weak, and the sick, leprous souls of the doomed—here was his answer!

The blade swept down. The prey turned at the last moment, its right hand rose instinctively, catching his knife hand above the wrist, gripping it with adrenaline fueled strength, contesting death like a man. He pushed the knife down, using all leverage to his advantage, grinning now in the utter rightness of it—in the world not of vitiated, cringing, Jesus-swooning door-mats but in his world—of Thrasymachus, Machiavelli, Nietzsche—the six-year world of prison, of reading philosophers who faced hard-edged truth not like sheep but like tigers—the truth, as one articulated, that life is assimilation, injury, violation of the foreign and the weaker, suppression, hardness, ingestion—and exploitation.

The sheep now pounded at his back, a female rose from beside his prey and dug her clawed nails into his throat, she bared her fangs and roared, a lioness not a deer, and he ignored her, ignored the outraged scream reverberating in his ears, consumed now by kill-lust, scorning the despairing wail of victim or family, inexorably he pressed the wicked blade downward toward his prey's exposed throat.

In transfixed horror, from the podium, Terry McGill watched the bloodied drama stagger toward its definitive climax.

Davy Friedman strained under the remorseless pressure of the knife hand descending toward his throat. Terry saw the tendons of his thick wrist bulge, the back muscles working visibly even under the tight contours of his shirt, he saw the ex-Marine plant both feet firmly on the floor and push upward with his powerful legs, rising fractionally at first, then a few inches more, his whole body resisting the blade's downward arc, rolling it back, marginally, and upward from his face.

The ex-priest gripped the sides of the podium—something was rising within, an internal force with which he had not been face-to-face in decades...befriend the beast, he had taught, know it, pet it, tame it. But it hit him now, like a studded fist to the larynx, that the beast, in undying residence, had its moments—as darker forces gathered in its purview—when playful petting was scorned as inauspicious to the season and it arose on hind legs preparatory to howl, flay, and rend.

Terry could not avert his eyes as Susan reacted immediately, not seeking to wrap and restrain, but to flail with claws, teeth, and pummeling blows at the foe who would efface her man—until with his left arm and hand, the black-studded killer flung her off, sending her spinning to the tiled floor where, with the wind knocked out of her, for a moment she lay until immediately rising and throwing her petite body once again at Davy's tormentor.

It hit Terry, like a building toppled on him, that the beast might properly have its day—and his eyes closed.

But the society of pacifists came now at the knife-wielding thug in waves. Paddy O'Neill, from his heels, with every ounce of his willowy frame, swung a savage right-handed blow that connected with a ringing thwack! on the right side of the murderer's skull, staggering for a moment the big man. The murderer roared and half-turned, across his body smashing Paddy's face with a studded fist that broke his nose and splattered blood on the boy's shirt.

Terry McGill heard that—and his eyes opened.

Davy Friedman was on his feet. His right hand checked the blade's downward motion, and his left was free. Terry saw Paddy slowly rise from the deck, he knew of Davy's Marines past, and of the unarmed combat in which the Corps trained its fighters. His eyes saw Davy's unhampered left fist and he thought, throw it, shatter the demon's visage, break its nose like it had broken Paddy's, and put a final resolution to this rampaging beast's blood-letting career.

But Davy did not throw it. He would not. Instead, he seized the creature's left fist—the studded fist that had just smashed Paddy's face—and gripped it with remorseless pressure, refusing to let it go. Davy had both of the creature's wrists in his powerful hands—he had the creature in his grip—and he would not let it go.

The two men, both on their feet, stared at each other— one with snarling death lust—the other with a calm of radiant newness, apparently birthed in the moment, a look without words that serenely stated to an unfailingly violent world that he had found an answer, the curing antidote, that he could face it unscathed, that it could no longer hurt him, and that he was free.

Throw it, Terry repeated the words to himself, and he started away from the podium. "Kill me," the fiend in the assistant principal's office had said aloud. "Kill me and be like me"—a killer. "A killer," the word pounded inside Terry's skull. He was down the stairs now from the riser, onto the tiled floor. He moved with purpose inexorable, adrenaline-fueled power coursing through his long lean frame, his massive hands formed now into fists—boxer's fists—for the first time in decades.

He strode through the shocked, milling attendees—they made way for him—his face, his fists, his towering size not to be impeded. He came up from behind, liberated of moral compunction regarding murderers. For an instant, he noted Davy's serene face as he held the savage at bay—but serenity in the ex-pacifist's soul had been displaced for the duration, and the beast rose in righteous fury from where it had lain dormant for so many years.

He swung from his shoulder, an arrow-straight right hand, devoid of loop, driven by two-hundred-and-twenty pounds of muscle harnessed now, surging from Terry's moral core. The crushing blow landed flush on the thug's right temple, who bellowed and slumped sideways, still grasping the knife, still in Davy's grip. Terry crouched, as though in the ring, his muscle memory reinvigorated. For a wild moment, he wished Davy would loose the creature from his grasp and let him, like that tameless youth from decades prior on Brooklyn's streets, pummel to bloody pulp this black-bearded fiend.

Terry stepped in and fired again, throwing from his legs, his buttocks, his shoulders, his entire lean frame. "That one's for Paddy," he breathed aloud. He hit the murderer again and again and again, lefts to the face, rights to the skull, pounding him, no longer distinguishing this thug from the brutes in Mary Jo's office, from the muggers who had savagely beaten him, from any of the subterranean creatures who preyed on innocent victims. "For Susan!" he roared at them all in thunderous defiance. "For Terry! For all of us!"

The murderer was going down, although Davy would still not loosen his grip. Terry was on his toes, swiveling at the hips—his youthful training reasserted—and swung a final left hook crashing into the murderer's cheekbone and snapping it with an audible crack heard across the auditorium. "I could kill you," he hissed aloud, the creature to which he spoke not in this room, no longer even on this earth—"but never be like you." The creature to which he spoke lived now solely in the memories of his victims, perhaps irrevocably effaced in this moment from Terry's.

The thug collapsed to the floor, his inert fingers loosening, the knife now safely in Davy's hands.

Terry stood over his battered form, half-crouched, fists still clenched, breathing heavily but under control. "Get up, you miserable f--k," he said, deliberately emphasizing the obscenity—"and let justice be done."

But the thug was done, motionless on the tiled floor. The eyes of the crowd ignored him, ignored Davy Friedman, ignored the barbed blade in Davy's right hand. They stared, with wide-eyed amazement, at Terry McGill.

Chapter Seven:
The Society of Humanity

Susan reacted first.

"Call the police!" she roared above the tumult.

Davy held the knife loosely, confident he could tighten his grip, if necessary, in a trice, and that nobody could wrest it away. He looked around the room and then at the would-be murderer stretched unconscious on the floor. He did not know him. But then, it was often that way in assault. There were no safe havens in the outer world. Looking for one was futile. You might barricade yourself in a stone fortress twenty feet high, lighted, alarmed, and guarded, but the guards themselves could turn against you...as myriad kings and emperors had learned...

Susan rushed to Terry but stared at Davy, and he nodded in affirmation. In their role reversal in violence, he knew, Terry needed her more.

He removed his shirt and undershirt, then put the shirt back on. Carefully, he rolled up the jagged blade in the undershirt, cushioning its bristling edge. He would hand it to the cops.

Mayhem, from this world, may well be ineradicable. He looked at the blanketed knife in his hand. From it, there was no safety. But there was inner control in how one faced it. No safety...but maybe...peace...

Susan reached Terry's side. In the moment, it was the ex-priest, not the ex-Marine, about whom she worried. Her shoulder was sore again from where she had landed on it, but, in the rush of adrenaline, she barely felt it.

The former pacifist had straightened now. But he still looked at the thug unconscious on the floor. "Terry," she wanted to cry in concern. But he turned and looked at her, as a father might, with a glance of protective strength so permeated with inner fortitude that she immediately sighed in relief. For one wild moment she thought that perhaps he would now open a gym to teach boxing as self-defense...but men pushing seventy did not open a gym. Did they?

He opened his arms and she came into them, wrapping her arms around his waist, laying her head on his chest, the chest of this man, this father, who loved her like she was his own. Briefly, tears came, of deliverance, and she welcomed them and permitted herself to weep on Terry's broad chest.

She turned then to face Davy.

She stood silently between these two men of her life and she recalled that they had never met. But the two men stared easily at each other and it occurred to her that two shared death struggles might be all the introduction they needed.

Terry took a deep breath. "You saved Paddy's life."

"It was the right thing to do."

Terry could read people, their eyes, their faces, the gateways to their souls...and he knew. "You paid a price."

Davy looked at the would-be murderer, moaning now as consciousness slowly returned. "Someone has to."

Terry nodded. "But not you any longer."

Davy turned back and smiled in relief and radiant deliverance. "No, not me."

"He's done more than his share," Susan said sharply.

Sirens sounded in the distance.

Terry stepped forward and reached for Davy's hand. "Thank you."

Davy nodded in acknowledgement and took the proffered hand. His chin pointed at the would-be murderer. "Who is he?"

"One subterranean creature of millions," Terry said bitterly.

"It's Warren Baker's older brother," Susan said. "His name is William...they call him 'Gash.'"

"You cannot avoid them," Terry said to Davy.

"You're right."

The sirens were coming closer. Their high-pitched whine rose to shattering crescendo as the prowl cars turned onto the block. In a moment, the room would be flooded with police officers, asking questions.

Terry tightened his grip on Davy's hand. "Pacifism is dead. It died at William Tecumseh Sherman High School."

"But it died a beautiful death."

The murderer stirred groggily on the floor. Paddy O'Neill stood over him and stamped his foot onto his chest, pinning him to the ground. He held a wad of white paper towels to his nose but still dripped blood onto the thug's chest.

"Pacifism is a lie," Terry said.

"But a noble one."

"It cannot protect the innocent."

"But it might transform the guilty."

"No guilty person has ever been transformed by love and logic."

"But the next one might be."

"Peaceful non-violence cannot save society."

"It saved me."

"Violence is necessary."

"When all else fails."

"It is hopeless."

"There is always hope for peace."

"I cannot go on."

"But you can pass the torch."

Terry loosened his grip and turned. Police officers, guns drawn, swarmed into the room. Dozens of by-standers pointed at the inert frame on the floor, and Paddy O'Neill stepped aside. The cops approached warily. Seeing the perpetrator had been beaten into submission, they holstered their guns and cuffed his hands behind his back. Two burly cops hoisted him to his feet. The thug spluttered slightly, and, for a moment, his head lolled. He regained consciousness slowly.

One veteran cop looked at the battered, swollen face. "William Baker," he said, nodding. "Gash." The other cops looked with interest. "Wanted on so many violent charges that he'll never again see the light of day." A brace of cops led him away.

The veteran cop, a sergeant, approached the three of them. "Father McGill. Is everyone okay?"

"Yes. Never better."

"You'll be needed at the station house, all of you...for questioning," the sergeant said. They nodded, and he walked away.

Paddy approached them. The wad of paper towels was reddened now and held in his left hand. He grimaced in pain. But he was not white in shock, he emanated ruddy complexion and athletic health. "Father." A crooked grin creased his face, and the broken nose manifested like a rogue-ish badge of honor. "Maybe we should teach the innocent to kick ass." He pounded his fist into the towels.

Terry smiled. "Perhaps we—"

"—The Society of Humanity is not finished," Davy said.

Terry stared, measuring Davy's words. "Most of those here

tonight were not at Sherman, although they know the horrific details. But what they saw from me tonight will be enough. The Society will dwindle to nothing.."

"It's the Society of *Humanity*. Who still believes that humaneness is best served by pacifism?"

"Nobody," Terry snapped. "What's your point?"

Davy looked at Susan. His words and tone were inclusive. "The great preponderance of what you did and taught: reaching out, love, logic, reason, restraint if possible—"

"—It's not always possible. One look into Warren Baker's eyes—one second of that creature's gaze—was sufficient to kill twelve years of dedication to the ideal that human disputes could always be resolved peaceably." He paused and breathed. "You were there, you saw, you know, you were the only one who did what was necessary."

"It's not always possible. But in the human world, what is?" He turned from Susan to Paddy to Terry. "Many persons want love, some find it—but do they always find it? Many yearn for freedom and risk their lives striving to reach it—do they always succeed? I could go on—but you see my point? Brute force, at times, might be necessary but always as final recourse. Prior to that, we utilize every instrument that the Society superbly teaches."

"You want to head the Society."

"It would be an honor."

"Who better," Susan said.

"The Kickass Society," Paddy said. "The Shoot-the Motherf--kers Dead Society."

Terry shook his head but Susan saw parental relief light his eyes: His son would not be at the mercy of subterranean creatures. Something lit her eyes, too. For Davy Friedman had come home. In out of the cold night in which, despite all her ministrations, he had shivered alone. She sensed somehow, her connection to him never more alive, that his nightmares were done, his demons vanquished, his inner battle won. Davy Friedman had carved out his proper niche in the world.

She turned to Paddy. "Before you kick any ass, let's get the nose attended." She led the young man away. She knew there were medical doctors in the Society.

Susan and Davy left together in silence. She leaned on his arm. At the bottom of the outside stairs she turned her head to him. "Someone must be the last line of defense against Terry's subterranean creatures."

Davy nodded. "Someone."

They walked slowly to her car. At the door, she fished the keys from her bag. "Do you want to drive?"

He nodded and took the keys.

"Davy," she said.

Some quality of her voice beyond seriousness caused him to turn.

"You've done more than your share. Much more."

He said nothing.

"I've resigned from the Society."

They stood together on the sidewalk in front of her car and he stared at her.

"Yesterday, I stopped at Grandmaster Kim's Karate Studio on Kings Highway."

She paused. He said nothing, waiting for her to continue.

"It will take five years. But with intensive effort I'll earn a Black Belt in karate." She looked around and breathed freely, letting in the scents and sounds of the soft June night, facets of the earth's beauty that resonated deeply in her healer's soul. "Whatever it takes to help innocent people, I'll do it." Involuntarily, her jaw stiffened and he sensed a hint of the righteous anger that burned within. "But I'll never be defenseless again. If someone again assaults me, I will rip his face off."

Davy let her words hang in the warm night redolent of blossoms and opening earth. She looked at him, her eyes soft, muted, defiant to the world's aggressors but to him inexpressibly tender and he knew that he was the one person on God's earth from whom she sought approval. He told her what he had told Terry. "Self-defense is a last resort."

"For you," she said quietly. "For me, a first resort."

"Killer, you'll protect me?"

"You need no protection. But if you do, yes, with my life."

He opened the passenger side door and held it for her. She got in the car and gazed at the man she loved. He felt her eyes on him as he closed the door and walked around the front and got in the driver's side. Together, they drove away.

Lightning Source UK Ltd.
Milton Keynes UK
UKHW022324241121
394517UK00011B/916

9 781951 943899